On The Third Day

Also by Piers Paul Read

Novels
GAME IN HEAVEN WITH TUSSY MARX
THE JUNKERS
MONK DAWSON
THE PROFESSOR'S DAUGHTER
THE UPSTART
POLONAISE
A MARRIED MAN
THE VILLA GOLITSYN
THE FREE FRENCHMAN
A SEASON IN THE WEST

Non-fiction
ALIVE: The Story of the Andes Survivors
THE TRAIN ROBBERS

On The Third Day

a novel by PIERS PAUL READ

Secker & Warburg
LONDON

First published in Great Britain in 1990
by Martin Secker & Warburg Limited
Michelin House, 81 Fulham Road, London SW3 6RB

Copyright © 1990 Piers Paul Read

A CIP catalogue record for this book
is available from the British Library
ISBN 0 436 40965 8

The author gratefully acknowledges the
kind permission of Penguin Books Ltd
to quote from *The Jewish War* by Josephus,
translated by G. A. Williamson.

Typeset in Linotron Palatino
Printed in England
by Clays Ltd, St Ives plc

On the third day, he rose again from the dead.

The Apostles' Creed

Prologue

The Israeli archaeologist, Michal Dagan, once Professor at
the Hebrew University on Mount Scopus, later director of
the Staedtler Institute of Archaeology in West Jerusalem,
lived with his wife in that leafy quarter of the city called
Rehavya. Their flat had three bedrooms – one for the parents
and one for each of their two children. Their daughter
Anna's was rarely used: she had been to school in the United
States, and was now studying in London.

Their son, Ya'acov, was in the army. In 1988 he was
stationed in Jerusalem, attached to a unit of Military Counter-
Intelligence headed by Colonel Yehuda Louvish. He worked
in plain clothes and lived at home, driving every day from
his parents' flat in Rehavya to a military compound on the
Ramallah Road. The Professor never asked what his son did
from day to day, content that it was undoubtedly of some
importance to the defence of the Jewish nation, not just from
external enemies, but from the enemies within who at that
time were organizing protests and demonstrations against
Israeli rule – the *intifada*.

One evening in late May, Ya'acov returned to have supper
with his parents and, as they were eating, abandoned his
usual discretion to tell them about his work. Because of the
intifada, it was necessary to eavesdrop on the Arabs in their
sanctuary on the Temple Mount. Existing devices on the hills
surrounding the Old City were proving inadequate. A
decision had been reached to go in from below.

Professor Dagan was familiar with the excavations which
had already taken place beside the retaining walls of
Herod's Temple. Since the conquest of the Old City in 1967,
a tunnel had been dug under the Muslim quarter, adjacent
to the Western Wall, linking the area around Wilson's Arch
with the cisterns under the Via Dolorosa. Israeli archaeolo-

1

gists had itched to know what lay on the other side of the wall, but they had always been prevented from excavating under the Temple Mount itself by the religious sensitivities both of the Muslims above and of the Orthodox Jews in the Ministry of Religious Affairs.

Now, the needs of security seemed to have overridden all other considerations, and a decision had been made to go through the Western Wall at the north-west corner, where it bisected an old cistern and blocked the Hasmonean water-course from the Damascus Gate.

The point Ya'acov made to his father was this: that if it was left to the sappers and engineers, they might overlook and inadvertently destroy things of great archaeological importance. He, Ya'acov, had some archaeological training, but he had neither the knowledge nor the experience to judge the importance of what his unit might find. He had therefore asked his superior, Colonel Louvish, to let his father in on the operation and allow him to go first through the Western Wall.

Michal Dagan could not refuse. His wife, Rachel, directed a doubting look from across the table, and asked Ya'acov who, beyond Louvish, had authorized the operation. Ya'acov's answer was vague, but it satisfied his father. Whether legal or illegal, dangerous or safe, it was a unique opportunity to gain access to the whole labyrinth of caves, conduits and cisterns which were known to be beneath the mosques on the Temple Mount, and had remained untouched since the destruction of the Temple by Titus.

The operation proceeded in great secrecy, with five young sappers in plain clothes working under Ya'acov and two fellow officers called Mordecai and Asher. It took more than three weeks to cut around one of the massive blocks of Herod's Western Wall, and another week to dislodge it. At the start, Dagan visited the site almost every day but, since progress was slow and he had other work to do, he began to visit the site less often, leaving it to Ya'acov to tell him when he was needed.

Almost a month after the work had started, Ya'acov came home and told his father that they hoped to remove the stone the next day. They both went early in the morning to the plaza in front of the Temple Mount, and were met there by Asher, Mordecai and the young sappers. They walked along the tunnel to where the massive block of stone protruded from the wall, held up by a tangle of chains, pulleys and scaffolding. It took another two hours to edge it out of the wall, and so tight were the blocks around it that, when it finally swung free, there was no movement whatsoever, but simply a black rectangular hole leading through to the other half of the bisected cistern.

Dagan looked through and inhaled the musty air. He shone a torch into the darkness to look for the level of the floor. They had assumed that it would be lower, and that they would need a ladder to reach it, but he found instead that there was a shelf of rock only a few feet down. He pulled himself through, followed by Ya'acov, Asher and then Mordecai, who carried with him a powerful lamp attached by a cable to the circuits in the tunnel.

This revealed a large cavern, similar to other cisterns of the Roman era which Dagan had seen before. The shelf of rock upon which they were standing was around fifteen feet above the floor. Dagan called for a ladder which was passed through to them from the other side of the wall.

Ya'acov went down first, to make sure it was steady for his father. Dagan went next, followed by Mordecai with the lamp, trailing the cable behind him. Once on the floor, they looked up to see if there was an entrance to the cistern from above, then shone their torches around the wall to find the outlet from which water would have flowed to other cisterns beneath the Temple itself. It was only when he was standing on shingle which had collected at the lowest point, that Dagan noticed a large earthenware jar, cracked and lying on its side.

The jar was not unusual. Like the cistern, it was of a kind common to the period, used for storing olives or grain, with a wide neck and a tapered stem. It was too heavy to have been used to draw water from the cistern, and perhaps for that reason had been left there, submerged under the surface.

It did not seem of immediate interest, and while Ya'acov and Mordecai looked up at the roof of the cavern for places where they might plant their bugs, Dagan searched for the opening that would lead on through a conduit to the cisterns beneath the site of the Holy of Holies. It was only after he had found it, walled up from the other side with masonry from the Herodian period, that Dagan returned to the jar.

He knelt and peered in. The beam of his torch fell on what remained of a wooden lid about halfway down the jar. There was something beneath it, but he could not see what it was. If he moved the lid before spraying it, the wood would undoubtedly crumble. He asked Mordecai to fetch tape and a plastic sheet, intending to bind the jar to prevent it splitting open where it was cracked, and then remove it from the cistern to the laboratories at the Staedtler Institute.

It was Ya'acov who pointed out that it would be difficult to carry the jar up the ladder and through the hole in the wall without disturbing the contents. Dagan agreed, and when Mordecai returned they put the tape aside, unrolled the plastic onto the shingle, and gently lifted the jar onto the transparent sheet. Then, while Mordecai held the lamp, Ya'acov and Asher separated the two halves of the broken jar, lifting one off the other like the lid off a box.

Dagan crouched to examine the contents. 'How curious,' he said. He took a magnifying glass from his pocket, then knelt, and looked more closely. Ya'acov, Mordecai and Asher watched in silence. Then the Professor looked up. His face was pale. 'Touch nothing,' he said. 'Leave everything exactly as it is. We must have a witness to this, another archaeologist; someone, above all, who is not a Jew.'

PART ONE

One

Among the world's most celebrated archaeologists was a Catholic priest called John Lambert. He was a monk of the order of St Simon Doria, a community founded in the Middle Ages to copy the Bible onto parchment. It had evolved over the centuries into a body of celibate scholars who ran schools and universities all over the world. In France the Simonites rivalled the Dominicans, in America the Jesuits. In Britain they had been exiled at the time of the Reformation, and had only returned towards the end of the nineteenth century when invited by Cardinal Manning to found a Catholic university in London.

A site had been bought in the borough of Paddington, and the money raised to build a large Gothic church, and a monastery for fifty monks. When the idea of a university came to nothing, the Simonites built a school instead. Some of the pupils later joined the order, together with other English Catholics who had been educated elsewhere. By the early 1960s, the small group of Irishmen, Frenchmen and Germans who had brought the Simonites back to England had grown into a community of thirty or forty Englishmen, renowned for their scholarship and Papist zeal.

By far the most distinguished of these was Father Lambert. He had entered the monastery in Paddington as a young man but had spent little time in London. In the 1950s, he had studied under the French Dominican, Roland de Vaux, at the Ecole Biblique et Archéologique in Jerusalem. Later, he had taught at Tübingen, and for a time at the Simonites' own Pater Noster University in Seattle. In 1969 he came back to Europe, to the Pontifical Biblical Institute in Rome, but only returned to England in 1975, as Professor of Archaeology at Huntingdon College, part of the University of London.

He was then aged forty – a tall, vigorous man with close-cropped hair, pale blue eyes, and skin that had grown tough and dark from the time he had spent digging under the burning sun. He was considered an ascetic by the other monks because he mortified his flesh in a way that was quite out of fashion. His expression was stern, and his manner remote, even forbidding. Few people called him John or even Father John: it was always Father Lambert. Yet, despite this austerity, he had a gentle manner; he was always kind; he was often funny. People crossed London when it was known that he was preaching, and his lectures at Hunting-don were so popular that they drew students from many different faculties, some of whom sat around the lectern like groupies at the concert of a pop musician.

His reputation went further than academic circles, and though several of the English Simonites were eminent in their fields, Father Lambert was the only one who could be described as a celebrity. He was often called upon for his opinion by the national press, and was invited to appear on television, but neither his fame, nor his dedication to uncovering the past, had ever distracted him from his obedience to his calling as a Catholic priest. He said mass every day, at an altar in a church or at a table in a tent; and when in London he would sit in the confessional for an hour every Saturday morning, waiting for penitents who rarely came.

Every summer he spent two months in Palestine, working on different excavations with Michal Dagan, a man he had known for twenty years and one of his closest friends. It was an unlikely friendship because Dagan was a committed Zionist and Father Lambert a Catholic of an uncompromising kind. Though each had always respected the other's learning and skill, they would never have chosen to work together had cooperation not been forced upon them by political considerations. The Israelis unquestionably ruled Palestine, but some of the most important archaeological sites had been controlled by the Catholics since the time of the Crusades. It had therefore been thought politic for Professor Dagan to work with a Catholic and for Father Lambert to work with a Jew.

Though they shared an enthusiasm for uncovering the Palestinian past, each was inspired by a different vision. To Dagan, God had made a Covenant with the Jews which gave them Palestine. To Father Lambert, God had made a new Covenant with all who believed in Christ which gave them the kingdom of Heaven. Dagan wanted to inspire the disparate groups of modern Israelis, by rediscovering what the Romans destroyed, to make a nation fit for the coming of the Messiah. For Father Lambert the Messiah had already come: he wanted to unearth the stage upon which he had played out the drama of his life. Their convictions were incompatible; if the one was right, the other was wrong; but when men work and eat together, and sleep under the same stars, a bond is forged between them, and after twenty years they were now such close friends that Michal Dagan had sent his difficult daughter Anna to study under Father Lambert in London.

In early June of 1988, soon after the feast of Corpus Christi, Father Lambert was telephoned by Michal Dagan and asked to come at once to Jerusalem. To Lambert, it was an odd request. The term at Huntingdon College, where he lectured twice a week, was not over. In addition, he had to prepare a paper for the Congress of Biblical Archaeologists in Oxford in July, and attend meetings of the organizing committee. Dagan was coming to the Congress, and Father Lambert had planned to return with him to Israel for his usual season of excavation. This was known to Dagan, yet he insisted all the same that Father Lambert should drop everything and take the next flight to Tel Aviv.

Father Lambert agreed to go because he trusted Michal Dagan. He asked the permission of his Prior, Father Godfrey – a formality – and told his secretary at Huntingdon College to cancel his appointments and reserve a seat. To neither did he give the reason for his precipitate departure: this he confided only to Brother Andrew Nash, who was both a Simonite monk and one of his graduate students.

Andrew, at the age of twenty-eight, had almost completed his seven years' probation as a member of the order. In six months' time he was due to take his solemn vows and be ordained as a deacon. He was considered by the other monks to be a valuable addition to their number. There were few vocations to the priesthood, and intelligent young men usually went into better-known orders like the Jesuits, Dominicans or Benedictines.

What had drawn Andrew to the Simonites was the personality of Father Lambert himself. He had first seen him on the podium of a lecture hall at Huntingdon College at a time when Andrew was not even a Catholic, let alone a would-be priest. His father was an agnostic, his mother an atheist; and the Anglicanism he had been taught at school had been so bland that he had gone up to London University with no beliefs at all.

The influence of Father Lambert had overwhelmed Andrew. It was not just his lectures which had impressed him, but the way in which his ambitions soared above the mediocre values of the times. While every other member of the older generation, particularly his parents, seemed to pursue banal objectives – more money, a faster car, a better job, a new wife – Father Lambert had devoted his whole life to a striving for sanctity and a search for truth.

Other students who were impressed in this way did not go on to become Catholics, let alone monks in the Simonite order, and some of those who knew Andrew's background felt that he had joined the Simonites only because he had found in Father Lambert a better father than the one nature had provided. It was also thought that perhaps the spectacle of his parents' unhappy marriage had led Andrew to consider a celibate life – something some of the young women at Huntingdon had reason to regret, because he was both good-natured and good-looking, with shaggy black hair and rumpled clothes which, as a concession to his calling, were dark in colour – grey flannel trousers, say, with a black corduroy jacket or a black jersey, and a blue denim, open-necked shirt.

Some doubts had been expressed by the novice-master, in the early years of his novitiate, as to whether Andrew's vocation was a genuine call from God, or the immature emulation of a man he inordinately admired. After he had

10

graduated from Huntingdon, he had been sent to study theology at the Simonite house in Rome. He had returned as determined as ever to become a Simonite monk, and had been considered sufficiently mature by the Prior both to proceed towards ordination, and to return to Huntingdon College as one of Father Lambert's graduate students. It had also suited the community to assign him as an assistant to the man who was now the most distinguished member of their order. This was why Father Lambert had told him of the mystery surrounding his summons to Jerusalem, and why Andrew was impatient for his return.

He was due back on the Saturday morning – exactly a week after he had gone – but when Andrew came in on the Friday evening from Huntingdon College he was told by Gerry, the old Irish porter at the monastery, that Father Lambert had already returned.

'When did he get in?' asked Andrew.

'This morning,' said the Irishman, 'and I can tell you, Brother, he looked terrible. I think I would say he was ill.'

'He always gets jet-lag,' said Andrew, 'and he may not have slept much on the plane.'

'Then you'd think he'd rest,' said the porter, 'but he was out again almost as soon as he came in, and then in and out, with hardly a cheerful word, which is very unlike the father.'

'Is he here now?'

'I think so, but I couldn't be sure because I haven't been at the door for most of the afternoon. They asked me to help them with moving the chairs down at Our Lady of Victories for the jumble sale, you know, which is tomorrow, so I went off with Father Godfrey's blessing . . .'

Andrew left the porter talking, as he had learned to do over the past few years, and walked along the clammy tiles of the monastery hall to the broad stairs of polished wood. Polish was the prevalent aroma around the place, sometimes mixed with the scent of incense wafting in from the church after high mass on a Sunday. He climbed the stairs to the first floor and went to his room.

11

It was not yet dark outside, but his window was over-shadowed on one side by the Gothic church and on the other by a wing of the monastery itself. He took out the books and papers from the Air France airline bag which he used as a briefcase. He then looked at his telephone, wondering whether he should ring Father Lambert's room, or should assume that he was resting and wait to see him at supper.

He decided to wait, and sat down to read at his desk. The light was weak. He reached forward to switch on his lamp, glancing as he did so up and out of the window towards the window of Father Lambert's room on the other wing of the monastery, thinking that if the older priest was there, perhaps he too would have switched on his lamp. No light shone from the window.

He looked back at his book and was dazzled for a moment by the bright light from his lamp reflected off the white paper; then, as his eyes focused on the print, his thoughts caught up with something he had seen when glancing towards Father Lambert's window.

He looked again. His eyes, used to the brighter light, took a moment to adjust to the gloom of the cloudy summer evening. When they did they confirmed what Andrew thought he had seen – a long shape like a large lobster net or an elongated kitbag apparently attached to the wall beneath Father Lambert's room. He stood and leaned out to get a better look, and then with a spasm of shock recognized the shape as a man's body hanging from the window by a rope.

He jumped up and ran wildly up the stairs, slithering in his haste on the polished wood. On the upper corridor he passed Father Thomas – a plump mathematician – and said to him breathlessly: 'Quick, get help.'

He reached the door of Father Lambert's room, raised his hand from habit to knock before he entered, but then lowered it to the handle, threw open the door and ran across the room towards the open window.

The bed blocked his path: it had been moved in front of the window, and a line of blue plastic-coated cable – the kind sold as washing-line in supermarkets – had been tied to a post at the foot and was stretched, tautly, over the sill. It was only by kneeling on the mattress that Andrew could look out of the window. He saw at once that the other end of the cable was tied around the neck of the suspended body and he knew, too, from the texture of the close-cropped hair on the head, that the body was that of Father Lambert.

In a frenzy he grabbed the line and tried to haul the body back into the room, but such was its weight that he could not lift it. Although his reason told him that the man was dead, and that there was nothing he could do to revive him, he became unreasonably convinced that there was still breath in the body and that he could save his Professor if only he could lift him back onto the bed. His weakness frustrated him and he began to sob, and shout at the same time: 'Wait, Father Lambert, wait . . . we're coming, we're here.'

At that moment three others came into the room behind him – Father Godfrey, the Prior, Father Thomas, the mathematician, and Gerry, the Irish porter. Father Godfrey climbed onto the bed beside Andrew, peered over the sill, turned pale, and whispered 'Dear Lord' between his teeth. He too took hold of the plastic-coated cable and with Andrew tried to lift the body, but given their awkward position on the bed, even their combined strength was not enough.

'Leave it to Gerry,' Father Godfrey said, as he always did when a fuse burned out or a door jammed. He moved back; so too did Andrew, and it was the turn of the porter to crouch on the bed with Father Thomas. They pulled for a moment at the cable, but then Gerry came away from the window saying: 'It'll be best to bring him in from below.'

The four men filed out of the cell and, while the porter went for some wire-cutters, the three monks descended to the unused room immediately below Father Lambert's. It was locked. Father Thomas ran to get the key while Andrew and his superior waited by the door. The younger monk, who had now mastered his sobbing, looked at the older one not so much to ask any specific question as to search for some explanation in the expression on the other's face. The plump face of the Simonite Prior, however, remained blank and severe. He avoided looking into Andrew's eyes as if knowing that his own had nothing to say.

13

Father Thomas returned with the key. He gave it to Father Godfrey, who opened the door. The furniture in the cell was the same as in all the others but there was a musty, airless smell like that in a loft or a cupboard. It was also dark, because the legs and torso of the hanging body shut out much of the fading evening light.

Father Godfrey went to the wide sash window, undid the catch and raised the lower half. Father Thomas, deferring to the greater strength of the younger man, let Andrew move up beside the Prior. 'Gerry wasn't sure if his cutters would cut the cable,' he said. 'He said he might have to use a hacksaw.'

Father Godfrey nodded.

'He'll give a shout when he's ready,' said Father Thomas.

Again Father Godfrey nodded. He reached out of the window to see where he could hold the body. Standing on the floor he could only reach the hip. 'I hope he can lower him slowly,' he said. He turned back to Father Thomas. 'Go and tell Gerry to cut the cable near to the bed and then lower it slowly. Tell him not to let it drop all at once.'

Father Thomas left the room. Andrew took a chair to the window to see if, by standing on it, he could get hold of the body higher than the hip, but he found that when he stood on the chair he was above the open lower half of the sash window.

'Should we open the top half?' he asked his superior.

'No, they always jam. This will do, if they lower it slowly.'

Andrew got off the chair, pushed it out of the way, and stood beside his superior by the window. For a moment they were silent, then Andrew asked: 'What can have happened?'

Father Godfrey opened his mouth to answer but at that moment a cry of 'Right' came from the porter on the floor above. The two monks – the young and the old – leaned out of the window and took hold of the body. As it was lowered, they guided it through the window until, at the last moment, the two men above let go, and the body fell onto the floor.

Andrew had fallen with the weight of the corpse and now found that its head lay half on his lap and half against the wall beneath the window. He shrank back, horrified to see a

14

face he had revered already blackened and distorted, with the tongue protruding from between the teeth and the unfocused eyes bulging from their sockets.

'God forgive him,' murmured Father Godfrey, whose face had gone a shade paler than before. Then he turned to Father Thomas who, puffing for breath, had come to the door. 'Quick, a stole and the chrism.'

Father Thomas disappeared. The porter came in and looked, astonished, at the body on the floor. 'Holy Mother of God,' he muttered.

As if inspired by this pious ejaculation, Father Godfrey now began to pray, but in a muttered whisper so that Andrew could not follow or join in. He floundered for a moment, searching in his mind for an appropriate prayer himself, then for something spontaneous to say to God; but the grotesque head on his lap seemed to drive out any other thoughts. No cry came from his heart and he could envisage no God to hear it.

Ritual enabled him to escape from that moment of desolation because Father Thomas returned with the paraphernalia of the last sacrament. It was clear, of course, that Father Lambert was stone dead – no attempts had been made to revive him – and so when the four men lifted his body onto the mattress, it was as if onto a bier, not a bed. 'He's been dead for a while, poor man,' said Father Godfrey as if voicing his own doubts, 'but there's no knowing when the soul leaves the body so we should anoint him all the same.'

He leaned forward and pulled the eyelids down over the bulging eyes, then took the stole from Father Thomas and placed it around his neck. Father Thomas opened the small silver box of chrism. Father Godfrey took some on his thumb and smeared it in the form of a cross on the eyelids he had just closed, saying: 'By this holy unction, and by his most tender mercy, may the Lord forgive thee whatsoever sin has been committed by sight.' He then did the same to his ears, nostrils, mouth, hands and feet, repeating the prayer each time with the words appropriate to each organ, and with a special emphasis when it came to the hands. 'May the Lord

15

forgive thee whatsoever sin thou hast committed by deed . . .'

When the ceremony was over, the four men stood quite still, either praying silently or simply wondering what to do next. As they did so the bell rang for the monks' supper. The sound seemed to make the Prior suddenly less constrained, as if the situation could be saved by a return to routine.

'Will you take these back,' he said to Father Thomas, handing him the stole and the chrism, 'and tell the fathers to start supper without us.'

'Should I say . . .' Father Thomas began.

'No, nothing at all.'

Father Thomas left the now darkened cell and Father Godfrey, with a last look at the corpse of his fellow monk, went out beside him and walked towards the stairs, followed by Andrew and the porter.

'Should I ring the sisters?' asked Gerry, referring to the nursing nuns who customarily laid out the corpses of the dead monks.

'Yes,' said Father Godfrey, 'but first, perhaps . . .'

'The police?' asked Gerry, his voice taking on a respectful tone as it mentioned an institution he revered almost as much as the Catholic Church.

The Prior frowned. 'I was thinking, rather, of Doctor O'Malley. I think we can leave it to him to bring in the police if he thinks it necessary.'

'I think that in cases of this kind . . .' began the porter.

'I dare say,' said Father Godfrey sharply, 'but we'll let the doctor decide.' He turned to Andrew. 'Would you come with me, now, for a word?'

Andrew nodded in a dazed way and followed his superior down the stairs to the ground floor and past the refectory – with its sound of clattering cutlery and the voice of Father Wilfrid reading from de Joinville's *Life of St Louis* – to the Prior's study.

This too smelt of polish, but tinged with tobacco, for Father Godfrey occasionally smoked a pipe. In most other respects it was similar to the study of the headmaster of a

16

public school – a large, half-private, half-public room with two old leather armchairs, a club fender, and in one corner a desk with two telephones, a dictating machine and a framed photograph of Father Godfrey's parents. On the wall behind the desk there was a reproduction of a painting by Titian of St Simon Doria, the order's founder, while over the mantel there was a large crucifix which made it clear that the room's imcumbent was a man of God.

Andrew, who had come in and out of this room on many occasions without remarking on the figure on the cross, noticed it now for the first time as a graphic depiction of agony and death.

'Sit down,' Father Godfrey said to him, pointing to an armchair on one side of the fireplace and sitting himself in the other.

Andrew did as he was asked, his eyes still fixed on the twisted figure of Christ on the cross.

Father Godfrey followed the direction of his glance and for a moment said nothing, as if unwilling to interrupt a silent prayer. But Andrew was not praying: he was not even grieving for his dead friend. He returned his eyes to the face of his superior and wondered almost idly what he was going to say. He watched as Father Godfrey raised the fingers of both his hands to rub the shining skin of his bald temples as if a massage might help to clarify his thoughts. When Father Godfrey looked up, it was with the kind of official expression which always accompanied the announcement of some administrative decision. He opened his mouth to speak, but before doing so he suddenly seemed to appreciate who it was who was with him, and a kinder look came into his eyes. 'This is particularly terrible for you,' he said.

Andrew shook his head as if to disown any selfish sorrow. 'I don't understand what can have happened,' he said.

Father Godfrey now blushed as if caught out in an impious assumption. 'It does seem,' he said, 'as if Father Lambert killed himself.'

'But that's impossible,' said Andrew.

'What other . . . interpretation can there be?'

'It could have been an accident . . .' Andrew began, but

17

then his voice faltered as if he realized that the suggestion was absurd. 'Or murder,' he blurted out, with a defiant look at his superior.

Father Godfrey hesitated, pretending to consider this last suggestion; but then, with an ironic smile on the edge of his lips, he asked: 'Can you think of anyone . . . or rather, any reason why anyone should want to murder Father Lambert?'

Andrew shook his head. 'No.' He looked down at his clasped hands to hide the tears which he now felt seeping into his eyes and blurring his vision. 'But I can't think why he would want to kill himself either.'

Father Godfrey sighed. 'It is a dreadful truth,' he said, 'but there are . . . occasional suicides among priests.'

'Why?'

'Because the Devil tempts us with moments of despair – us, above all, whom he loathes and envies because God has chosen us to be higher than the angels.'

'But surely, after so many years . . .'

'If a priest's faith falters, it is precisely his age which deepens his despair, because he has given up so much – a wife, a family – all for a reward which he no longer believes will be his.'

'I can't believe that Father Lambert ever wanted that kind of life,' said Andrew fiercely.

Father Godfrey hesitated, and when he spoke chose his words with some care. 'He was an exceptional man, as you know – learned and holy – and he was already that way when you met him, but just as he only became learned after many years of study and concentration, so he only became holy after many trials and temptations.'

Andrew lowered his head and mumbled: 'Of course. I should have realized.'

'I cannot believe,' said the Prior, 'that almighty God will condemn him because he faltered in one moment of despair. Remember the words of St Paul. "In Jesus, the Son of God, we have the supreme high priest who has felt our weaknesses with us – who has been tempted in every way that we are, though he is without sin. Let us be confident, then, in approaching the throne of grace, that we shall have mercy from him" – and mercy too for Father Lambert.'

'Yes.' Andrew kept his head lowered, and for a moment the words of the older priest did calm his chaotic thoughts.

'Now,' said the superior, reverting to the practical tone of voice with which he clearly felt more at ease, 'we must think of what is to be done.'

'Doctor O'Malley will be on his way.'

'Yes, and he may feel it necessary to call in the police. What is important, however, is to make sure that no newspaper finds out what has happened. There are all too many enemies of the Church who take delight in reporting cases of this kind.'

'But won't there be an inquest?'

'There will, yes, unless Doctor O'Malley decides that no good purpose could be served by calling in the police or putting suicide as the cause of death.'

'But we could hardly expect him to make out a false death certificate.'

A small frown wrinkled Father Godfrey's bald brow and a trace of irritability sharpened his tone of voice. 'It is not what we would expect of him, but what he would expect of himself. He is a good Catholic, after all. He would not want to harm the Church.'

Andrew said nothing, but his superior seemed to take his silence as a form of rebuke because he went on, again in a tetchy tone of voice: 'As you will discover as you grow older, Andrew, we are often tested by choices not of good and evil but of the greater or the lesser evil. No doubt it would be wrong for Doctor O'Malley to say that Father Lambert had died from natural causes if he had not, but first of all we cannot be absolutely certain that some kind of embolism or brainstorm – perhaps sunstroke from his visit to Israel – did not lead him to behave in this irrational way, and secondly we must weigh against the lesser evil of a small deception the certain and substantial evil that will result if it becomes known that Father Lambert – Father Lambert, of all people – has taken his own life.'

19

Again Andrew said nothing, but his silence was more hesitant and less sullen.

'It isn't just his fame as an archaeologist that matters – though that would make sure the story went on the front page: it is his standing as a priest and a man of faith. Imagine the gloating of our detractors, and think of the demoralization of all those men and women who have looked to him as a heroic exponent of the Catholic religion. Think of our fellow priests, and the danger that this advertisement of his one brief moment of despair might induce the same in one of them and inspire him to do likewise.'

He argued with increasing agitation, as if to persuade himself as much as Andrew, and Andrew, who, ever since he had seen the body dangling from the upper window, had been gasping and struggling in his own mind not to be sucked under by the current of his despair, could not but see the force of this argument. He looked up at his superior, and in his eyes there must have been a sign that he was persuaded, because the Prior now sat back with a sigh as if Andrew's concurrence was that of a whole committee.

At that moment there was a knock at the door. Father Thomas entered and said: 'The doctor is on his way.'

'Good,' said Father Godfrey. 'Come in, please, and close the door.'

Father Thomas did as he was instructed and came to sit on the club fender. Father Godfrey stood up, went to his desk, picked up one of the telephones and dialled a single number. 'Gerry,' he said when the call was answered. 'Would you come to my study at once, please.'

He put the telephone down.

'Father Gervase asked if you were coming to supper,' said Father Thomas in the voice of one terrified that he has done the wrong thing. 'I said I thought not.'

'Quite right.'

Again there was a knock on the door and the porter entered. 'Doctor O'Malley will be here in a jiffy,' he said.

'Good,' said the Prior. 'Thank you.'

Gerry hovered near the door.

'Please sit down for a moment.'

The old man crossed to the leather armchair that the Prior had vacated.

'We have all been the witness to a very tragic and shocking event,' Father Godfrey began, leaning his body against his desk. 'There is no escaping the fact that Father Lambert, in a moment of terrible despair, has succumbed to the prompting of the Devil and has taken his own life.'

'Indeed, indeed,' muttered the porter.

'Now I have told Brother Andrew, and I will tell Doctor O'Malley, that if news of this gets out to the wider world it will do incalculable damage to our holy mother, the Church.'

'Of course,' said Father Thomas.

'It is therefore incumbent upon us to make sure that it does not.'

'Indeed,' said Gerry.

'I shall therefore propose to Doctor O'Malley that it be given out that Father Lambert died of a stroke.'

'And no police?' asked Gerry.

'And no police. But clearly, if Doctor O'Malley is to risk his professional reputation for the greater good of the Church, then it is our duty to support him by saying the same thing.'

'You can count on me,' said Gerry.

'Even our brothers in the community?' asked Father Thomas.

'Must not know.'

The old mathematician bowed his head. 'Very well.'

'I take it upon my own conscience,' said Father Godfrey, 'and as your superior I instruct you on pain of sin never to divulge to anyone how Father Lambert met his end.'

Two

Father Godfrey awaited the arrival of the doctor, alone at his desk, his eyes closed, his face pressed against the palms of his hands. He too tried to pray, but the only words that came to him were those of Christ on the cross: 'My God, my God, why hast thou forsaken me?' The suicide of Father Lambert appeared to undo everything he had achieved since the community had chosen him as their Prior.

His election, seven years before, had marked the end of the long period of turmoil which had followed the Second Vatican Council. When the genial Pope, John XXIII, had summoned all bishops in communion with the Catholic Church to the Vatican in 1962, none among the London Simonites had envisaged the revolution this would bring about. Certainly the Church had become isolated, even aloof, from the outside world. Its light was hidden under a bushel of institutional conceit. The talent of a composer like Elgar, or a writer like Evelyn Waugh, was ascribed by the Simonites to their religion. Those outside the Church – even fellow Christians in the Church of England – were thought damned, if not for what they believed, then for what their forefathers had done to the Catholic martyrs of Elizabethan times. When all the Simonite monks were joined by the boys from their school, and the lay people who belonged to the parish, to sing the Credo in Latin, or a hymn like 'Faith of Our Fathers', there was hardly a heart which did not swell with pride, or face flush with triumphalist fervour.

All that changed. First it was ordained that the mass was to be said in English instead of Latin; then, that the celebrant should not face God in the tabernacle but the people in their pews. The mystery of the consecration, once hidden behind the hunched shoulders of the priest, now became a spectacle for all to see, like the feeding of the animals at the zoo. Many of the old moral certainties, so painstakingly transcribed from parchment to parchment by Simonites over the ages, were thrown aside. No sins were now mortal or venial, or even sins at all, if they were done with a comfortable conscience. The relics of the saints, once venerated, suddenly became so many bits of bone. Terms like 'transubstantiation' and 'consubstantiation' became meaningless distinctions: the only difference in the eucharistic bread of the various Christian denominations was in the way it was baked.

Father Godfrey had not blamed the Council itself for what happened in its wake. It started and finished with the best of intentions, and nowhere in its promulgations can be found the texts and statements which explain why tens of thousands of priests, friars, monks and nuns suddenly threw off their habits and abandoned their calling. Or, more confusingly, threw off their habits without abandoning their calling. Or, most confusingly of all, abandoned their calling without throwing off their habits, remaining as priests, friars and nuns to reform the Church so radically from within that it would bear no resemblance to what it was before.

The English community of Simonites suffered the full force of this hurricane of change. In 1965 there were forty-seven monks in their monastery in London – forty-one priests and six novices. Twenty years later there were twelve. Of the missing thirty-five, nine had died, five had been transferred to the American province, two had defected to the Dominicans, while the remaining seven had been laicized, six of them marrying, two of those to nuns.

The statistics, however, do not tell of the terrible quarrels and conflicts during those twenty years. Rival camps were formed within the community whose mutual antipathy was so great that they would barely speak to one another. A strong Prior might have prevented this degeneration of a community supposedly based upon love; but it was a tradition among the Simonites not to waste the talents of their eminent scholars on administration, but to elect as their superior a monk who had nothing better to do. In untroubled times, this arrangement worked well. Most of the Simonites pursued their careers in secular universities, and the rule of the Prior was a formality.

Suddenly, however, some of the younger monks began to behave in ways which outraged their older and more conservative brethren, discarding the grey habit which had been the uniform of the Simonites since the eleventh century, and even the black suit and clerical collar which was worn in the world outside, and appearing first in suits, with collars and ties, and later in jeans, with shirts open at the neck.

The Prior at the time tried chiding, gently, these rebellious monks, only to be subjected to a counter-blast of progressive theology – Karl Rahner, Hans Kung and 'the spirit of Vatican II'. He would retreat only to find himself prodded in the rear by the indignation of the conservatives. The matter would then be raised in Chapter, leading to painful debates in which insults were thrown from one side to the other, all couched in convoluted theological jargon. The Council had decided that the Church should be open to the world. How could the monks follow this teaching, the progressives argued, if they wore fancy dress dating from the Middle Ages? How could they keep themselves informed of what was happening in the world if they were not allowed televisions in their cells? Or stereos to listen to the kind of music that was an integral part of contemporary culture?

The community capitulated on the question of clothes and televisions, but worse was to come. One of the progressive monks, a middle-aged man, was seen entering a restaurant with a nun – neither wearing habits, both in lay clothes; and not at midday, but at eight in the evening; and not a straightforward kind of restaurant where two hungry people might go to get something to eat, but somewhere expensive and dimly lit with pink table-cloths and the menu in French.

Then a second monk, who taught Medieval History at Bedford College, began holding tutorials in his cell. Since his students were all girls, and it was an ancient rule that no women were allowed in the monastery, this aroused such indignation that the Prior was forced to call a special meeting of the Chapter. Here the Medievalist argued that the bar against women was the expression of the sexist, paternalist, misogynistic, gynophobic prejudices of the Church which were most emphatically at variance with the spirit of Vatican II. He was supported by the monk dating the nun who, since he was not only the senior theologian in the community, but had also served as a *peritus* at the final session of the Council itself, persuaded a majority of the community that to bar women from entering the monastery was to disregard the promptings of the Holy Ghost.

It was decided that women should be admitted, but not after dark for fear of scandal. The Medievalist continued to hold afternoon tutorials for his students from Bedford College, one of whom, in particular, seemed to need more supervising than the others. It was reported to the Prior that music was heard from behind the door when she was there. The Medievalist said that it was a tape of *Carmina Burana* which was relevant to the subject. Later still, some of the monks heard other sounds of a kind they dared not interpret; but when the Medievalist was laicized, and then married the student, it came to them as no surprise.

There were other sources of dissension, particularly when some of the young monks heard the call of the South American bishops to exercise a preferential option for the poor. Under their influence the community changed their school from a good grammar school to a bad comprehensive where monks who were authorities on the poetry of Catullus or the Theory of Relativity tried to teach Maths and English to the rough little ragamuffins who lived in neighbouring council flats.

There was also the question of the order's endowments, bank deposits and stocks and shares, and some valuable paintings which had been bequeathed to the Simonites over the years. It was proposed in Chapter – and the motion was carried – that all should be sold and the proceeds given to the poor; and it was only through the deft, and somewhat duplicitous, transactions of the stubborn and conservative procurator that the English province of the Simonites remained solvent.

This procurator had been Father Godfrey who, together with Father Thomas and one or two others, made up the conservative faction. None of them, however, had the qualities to wrest the moral initiative from the progressives. Father Thomas was shy, and could only see the hand of God in the formulas of higher mathematics. Father Godfrey was good at finance and administration, but had a weakness for lunching with rich benefactors of the order, and knew rather too much about wine.

Their fortunes had changed with the return of Father Lambert to be Professor at Huntingdon College. He brought with him not just his prestige as an archaeologist, but also his distinction as a theologian and reputation as a monk of an uncompromising kind. He was known to fast. He was seen to pray. He made a personal confession every week. Yet he accepted whole-heartedly the doctrines of the Council. He was open to the world, teaching at a secular institution. He was also ecumenical in spirit, with more friends than any of the other monks among Anglicans, Muslims and Jews.

Where he differed from the progressives was on the question of what it meant to be holy. Their interpretation of the law of love led them to support famine relief, nuclear disarmament and the Sandinistas in Nicaragua. Father Lambert could see love in a kind word from a duchess to her servant, or the prayer said by a general with nuclear missiles under his command. It was faith, not good works, which saved man from damnation. To those Simonites who dismissed the 'cultic priesthood' in favour of helping the poor, he would say, like the Curé d'Ars, that welfare was merely the work of men, whereas Christ's sacrifice in the mass was the work of God.

It was not so much what he said, however, as the force of his example which won over the Simonite monks. Under his influence, they revived ceremonies like Benediction which had been abandoned after the Council. On his advice, they dismissed the ineffective headmaster of their school and appointed one of a sterner kind. When their Prior died in 1981, many wanted Father Lambert to take his place. He asked not to be put forward, because, if elected, he would have had to give up his post at Huntingdon College. The candidate he suggested was Father Godfrey, and Father Godfrey was duly chosen.

Three

Andrew, as he left his Prior's study, felt no appetite for supper – indeed nausea overwhelmed him when he smelt the aroma of sausages, cabbage and coffee from the refectory. He returned to his own room and to the desk where he had placed his books in what now seemed a different life. His window was still open and the lamp switched on, but he went neither to the window nor to his desk but knelt down at his bed and raised his eyes to the crucifix on the wall behind it. Instead of any prayers coming onto his lips, however, or pious thoughts into his mind, the tears which had been seeping into his eyes for some time now flowed freely down his cheeks, and his torso began to shake as he sobbed with an abandon he had not known since he was a child. The image of the leathery cheeks and smiling face of his beloved Professor kept changing to the grotesque grimace of the strangled corpse. He hid his face in the cotton bedspread which covered the blankets on his bed, not so much to muffle the sound of his sobbing or sop up his warm tears as to shut out the light, as if darkness would obscure the reality of what had happened.

In time this physical expression of grief ran its course. The sobbing stopped. He raised his eyes from the bed, though not to the crucifix which, rather, they avoided; and because, at that moment, he felt far from God his thoughts turned instead to his older brother, Henry, who had always been his closest friend.

He went to his desk and put his hand on the telephone, intending to ring Henry and say what had happened. Then he remembered that the Prior had forbidden it and wondered if it would not be worse to tell Henry half the truth than to tell him nothing at all. Yet the thought of never confiding in him, and so never getting the kind of comfort that his sardonic brother always provided, seemed to add to the already intolerable weight of his suffering; for though Henry was not a Catholic, and thought Andrew almost insane for wanting to become a priest, he had nonetheless witnessed the drama of his vocation and so could hardly be excluded from knowing the present tragic turn of events.

As he wondered what to do – whether to ring his brother now, or wait to tell what had happened until they met the next day, or not to tell him at all – Andrew was distracted by a moth which had flown in through the open window and was throwing itself erratically at the bulb of the lamp on his desk. He went to close the window, and as he did so looked up to the spot where he had seen the body hanging from the wall. A light shone in the room below – perhaps the doctor had arrived and was studying the body – and above, Andrew noticed, the window remained open. A reflex sense of responsibility for Father Lambert's affairs made him decide to go up and close it.

He passed no other monk as he climbed the stairs to the floor above and walked the length of the long corridor to Father Lambert's cell. He opened the door, switched on the light and went to close the window, squeezing between the bed and the wall. He then turned to push the bed back to its proper place away from the window. The end of the cable remained tied to the bedpost, a short length jutting out to the point where Gerry, the porter, had cut it. Andrew worked the knot loose and, having freed the piece of cable, tied it in a coil and dropped it in the wastepaper basket by Father Lambert's desk.

He looked around the room, half hoping to see something that might explain why Father Lambert had taken his own life. Everything was so familiar to him that he could see at once that nothing was out of place. There was a crucifix on the wall by the bed, as there was in each of the cells; the narrow bed with its posts of stained pine; the wardrobe, made of a heavier wood – oak or ash – and decorated with the same kind of Gothic embellishments as the banisters of the stairs and the confessionals in the church.

The walls were white, but one was obscured by the books stacked against it from floor to ceiling. On the other three, the only decoration was the crucifix above the bed. There was a sink in the corner of the room, as there was in Andrew's, with the same small mirror above it; a chest of drawers with Father Lambert's hairbrush and comb lying on it, together with a small leather box containing his collar-studs and cuff-links; a bedside table, constructed to contain a chamber-pot; and a desk at the book-lined wall, with a filing cabinet at either side, an Anglepoise lamp at one corner and at the other two telephones – one linked to the exchange at the porter's lodge, and the other a direct line.

He had also had an office at Huntingdon College, but he had preferred to work here in his cell. The desk was therefore covered with papers – issues of archaeological reviews from America, France and Germany; offprints sent by colleagues in different countries; theses sent for an opinion; and letters that were yet to be answered. They were not scattered in disorganized piles as a description of them might suggest, but were laid out either on the large desk or on a shelf behind it which had been cleared of books. Andrew, having acted as Father Lambert's secretary, knew the significance of each particular pile and glanced cursorily over them to see that each was in place.

In the back of his mind was the thought not that Father Lambert would have left a note that was meant for him, or indeed for anyone else, but that there might be something which would explain his state of mind. He had not worked out quite what that clue could be, and so he was not looking for anything in particular when it suddenly struck him that there was something odd about the arrangement of the papers on the desk. They were not displaced but rather lay a little too neatly in their various piles. It was not a difference that anyone could have noticed who was not entirely familiar with Father Lambert's habits. He had been orderly but not tidy, always able to find what he was looking for among the papers scattered on the desk and shelf.

Now, however, the piles were all neatly stacked, as if a cleaner had been dusting the room. He wondered for a moment whether the old Pole who cooked for the monks and polished the corridors might have broken the rule under which each monk had to clean his own cell; but by lowering his head at an angle to the light from the lamp, he could see that while a thin film of dust had been disturbed around the piles of papers, it had not been wiped away.

The obvious supposition was that Father Lambert himself had rearranged his own papers before taking his life; but to Andrew's eye the neatness of their arrangement suggested someone else's hand. Why, moreover, would a man who was about to kill himself tidy a pile of back issues of the *American Journal of Archaeology* and the *Revue d'archéologie Biblique*? Yet why should anyone else have moved the magazines, unless looking for something they had not found among his papers?

Andrew went to the desk and opened the drawers. Here too his eyes fell upon familiar objects – paper, pens, a bottle of ink, a magnifying glass, pins, paper-clips and postage stamps – and he stared at them for some time, unable to decide whether they had been moved or not. It seemed once again as if they were all rather more neatly arranged than he had imagined them, but then perhaps they were in exactly the same position as before. He could no longer tell whether he was noticing some subtle change in the arrangement of things or imagining evidence to feed his suspicions. But suspicions of what? If he was searching for anything it was for a note, but he was hardly searching even for that: Father Lambert had considered himself answerable to God alone.

He took up Father Lambert's diary, which was in the top drawer of the desk. In it was written only the details of his flights to Tel Aviv and back again. He had not altered it following his precipitate return, and no appointments were entered for that Friday, even though the porter had said that he had been in and out all day. Nor were there any marked down for the days he had spent in Jerusalem: he had clearly left his programme to Dagan.

What interested Andrew was less this diary than Father Lambert's canvas-covered notebook in which he always

wrote down what was passing through his mind – obser-
vations from books he had been reading or discoveries made
during an excavation. If Dagan had called him to Israel to
witness some startling find, then Father Lambert would
almost certainly have written something about it in the
current volume.

He searched quickly through the drawers, and then in
Father Lambert's briefcase which was beside the desk, but
did not find the notebook. Its absence, together with
Andrew's suspicions that someone had been through his
things, suddenly made it seem possible that Father Lambert's death was not as straightforward as it seemed. The
idea that perhaps, after all, he had not killed himself filled
Andrew with great joy, and feeling that he must immediately
share the good news with the Prior, he rose and ran from
the room, along the corridor and down the stairs to the
study of his superior, where he knocked and waited, puffing
for breath. He heard the word 'Come' and entered to find
Father Godfrey sitting at his desk. Doctor O'Malley had
apparently gone, and the Prior looked up with relief on his
face as if Andrew had come at an opportune time.

'Yes, good. Come in.'

'His notebook's gone,' Andrew blurted out.

Father Godfrey frowned. 'How do you mean?'

'His notebook, where he wrote everything down – it's
gone.'

The frown deepened. 'What does that signify?'

'That someone took it from his room.'

'Why should someone take it?'

'I don't know, but I noticed too that everything has been
neatly rearranged . . .'

'*Rearranged?*'

'Yes. As if someone had been through his papers.'

'But you are the only one who . . . or Father Lambert,
before he died.'

'That's just the point,' said Andrew, his agitation sounding
a little like exasperation. 'I am almost certain that someone
else – some third person – has been through his papers and
has stolen his notebook.'

31

Father Godfrey sighed – a sigh which also had a touch of exasperation. 'Who would want to do that?'

'I don't know.'

'And why?'

'I don't know that either. But there might have been some clue in the notebook as to why he . . . he died.'

The Prior looked wearily at the window, then back at Andrew who remained standing in the middle of the room. 'I can understand,' he said, 'that you in particular should be upset by what has happened, and that consciously or unconsciously you will search for some explanation of a rational kind. But you must accept that men act irrationally – even men like Father Lambert – when they suffer inordinately or are tempted to the limits of their endurance.'

'If someone was there . . .' Andrew interrupted as if he had been listening to his own thoughts, not his superior's advice.

'No one was there,' said Father Godfrey.

'. . . then we should call the police.'

Now the Prior lost patience. 'We cannot call the police,' he said in a weary, irritable tone of voice, 'because Doctor O'Malley has signed a death certificate giving a stroke as the cause of death.'

'I'm sure he was killed,' said Andrew, tears returning to his eyes.

'Of course,' said Father Godfrey, his tone of voice kinder as he heard the choking of the younger man. 'It is natural and noble of you to refuse to accept that Father Lambert succumbed to such a serious sin. But even if you are right – even if he was killed – you must see that the absence of his notebook, which he may well have left at Huntingdon College or in Israel – and your sense that his papers were too neatly arranged – would not constitute evidence worth showing to the police.'

Andrew swallowed to control his tears. 'No. Of course. I'm sorry.'

Father Godfrey stood and with a paternal hand on Andrew's shoulder guided him towards the door. 'If anything else turns up – anything concrete – come to me again.

32

I too would love to be able to believe that Father Lambert did not die by his own hand.'

It was now around ten o'clock, a time when most of the monks went to work in their own rooms. Andrew, however, returned to Father Lambert's to test his perception a second time. He switched on the light, closed the door and sat on the edge of the bed looking at the desk from a distance, comparing the books and the papers with how he remembered them the week before. They still seemed a fraction too tidy but nothing was out of place. Whether or not someone had been there, Andrew remained calm enough to recognize the force of the Prior's argument: it would be absurd to suggest that Father Lambert had been murdered simply because he, Andrew, sensed something odd in the arrangement of the papers on his desk, or the absence of his notebook.

The weakness of the evidence led to a collapse of the hypothesis in his own mind, and all at once he was overwhelmed by another, larger wave of sadness. The idea that such a strong and vibrant man had so suddenly and so totally fallen into despair that he had gone out to buy a washing-line, had tied one end to his bedstead and the other around his neck, had moved the bed to the window and had then jumped out – that idea, once admitted to Andrew's mind, conjured up in him at one and the same time an oppressive sense of the power of evil and an acute feeling of pity. Certainly, since Father Lambert had been a much older man, his feelings for him had been like those of a son; but sons can feel protective towards their fathers – particularly those who care for them in the way that Andrew, as Father Lambert's secretary, had cared for him – and with a certain bravado he now felt that he could have helped him if only Father Lambert had confided his despair.

Inadvertently he started to pray – not kneeling before the cross but sitting there on the edge of the bed. Before, when he had tried, no words of prayer had come onto his lips and no image of God into his mind. Now, however, when he had not formally intended to address his invisible creator he

33

found himself pleading for the soul of his dead friend, begging Christ to judge him not by the despair of his last moments but by the heroic virtue of his life before.

These pious thoughts were interrupted by the ringing of one of the telephones on his desk. Andrew jumped up, startled not just by the sound itself but by the fact that a dead man's telephone should be ringing at all. It was the direct line. He watched it for a moment, wondering whether he should answer. Then, realizing that he remained in charge of Father Lambert's affairs, he picked it up and said: 'Hello.'

'John? Is that you?' asked the soft voice of a woman.

'This is his secretary, Brother Andrew.'

'Ah. I had hoped to speak to Father Lambert.'

'I'm afraid he . . . he's not here.'

'I see.' She paused, then asked: 'Is he all right?'

'He's . . . he's . . .' Andrew tried to say that he was dead but felt unable to do so over the line. 'He's not well,' he said.

'I see.' She replied as if she had expected him to say something of the kind.

'May I ask who is speaking?' asked Andrew.

'Veronica Dunn. You don't know me. I am a friend of Father Lambert's. I saw him this afternoon and . . . he didn't seem well.'

'You saw him today?'

'Yes. He came to lunch.' She said this with a nonchalance as if he had been one among other guests.

'Where?' Andrew asked. 'Where did he have lunch?'

'In my house. Why? Has he got food poisoning?' She asked this with a trace of humour.

'No, no,' he said, 'but I wonder . . .' He hesitated, uncertain as to how to go on.

'What?'

'Could I come and see you?'

'Tonight?'

'No. But perhaps tomorrow. I could tell you how he is.'

'Of course. I live in Edwardes Square.' She gave the address. 'I'll expect you any time after ten.'

Andrew was now exhausted, worn out by the series of

shocks he had received in the course of the evening. This call itself was extraordinary because Andrew, having been privy to Father Lambert's affairs for the last two years, had never heard him mention a woman called Veronica Dunn; yet here she was, ringing him on the line whose number he had kept secret from all but a very few.

Andrew picked up Father Lambert's address book, which lay next to his diary on the desk, and looked under the letter D for Dunn. It was not there. This suggested either that he had known her very well or that he had known her hardly at all. If well, why had Andrew never heard of her? And if little, why had Father Lambert not only given her the number of his private line but also had lunch with her on a day he had expected to be in Jerusalem?

Tired as he was, Andrew was impatient to see her the next day. However, before he saw her, he wanted to know something about her, so he picked up the same telephone and dialled his brother's number.

'Henry?'

'Yes.'

He could hear *Newsnight* on the television in the background. 'Is this a bad moment?'

'No. Wait a minute.'

There was a clunk as Henry put down the telephone and went to turn down the sound of the television.

'I thought you'd be out,' Andrew said when his brother returned.

'I've just got back.'

'Something dreadful has happened.'

'What?'

'Father Lambert is dead.'

There was a pause before Henry said: 'I'm sorry.'

'It has come as a most terrible shock and there are various complications . . .' He longed to tell his brother how the priest had died, but remembering the command of his superior he let his voice tail off.

'What kind of complications?'

'I can't tell you just now. Perhaps we could meet tomorrow?'

'Do you want to meet for lunch?'

'Perhaps in the evening?'

'I'm out for supper, but come for a drink around six.

'At six. Yes. Thanks. And there's another thing . . .'

'What?'

'Have you ever come across a woman called Veronica Dunn?'

'I've met her, yes. She was married to Tom Dunn.'

'Who was he?'

'A businessman – chairman of CDT.'

'And now?'

'I don't know. They divorced and I think she took a degree at Birkbeck College.'

'Is she a Catholic?'

'Yes. So was he.'

'Were there children?'

'I dare say, but they'd be grown up by now.'

'So she's not young?'

'No. Why? Haven't you met her?'

'No. I'm going to tomorrow.'

'I seem to remember she's fairly dreary.'

'It's all very strange.'

'What is?'

'I'll tell you tomorrow.'

Four

Andrew was awoken at six the next morning by a knock on the door of his cell, and the shout of *'Benedicamus Domino'*, to which he mumbled *'Deo Gratias'* in reply. He stumbled out of bed, his head aching after a restless night. He sat, dazed, through matins and mass, and at breakfast was glad of the rule of silence which prevented his fellow friars from discussing the death of Father Lambert. He wondered, as he ate a bowl of cornflakes, whether or not he should tell the Prior about Mrs Dunn, but, remembering his irritability the night before, decided that it would be more charitable to spare him further complications.

He left the monastery at half-past nine carrying his Air France bag, as if to go to Huntingdon College, but instead of taking a bus to Bloomsbury he caught one going to Kensington. He got off at the High Street, and walked from there to Edwardes Square, arriving at the address he had been given at five minutes past ten.

The door was opened by a tall woman of around fifty with shoulder-length grey hair and kind blue eyes. She did not ask who he was or introduce herself, but invited him in, and, as she did so, Andrew recognized her voice as that of the woman he had spoken to the night before.

'Go upstairs,' she said, leading him into the narrow hallway. 'I'll bring some coffee.'

He went up to the drawing-room on the first floor which had two long windows looking out over the square. There was a deep sofa and two armchairs with clean yellow covers and plump cushions. On the walls there were two eighteenth-century paintings – dark canvases with fat gilt frames – and a Piranesi print. On the well-polished surfaces of the antique cabinets and tables there were little clusters of bric-à-brac – silver snuffboxes, china figurines – and two silver-framed photographs, one of Veronica Dunn as a younger woman, the other of two grinning thirteen- or fourteen-year-old children.

He heard footsteps on the stairs and a moment later she came into the room carrying a silver pot of coffee and two cups on a tray. She placed it on a low table and sat down, perched on the edge of the sofa. Her blue skirt and purple jersey, like the furniture in the room, were elegant and clean; there was a brooch pinned at her throat – a golden swallow on a little diamond-studded branch – and her hair, as he had seen when he entered, was carefully moulded around her melancholy face. Comparing her to the silver-framed photograph of her younger self, Andrew saw how her beauty had faded with age; yet, when she smiled, he recognized the residue of great feminine charm.

37

'I'm so glad to meet you,' she said, handing him a cup of coffee. 'John has talked about you from time to time.'

Andrew blushed, not from modesty, but to hide the confusion he felt that she should know about him when he knew so little about her. 'It's kind of you to let me call on you . . .' he mumbled.

She smiled again. 'How is he this morning?'

It was a sign of Andrew's confused state of mind that he had not prepared himself for this question, which he knew would be asked almost as soon as he set foot through the door. 'I'm afraid,' he said, 'I'm afraid that he's . . .'

The smile left her lips. 'Is he worse?'

'No. He's dead.' The words came out abruptly only because he could think of no others.

The woman turned pale. 'He's dead?' she repeated in a whisper.

'Yes.'

'When? What was wrong with him?'

'I'm afraid that last night . . . I felt I couldn't tell you over the telephone. He wasn't ill. He was already dead. He died . . . in the afternoon.'

'Dear God.' She hid her face in her hands.

'I'm sorry. I'm terribly sorry.'

For a moment they sat in silence. Then, suddenly, Veronica Dunn uncovered her face and looked up at him with an expression of horrified anxiety. 'But he didn't kill himself, did he?' she asked, her voice both pleading and emphatic.

'Yes, I'm afraid he did. He hanged himself.'

He answered in this way only because he was so taken aback by her question that he forgot both his own suspicions that Father Lambert had been murdered and his promise to his superior that he would tell no one the truth.

Her face, already pale, now became quite grey, and the features which had seemed so bland and expressionless took on a look of alarming desperation. Her lips moved as if she was about to exclaim or whisper, but no word came out. She glanced almost angrily at Andrew, stood up, went to the window and, with one hand clutching the other, looked out over the square.

Andrew, feeling that it was his duty to console her, searched for something appropriate to say; but as he did so he realized that, if she had suggested that Father Lambert might have killed himself, she might also know what had put him in a suicidal frame of mind.

'It was a terrible thing to have happened,' he said awkwardly.

She said nothing but remained looking out of the window.

'We feel, however – at least, our Prior has decided – that it should not be known that he died in that way.'

Now she turned to face him, her features more composed. 'Of course,' she said. 'I shall tell no one.' She came back to the armchair and sat down.

'I would be grateful,' said Andrew, 'because I was told to say that he had died from a stroke.'

She turned to him, hesitated, then asked: 'Did you find him . . . hanging?'

'Yes.'

'How terrible for you.' She glanced at him kindly.

'I loved him very much.'

'So did I.'

'May I ask . . . what made you suspect that he had killed himself?'

She looked grave again. 'I was afraid that he might . . .'

'Why?'

'He came to lunch and behaved in a quite unusual way.'

'How do you mean?'

Once again she looked intently at Andrew as if trying to decide how much she should say. 'I thought that perhaps in Israel the sun had affected him.'

'You knew that he had been to Israel?'

'Yes. And something happened there to change him.'

'To change him? How had he changed?'

'He no longer believed.'

'In what?'

'In God. In Christ. In the Church. I don't know quite what. But he had changed. He was no longer calm or

39

cheerful. Do you remember how calm and cheerful he always was?'

'Yes.'

'There was a time – you won't remember, you are too young – but when he was younger he could become agitated and morose. That calm and that cheerfulness only came with time. And yesterday it was as if he wanted to go back to the past, to go back and begin again.'

'How could he go back?'

'Of course he couldn't, but he thought he could and I . . .' She stopped, blushed and looked away. 'He was worried about you.'

'About me?'

'Yes. He thought that when you knew . . .'

'Knew what?'

'That he no longer believed – or *why* he no longer believed – then you would suffer a dreadful disillusion.'

'At least I have learned,' said Andrew quietly, 'that my faith does not depend on his.'

'No. Nor does mine.'

'Weren't you upset by what he said?'

'Yes, of course, of course, but for him, not for me.'

'You thought that he might kill himself?'

'Not at first, no, although for a man to abandon what he has lived for for so long . . . But after . . .'

'After?'

She looked down at her hands. 'I knew . . . I told him, that you can't go back and begin again.'

Now, for the first time, a few tears ran down her cheeks, but her grief was as reserved as the rest of her behaviour.

'I don't really understand,' said Andrew.

She looked at him kindly. 'How could you? You are so young.'

'I . . . I would like to,' he said, 'because it is important to me to know why Father Lambert took his life.'

'But if I tell you . . . if I tell you everything . . .' Her voice petered out.

'What?'

'Then your memory of him . . .'

'That is secure.'

'You are not a priest yet, are you?'

'No.'

'But I could trust you, as if you were?'

'Of course.'

She sighed – the sigh of a child. 'Some years ago, when my husband left me, I was very unhappy. I went to your church to speak to a priest. Quite by chance it was John. I saw him from time to time and I ceased to be unhappy because, well, because I fell in love with him.'

'But you were married,' said Andrew.

She looked at him coolly. 'Yes. My husband had left me for another woman, but in the eyes of the Church I was still married and had two children. Nevertheless, I fell in love with him and he . . . he fell in love with me.'

'How terrible.'

She smiled bitterly. 'Yes. It was terrible. Terrible is just what it was, for us both, because I was married and he was a priest, and we could so easily have become lovers but we didn't. God triumphed over the Devil. We stopped seeing each other. We lived only a mile apart but we never met alone until nine or ten years later when we both felt old enough and safe enough to be friends once again.'

She paused and glanced at Andrew, but the young monk's face was hidden in his hands – to conceal an expression not of disgust or disapproval but of outright astonishment that Father Lambert had ever been tempted by a woman, particularly a woman as conventional as Veronica Dunn. He looked up, glanced at her, then looked away – revealing the very thoughts he had hoped to conceal. 'It must have been hard,' he said lamely.

She smiled with the sour understanding of a woman who is past her prime. 'Other people's passions are always difficult to imagine,' she said, 'particularly when you are young and they are middle-aged.'

'Not at all,' he said chivalrously.

'They are even harder to remember,' she said, 'and, as I told him, impossible to revive.'

Now an unpleasant feeling overcame Andrew, similar to

41

that he had felt the day before when he recognized the body hanging from the window. He became afraid that the woman in front of him was about to tell him something he did not want to know; but as strong as his reluctance to listen was her urge to confess. 'I told him, yesterday,' she went on, hesitating, blushing, but continuing inexorably all the same, 'that we could not go back and relive the past in a different way, but he said that our love was now the most precious thing in his life and that he did not want to die with it unfulfilled.'

Andrew looked at her, appalled, but she had moved her gaze towards the window and did not catch the expression in his eyes. 'He was so agitated, so determined, and I felt, still . . . well, that if it mattered to him so much . . . The house was empty, so I agreed.' She turned back from the window and glanced, involuntarily, at the sofa upon which Andrew was sitting, then was silent.

Andrew, too, said nothing as he tried to digest the disgust he felt at the image she had conjured up – not just of a priest and a woman untrue to their vows, but at two aged bodies making love in the middle of the day.

'It was a matter of a moment,' she said quietly, 'and I am afraid that he was dreadfully disappointed. He had imagined, I think, something altogether more magnificent.'

'And did he show remorse?' asked Andrew.

'I don't know. He apologized . . .'

'For what he had done?'

She shrugged her shoulders. 'Or for what he felt he had done . . . badly. He said it would take time, but I knew from the look in his eyes that it would never happen again, and that was why I was afraid that after this second disillusion . . .'

'Yes, of course. It makes suicide more certain.'

She looked at him, puzzled. 'Why more certain? Was it ever *un*certain?'

'I thought that there was room for some slight doubt.'

'Could it have been an accident?'

'No, not an accident, and at first sight, clearly, he seemed to have hanged himself; but I noticed – or I thought that I noticed – that his things were tidy. That is, they were always tidy, but that they were tidy in a particular, unusual way.'

Mrs Dunn frowned. 'Are you suggesting that someone might have killed him?'

'No.' His brow, too, was wrinkled as he tried to see the implications of what he was saying. 'One can't really suggest that someone could have killed him – like that, to make it seem like suicide – because one cannot think of any reason why they should. But if someone *had* been there, going through his things . . .'

'Was anything missing?'

'Yes. His notebook.'

'Stolen?'

'Not necessarily, no. He might have left it in Israel.'

'You should surely have called the police.'

'The Prior thought that the greater good was served by avoiding scandal.'

'But if he was murdered . . .'

'It is very hard to think of a motive for murder, whereas suicide, well, you yourself felt that he may have had it in mind.'

'I know, I know. So the mystery is not how he died, but how he lost his faith.'

'There are apparently priests who do.'

'Of course. I know. And he knew that too. So many of his friends abandoned the priesthood in the years which followed the Council; and John himself was pessimistic at times about the direction in which the Church seemed to be going.'

'I know.'

'That's why he placed so much hope in you. He told me that so many of the younger priests had been corrupted in the seminaries by the liberal theologians. They were no longer taught to believe in Hell, but without Hell the whole idea of salvation loses its meaning and there is no point to the suffering of Christ.'

'*He* believed in Hell,' said Andrew gravely.

'Until yesterday, yes, he believed in Hell, but then suddenly he behaved as if he knew for certain that there was nothing beyond the grave.'

*

Andrew left Edwardes Square soon after eleven and, catching a bus which went towards Huntingdon College, he sat down on the front seat on the top deck trying hard to make sense of what he had just heard from Veronica Dunn.

That Father Lambert had slept with her hours before he died was an appalling revelation, but it was only further evidence of that dreadful doubt and despair which had clearly overwhelmed him upon his return from Israel. More astonishing to Andrew, and far harder to digest, was the discovery that nine or ten years before, shortly before Andrew had met him and when Father Lambert had been in his prime as a priest, he had been deeply in love with a woman.

Of course, Andrew knew that many priests found celibacy an ordeal. He himself, when considering the priesthood, had had misgivings on this account. He had instincts common to a man of his age, and novices were then encouraged to be candid about their sexuality. Indeed his novice-master, a veteran of Vatican II, had even expressed doubts about the Church's wisdom in insisting upon celibacy in all its priests. It had been Father Lambert who had persuaded him that it had a value beyond the sacrifice of something pleasant for God, or the avoidance of the encumbrance of a wife and family so as to dedicate oneself entirely to the Lord.

In a priest, he had said, the man must transcend the male: holiness was incompatible with the qualities which women sought in their lovers. That was why Jesus had been celibate, and had asked those who would follow him *à outrance* to make themselves eunuchs for the sake of the Kingdom of God.

Andrew had been readily persuaded. The only contrary opinion came from his brother Henry, whose cynicism about women had always made Andrew feel that it would be as well to leave them alone. There were times when he had wondered what it would be like to know the warmth and comfort of a woman's love; but, by and large, he had accepted that the great reward for renouncing a wife and family of his own was the freedom to love both God and his

44

neighbour in an entirely unstinting and unselfish way. Although called to serve God principally as an archaeologist, he had also worked as a stretcher-bearer at Lourdes, helped at a hostel for down-and-outs in Waterloo, and was always ready, at Huntingdon College, to listen to the troubles of his fellow students when their love affairs went wrong or their parents let them down.

Now, sitting on the bus, and digesting what he had just learned about Father Lambert's passion for Veronica Dunn, he could not suppress the feeling that somehow he had been misled, if not actually deceived. He felt like a boy who had caught his teacher reading a pornographic book. Did it mean that the teacher was depraved? Or that the lewd passages were not as corrupting as he had been told? Was it possible that when Jesus had said that only the man who hates his life in this world will keep it in the next one, he had not meant it to be taken as literally as he had supposed? Was there some way, perhaps, in which a Christian could have his cake and yet eat it?

Five

Andrew got off the bus at Holborn, still in some confusion, and walked through the elegant streets and squares of Bloomsbury to the ugly post-war buildings which housed Huntingdon College. There he went straight to the Master and told him how his Professor of Archaeology had died from a stroke. He then broke the news to those who worked in Father Lambert's own department. One of the older lecturers, who happened to be in the office, blanched as if struck by the thought that it could very easily have been him, while the secretary sobbed quietly into a paper handkerchief.

Andrew went in search of Anna Dagan, and caught sight of her coming out of a seminar which he himself should have attended. From the way she greeted him, and the

45

cheerful look on her face, it was clear that she had not yet heard the news. He walked with her down the corridor without saying anything in particular, past the notice-boards towards the canteen where both picked up trays and helped themselves to some lunch. It was only when they were seated at a table in the corner of the canteen that Andrew told her that Father Lambert was dead.

Anna looked at him quizzically as if he was playing some kind of joke, but seeing the grave expression on his face, she sank back, shaken, on the hard canteen chair. 'But he always seemed so well,' she said. 'I can't believe he died just like that.'

Andrew did not answer. He faced a dilemma. He had just told everyone at Huntingdon College, in obedience to his superior's instructions, that Father Lambert had died of a stroke. With Anna, however, he was tempted to tell the truth, not just because she was his friend, but because she was well placed, as Michal Dagan's daughter, to find out what Father Lambert had done in Israel. With the kind of quick casuistry which comes easily to the young, he decided that, since the secret had innocently escaped him in the presence of Veronica Dunn, it was no longer as such a secret. Just as Father Godfrey in good conscience could decide that a greater good would be served by lying, so he, Andrew, could equally well decide that a greater good would be served by telling the truth. He therefore repeated the whole story to Anna who, for the first time since Andrew had known her, listened without interruption to every word he had to say.

In normal circumstances, she would tease Andrew almost every time he opened his mouth. She made the most of the fact that he was a Simonite monk, saying that she had been sent by God to test him. She was small, with short black hair, sallow skin, brown eyes and an innocent, child-like face. She was often taken for sixteen instead of twenty-two, and part of her sharpness was undoubtedly to disabuse those who thought her as innocent as she seemed. She was clever, but also contrary, and had made life so difficult for

46

her parents in Israel that they had sent her to study for a postgraduate degree with Father Lambert in London.

Here Andrew had befriended her, putting up with her relentless teasing and her occasionally cruel moods because he was amused by her jokes and enlivened by her intelligence. He also felt sorry for her, sensing the uncertainty behind the shield of her caustic humour. He knew from Father Lambert that she got on badly with her family, particularly her brother Jake, and so came to regard her as an adopted sister. As a result, it seemed entirely proper to tell her not only about Father Lambert's suicide, and the possibility that someone had searched his rooms, but also about his fall from grace with Veronica Dunn.

Anna, who could not stop a slight smirk coming onto her face when she heard this last piece of news, said: 'Well, it's good to know he had it in him.'

Andrew frowned. 'That's a banal thing to say.'

'Yes. I'm sorry.'

Since she rarely apologized, her words dissipated his irritation. 'What is odd, surely,' he said, 'is not that he fell in love with a woman – that can happen to any priest – but that he went back to her yesterday after ten years.'

'You say she had *grey hair*?'

'Yes. She was really quite old.'

'I guess people keep at it longer than you'd think.'

Andrew blushed. 'I don't think . . . I mean, she seemed to think it was . . . unusual. It was almost as if it was symbolic.'

She wrinkled her nose. 'Symbolic sex. Yuk.'

'I do see that if he had lost his faith . . .'

'He'd want to lose his virginity?'

'He might want to know what it was he had missed – from curiosity as much as . . . desire.'

'One of the things I can never understand about your creepy religion is why faith and sex are incompatible.'

'They aren't,' said Andrew.

'I know, I know,' said Anna in a tone of affected weariness. 'A married couple with the blessing of the Church can do it so long as they bear in mind that it might lead to a baby and don't take any precautions to make sure that it won't.

47

Great. That damns ninety-nine point nine per cent of all lovers. So my statement stands. The Catholic Church hates sex.'

This was not one of Andrew's favourite topics of conversation. He sensed that Anna knew more about the subject than he did, but he preferred not to know the details of her experience. 'You shouldn't see it as being *against* sex so much as *beyond* sex,' he said. 'The full Christian life, which is what a priest aspires to, transcends our natural condition . . .'

'Then why are you eating those sausages?'

'I have to keep alive.'

'You could have had bread and water.'

'One can legitimately take pleasure in God's creation.'

'As the bishop said to the actress, or Father Lambert to Mrs Dunn.'

Andrew blushed. 'Please don't.'

She opened her mouth to say something more but shut it again before a word had escaped, and looked from under her fringe at Andrew as if to gauge whether or not he was genuinely upset. Seeing that he was undoubtedly in a vulnerable condition, she said, in a much softer tone: 'I really am sorry he's dead, you know. I loved him too.'

'Of course.'

'And I think, for your sake, we ought to try and find out why he suddenly threw all his eggs out of his one basket.'

'I would like to know.'

'Even psychologically it's interesting . . .'

'Yes.'

'I'll call Dad and ask him what happened in Israel.'

'Do you know why he wanted Father Lambert to come to Jerusalem?'

She shook her head. 'Not exactly. It was something to do with a dig by the Western Wall.'

'When will you ring him?'

She looked at her watch. 'We could try him now.'

They left the canteen and went up to the Department of Archaeology where the secretary, who was used to Andrew acting as Father Lambert's assistant, let them into his office. Anna took the telephone and dialled first for an outside line, and then the code and number for her father's office in Jerusalem. When she got through she asked, in halting Hebrew, to speak to Professor Dagan.

When her father came on the line she reverted to English. Andrew stood looking out of the window into the street as she gave him the news of Father Lambert's death. He heard her say that he had had a stroke, and then abruptly ask: 'Can you tell us, Dad, if anything happened to him while he was in Israel? I mean, did he seem OK to you?'

There was a pause as she listened to her father. Then she said: 'Sure, he's here,' and held out the telephone to Andrew. 'He wants to talk to you.'

Andrew took the telephone and heard the deep, gentle voice of Michal Dagan on an extraordinarily clear line.

'Andrew, I am so sorry. This is terrible. I cannot believe it. But it is true?'

'Yes.'

'He was a wonderful man. It is terrible, terrible, and for you especially. You were like his son, I know.'

'We wondered,' Andrew began, uncertain about what words to use. 'We wondered whether anything might have happened to him in Israel?'

There was silence from the other end of the line. For a moment Andrew thought that he might have been disconnected. Then Michal Dagan asked, in a cautious tone of voice: 'Why? Why do you ask?'

'The doctor thought that perhaps the sun, or some sudden shock of some kind . . .'

Again there was a pause and finally Dagan asked, in a tone of voice even cagier than before: 'It was a stroke, was it? Are you sure?'

Andrew blushed as he lied. 'Yes. They seem to think so.'

'There is no question of foul play?'

'Foul play?' He repeated the odd, old-fashioned words while looking at Anna.

'It was only a thought,' said Michal Dagan.

'Do you mean, was he killed?'

'No. It is far-fetched.'

'Who would have wanted to kill him?'

49

Again there was a silence. Then the Professor said: 'Listen, Andrew, there are things I cannot talk about on the telephone.'

'But should we tell the police that Father Lambert might have been murdered?'

'No, no. I should not have said it.'

'His notebook has gone,' said Andrew.

'Ach.' Another pause.

'Can he have left it in Jerusalem?'

'I don't know. Not here, certainly, but perhaps with the monks. You should call them. It should be found, definitely, it should be found, unless, of course, it has been taken . . .'

'I'll write to the Prior,' said Andrew.

'No. Better not. They may think that you know what is in it.'

'I don't understand.'

'There were many things. Many difficulties.'

'About what?'

'I cannot tell you now. Perhaps Ya'acov, if you see him . . .'

'Is he in London?'

'He is, yes. Let me speak to Anna again.'

Andrew gave the telephone to Anna who, after a few more words with her father, rang off. She seemed melancholy, as she often did when reminded of home. 'Apparently Jake's in London,' she said.

'Did your father say why?'

'No. He sounded really confused.'

'They were very good friends,' said Andrew.

They walked out through the gates of Huntingdon College into the street.

'What was all that about foul play?' asked Anna.

'He seemed to think that Father Lambert might have been murdered.'

'Then something *did* happen in Israel.'

'It would be wonderful, wouldn't it?'

'What?'

'If he *had* been killed.'

'*Wonderful?*'

Andrew blushed. 'No, not wonderful in itself, but wonderful that it wasn't suicide.'

'Only he'd still be roasting in Hell because he'd just jumped the old lady.'

Andrew blushed again before the first had faded. 'At least he would have had the chance to repent.'

'Sure. It doesn't sound as if it was much fun.'

They reached the gates to the college. 'Are you going home?' he asked.

'I guess so,' she said. 'Or I might go for a walk. Why don't you come?'

'I ought to get back to the monastery, and sort out Father Lambert's affairs.'

'You can do that later. It's such a lovely afternoon.'

The clouds had cleared since the morning to show the blue sky above the buildings, and Andrew, as he looked up, suddenly longed to fly above the ground mist of fumes left by the traffic in the street. Thinking, with an inward shudder, of his dark cell and its morbid memories, he changed his mind and went with Anna on a bus to Chalk Farm.

From there they walked to Primrose Hill. Here, other people were sitting on the benches or lolling on the grass, but the two found a spot on the steep bank with its vast views over London. They sat down facing the spires and steeples and glinting glass towers rising from the mauve mist of carbon monoxide. The ground was dry, the air was warm, and Andrew, who had slept badly the night before, suddenly felt tired and sad. The fatigue undermined his control over his emotions and, while he did not cry, he sat, crumpled, with a miserable look on his face.

At first Anna did not notice his dejection – her eyes were on the view – but when she finally looked around and saw an almost old expression on her young friend's face, she said in an unusually gentle tone: 'I guess it is really hard for you – him dying and you not knowing how or why.'

He smiled gratefully. There were tears in his eyes. 'We're trained to be detached,' he said, 'and taught to love God so much that we only love others for his sake, but it was always hard for me, with Father Lambert. He was such a wonderful man.'

'Sure.'

'He knew, of course, and so did the Prior and the novice-master, that I looked on him as an adopted father. Neither of them thought that there was anything wrong. St John, after all, loved Jesus in a special way. And I always knew that he would die – in fact I almost looked forward to the moment because I felt sure that he would die cheerfully and serenely. He was so sure of the life to come. What's difficult now is not so much that he's dead, as that his death was so ugly and his fate now . . . uncertain.'

'But can you really believe, even for a moment, that he might be in Hell?'

Andrew clasped his hands and kneaded them together as if the twisting fingers were mimicking his contorted thoughts. 'Of course, in a way, I don't. I mean I believe, above all, in the mercy of God, and Father Lambert was so sure of God and so loyal to God for so long that it seems impossible that God would abandon him now.'

'So doesn't that mean he's OK, scratching around in some archaeological happy hunting ground?'

'No. Because I also believe – I have to believe – in the power of the Devil to tempt us, and in the possibility that we might succumb to that temptation and fall.'

'Why do you have to believe that?'

'If that *wasn't* possible, then we would have no choice and without choice we would have no value.'

Anna gave a funny little frown, unseen by Andrew, as if ready with some squashing rejoinder, but again, if she had something of that kind in mind, she held it back and said simply: 'I don't know what's so great about choice if you end up roasting in Hell.'

'Well, of course, there are times,' said Andrew, 'when one would much rather not have that burden of living for ever and just settle down to the cosy life of an innocent beast. But having eaten the fruit of the knowledge of good and evil, we cannot escape what we now know.'

'Can't we live in blissful ignorance?'

52

'You can pretend to. You can even behave as if you do. But in the end even the atheist succumbs to original sin and suffers the more because he can't recognize it for what it is.'

'Give me an example.'

'Well, there's my brother, Henry. You met him that time . . .'

'I remember.'

'He takes the line that man is just a superior baboon and that any claims that he is anything more are pretentious nonsense. However he himself doesn't behave like a superior baboon, but more like a fallen angel.'

'In what way?'

Andrew hesitated. 'I don't want to betray his confidence, but . . . well, you don't know him, and anyway, I don't think he'd mind. You see, he has made a lot of money, just as the baboon might amass a lot of bananas, and he has had a series of beautiful girlfriends just as the baboon might accumulate mates; but while the baboon would go on, in obedience to instinct, to procreate his species, Henry has never married and never had children. His life is totally barren, and whenever it looks as if it might bear fruit in terms of a long-lasting love or a family, then he abruptly alters course . . .'

'He ditches the girls?'

'He ditches them, yes, even if he still likes them.'

'Why?'

'Because they have come to the end of their three months.'

She frowned. 'Their three months?'

'As soon as he starts up with a girl he sets a timer and when three months are up he ends it.'

'Even if they're getting on?'

'Especially if they're getting on.'

'Why?'

'So as not to become dependent upon another human being.'

'He sounds a cold fish.'

'Of course he does, but what's so sad is that by nature he's so affectionate and so good.'

'Some men don't want to get involved,' said Anna.

'I know. But Henry has made his philandering into a kind

53

of religion and it hasn't really made him happy. And that's really the point I want to make – that the Christian hypothesis makes more sense of our moral condition.'

'For Christians, perhaps.'

'And for Jews. The whole story of the Fall, after all, comes from your religion.'

'It's not my religion. I'm not that kind of Jew.'

'Of course. I know. You don't believe it. And sometimes I envy those like you or Henry who don't have to worry quite so much about whether what they are doing is right or wrong. But if you *do* believe – if you look at humanity and sense that there is much, much more to it than a herd of animals of different species – if you see in it such extraordinary extremes of beauty and ugliness, virtue and vileness, such inhuman cruelty and at the same time such equally inhuman unselfishness and self-sacrifice – then one is bound at least to consider that there *is* more to our condition than the cosy life of an animal.'

'You can think there is more, can't you, without swallowing the idea of eternal damnation?'

'One could, yes, if one could explain away what Jesus had to say. I promise you, Anna, if it wasn't for him it would be easier, much easier, but there he is. He lived and died, and he said he died to save us from the consequences of our sins, and when you think *how* he died and what he suffered and how easily, even in human terms, he could have avoided it, then he must have felt that he was saving us from something unbearably dreadful.'

'Sure, he may have thought so, but his delusion doesn't have to become your delusion.'

'But was it a delusion?' They had had discussions of this kind before, but now, since the fate of Father Lambert seemed to depend upon the conclusion they reached, Andrew spoke with an anguished urgency. 'You see it is easy enough with our knowledge of the human mind to dismiss Jesus as a neurotic and a hysteric with, perhaps, some kind of hypnotic power over his followers. That's certainly what Henry would do. But then you read the Gospels and you realize that such a hypothesis won't stick because what he said is so subtle and so convincing, and it is not only backed up by miracles which show an extraordinary power over nature, but by the final miracle of his resurrection from the dead.'

'Sure,' said Anna. 'If you can swallow that, you can swallow the whole caboodle.'

'And if you can't swallow it, then clearly Jesus is no more than another Jewish prophet.'

'I don't see what's wrong with living decently and hoping for the best in an afterlife, if there is one, without taking on board the whole paraphernalia of Heaven, Hell, judgement, resurrection, and the Catholic Church.'

'There's nothing wrong with it as far as it goes, and it is what most of us do, but fundamentally it is irrational because it implies that if there is a God who has created us, he is either unable or unwilling to communicate with us – in other words, that he is neither the jealous God of your Bible nor the loving God of ours, but a lazy or indifferent God who, having made us, leaves us to our own devices.'

'In a way that seems safer,' said Anna, 'because whenever people do believe in a God who communicates his will, they start slaughtering the people who appear to defy it. Jews stoned the Christians, Christians burned the Jews and the Muslims massacred everyone.'

Andrew shook his head sadly. 'I know, I know. But that doesn't mean that he isn't there, or that he doesn't wish us to know him and love him and go to him when we die.'

'Or to the Devil.'

'If we so choose.'

They were back to where they had started – the death of Father Lambert – and the very fact that they had come full circle deterred them from going on. It was also time for Andrew to make his way back towards Paddington. 'I'd better go,' he said, looking at his watch. 'I've got to meet Henry.'

'Don't forget your long spoon.'

He looked puzzled. 'My long spoon?'

'If you're supping with the Devil.'

He laughed. 'I'm only going for a drink. He's supping with someone else.'

Six

While Andrew travelled back towards the centre of London, Anna returned to Belsize Park where she lodged with her aunt – her father's sister – Miriam Lilien. She lived in a substantial Victorian house which she had bought after the war with compensation paid by the German government to the children of those killed in the concentration camps. The Liliens had never occupied the whole house – they had always let the top floor as a flat – and now that Peter Lilien was dead and their two children had homes of their own, Miriam had retreated into the ground floor and the basement. The entrance was still through the front door at the top of a flight of steps; but the main staircase now went up to the flat above. A second door led into an inner hall beyond which was the drawing-room. This was sparsely furnished and rarely used, serving as a gallery for the modern paintings which Anna's uncle, Peter Lilien, had collected in the 1960s.

He had worked in the modern paintings department of the auction house, Christie's, and seeing the rapid rise in the value of some contemporary painting, had backed his own judgement by buying the works of living artists. Unfortunately, his judgement was not shared by the market, and the paintings he had bought were now uniformly worthless. They were also, in the opinion of his widow, uniformly bad, but she could not bring herself to burn them or give them away and, having nowhere to hide them, had left them hanging on the walls of this large room while she herself retreated into the kitchen on the floor below.

Here she concentrated all the *Gemütlichkeit* of which her husband, when he was living, had disapproved – a plump sofa, an upright piano, a Welsh dresser with cups hanging from the hooks and, in place of the saucers, a large library of paperback thrillers. The room next to the kitchen, once the dining-room, was now her bedroom. Like the kitchen it looked out onto the garden. Anna had one of the four bedrooms on the floor above which had been that of the Liliens' daughter, Rosie, now married and living in Bristol.

When Anna got back that afternoon she came in at the front door at the top of the steps, left her books in her bedroom, then went down the inner staircase to find her aunt sitting at the kitchen table – a small, beetle-browed woman who looked quite unlike her brother Michal. She was now over sixty but in no way decrepit, and followed Anna's life with as much interest as she had shown in the lives of her own children. Hearing Anna come down the stairs, she immediately filled the electric kettle and, when it had boiled, made tea as Anna told her about the death of Father Lambert.

'The poor man,' said Miriam. 'Michal will be sorry.'

'We called him from the college,' said Anna. 'He asked if he might have been *murdered*.'

'Why should anyone want to murder him?' asked Miriam in an undramatic tone of voice.

Anna shrugged. 'It seems crazy, but that's what he told Andrew.'

'It's because there's so much violence in Israel,' she said. 'They cannot imagine anyone dying of natural causes.' She poured tea into a cup and gave it to Anna.

'Andrew actually wants him to have been murdered because suicides go straight to Hell.'

'Well, I wouldn't pay too much attention to *his* opinion.'

Miriam Lilien had met Andrew on a number of occasions and she disapproved of him – not because she disliked him, or because he was a Catholic monk, but because she felt that his friendship distracted Anna from finding a man she could marry. She was, in this way, somewhat old-fashioned – she felt that a woman's destiny inevitably lay in a husband and a home. However, she knew her niece better than Anna knew herself and understood that in her case this destiny might be difficult to achieve.

'Did Jake call?' Anna asked her aunt.

'No. Why should he?'

'Dad thought he might be in London.'

She shook her head. 'I've heard nothing.'

'Doesn't he usually stay here?'

'He prefers not to. He feels uncomfortable.'

'Why?'

'He doesn't feel it should be like this.'

'Like what?'

'Like a home, here in England, with his aunt English and his cousins all English. He doesn't like it. He's like a caged lion, pacing up and down. He's only happy in a kibbutz or in a tent.'

Anna smiled. 'With a rifle under his bed.'

Miriam nodded soberly. 'You laugh, Anna, but, last time he came, he *had* a gun – not under his bed but in his bag in the wardrobe. I saw it when I was cleaning his room.'

'He sees the PLO behind every lamp-post.'

'He frightens me, Anna.'

'He frightens me. The whole thing frightens me. That's why I left.'

Miriam sighed. 'But to do what, Anna?'

'A degree.'

'Yes, a degree.' She sighed again as if to pass judgement on higher education.

Anna smiled. 'Just because you got married when you were twenty doesn't mean that we all have to do the same thing.'

'It certainly won't happen to you if you spend all your time with that priest of yours.'

'He's cute, and a good companion, *faute de mieux*.'

'And how are you going to find the *mieux* if you're always with him?'

Anna took her aunt's hand in hers and patted it fondly. 'Don't worry, Auntie. I'll find a nice Englishman just as you did. In fact I've got a date tonight.'

Her aunt looked doubtful. 'May I ask who?'

'You don't know him.'

'Is he Jewish?'

'Does he have to be?'

'It would be better. My Peter was English but he was also Jewish and that made many things much easier.'

Anna laughed. 'Thanks for the advice,' she said, getting to her feet and kissing Miriam Lilien on the cheek before leaving to go upstairs to her room.

There, for a moment, she felt happy as she always did after talking to her aunt, who was the only member of her family with whom she felt in sympathy or who she felt was in sympathy with her. For Anna, like Miriam, had rejected the Zionism which the rest of her family had espoused. This had not been just an expression of adolescent rebellion but came from the confusion of her upbringing. Unlike her brother Jake, who had been brought up in Israel, Anna's childhood had been spent largely in the United States. She had been born in Israel, but at the age of four had gone to Princeton with her parents. Throughout the 1970s, when Michal Dagan had held different posts in American universities, Anna had gone to American schools. Since her mother was originally American, English was spoken in the home. Anna had never learned more than a smattering of Hebrew, and often, when Michal and Rachel went back to Israel, she had remained with her grandmother in New York.

After graduating from Brandeis, her reassimilation into Israel might have been easier if there had been a more tolerant atmosphere in the Dagan household. Her father who, upon coming to Israel in 1952, had espoused the old-fashioned, secular, socialistic Zionism of the founders of the Jewish state, changing his family name from Fischl to Dagan, now attended the synagogue every Sabbath and observed many of the precepts of the Mosaic Law. Unclean food was banned from the kitchen and, to avoid the servile work of boiling a kettle on the Sabbath, water for making tea or coffee was kept simmering in an urn from sunset on Friday to sunset on Saturday.

All this, Anna knew, came from the influence of her brother Jake. Six years older than Anna, he had been left with friends in Israel whenever the Dagans had gone to America. His first language was Hebrew and, just as Anna hardly knew Israel, so Jake had little experience of the outside world. Raised on stories not just of Joshua's conquest of Jericho, or David's defeat of Goliath, but also of the assassination of British soldiers by the Irgun and the Stern Gang, Jake gloried in the military triumphs of his people, and never doubted their right to populate the territory that in antiquity God had given to the Jews. He supported the Likud, under Begin and then Shamir, and the policy of Jewish settlement on the West Bank. He also believed in an inner commitment to the Jewish cause, and had persuaded his agnostic parents to call him Ya'acov, and to reintroduce the pious practices which had been unknown in their family for three generations.

If strict observance of this kind had always been part of the Dagans' way of life, Anna might have accepted it; but, as she scornfully pointed out to her parents, the tradition of the family was rather to play down the kind of scrupulous observance of the law of Moses which had so isolated the Jews in Gentile societies. The atmosphere of her grandmother's flat in New York had been German as much as Jewish, and her father's original commitment to Israel had been as a homeland for his people, not a colony of crazed fanatics like her brother Jake.

Michal Dagan had defended himself a little lamely on the grounds that a greater dedication to the Jewishness of Israel had become necessary 'under pressure of events'. His wife Rachel, too, seemed now to accept that observance had always been part of the faith of the Jews. Anna, however, not only ridiculed this Jewish fundamentalism, but also flaunted her own secularism in any way she could. She would make herself bacon sandwiches and cheeseburgers, and go to the movies on a Friday night, just to exasperate Jake. The brother and sister had violent arguments, to the distress of their parents. Rachel Dagan would take her son aside to ask him to try to understand that, after so many years in America, Anna was bound to have a different point of view, while Michal would explain yet again to Anna how Israel could only survive if the Jews deepened their sense of who they were by observing those laws and customs which had preserved their identity over the centuries of the diaspora.

Neither child was convinced, and the arguments became so unpleasant that it was finally decided that Anna should study for a postgraduate degree abroad. If her grandmother had still been alive she would have returned to New York; instead, she went to London to lodge with her Aunt Miriam and study under Father Lambert. She told herself that she was happy to go: she found Israel provincial and claustrophobic and had no intention of serving in the army; but she felt, all the same, that she had somehow been driven out of her home by her older brother and that her parents had allowed it to happen because they loved her less than they loved him.

The room she had been given in her aunt's house was large and light, looking out over the garden to the backs of the houses in the adjacent street. Having been that of her cousin Rosie, it had a girlish look with blue and white striped wallpaper and a shelf of china ornaments; and Anna, though her taste was different, had done little to change the décor – substituting only a poster of a Bonnard exhibition which she had seen in Paris for a picture of Rupert Everett, an English actor she did not know.

Now, with time to kill before she left for her date, she started the kind of footling around with which she always wasted an hour or so in the evening – arranging the work she meant to do rather than doing it; skimming through an article to see if she wanted to read it, but, upon deciding that she did, putting it on one side, preferring to tidy her clothes which were either draped over her chair or hanging out of the open drawers and cupboards.

In doing this, she would come across some garment – a skirt or a waistcoat or a blouse – which she had forgotten about, and she would try it on to remind herself how she looked in it, turning first in profile and then to face the cheval mirror in the corner of the room, looking less at the clothes which were her excuse for this narcissistic study than at her own childish face – the tiny nose, large eyes and black

61

hair; and at the still adolescent figure – narrow hips, thin legs and barely perceptible bosom.

She studied herself with alternating admiration and despair – at one moment thinking that she was really rather pretty in a waif-like way, and at the next concluding that no man could possibly want someone so skinny and small. She knew, of course, that strictly speaking the second statement was not true. She had been to bed with half-a-dozen boys – fellow students in America, young soldiers in Israel and, most recently, Andrew's brother Henry, who was taking her to the opera that night.

This current affair had been complicated by Henry's insistence that it should be kept secret from Andrew, and her own determination that it should also be hidden from her family. That was why, until that evening, she had always pretended to her aunt that she went out with Andrew rather than Henry; and why she had listened to Andrew talk about his brother as if she hardly knew him. She disliked deceiving someone who, she knew, would never deceive her, but, just as she knew that it would upset her aunt to know she had a Gentile lover, so she accepted from Henry that Andrew would suffer if he thought she had been seduced by his degenerate brother.

She also knew that Andrew would not understand how she could sleep with a man she did not love. He would assume, if she slept with him, that she must love him, when she knew she did not. She had never, since her adolescence, considered herself to be in love. Few of her earlier affairs had been one-night stands, but none had lasted for more than a couple of months. If Anna had let them, one or two of the young men she had slept with might have followed up the casual encounter with the kind of friendship that could have led to love; but invariably they had been dismissed – or had felt themselves to be dismissed – by the harsh things she had said to them later; for she was caught in the trap of desiring the kind of man she despised – someone physically large and mentally slow – as if the demands of natural selection obliged her to balance her own quick wit and small stature in the genes of the next generation.

When Andrew had first introduced her to Henry, she had found him snobbish and affected. He was taller and better-looking than his younger brother and in almost every way created a contrary impression. While Andrew was naïve, unkempt and cheerful, Henry was cold, secretive and demanding. He dressed formally and fastidiously – he had appeared almost foppish to Anna – and always seemed on the brink of exasperation, as if expecting everyone and everything around him to fall short of the exacting standards which he set for himself.

He was aged around thirty-three but seemed older to Anna, partly because of the severity of his manner, partly because he was rich and so had all the appurtenances of the older generation, like a well furnished flat and a silver BMW with telephone and electric windows. He also wore suits and took her to restaurants where he never ordered the house wine but chose some rare claret with a musty flavour which doubled the already considerable bill.

Anna was not seduced by these luxuries – indeed, she found them unnecessary and absurd – but she had been pleased at first that a man of his kind should feel that she merited his attention. She had then become curious because he was English in the way she had expected Englishmen to be – not cheerful and casual like Andrew, but formal and reserved. Getting to know Henry better had seemed like going to see the Tower of London or a Shakespeare play at Stratford-upon-Avon.

The more she saw him, the more she felt drawn to him without quite knowing why. She could not say that she had become fond of him because he would not allow her to come close enough to feel affection. She could not say that she was attracted to him – not, certainly, with the kind of straight-forward lust she had felt for some of her previous lovers. It was rather that she was fascinated, even challenged, by a man of a sort she had not come across before; and, while most of her earlier boyfriends had been wholly preoccupied

63

with themselves, boring her with long, introspective monologues and demanding constant compliments to bolster their
egos, Henry never spoke about himself or looked for reassurance. It was from Andrew that she knew about his unhappy
childhood and his successful career. If Anna herself put any
question to Henry of a personal kind, it either returned like
a boomerang, or it was simply ignored, as if she was a
Delilah seeking the secret of his strength.

Yet he was constantly asking about her past life, not with
the solicitude of a psychoanalyst or a confessor but with the
cold curiosity of a scientist or a collector. This detachment
did not offend her. Instead, it stimulated a desire in her to
seem interesting enough to form part of his collection, to
help prove or disprove whatever hypothesis about human
nature was running through his mind. She realized, when
she had first set foot in his flat, that there was more to him
than an up-to-date version of the classic bowler-hatted English gentleman. Many of his books, for example, were in
French, and by writers she had heard of but never read. The
paintings, too, were strange – some large and colourful,
others figurative and weird, and all quite unlike the dreary
works in her parents' flat in Jerusalem, or the restrained
abstracts in her uncle's collection in Belsize Park.

These manifestations of his taste, taken with the imper-
sonal elegance of the clothes he wore and the furnishings of
his flat, formed an image in her mind of an intriguing man
whom she would like to intrigue in her turn. Sex seemed an
obvious way to establish that she had succeeded. She was
feminist enough to feel that a casual affair could be an
adventure for a woman as well as for a man; and emanci-
pated enough from Jewish ethics to discount any qualms she
might have about going to bed with a man she hardly knew.

If she had hoped, by sleeping with him, that she would
get to know him better, she was quickly disappointed; for,
when they did make love, he remained as detached as he
had been before. He caressed her naked body as if he was
repelled by what he desired and despised her for responding
to his gestures of affection. Even as they made love, he
seemed removed, watching what they were doing with

distaste; but, far from offending Anna, this ambivalence had enhanced her own pleasure, for she too felt the same blend of excitement and shame.

That evening, since she was going to Covent Garden, she chose the clothes she was to wear with great care, changing back and forth two or three times, wanting to look elegant yet also to give Henry the impression that she had not bothered much at all. It was the same when she came to make up her eyes – adding a barely perceptible line of mascara to her already dark lashes and a small smudge of shadow. All the time, while she was doing this, she was brooding about Henry's 'three-month contracts', but it was only when she was ready to leave that she went to her desk, looked at her diary and flicked back through the pages to find out if her time was up. She found the entry for their first dinner together at the beginning of February: she had written his name out in full. Then, on the pages which followed, there were increasingly abbreviated entries until it had become simply an H.

She knew the date she had first slept with him: she had made an appointment to see a doctor two days later to get a new prescription for the pill. It had been at the beginning of March. Now it was early June. Her three months had run out at the weekend.

Seven

She caught the tube at Belsize Park and emerged forty minutes later at Sloane Square. It was an area of London where she felt ill at ease. Hampstead had something cosmopolitan about it while Belgravia, for all the foreign embassies, felt alien and English. Eaton Square in particular, with its classical façades of white stucco, seemed as cold and aloof as the lover who lived there.

When she reached the entrance to the building whose top floor formed his flat, she rang the bell and waited for his voice to ask harshly who it was. When it did, she barked back, 'Anna', regretting, as she always did, that the evening should start by shouting her name into a microphone embedded in a wall.

The buzzer sounded. She pushed the door and went up the carpeted stairs to the top floor. Henry was waiting by the entrance to his flat. She glanced at his thin face to assess his mood, but he greeted her, as he always did, with a mask of courtesy – an empty smile, a brushing kiss on her cheek – before closing the door behind them and guiding her into his living-room, where the flames of a gas fire flickered soundlessly over asbestos logs.

She had no coat, and sat down at once on one of the large sofas while Henry crossed the room to pour her a drink. He was wearing, as he always did, a double-breasted, grey pin-striped suit which somehow suited his tall, slightly stooping figure.

'Have you heard about Father Lambert?' she asked.

He handed her a glass of white wine. 'Yes. Andrew told me.'

'Isn't it sad?'

'Particularly for Andrew.' He returned to the tray of bottles and glasses to fill his own glass with whisky and water.

'Did he tell you that it was suicide?'

'Yes. Or murder.' He sat down on an armchair which faced her.

'And about the woman?'

'Yes.' He gave a sour smile.

She smiled too. 'Poor Andrew.'

'It had to happen, sooner or later.'

'What?'

'A crisis of this kind.'

'Why?'

'Because sooner or later, anyone in religious orders suffers a breakdown of some sort. With Lambert it came later, that's all.'

'How can you be so sure?'

'Because a religious vocation is the symptom of a psychosis.'

66

'Always?'

'What else can it be?'

She shrugged. 'Well, I sure don't want to be a nun, but that doesn't mean that anyone who does is crazy.'

He frowned. 'By definition, isn't it demented to lead a life in which you suppress all your natural desires?'

She thought of the bed next door where they so often ended the evening, and acknowledged to herself that it did seem odd. She was irritated, however, by the confidence with which Henry passed judgement on others and said: 'Perhaps you just don't have the imagination to envisage a life that is different from your own.'

This appeared to irritate Henry. He swirled the ice in his glass of whisky. 'I can envisage a different life only too well,' he said with a sidelong glance at Anna. 'I can also envisage a different life for my brother.'

'Well, so can I, I guess,' said Anna.

'It's so patently obvious to me that after being deserted at a vulnerable age by our weak father, and then bullied in adolescence by our emasculating mother, Andrew found a psychological haven in the Catholic Church with its strong but kindly God the Father and passive, patient and ever-loving mother of Mary.'

'Sure.'

'Add to that the personal influence of Father Lambert, who was determined to bring fresh blood into his decrepit order, and at the same time recruit a secretary without having to pay for one . . .'

'That's very unkind.'

'I think he was unkind to bamboozle my brother. And now, having led him up the garden path, he confesses, if not in word, then in deed, that the whole thing was a grotesque fraud.'

She sighed. 'I really think he seems OK – Andrew, that is.'

'For the time being, maybe. He's clinging to the idea, which your father seems to share, that Father Lambert did not kill himself but was murdered.'

'I don't know why Dad thinks that.'

'Andrew feels frustrated because he can't call on the police. He wants me to play the detective.'

'And will you?'

'I'll do anything to help my brother.'

'That's the . . .' She faltered. 'It's one of the nicest things about you,' she said.

'The only nice thing?' he asked, finishing her first sentence. He stood up before she could answer and moved towards the door.

They drove to Covent Garden to see Mozart's *La Clemenza di Tito*. She had been to the opera with Henry twice before, and on neither occasion had she enjoyed it – not because she had disliked the music or the production, but because she had felt Henry was uneasy at being seen with her in public. In the four months since she had known him, she had never met any of his friends. She knew that they existed because the telephone often rang when she was in his flat, but it had soon become clear that he did not intend to introduce her into his circle.

At first she had thought this was because he wanted to keep her to himself, but later she decided that he was in some way ashamed of her or, if not ashamed, then embarrassed to be seen in her company. She wondered, without minding much, whether it was because she was Jewish or American or small; or whether he was conducting a parallel affair with some tall English rose who belonged to the group of his regular friends.

The idea did not upset her because she herself felt detached from Henry. She found him interesting and attractive but entirely alien in a way that Andrew, for example, was not. She was fascinated by him, and flattered to be taken up by someone so rich, successful and decidedly grown up. She also appreciated the skill and the style with which he made love to her. Yet, once he had done so, she never felt close to him, or wanted to remain around. Once he had put on his cotton boxer shorts, his silk shirt and grey, pin-striped suit; once he had opened his mouth to speak in that sneering British drawl; once he had begun to move around in the stage-set of his grandiose apartment – she felt

68

estranged, and as inappropriate and out of place as the jeans, tee-shirt, socks and sneakers which she picked up off the carpeted floor.

It was the same that evening at Covent Garden. She had taken trouble to dress as smartly as she could, but when she caught sight of herself in a mirror she saw just how preppy and teen-aged she looked, how out of place in the long gallery where the bankers and businessmen with their elegant wives walked up and down while waiting for the next act.

He had bought her a glass of champagne which she drank, even though she disliked champagne, while Henry, with a glass of whisky, asked her what she thought of the opera.

'Well, it isn't quite what you expect from Mozart, is it?'

'It is apparently one of his last.'

'You never saw it before?'

'No.'

'It's certainly interesting . . .'

'Why? To see that even a genius can be a bore?'

She laughed. 'My father wouldn't like it.'

'Why not?'

'Titus destroyed Jerusalem. He wasn't very clement to the Jews.'

'Yet Bernice was Jewish and she loved him.'

'Sure. Titus and one or two others.'

'Who else?'

'His father, Vespasian. Three husbands. And her brother, Agrippa.'

The bell rang for the second act.

'She also met St Paul,' said Anna, 'but he was in chains so I guess he was safe.'

'How did she arrange that?' asked Henry, taking her empty glass.

'She and Agrippa were visiting Festus, the Roman procurator, in Caesarea. St Paul was waiting to be sent off to Rome. Agrippa asked to hear him preach.'

They went back into the auditorium.

'How do you know all this?' asked Henry.

'From Father Lambert's lectures,' said Anna. 'It came into his course on Biblical Archaeology.'

After the opera they drove back to Belgravia and had supper in Henry's flat. This, too, was far from a simple bite to eat. Instead of the glass of milk and peanut-butter sandwich which Anna, on her own, would have eaten in her Aunt Miriam's kitchen, Henry always arranged a three-course dinner, beginning with soup and ending with a sorbet, with smoked salmon, gravadlax or game pie in between. He did not prepare it himself; someone else came in during the day; but he served it methodically by candlelight at the polished antique table in the corner of his living-room.

There was always, too, a half bottle of Meursault or Montrachet and a full bottle of some fancy claret, then a choice of liqueurs to drink with their coffee; and, while Anna at first found the formality of such suppers a little absurd, particularly after going to a film, they had the effect of arousing a pleasant anticipation of what was to follow in bed.

Before they reached that point, Henry always behaved as if it might not happen; or, at any rate, he never referred to it with languorous looks or gestures. She sensed that for her to do so would offend Henry's sense of decorum – like ogling the sorbet while sipping one's soup. She therefore made conversation and, on that evening, returned to the history behind the story of *La Clemenza di Tito*.

'I shall miss that course of Father Lambert's,' she said.

'What was so special about it?'

'He made the whole ancient world come alive and make sense. I hadn't realized, for example, how tight things were . . .'

'Tight?'

'Well, I'd always kind of thought of Caesar and Cleopatra in one compartment, like History or Drama, and Herod the Great in another, like Scripture Studies. In fact Herod was a friend of Cleopatra's, and of both Julius and Octavius Caesar. He named the Antonia fortress after Mark Antony. His son Antipas was deeply involved with John the Baptist, Salome

70

and all that; and his great-grandchildren, Agrippa and Bernice, turn up listening to St Paul.'

'And what did they make of him?'

'Of St Paul?'

'Yes.'

'The procurator, Festus, thought he was crazy, but Agrippa was quite impressed. Father Lambert used to say that if you read between the lines, it looks as if Bernice dragged her brother away before he could be converted.'

'I would have reacted in the same way as Festus.'

'You've never been tempted to believe?'

'If I was, I would resist it.'

'Why?'

'Because it degrades the mind to fall back on superstition.'

'I don't believe either, but I don't think it's degrading. You could look on it as a kind of poetry, a way of letting something ancient and beautiful suffuse your being so that you are not in fact degraded but ennobled by it.'

'Like marinating a fish?' He smiled sourly.

'Sure. We Jews, after all, are a people moulded by our myths, and I don't have to believe that Moses heard God speak from a burning bush to be glad all the same that I'm part of that tradition. And Andrew, whatever may be the reasons for his believing, gets something very beautiful from his faith. He really is gentler and kinder than anyone else I know.'

'That's not thanks to Christ.'

'Thanks to what, then?'

'His fear of life. He's like a monkey, threatened by a stronger monkey, who lies down and proffers his genitals to deflect the other's aggression.'

'That's a horrible thing to say.'

'It doesn't help Andrew to shy away from an impartial analysis of his condition. Clearly his commitment to poverty, chastity and obedience is a way of saying: "I won't compete for your money or your women, and I'll do anything you say."'

'That's what makes him nice.'

'It makes him a victim.'

'Of whom?'

'Of all those repressed pederasts and menopausal spinsters who run the Roman Catholic Church.'

'He's nice to me too.'

'But you don't sleep with him.'

She blushed. 'Liking and . . . loving are different.'

'They are indeed. Different and probably incompatible.'

'Why?'

'Because love is just a gloss on the crude instincts which ensure the survival of the species.'

Anna looked down at her plate, wondering if this cynicism was meant to soften her up for the ending of their affair. 'Can't you love and like people at the same time?' she asked.

He shrugged his shoulders. 'Perhaps. But even liking, in my experience, has some ulterior motive behind it.'

'Like what?'

'We choose our friends like our possessions, to enhance the image we want to present to others.'

'You have a very low opinion of human beings.'

'Vanity, vanity, all is vanity, as one of your prophets put it.'

'Then why aren't you pleased that Andrew has climbed out of this cesspit?'

'Because you can't climb out. We are what we are – isolated individuals in relentless pursuit of gratification and power. The only way to be content is to own up to it, and enjoy the chase.'

'And *do* you enjoy the chase?'

He looked at her briefly as if assessing the prey. 'Do I? Yes, I do. The fittest are always happy to survive.'

'Whereas your unfit brother is unhappy?'

'Yes, because of Lambert.'

'But in general?'

'The general and the particular are linked. That's the point I am trying to make. He imagined that he had escaped the struggle by joining the Simonite order. Sooner or later he was bound to discover that you can neither change human nature nor deny it; you can simply pervert it. Most dangerous of all is the celibacy of priests, because all that energy which should be dissipated in sex is obliged to find other outlets like pride, ambition and the sinister pleasure which priests take in exploiting and manipulating the weakness and uncertainty of others.'

'Do you say this to Andrew?'

'No. It would upset him. But you – well, I should have thought that you would sympathize with my point of view.'

'Because I'm a Jew?'

'Yes.' He answered at once but she could tell, from his slight confusion, that he would rather not have been caught labelling her in that way.

'My brother would,' she said, 'but the only Catholic I have ever known besides Andrew was Father Lambert, and he always seemed to me to be kind, cheerful and completely unselfish.'

'But now you know you were wrong.'

'How?'

'Because suicide is at the apex of egoism.'

'Perhaps he didn't kill himself,' she said. 'Perhaps he was killed.'

'Even if he was killed, he went to bed with that woman before he died.'

'That, well, in a way it's kind of romantic. And it proves your theory wrong.'

'How?'

'Well, you can hardly say that he did it to improve the species.'

'No. He was probably just curious to know what he'd been missing all those years.'

'And had he been missing much?' she asked, attempting the kind of ironic smile that she saw so often on Henry's face.

'By definition,' he said.

'Why by definition?'

'Because if our genes are programmed for survival, not just as an individual but as a species too, then those things which ensure our survival must be pleasurable.'

'Like eating?'

'Yes.'

'And screwing?'

'Yes, except that it is complicated by psychological factors.'

'Like love?'

'Love, yes. Or the lack of it.' He looked at her sadly.

'It's a pity,' she said.

'What?'

'Well, that I don't inspire love.'

'And do I?'

'No.' She lowered her head and shook it at the same time so that strands of hair fell over her face and hid the tears which had come into her eyes.

'It's better, don't you think?' he asked.

'What?' She understood what he meant but wanted him to say it.

'That we stop.'

'Don't you like it any more?'

'It's not as simple as that.'

'It seemed perfectly simple up to now.'

'For the body, perhaps, but not for the mind.'

'You shouldn't take it so seriously.'

'Perhaps not.'

'It's just sex, for God's sake.'

He looked at her from across the table with no particular expression. 'I'm sorry if you feel let down.'

'No.' She turned away. 'I always knew, well, that there were no strings.'

He stood up and went to the kitchen to fetch the coffee.

When he returned, she asked: 'Is it true that you always end things after three months?'

He frowned. 'Who told you that?'

'Is it true?'

'In my experience, it's always wise to quit while one's ahead.'

'Why?'

'Because familiarity breeds contempt.'

'Always?'

'Always. But I wish . . .'

'What?'

'That it didn't.'

She sniffed and stood up. 'I guess it's good for me to get dumped, once in a while, since it's usually me who does the dumping.' She moved towards the door.

'Don't you want any coffee?'

'I'd rather get home.'

'Are you sure?'

She nodded, and sniffed again.

'I'll call a cab.'

'I can find one in the street.'

'No, wait.' He went to the telephone. 'If I book it from here, you can charge it to my company account.'

Eight

After he had seen Anna into a cab and had given the driver her aunt's address in Belsize Park, Henry returned to his flat, where he refilled his glass with whisky and water and sat down on the sofa facing the blank screen of his television. He remained like this for some time – a man in a suit, now crumpled, with tired features and bloodshot eyes. Occasionally his head would turn, and he would look at the fabrics and artefacts which furnished and decorated his flat – at the beige walls with olive-green borders to match the sombre pattern of the heavy curtains and the piping on the sofa.

To Anna it had seemed grand. To Henry it was meant to seem grand – even aristocratic. He had paid a designer, after all, to create such an effect. In the four years since he had moved in, there had been, he knew, many who had been convinced – and not all of them as impressionable as Anna. However, he had never been convinced himself, any more than an actor who plays Hamlet on a stage set of Elsinore believes that he is a prince of Denmark.

He intended, now, to replay the tape of *Newsnight* which had been recorded automatically earlier in the evening; but he did not reach for the controls which, with the press of a couple of buttons, would have brought sound to the speakers and an image to the screen. Instead, he sat in quiet obeisance before the dead set as if praying before his household god. It was a fine god – a Bang and Olufsen: when it was switched on, its colours outshone the flames of the gas log fire. So, too, the video recorder was the best of its kind, slim and grey like a revolver, with twinkling numbers and symbols waiting to obey those invisible rays which emanated from the small box which Henry held in his hand.

That box was not the only magic wand in his possession. There was another for the television, and a third for the music centre which, again at the touch of a button, would instantly bring into his living-room the finest choirs and orchestras playing the loveliest sounds contrived by the human mind. So too in his car, the gleaming silver-grey BMW 635 CSi, he would listen to the same tapes and, like the fine lady riding to Banbury Cross, could have music wherever he went. And from his car, or in a restaurant, he could speak through his portable telephone to anyone anywhere in the world. There was no invention of modern man which Henry did not exploit – to wash his clothes or his dishes; to clean his flat or his car; to transpose his thoughts into words, his words onto disks, then back onto paper, and from paper, by telephone, to another sheet of paper at the other end of the line.

His clothes, too, were the best – cashmere sweaters, cotton or silk shirts, hand-made shoes. Nothing he touched was cheap: even the women, before Anna, had worn exquisite dresses from the fashion houses of France; and beneath them, silken, lace-edged lingerie, smelling sweetly of heady scents which mingled luxuriously with the musks of nature.

Now, when he thought of Anna's childish underclothes, and how touching her little brown body had looked on the white sheets of his large bed, he felt a sense of regret which joined, but did not supplant, the relief he had felt at seeing her go. Indeed, the question he asked himself – or waited to have answered by his household god – was not why he had dropped her, but why he had taken up with her in the first place.

He remembered how, when he had met her with Andrew, he had, as he always did when meeting a woman, appraised her for her sexual potential; and how he had disqualified her, as indeed he disqualified most of them, not because she was ugly – her face was unquestionably pretty – but because she was socially irrelevant and physically out of scale.

It was not snobbery which led him to consider her irrelevant, but rather the sage which spoke through the flickering, multicoloured 24-inch screen, and valued only long-legged, well-dressed, upper-class girls. Her size, too, put him off, not because she was squat or built in inelegant proportions, but because, dressed as she was at the time in a duffel-coat, trainers and jeans, and glancing at him furtively with impish eyes, she seemed too fragile and childlike to be eligible for a grown man's bed.

He had been amused, certainly, by the way she had tormented his pious brother with her sharp answers and the kind of casual obscenities with which young Americans spice their speech; but the only reason why he asked where she lived, and had later invited her to lunch, was because he had learned from Andrew that her brother Jake worked for Military Counter-Intelligence in Israel's army, the IDF.

Henry owned and edited a series of newsletters providing inside information on business and trade. At the time he had been preparing an issue on the arms industry, and Israel, he knew, had one of the largest arms budgets in the world. He already had contacts in Tel Aviv, but another would be useful. It had certainly seemed worthwhile to try and find out from the sister what her brother might or might not know.

It turned out that she knew nothing, but she had amused him sufficiently – or so he told himself – to ask her out again, once to the theatre, then to the opera, and finally to the kind of restaurant where the expense was a compliment and the atmosphere enticing. When, a month after meeting her, he had asked her back to his flat, he still did not fancy her in the usual way, but was partly curious to know what she would be like in bed, and partly conscious that it would be

77

almost insulting if their candlelit dinners did not end in this way.

From the start it had been a shallow commitment. Henry's chief concern had been to keep the whole thing a secret from Andrew, fearing that, if he discovered about their affair, he would blame himself for leading Anna into sin. He loved Andrew and wanted to protect him from the coarse realities of life. He loved him and he pitied him profoundly, having seen what he had suffered as a child. It was not so much the divorce which had hurt him, as the humiliation they both had witnessed, during the years which led up to it, of their weak father by their embittered mother.

James Nash had been an officer in the Royal Navy, and, in their infancy, both boys had seen him as a hero. Failing, in middle-age, to gain the promotion he felt was his due, he had retired from the Navy to work as a management consultant. This was intended to make him rich, but he was no more successful on land than he had been at sea. His wife, having suffered from the sneers of the naval wives whose husbands had risen faster than hers, now languished in genteel poverty in a villa in the suburbs of London.

Doubtless, there was sexual dissatisfaction too, but the complaints Henry remembered being shrieked at his father by his mother were more about the career she had sacrificed to marry him and the drudgery of domestic life. How he had longed for his father to answer her charges; instead, he had stayed silent, and, to escape his wife's nagging, went to sleep on a narrow bed in the attic.

At the age of thirteen, Henry had been sent to a boarding-school that was both cheap and second-rate. Andrew had joined him three years later. It was here that they learned that their father had gone to live with his secretary, whom he later married. They now saw him only at odd weekends, and for a fortnight in the summer when he took them camping in Wales.

His departure exacerbated their mother's discontent. She took a job as a receptionist in a doctor's surgery, but this only reminded her of the career she might have had if she had gone to university instead of marrying and raising a family. With no husband to blame for her condition, she turned instead upon her two sons, making clear how much she resented having to cook their supper and wash their clothes. Her social circle contracted to a few other embittered single women and the boys themselves, after going to boarding-school, no longer had friends in the neighbourhood. As a result, the holidays in Wimbledon became tedious and tormenting. They were no happier with their father and stepmother in their cramped flat, and they both came to look forward to going back to the school which most of the other pupils found grim.

It was at school that the boys had their friends, and that there were also some inspiring teachers. As a result, they did well – Henry going on to study economics at Leeds University, and Andrew, four years later, archaeology at Huntingdon College in London. Nor, while they were at university, was there anything in particular to tell them apart from students from happier homes. Certainly, the qualities which Henry was aware of in himself, as he started out in life, did not appear as either strengths or weaknesses, but simply as features of an interior physiognomy. He did not feel, for example, that he loved Andrew because he pitied him but only because brothers loved brothers and Andrew, anyway, was a patently lovable young man. Nor did he ascribe his own determination to make money to the humiliation he had suffered in witnessing his father's penury: it was a normal enough ambition in a young man at the time.

His attitude towards women, too, seemed not the fruit of a neurosis but the application of common sense to relations between the sexes. Desire, after all, was a given factor. Not only the promptings of his own instincts, but also the propaganda implicit in every book, every magazine, every film and every advertisement on television, confirmed the view that nothing equalled the delights of sexual love. If, on the first few occasions, the nervous fumbling in student hostels or shared flats in Leeds had not quite matched the ecstasy he had imagined, it did not deter him from continuing his pursuit of girls: seducing them brought about a catharsis which satisfied more than his senses.

79

In the isolation of his own ego, it did not occur to Henry that others found sexual encounters simple and fun. To him, just as nakedness was shameful, so copulation was degrading. It was the defiling of women which excited him, and led him to prefer those who were reluctant to sleep with him. To shift the source of a woman's will from her mind to her groin, and see her shed the pose of an intelligent being to rut like a beast, filled him with a dour satisfaction. He did not feel that he was himself degraded as the other half of the copulating couple; he remained detached – not merely from what he was doing but from the very part of his body which was ramming home the resentment he felt against the whole female sex.

After graduating from Leeds, Henry worked for some years as a financial journalist and researcher, first for the *Investor's Chronicle*, then the *Economist*, and finally the Economist Intelligence Unit, before leaving with a colleague to start a series of newsletters of his own. These picked the brains of dons, diplomats and international civil servants to provide both legal and technical data about trade to those who paid the subscription.

At first this enterprise had gone badly: it was too limited in its application and was inadequately financed. Understanding this, Henry persuaded his partner to sell him his shares, which he bought with borrowed money. He borrowed more to buy the lease on an office in Soho. He expanded the range of the newsletters, and took them to the limits of the laws on official secrets and industrial espionage. As a result, the Soho newsletters became essential reading for investment analysts and export managers wanting to know, for example, what standards were required for electrical equipment in South Korea, what products were being prepared by rivals in Singapore, or what bribes should be paid and to whom to get goods through customs in Ghana. As the newsletters grew both in size and scope, Henry increased the number of subscribers and the cost of the subscription. After two years, he was making a profit; after four, he had paid off his loans. By the age of thirty, he was a rich man.

This success had enabled him to acquire all the material appurtenances of a pleasant life, such as a flat in London and a house in France; but it meant that he lost through envy some of his oldest friends. He made others, of course, but of a more superficial kind – men who had also made money, usually in the City, and who were ambitious and selfish in the same way. It also enabled him to extend the range of his philandering into circles which had hitherto been out of his league; but he found, to his disappointment, that one woman's body was much like another's – and their minds not so very different. It was then that he decided all love affairs should end after three months: prolonging them invariably led to ragged and painful endings. As the length of each liaison was limited, so the period between them became longer. He grew bored by love as he had grown bored by business, and he looked for something new to engage his interest.

For a while Henry considered a career as a Conservative politician. He had grown rich as a result of his own initiative and hard work; he believed strongly in the Darwinian ethos of the government of the day. He joined the local Conservative association, went to one or two meetings and canvassed at a local election; but soon he realized that he was too easily exasperated to listen patiently to a constituent's complaints, or to spend a lifetime trimming his opinions and kowtowing to people he despised – all for the remote chance that in due course he might exercise political power.

What was left? More money? To build his business into an empire? To fatten his fortune into twenty or even two hundred million pounds? For what? He was content with his flat in London and found his house in France a time-consuming encumbrance. He had more clothes than he could fit into his wardrobe and travelled whenever and wherever he liked.

He liked painting and sculpture and bought one or two works of art. He also liked reading, as Anna had noticed from the books on his shelves, and had taught himself French because French literature appealed to him, or had done when he was in his twenties and could relate his own experience to the escapades of Stendhal's or Flaubert's young heroes.

As he grew older, he found that he had more in common with the nihilistic and pessimistic characters in the novels of Sartre or Céline. However, the more he became absorbed in a novel, the more he suffered from the banality of his own life. Films frustrated him in the same way. He felt he was watching life from the auditorium when he should have been on stage. He was sure that there must be more to achieve than what he had achieved already. At times, a sense of destiny convinced him that something glorious and extraordinary lay ahead; but, even as he felt this, the voice of common sense would remind him that man was no more than an evolved baboon.

This conflict between the vague but grand aspirations of what was poetic and romantic in his nature, and the prosaic expectations of the realist, came to torment him. He was determined that a man equipped with reason should be able to master his own mind, and refused to believe that we are all subject to the dictates of our subconscious. Such a hypothesis seemed to undermine the foundation upon which all science and philosophy depended; yet he had read the works of psychoanalysts and felt he understood quite clearly what had driven Andrew to become a priest. He was obliged to recognize that, if Andrew had been conditioned by his childhood, he too must have been affected – that his vengeful feelings towards women, for example, and his reluctance to commit himself in love, came not from an impartial assessment of the character of women or the drawbacks of marriage, but from the harm done by his irascible mother.

His affair with Anna might have been his salvation, or, at any rate, might have marked a change of direction, because she was so different to the girls he had gone out with before – different in size, different in style, simpler, funnier, cleverer and more serious-minded. For the first time in his life he had slept with a girl whose views he respected, not just on history or archaeology, but on general matters like politics and art. Her vocabulary was limited, and it irritated him that she so often expressed herself in cute college-girl slang, but her opinions were original, her judgements sound, and her gibes often painful to his self-esteem.

These qualities, however, which made him like her, made loving her out of the question. Courtesy and curiosity had led him to sleep with her in the first place. He had persisted only because, after the coffee and the Cointreau, it seemed the proper thing to do. The sex itself had passed off to her apparent satisfaction; he had found that, for all her delicate proportions, she had the appetites and attributes of a mature woman. However, she lacked the voluptuousness which in other women aroused his lust. She was too likeable and intelligent to be credible as an object of resentment and contempt, and, where sex did not express his vengeful passion for women, it became nothing more than a banal routine.

That he might love her, despite this absence of desire, was inconceivable; it went so radically against the teaching of that religion, preached not by priests from a pulpit, but from advertising copywriters through the flickering screen. Love was an appetite which, once satisfied, came to an end. That was why it never lasted; why most of his married friends were unfaithful and unhappy, their children millstones around their necks.

Yet, the more he raged against love, marriage and family life, the more he himself longed to love someone other than himself. He began to imagine a love that went beyond the tempestuous egoism of sexual passion – something like the idealism which had led patriots to die for their country or revolutionaries to fall at the barricades. But he was trapped by the disillusion of his generation which found idealism impractical and patriotism absurd. His yearning had no object. He had to live with it unfulfilled.

PART TWO

Nine

Anna Dagan had a friend from Brandeis called Naomi Sherz who was writing a thesis on Brancusi at the Courtauld Institute of Art. She was the closest thing to a confidante that Anna had in London – or, indeed, anywhere else in the world; and though she did not know the identity of Anna's mysterious lover, she at least knew that he existed.

Waking the next morning feeling miserable, Anna telephoned Naomi and arranged to meet for lunch. She liked the idea of telling her how she had lost both her lover and her professor in the space of a day; and though, to judge from the mess that Naomi had made of her own life, Anna did not expect any valuable advice, she knew she could count on some sympathy in return for the sympathy she had shown to Naomi on many occasions at the break-up of her own unfortunate affairs.

She spent the morning at Huntingdon College, hoping to see Andrew, but he did not come in. At noon she took a bus to the Courtauld. Reaching Oxford Street early, she went into Selfridge's to kill time. She wandered through Miss Selfridge, wondering wistfully whether Henry might have kept her on if she had worn more elegant clothes, then she went up to the book store to look for a paperback novel.

Even as she had been strolling between the racks of dresses, she had felt she was being watched. Now, by the book-shelves, she sensed that a man was hovering only a short distance away from her. She turned. There was no one, or whoever was following her had ducked behind a pillar or a stack of books. She looked at her watch. There were still ten minutes to kill. She continued to browse among the books, still with the odd sensation that she was being observed.

When it was time to meet Naomi, she picked up a book

almost at random – it was Jean-Paul Sartre's *Words* – and went to the cash desk to buy it. She remained aware, as she stood there, that someone's eyes were on her, and the feeling grew until she was certain that whoever it was stood directly behind her in the queue. Suddenly angry at being pestered in this shadowy way, she turned abruptly and found herself face to face with her brother Jake.

'Hi,' he said with an amused look in his eye.

'What are you doing here?'

'Buying a book?' He showed her the paperback he was holding in his hand.

She stepped back to let him get to the cash desk and waited while he made his purchase. Then they both walked out of the department store and into the street leading to Portman Square.

'But what are you doing in London?' she asked.

'I came to see you.'

'Huh.'

'Let's say I was offered the trip and thought how nice it would be to see my sister.'

'Why didn't you call?'

'I was busy.'

'And Aunt Miriam? She thought you might stay.'

'She knew I was here?'

'Dad told us yesterday.'

He nodded. 'Shall we go eat?'

'I'm having lunch with a friend.'

'Couldn't you cancel it?'

She frowned because Jake had always taken it for granted that he would get his own way. 'I could, I guess,' she said, 'but I'm not sure that I want to.'

'I fly back this evening.'

'So?'

He smiled sourly to acknowledge that there was little affection between them. 'There are things to talk about,' he said.

'Like what?'

'Like the death of Father Lambert.'

'You heard?'

'Yes.'

'Do you know what happened in Israel?'

'I know, yes.'

'OK,' said Anna. 'I'll go tell Naomi that I can't make it.'

They walked to the Courtauld Institute where, rather than wait for Naomi, Anna left a message at the desk. She rejoined Jake outside and went back with him towards Baker Street.

Anna felt ill at ease, as she always did when she found herself alone with her brother. She was particularly suspicious when he was friendly, as he seemed to be now, because she knew from experience that it meant he wanted something out of her. His usual manner was that of the sneering older brother who had resented her presence in the Dagan family ever since she was born. When they were young he had bossed her and bullied her in the ways boys often do; but maturity had not mellowed his behaviour. When they were apart – Anna in the United States, Jake in Israel – each had envied the other the company of their parents. Every time Anna had returned to Israel, Jake's disdain for his younger sister had become ideologically more explicit. She had grown into an easygoing American, he a determined Israeli; but it was not until he had joined the army that she had actually come to fear him.

He had always been older, taller and stronger than she was, and had dominated her when they were children with his greater aggression and superior strength. As a recruit in the Israel Defence Force, he had learned to use this strength and aggression in a lethal way. He was trained in the use of weapons and came home on leave with a machine-gun, which he left hanging over the back of a chair in the kitchen – all of which was normal enough in Israel, but alarming for a girl raised largely on the East Coast of the United States.

More disturbing to Anna than Jake's familiarity with guns, was the training his mind had received in the army. He had chosen to serve for four years, and thereby gained a commission. Together with her parents she had witnessed his induction as an officer in the Armoured Corps in a torchlight ceremony held in the ruins of the fortress of Masada. When she had heard him take the oath that 'Masada will not fall again', she could imagine him like El'azar, the leader of the resistance to the Romans, killing the whole of his family, and then himself, rather than surrender an inch of the land of Israel to the Arabs.

Later, he had gone to the Lebanon and fought in the siege of Beirut. Once, when she had asked what he knew about the massacre of the Palestinians in the Sabra and Chatila camps, he had answered first that it was nothing to do with the Israeli army, and had then added, with a cold smile: 'And where would Israel be without Deir Yassin?' This massacre of Arabs by the Irgun and the Stern Gang in 1948, which had led to an exodus of refugees, was defended by Jake as the only way to get them off the land that God had given to the Jews. Anna had talked about self-determination and human rights, but always came up against her brother's unshakeable conviction that no human concept of justice could override a divine gift to a chosen people.

She had appealed to her father and mother, but they had given her little support. They had been less happy than Jake to relish the triumphs of modern Israel, and they expressed their opinions in a gentler way; but they too believed that the land, like the Law, was the birthright of the Jewish people.

These arguments had been largely academic until the *intifada*, when the Palestinian Arabs had started to protest against the Israeli occupation of Gaza and the West Bank. Then, when every day in the *Jerusalem Post* there were stories of riots by the Arabs and of rioters shot dead by the IDF; when there were pictures on television of soldiers using rocks to break the bones of their young Palestinian prisoners, and of the razing of houses of those active in the uprising; when the Arab schools and universities were closed, and the refugees in Gaza confined by curfew to their wretched shacks in the burning heat; then their arguments had become less theoretical and so impassioned that the atmosphere in the Dagans' home became impossible for them all. When Anna had announced that she was going to refuse to serve in the army because of what it was doing to the Palestinians, her father had at once applied for a deferment, and then had called Father Lambert and his sister Miriam to arrange for Anna to go to London.

It was now almost a year since she had seen Jake, but neither the time nor the distance which had separated them had lessened his ability to irritate her. She acknowledged to herself that if, as everyone suspected, he still worked for Mossad or Shin Bet, he had reasons to be secretive about his movements. But why had he had to follow her into Selfridge's instead of telephoning her at Aunt Miriam's? Why, now, did he have to walk along Baker Street as if he was on patrol in Gaza or East Jerusalem? She was even annoyed that he knew that there was a kosher sandwich bar on the corner of George Street where he could eat lunch without being defiled.

As they went in, she intercepted the look of a girl at the counter and recognized, reluctantly, that her brother was handsome, almost heroic. Even here in London, wearing beige Chinos, a check shirt and trainers, no one could mistake him for an off-duty accountant from Golders Green. His eyes were too quick and their expression too hard; his body was too fit and its movements too controlled; and there was something indefinable in his bearing which suggested a man who knew neither scruple nor fear.

'So how did Lambert die?' he asked Anna as he sat down with a salt-beef sandwich.

'Officially?'

'I know. A stroke.'

'He hanged himself.'

'He *hanged* himself?'

She nodded.

'Who found him?'

'Andrew.'

'Was it suicide?'

'Yes, though for a while Andrew thought he might have been murdered.'

'Why?'

'He couldn't find his notebook.'

'He might have left it in Israel.'

'Of course. But he also noticed, or he thought he noticed, that Father Lambert's things were too tidy.'

'Did he call the police?'

'No.'

'Why not?'

'The Prior wanted to avoid a scandal.'

'But if Andrew thinks he was murdered . . .'

'He doesn't now.'

'Why did he change his mind?'

'Because, well, he discovered that Father Lambert, just before he died, did something which seemed to prove that he had lost his faith.'

'Did what?'

'Never mind. But it was more than enough to convince Andrew that he was in a real state of despair.'

Jake put down his sandwich, licked his fingers, then said, nonchalantly: 'I think it's quite possible that he *was* murdered.'

'Why would anyone want to murder him?'

'To silence him.'

'To silence him?'

'To stop him speaking at the Congress.'

'Why? What was he going to say?'

'That Dad's dug up the body of Jesus.'

She looked at him oddly. 'Why should he want to say that?'

'Because he has.'

'Dug up *Jesus*?'

He put a finger to his lips. 'Not so loud.'

'How can Dad have dug up Jesus?' she whispered, half giggling as she spoke.

He went on munching. 'We found him in a cistern under the Temple Mount.'

'Jesus? Jesus Christ?'

'Sure.' He took another bite.

'You mean the remains of a crucified man?'

'As described in the Gospels.'

'There are marks?'

'Yes. On the wrists, the ribs, the skull. And a long nail through the ankles.'

'What kind of marks on the skull?'

'Scratches.'

'The crown of thorns?'

He shrugged. 'I guess so.'

'But this is ridiculous,' said Anna. 'Even if you've dug up the skeleton of a crucified man, how can you possibly know that it's Jesus?'

'Because of the Codex.'

'What Codex?'

'Four or five years ago, in Vilnius, they found a fragment of the Slavonic version of Josephus' *Jewish War*.'

Anna frowned. 'I remember Father Lambert telling us something about it.'

'It contained a passage not found in any of the other editions, to the effect that the Romans might have smuggled the body of Jesus out of the tomb hidden in a storage jar and had built it into a cistern beneath the Temple.'

'And Dad found the cistern?'

'We've known it was there since they dug along the side of the Western Wall. The wall cuts right through it. What we've never dared do until now is go through the wall into the other half of the cistern.'

'And when you did, you found the jar?'

'Yes. With the body inside.'

She shook her head. 'I don't understand. I thought you were excavating beside the Western Wall, not under the Temple Mount?'

'Of course. We had to say that because the Muslims would go berserk if they thought we were digging under the Haram. But once the Department of Religious Affairs had dug their passage alongside the Western Wall, and linked up with the cisterns under the Via Dolorosa, Dad had always wanted to go through Herod's Western Wall and see what there was between that and the retaining wall built by Zerubbabel and Solomon.'

'But who sanctioned it?'

'Certainly not the Department of Antiquities.'

'Religious Affairs?'

He shook his head. 'No. To them it would be desecrating the Temple. It was authorized on grounds of national security.'

'And who did that?'

He grinned. 'Let's just say there was a common interest between those who wanted to listen to what was being said by the Arabs on the Temple Mount, and those who wanted to know what was on the other side of the Western Wall.'

This irritated Anna, but not enough to smother her curiosity. She was, after all, the daughter of Michal Dagan and an archaeologist in her own right. 'But isn't it just bedrock?'

'In parts, yes. By Warren's Shaft, bedrock. By Wilson's Arch, probably infill. By Robinson's Arch, infill and the stables of Solomon. What had always interested Dad was the northern corner, at the very end of the new tunnel.'

'Why?'

'Did you ever go down there?'

She shook her head. 'No.'

'Herod built the Antonia fortress overlooking the Temple, right?'

She nodded.

'He built it on the site of a Maccabean fortress which had stood on bedrock. Some of that had to be cut away for the Western Wall of the Temple.'

'So what was the point of going through the wall into bedrock?'

'No point at all. But at the very end there is a break in the bedrock where the wall cuts through the old cistern.'

'Fed from where?'

'The same source as the cistern beneath the Via Dolorosa – the water which ran down from the Damascus Gate to the Antonia and the Temple, until it was blocked off by the Western Wall.'

'So the other half of the cistern . . .'

'Must link up to the entire network of cisterns serving the Temple.'

'But how did they fill them after the building of the Wall?'

'We don't know. Possibly with water collected from the

Temple precincts themselves. But those on the higher level – certainly the other half of the cistern cut in half by the wall – would be dry.'

'And it was there that you found the body?'

'Yes.'

'In an ossuary?'

'In a jar.'

'What kind of jar?'

'An ordinary storage jar, for olives or grain.'

'From what period?'

'Early first century.'

Anna sat back, her face flushed with excitement. 'But that's . . . that's fantastic. I mean, if it really is – if it can be shown to be the skeleton of Jesus, it beats the mask of Agamemnon or the tomb of Tutankhamun.'

'Sure, it's fantastic,' said Jake, 'but it's also kind of awkward.'

'Why?'

'Think about it.'

'Jesus, of course, Father Lambert. Dad showed it to him and he believed it.'

'He had to believe it.'

'So he came back and . . . of course, now it all makes sense.'

'It was really very unfortunate for Dad,' said Jake, 'because he not only liked Father Lambert, he counted on him to break the news.'

'He said he would?'

'Yes. At the Congress at Oxford.'

'Why can't Dad announce it himself, now, in Jerusalem?'

'Because Christians won't believe a Jew.'

'They'll think Dad faked it?'

'What do you think?'

'I guess they would.'

'It's got to be announced by a Christian, and not just by any Christian either, because half of them don't believe in the Resurrection anyway. It has to be a hard-line, old-fashioned Catholic like Father Lambert.'

95

'And he was definitely going to announce it?' she asked again.

'Yes. That's why we think he might have been killed.'

'Who could have killed him?'

'Catholics.'

'One of their own priests?'

He laughed. 'They've done as much before.'

'Who?'

'The Jesuits. The Dominicans. The Franciscans. They've always believed that the end justifies the means. Or one of these new groups of fanatics like Opus Dei or the Society of Pius X. If they had got wind of what Lambert was going to do, they could well have decided to stop him.'

She shook her head. 'If you knew what I knew,' she said to Jake, delighted to be able to remind him that he did not know everything, 'I think you'd come to the conclusion that he took his own life.'

'Perhaps.' He did not seem irritated to have his opinion contradicted. 'But it leaves us with a problem.'

'You've got to find someone else?'

'Precisely. And that's where you come in.'

'Me?'

'We don't know who to approach.'

'The Vatican, I guess.'

'But who in the Vatican?'

'I don't know.'

'But Andrew would.'

'Sure. He'd know. Do you want me to ask him?'

'Yes. Tell him it's got to be someone like Lambert who is known to believe in the actual Resurrection of Christ, but has the integrity to accept the implications of what we've found.'

'OK. I'll see what he says.'

'Take care . . .'

'Why?'

'We don't want anyone else found hanging out of a window.'

Ten

She went back to Huntingdon College, hoping to find Andrew in Father Lambert's office. He was not there, but the secretary said that he had telephoned to say that he was on his way.

To prepare for his arrival, Anna went down into the library of the Department of Archaeology to find the references to the Vilnius Codex. She looked first through the back numbers of the *Review of Slavonic Studies*, then the *Cahiers d'études d'archéologie Biblique* and finally the *Soviet Archaeological Review*. Here she found what she wanted – the translation into English 'of the original article by N. Vesoulis of the Lithuanian State Archives in Vilnius.

She took it to a desk by the window and went through what she had read the year before for a seminar on the literary verification of archaeological data. She now remembered the whole controversy about the Slavonic additions to Josephus' *Jewish War*, those which mention both Christ and John the Baptist and were said by some to be forgeries by Byzantine monks, and by others to be part of the first draft of Josephus' *Jewish War* which was later censored at a time of Christian persecution.

Father Lambert had mentioned the later 'addition to the additions' only as an instance of how fragments like this, or the Dead Sea Scrolls, could turn up even in our own time. He had accepted, certainly, that the Slavonic additions were genuine, but had not considered that the rumour in the later addition could be true. Nor, when it was discovered, had anyone else, because no one had any reason to envisage finding a jar in a cistern containing the remains of a crucified man.

She photocopied the article so as to be able to show it to Andrew, but, as she stood by the machine in the library, she suddenly wondered how Andrew would react when told of her father's find. Until that moment, elation had over-whelmed any misgivings. Now, she remembered the effect the news had had on Father Lambert. Andrew might react in an equally dreadful way. Had he not, only the day before on Primrose Hill, told her that the Resurrection was the corner-stone of his religious belief? Had not Henry explained how his brother's religious convictions had saved him from the consequences of a miserable childhood? She took the pages of the article as they came from the copier and quickly folded them, as if afraid that Andrew might come up behind her and read them over her shoulder. When the copying was complete she quickly put the issue of the *Soviet Archaeological Review* back onto the shelves and hurried out of the library.

She went up the stairs towards the faculty offices uncertain as to what to do. She had promised Jake to ask Andrew who could replace Father Lambert as the herald of her father's momentous find; but, if she did so, she risked destroying the illusion upon which Andrew's peace of mind depended.

Only one man could advise her how to deal with this dilemma, and that was Henry. She did not want him to think that she had seized upon the first pretext she could to see him again, but her anxiety about Andrew overcame her embarrassment, and she went to the public telephone by the notice-board in the passage and rang Henry at his office.

He was not there. She tried his flat. He answered. She told him briefly that she had to see him at once, and added, to reassure him: 'It's not about us, it's about Andrew.'

He was neither friendly nor unfriendly when he opened the door and greeted her, as he always did, with a brief kiss on her cheek. He had been working at home, and his eyes had a glazed expression from focusing for many hours on the screen of his word processor as well as on the papers and reports which, as she came into his living-room, Anna saw laid out over both the desk and the table in front of the sofa.

'I'm sorry,' she said. 'I guess you were working.'

'I needed a break. Would you like some coffee?'

'Only if you want some.'

'I do.'

She followed him into his small kitchen, which looked out over Eaton Square, and sat down on one of the high stools at the counter while Henry filled the electric kettle.

'Jake's in town,' she said.

'When did he arrive?'

'I don't know. Yesterday, or the day before.'

'Have you seen him?'

'Yes. We had lunch.'

'Did he know about Lambert?'

'Yes. Dad must have told him.'

'What did he say?'

'It's all kind of unbelievable . . .'

'What is?'

'In a nutshell, Dad's found the body of Christ.'

For a moment Henry hesitated, his hand holding the packet of Colombian coffee. Then he frowned and said: 'You mean he has dug up the body of a crucified man?'

'They know that it's Jesus.'

His frown deepened. 'How can they know?'

'It's a long story.'

He put three spoonfuls of coffee into the glass jug. 'Tell me.'

'Do you know who I mean by Josephus?' she asked.

'The historian?'

'Yes.'

'Not much. Wasn't he a Jew who changed sides in the middle of the revolt against the Romans?'

'Precisely. He was an aristocratic Jew, Joseph ben Matthias, born around forty years after Jesus. During the revolt against the Romans, he was sent to organize the resistance in Galilee. At the battle of Jotapata he changed sides. He surrendered to the Romans and became a big-time collaborator. He helped Vespasian with the siege of Jerusalem, and after its fall, while the Jews were either slaughtered in the arena or led off as slaves, he retired to Rome on a pension to write his histories justifying what the Romans had done.'

'Did the Romans have doubts?' asked Henry, pouring boiling water onto the coffee in the glass jug.

'That's just the point. The Romans themselves didn't need convincing, but there were large numbers of Jews who lived under the Parthians in Babylon. So his first draft was not written in Latin or even in Greek, but in Aramaic. Only the version of Josephus' *Jewish War* which became known in the West was not this original draft, but a later edition, written in Greek some twenty years later under the Emperor Domitian. It wasn't until the end of the nineteenth century that some German, working in Latvia, then ruled by Russia, discovered a version of *The Jewish War* written in old Slavonic which looked like a translation of that first Aramaic edition. It lacked passages from the later version, and was written in a more primitive style. But it had seven passages not found in the later edition which refer to John the Baptist and Jesus Christ.'

'What did they say?' asked Henry, leading her back into the living-room with the pot of coffee on a tray.

'Nothing very extraordinary, but they confirm, if they are genuine, that Jesus and John the Baptist actually existed.'

'Are they genuine?'

She sat down. 'Who knows? You see, there were already two passages of the same kind in Josephus' *Antiquities of the Jews*, which some scholars thought had been inserted by pious monks in the Middle Ages. So the same was said of these Slavonic additions to his *Jewish War*. But the evidence that they are genuine is strong. They are very much in the style of Josephus, and they mention both Jesus and John from the standpoint of a sceptic.'

'Perhaps they were just being cunning?'

'Sure. But the only reason for doing that would be to prove that Jesus and John had existed which, at that time, no one doubted.'

'Then why,' asked Henry, 'were there no similar passages in the Greek version of *The Jewish War*?'

'That is easier to explain. By the time Josephus wrote his second edition, under the Emperor Domitian, the Christians were regarded as enemies of the state. It would have been crazy of Josephus, still living on an imperial pension, to refer to the founder of their religion as a miracle-worker and demigod who was executed unjustly by a Roman official for a bribe.'

'But what has all this to do with the death of Father Lambert?' asked Henry, handing her a cup of coffee.

'Wait. I'll tell you,' said Anna, first taking a sip of her coffee. 'This German scholar, Alexander Berendts, who had pieced together the Slavonic edition of Josephus from several different manuscripts, published his preliminary findings in 1911, but his work was not complete when he died the following year. He had got hold of bits of manuscript from monasteries and museums in Russia, and after his death his work was continued by a colleague called Konrad Grass. The First World War put a stop to Grass' researches. Then came the Russian revolution, the German invasion of the Baltic states, and the loss of some of the old Slavonic texts – in particular, a certain Codex 109 in which parts of Josephus' *Jewish War* were mixed with bits of the Gospels and various apocrypha. This Codex was thought to have been taken by the retreating Russians to the public library in Leningrad, and supposedly lost in the fire of 1919.

'Three or four years ago, it was discovered in Lithuania – or, more exactly, it turned up among other manuscripts given to the State Library in Vilnius by some Orthodox monks. A woman working at the library who knew old Slavonic noticed almost at once that this Codex differed in one small way from the others from which Berendts' translation of the Slavonic version had been made. There was, as it were, an "addition to the additions", to the sixth, which dealt with the rending of the veil in the Temple.'

'What did it say?' asked Henry.

'You can read it yourself.' She took the photocopy of the article from her bag. 'This is a translation of the article by Miss N. Vesoulis which was published in a Soviet archaeological review. It was Father Lambert who first showed it to me.'

'Must I read it all?'

'No. Just the passage from Josephus. The words in italics are those found in the new Codex.'

Henry took the article and read the text under the title 'The Rending of the Veil':

> In the days of our pious fathers this curtain was intact, but in our own generation it was a sorry sight, for it had been suddenly rent from top to bottom at the time when by bribery they had secured the execution of the benefactor of men – the one who by his actions had proved that he was no mere man. Many other awe-inspiring 'signs' happened at the same moment. It is also stated that after his execution and entombment he disappeared entirely. Some people actually assert that he had risen; others that his friends stole him away: *and others still that Pilate himself had his body taken from the tomb in a jar and then hidden in a cistern under the Antonia.* I for one cannot decide where the truth lies. A dead man cannot rise by his own power; but he might rise if aided by the prayer of another righteous man. Again, if an angel or other heavenly being, or God himself, takes human form to fulfil his purpose, and after living among men dies and is buried, he can rise again at will. Moreover it is stated that he could not have been stolen away, as guards were posted around his tomb, 30 Romans and 1,000 Jews.

When Henry had finished reading this he looked up at Anna. 'And your father has really found the body of a crucified man in a jar in a cistern under the Antonia?'

She nodded. 'Yes. Or, to be more precise, under the Haram – the Temple Mount – which at its north-west corner was connected to the Antonia. Two weeks ago they broke through the wall of an old cistern and found this jar containing the skeleton of a crucified man.'

'From what period?'

'The first century AD.'

'But thousands were crucified at that time.'

'Of course. But on the skull of this skeleton are marks consistent with a crown of thorns, and between the ribs on the left side there is the mark made by a sword or a spear.'

'And they showed all that to Father Lambert?'

'Yes. And apparently he realized at once that what Josephus had suggested in the Vilnius Codex was true.'

Henry frowned. 'One would have thought he would wait before jumping to any conclusions.'

Anna frowned, irritated that Henry should seem to doubt the veracity of her father's momentous find. 'He didn't jump to any conclusions. He had the evidence of the find.'

'It still seems . . . improbable.'

'Father Lambert didn't think so.'

'No. That's true. And it explains his suicide.'

'Or his murder.'

'How . . . his murder?'

'He was going to announce the find at the Congress.'

'Why him? Why not your father?'

'They thought it should come from a Catholic.'

'Of course.'

'But Jake thinks that some of his fellow Catholics may have got wind of what was going on, and may have killed him to shut him up.'

Henry put down his empty cup on the tray. 'Killing Father Lambert could hardly prevent the find from becoming known.'

'No, but it would make it less likely that people would believe it.'

'Why?'

'Because if Dad or any other Jew breaks the news to the world, then everyone is going to say that it's a forgery.'

'Why should your father pretend to dig up the body of Christ?'

She shrugged. 'To get at the Christians, I guess.'

'So they called in Father Lambert, who was not just a distinguished archaeologist but a Catholic priest of a most conservative kind?'

'Exactly. And now that he's dead, they want me to ask Andrew who they can ask in his place.'

'Wouldn't your father know better than Andrew?'

'About the archaeology, yes, but not about the theology.'

Henry smiled. 'No, of course. It would be no use asking a liberal theologian.'

'Why not?'

'They don't believe in the empty tomb. But Andrew does, so you must be careful how you break it to him.'

'Sure. That's what I wanted to ask you. How do you think I should tell him?'

'Try and seem a little less pleased.'

She blushed. 'I'm not pleased, I mean, not that it's Jesus, but you've got to agree that it's great for Dad.'

'It'll certainly make his name,' said Henry, offering Anna more coffee.

'It's very hard for me to imagine,' said Anna, holding out her cup, 'how the news will affect someone who really believes that Jesus literally rose from the dead.'

'It'll be painful.'

'I'm also afraid that he'll hate me for telling him – whether he believes it or not.'

'No one likes the bringer of bad news.'

'And I know that he'll think I'm pleased because I'm a Jew, even though I couldn't care less about being a Jew and that it's only because of Dad that I'm a little excited.'

'Would you like me to tell him?'

'Then he might hate you, and he'll think you're pleased because you've always said it was nonsense.'

'I hope it would take more than that to turn Andrew against me.'

'You mean he'd take it from you but not from me?'

'I've known him longer.'

'But if I leave it to you, he'll know that I've ducked out of telling him and he may think that I don't trust him.'

'Perhaps.'

'So if you don't mind, I think I'll tell him.'

'As you like.'

She looked at her watch. 'He'll probably be at Huntingdon. I'll catch him there.'

Eleven

Anna left. Henry returned to his desk. His eyes fell on the columns of print from which he was drawing up an abstract on the regulations governing the import of tinned meats into the United Arab Emirates, but his mind – normally able to concentrate at his command – remained preoccupied with Anna and what she had just told him.

When she had telephoned he had assumed – despite her assurance to the contrary – that she was coming round to try and repair the rupture of the night before. How many times had his girlfriends contrived to reappear in a sexy dress or with their hair done in a different way, as if the glimpse of a breast or a cascade of tinted curls could reanimate a dead affection? In reality, the very crudity of their assault upon his senses only exacerbated the revulsion he felt for the body which had once inspired desire.

As soon as she had entered his flat, Henry had known that his assumption was wrong. Not only had she taken no trouble with her appearance, but she hardly looked him in the eye – and when she did, it was not with any lingering innuendo, but with a strange, mixed look of anxiety and triumph. He wondered whether perhaps she thought she had done something which might impress him, but, again, as she had told him about her father's find, she showed none of the conceit which girls sometimes feel because of their father's celebrity or their family's distinction.

She was excited, of course, and proud on her father's behalf; and, undoubtedly, it was momentous news if Dagan had discovered the skeleton of Christ and could prove it. There remained enough of a journalist in Henry to be intrigued by such a sensational story. He was also amused by imagining the effect the news would have on the clergy up and down England – the sermons that would be preached, the articles written and the learned correspondence in the columns of *The Times*. He was anxious, all the same, as Anna had been, about the effect the discovery would have on his brother. However convinced he was that his beliefs were false, and however contemptuous he was of the Catholic Church, he saw the value to Andrew of his religious convictions.

He had always known his brother would discover, sooner or later, that his faith was no more than a means of avoiding unpleasant truths about human nature, but he had hoped he would be eased into this understanding when he was more mature. Andrew might be twenty-seven or twenty-eight years old, but the monastic life had protected him from the coarse realities of life. To the monks, his naïveté might be evidence of spiritual strength: to Henry, it was the sign of someone fragile who, upon being obliged to admit that his beliefs were bogus, might retreat into an unsound mind.

Eventually, he forced himself to return to work on the digest of trade regulations. Sometimes he rang his office to check a fact, or answered the telephone when it rang, but he kept the calls short, wanting to leave the line open in case Andrew should want to reach him. Towards six, his head tight from prolonged concentration on facts and figures, and his eyes bleary from gazing at the small points of light on the screen, he longed to leave his flat and go for a walk before it became too dark; but his anxiety about Andrew took precedence over his desire for fresh air, and so he went to the window and leaned out over Eaton Square.

At eight, Henry rang the friends who were expecting him to dinner to say that he could not come. At nine he ordered a pizza to be delivered to his flat. Soon after, Andrew rang, as Henry knew he would, and asked if he could come round at once.

He arrived at the same time as the pizza, his tousled appearance and demented expression contrasting with the neat, bored look of the uniformed delivery boy who stepped aside to let Andrew in. Henry bribed the boy to give him a second pizza from the box on the back of his bike and then took both of them into his living-room with a bottle of wine and two glasses.

Andrew turned as he came in. 'You can't imagine what has happened,' he blurted out at once. 'Really, things have been said which, well, if anyone else had said them, or they'd been said without my knowing – without my having *seen* what had happened to Father Lambert – well, if it hadn't been for that, I would simply have thought them a joke in poor taste, or not even a joke – more a kind of silly science-fiction fantasy . . .'

Henry sat down with the wine and the pizzas, wondering at first how convincing he could make his pretence that he had not already heard what Andrew was telling him. Then he saw that his brother was oblivious to his reactions – gazing wildly into mid-air and talking in an unusually loud voice, not as if addressing an audience but as if he wished to shout down some other voices which were attempting to interrupt him.

'You see, everything which is incredible in itself is proof of the next incredible thing which in turn proves another until you have a complex circle of facts which are established, which cannot be discounted, at least not by me who saw with my own eyes his dead body and heard with my own ears the confession of Mrs Dunn.'

'What have you learned now?' asked Henry.

'It seems – it will seem absurd to you if I tell you just like this, but there's no other way – it seems that Father Lambert killed himself because he saw the body of Our Lord – a skeleton, I mean, which he believed to be that of Our Lord, not just because it had a nail through the feet and the marks of thorns on the skull, and a spear between the ribs, but because it was found in a storage jar just like that described by Josephus in the old Slavonic version of his *Jewish War*.'

Henry was ready to ask for more details of this revelation, as he would naturally have done if he had not known them already, but again it was quite clear that Andrew was beyond suspicions of any kind, so Henry simply allowed him to continue talking.

'Of course, no one thought the new addition particularly

107

significant at the time. I remember Father Lambert mentioning it, and I think he referred me to the articles which described it, but I never read them because it never occurred to anyone that the body of a crucified man would be found in a jar in a cistern. But now it has been found, and it seems quite plausible that Josephus should have known because he had access to all the imperial records in Rome, and it is accepted that procurators like Pilate reported what they were doing in great detail. If it existed, he would certainly have seen a copy of the *Acta Pilati* – he might even have known old men who had served under Pilate in Palestine as young officers in the Roman army.'

'But Josephus mentioned other possibilities,' said Henry, 'even that Christ did rise from the dead.'

'Yes, I know, which is why until now it occurred to no one to take this new addition seriously. But if they have found a skeleton with those marks in a cistern just like the one described by Josephus – well, it is very hard to know what to think. And I have been thinking very hard of how it could not be the body of Our Lord, but just that of an ordinary criminal. But why would an ordinary criminal have been buried in such an obscure place?'

'Both could be forgeries.'

Andrew frowned. 'But how?' That would presuppose collusion between Professor Dagan and Russian Orthodox monks in Lithuania; and even if that is theoretically possible, it is extremely improbable to anyone who knows Professor Dagan.'

'That is presumably why Father Lambert accepted it.'

'Exactly. That is the most telling evidence, because, if Father Lambert had had any excuse to doubt the validity of the find, he would surely have taken it; but, instead, he came back feeling that everything he had done, everything he had sacrificed, everything he had stood for, was in vain.'

'Do you feel that?'

Andrew laughed. 'I haven't really had time to be affected one way or the other. Anna gave me the news at Huntingdon. Then we rang her father again in Jerusalem. He couldn't say much over the telephone, but he seemed very upset about Father Lambert, and is in something of a quandary about his find. Naturally, the archaeologist in him is very excited – one can hardly blame him for that – but the death of Father Lambert, whether it was murder or suicide . . .'

'Doesn't this prove it was suicide?'

'Jake apparently thinks he may have been murdered by some Jesuit, but that's very improbable. Anyway, whether he killed himself or was murdered, he was the first Christian to be told. Michal Dagan is, quite naturally, alarmed by what will happen when it is announced to the world. He even wonders whether it *should* be told, and has asked me to advise him.'

'What did you suggest?'

'How could I advise him? I'm not even a priest. I asked him, instead, if I could tell my superior.'

'Did he agree?'

'In the end, yes. So I went back to the monastery and told Father Godfrey. At first, he thought it was a joke, but he too had to face the fact of Father Lambert's death and all that it implied, so he thought for a moment and then said, as I had said, that *he* couldn't decide what should or should not be done, and that he would have to consult the Papal Nuncio or Cardinal Hume, and he picked up the telephone to ring one or the other. Then he realized how absurd it would sound to say, *tout court*, that some Israelis had dug up the body of Christ, particularly since the only thing which made *us* take it seriously was that Father Lambert, whom we knew, had taken it seriously enough to hang himself, but neither Cardinal Hume nor the Nuncio knew that Father Lambert had hanged himself because Father Godfrey had announced that he had died of a stroke and was reluctant now to change his story.'

While Andrew was talking, Henry had been eating his pizza. He now pushed the plate towards Andrew, who took a slice into his hand, but instead of biting into it, used it like a conductor's baton to gesticulate while he talked.

'Father Godfrey therefore decided to call Cardinal Memel in Rome.'

'Who is Cardinal Memel?'

'The head of our order.'

'Is he a German?'

'No, an American. He was the rector of Pater Noster University for ten or fifteen years. Father Lambert didn't think much of him, but he is our General, and I suspect that Father Godfrey had told him already about the suicide of Father Lambert. He got on to him almost immediately and told him what had happened. He then handed me the telephone, and I had to repeat the whole thing myself. Then the Cardinal said: "You think there's something in this?" And I had to say yes. He hesitated for a moment, then told me that I was to go to Jerusalem at once and that he would fly out to meet me there.'

Now, at last, Andrew bit into the slice of cold pizza, and drank, in one gulp, his glass of wine. Henry realized, with some relief, that his brother had been saved from the full shock of what the news implied by being swept up into the centre of such momentous events.

'Is Cardinal Memel an archaeologist?' he asked, filling Andrew's glass.

'No, a biblical scholar.'

'Then how will he be able to form an opinion about the find?'

'I dare say he'll bring in a team from the Pontifical Biblical Institute, which will carbon-date the skeleton and all that kind of thing.' He drank from his glass of wine. 'The difficulty, of course, will be to prevent the news from getting out before the tests have been done. In fact it won't be possible, and that's why Professor Dagan thinks that if it is to be announced, then someone should do it at the Congress in July.'

'Cardinal Memel, perhaps?'

'Yes.'

'There will inevitably be people who won't believe it.'

'I know. All those fundamentalists in America, and even Catholics . . .'

'Wouldn't they have to accept a ruling of the Pope?'

'Not people like Archbishop Lefebvre – particularly not if that ruling was made on the advice of Cardinal Memel.'

'Why not?'

'He's very liberal and ecumenical.'

'Is that why Father Lambert didn't like him?'

'Yes.' He emptied his glass again and Henry filled it – noticing, however, that the wine, rather than making Andrew cheerful, was changing his mood from elation to anxiety. 'It's so difficult to know,' he said, 'what effect it will have on the Church if it *is* established that the skeleton is that of Christ. Clearly, those theologians who presumed a purely spiritual Resurrection will be delighted. And even those of us who believed in a more literal way . . . well, it's not the only article of faith in the Christian religion.'

'No.'

'There are still the many sayings of Our Lord which, I should have thought, have a value in themselves, and so people will still be able to model themselves upon him.'

'Of course.'

'But it would seem to suggest that, despite the inherent moral values in what he said about loving one's neighbour and all that kind of thing, Jesus did have illusions about himself and his immortality, and his kingdom in another world.'

'Yes,' said Henry carefully, 'but perhaps that aspect of his teaching will turn out to have been less important than had been imagined.'

'Of course, but there are several aspects, not of Christian teaching but of the practice of the Church, particularly the Catholic Church, which do depend, finally, upon Jesus being the Son of God, and speaking with the authority of God.'

'You mean the Eucharist?'

'Yes. Clearly, an ordinary man, however wise and good, cannot turn bread into his body, or wine into his blood.'

'No.'

'And the same goes for the forgiveness of sins. We cannot presume, as we have done up to now, that the priest in the Confessional can forgive sins in the name of God if Jesus himself had no power to do so, because it was he who delegated that power to the Apostles and through them to the clergy today.'

'It would be a pity to abandon a practice which serves a therapeutic purpose,' said Henry.

'But will it serve a therapeutic purpose if the penitent no longer believes that it is God, through the priest, who is forgiving his sins?'

'I don't know. I have never been to Confession.'

'No, of course not.' Andrew blushed and looked apologetically at his brother as if realizing suddenly that he was not talking to himself.

'But I can see its value,' said Henry, 'and I sometimes wish . . .'

'What?'

'That there was some equivalent for non-believers.'

Andrew smiled. 'I may soon be looking for something of the sort myself.'

'Have you ceased to believe already?'

'No, no, certainly not. At least not in Jesus or his teaching or the value in his suffering and death. But I suppose that the finding of this skeleton, and the possibility that it might be his, has made me wonder whether there is that much point in being a priest.'

'That seems to be the effect it had on Father Lambert.'

'Yes. But for him it was too late, whereas I am young enough to change the direction of my life.'

Henry emptied the bottle of wine into his own and his brother's glasses. 'You know,' he said – again choosing his words carefully – 'that because I didn't accept the premise upon which it was based, I never saw much point to your life as a monk. All the same, I should be cautious about making any sudden decisions. Give yourself time to take it all in.'

'Of course. I don't meant to leave the order tomorrow. Quite apart from anything else, it'll pay for my ticket to Tel Aviv. But I am glad, all the same, that I have my academic qualifications to fall back on. Think of all those poor priests who have never done anything but administer the sacraments and preach the Gospel of the Risen Lord.'

Twelve

The next morning Andrew rang Anna and asked her to go with him to Israel. At first, she was reluctant – she still felt sour towards her parents and was afraid she might be in trouble for avoiding the draft – but Andrew argued that as an archaeologist she should grab the chance to study her father's find, and that he would find it very useful to have a second opinion from someone he could trust. When she still hesitated, he said that he would be glad of her company in case he was affected in the same way as Father Lambert. 'I know I'll be all right,' he said, 'but Henry thinks I should have a chaperon, and he's offered to pay for your ticket.'

She agreed to go, and on the El Al flight to Tel Aviv she chatted cheerfully to Andrew as if they were going on holiday to the Red Sea. Her mood changed as soon as they arrived at Lod, and were met by Michal and Jake Dagan; for, though her father greeted her with all the conventional gestures of affection, it was apparent, even to Andrew, that there was a certain reticence and artificiality in both his kiss and his embrace.

Like Jake, Michal Dagan was a slim man of medium height with brown eyes. His hair, once black, had thinned at the temples and turned grey. Unlike his son's, his features were small and precise – almost feminine – and they alternated between a look of petulance and a roguish, boyish smile. He could look distinguished on a dais – Andrew had heard him lecture; but his eyes avoided the eyes of others, as if Dagan was afraid that something might be read in his expression which he did not want to be known.

He also hid whatever thoughts might be passing through his mind behind a patina of irony which Anna had either inherited or learned to imitate as a child. It was this that made his kiss less than a kiss and his embrace a false embrace – as if he were saying to Anna, as he welcomed her: 'Isn't this how fathers greet their daughters? Isn't this the way it's meant to be done?' And Andrew, knowing how, behind the same ironic manner, Anna longed to be enveloped in an instinctive, unselfconscious hug, winced as he witnessed her disappointment and trembled as he anticipated her disgruntled mood.

Professor Dagan was more friendly towards Andrew than he was towards his own daughter – not, Andrew recognized, because he was fond of him but because he was the protégé of one of his closest friends. Yet it was Father Lambert who had once described Dagan to Andrew as the archetypal wandering Jew – part German, part American, part Israeli; eminent in all these countries but at home in none; dreaming of a *Heimat* which could only exist if Central Europe were to be recreated in the Middle East.

Now, as they left the airport, he said no more about the death of his friend than he had said over the telephone to London. He led Andrew and Anna to a white Volvo in which a swarthy man, who to Andrew might have been either an Arab or a Jew, sat waiting in the driver's seat. He got out to put their luggage in the boot. Jake sat next to him in the front, while the others got in behind.

The car was air-conditioned, but outside it was so hot that the driver, as they drove out of the airport, looked anxiously at the temperature gauge on the instrument panel. Jake talked to him in Hebrew, which Andrew did not understand, but because of his presence and because Dagan himself did not bring the subject up, Andrew felt unable to discuss either Father Lambert's death or Professor Dagan's find.

He therefore sat in silence as the car followed the motorway across the coastal plain towards Latrun, then curved up into the Judaean Hills towards Jerusalem. As they passed the burnt wrecks of armoured cars, which had been preserved at the roadside as memorials to the battle for the city, Anna scowled and said: 'Why don't they clear those hulks away?'

'Why should they?' asked Professor Dagan.

'They kind of spoil the landscape.'

'People want to remember.'

114

'What? How they clobbered the Arabs?'

'What they sacrificed to recover Jerusalem.'

They reached the outskirts of the city. Jake directed the driver towards East Jerusalem, and all at once Andrew caught sight of the domes and spires and minarets of the old walled city and was moved, as he always was, by the sight of this paradigm of Heaven. It did not matter that the walls had been built by a Turkish sultan, not a Jewish king; or that the breach in the wall by the Jaffa Gate was not made by the legions of Titus to storm the city, but by the Turkish caliphs to enable Kaiser Wilhelm to enter in his landau. The city's setting was as dramatic now as it had been when King David chose it for his capital three thousand years before; and the jumble of churches, mosques and white, flat-roofed houses brought to Andrew's mind not just scenes from the Gospels but also those fables of the Orient like Sindbad the Sailor or Ali Baba.

It was difficult for the car to enter the narrow streets of the Christian quarter, so, at Andrew's suggestion, the Dagans dropped him at the New Gate. From there it was only a short walk to the Simonite monastery and church. Both had been built by the Crusaders in the eleventh century, destroyed by the Saracens in the twelfth, rebuilt under the Mamelukes, left to decay under the Ottomans and restored to their present condition only in the nineteenth century, with small, barred windows on the ground floor, a thick studded door beneath a Venetian arch, and an old-fashioned bell which jangled within as Andrew tugged at the iron lever.

The door was opened by a sallow monk and Andrew stepped into a cloister which was much gentler and prettier than the exterior of the monastery had suggested. It had the fat pillars and barrel vaulting of the twelfth century and looked more like a monastery in Normandy or Burgundy than anything indigenous to the Middle East. The monk too was not an Arab but an Italian, and spoke to Andrew first in his native language but then, when he realized that Andrew was one of that rare species, an English Simonite, changed with greater enthusiasm than skill into English as he led him towards the office of the Prior.

Andrew had been to the monastery before on several occasions and it saddened him to remember that on almost all of them he had been in the company of Father Lambert. The news of the death of this eminent archaeologist had already reached Jerusalem, and the Prior – a German Simonite called Father Manfred Stott – said at once how sad he had been to hear the news. 'And he seemed so well when he was here,' he said. 'A little affected by the heat towards the end, perhaps, but no one could have imagined that one day after his return he would die.'

It was clear from the way in which the Prior expressed his sorrow that he had no inkling that Father Lambert's death was caused by suicide or murder. He knew, of course, that their General, Cardinal Memel, was coming to Jerusalem, and that Andrew's arrival was somehow linked to this, but it was part of the discipline of the order to curtail unnecessary curiosity. He informed Andrew simply that the Cardinal was expected later that night, and then asked the Italian brother to show him to his room.

It was a pleasant cell, in which Andrew had stayed before, with old-fashioned furniture, an enamel wash-stand and a jug of water. There were clean sheets, a clean towel and a view from the window over the roofs of the Christian quarter towards the two domes of the Church of the Holy Sepulchre.

Andrew unpacked his few belongings, then went along the wide corridor to take a shower in the huge, archaic bathroom. He was sticky and smelly after his journey and was relieved for once, after washing in this way, to change his trousers and jacket for the cotton habit which had been laid out for him on his bed. He put it on not just because it was cool, but because he dared not greet Cardinal Memel wearing anything but the robes of the order.

It was now five in the afternoon. At six there would be vespers, and at seven supper. Andrew therefore had an hour free to go out into the streets of the old city. Although the shops were shut, because of the strike called by the leaders of the *intifada*, some Arabs had come out into the streets to take advantage of the cooler evening air. Andrew did not feel conspicuous in his grey habit, because here, in the Christian quarter, it was common to see priests of every known denomination – Catholic, Orthodox, Maronite, Coptic – as well as monks and friars from the different orders, and pilgrims from every country in the world.

This evidence of the universality of the Christian Church had always exhilarated Andrew when he had been to Jerusalem before. Now, however, as he passed through the gate into the paved forecourt in front of the Church of the Holy Sepulchre, he wondered what would happen when the news leaked out of Professor Dagan's find. Here, since the time of Constantine, pilgrims had come to pray over the very tomb from which Jesus was said to have risen from the dead. Would the church be abandoned? Or change its name to the Church of the Crucifixion, for Golgotha, too, was under its dome?

He stepped between a group of American pilgrims and a party of German nuns, to pass beneath the Romanesque arch into the gloomy church. He had never liked the hotchpotch of its architectural styles – the Latin pillars, the Byzantine icons – nor the shabbiness which came from the inability of the different denominations to agree about its repair and redecoration. Nor, in the claustrophobic little shrine within the church built over the tomb of Christ, with its suffocating smell of burning oil and stale wax, had he ever felt moved to pray.

Now he did not even try, but simply watched the tourists and pilgrims file in to light a taper handed to each of them by an Orthodox monk. He turned back towards the door, but before leaving the church, he climbed the narrow staircase to the ornate altar built over the spot where the cross had stood. Here, again, where once he had knelt to pray, he merely studied the intricate silverwork which surrounded the painted faces of the Greek icons; looked up at the twinkling vulgarity of the candelabra; and noted the naïve depiction of Christ on the Cross.

It was not that he doubted the fact of the crucifixion, but, if it was to turn out that there had been no resurrection, then

117

it became a public execution of a more ordinary kind. He went back down the steps, and out of the church, thinking quite calmly of Jesus, and of the suffering he had endured. He felt he could love him and revere him, whether or not he had risen from the dead; indeed, he could love him even more if, as now seemed possible, he had been merely human after all, because always, since his conversion, Andrew had felt daunted by those passages in the Gospels in which Christ claimed to be the sole means of human salvation. Henry, after all, did not believe in him. Nor did Anna. And it had been difficult for Andrew to accept that his brother, and his closest friend, might both be damned.

He left the forecourt and walked south, past the Muristan, towards the Jewish quarter, remembering how he had put this problem to Father Lambert, and how Father Lambert had given a somewhat evasive reply, saying that what was just to God might seem arbitrary to man; and referring, rather drily, to the recurring theme in Scripture of God's apparently gratuitous exercise of choice – of Jacob rather than Esau, of Judah rather than Joseph, indeed his choice of the Jews themselves.

Now, if it was to be established that Jesus was not the Son of God, it seemed to offer the possibility that any man of good will might be saved. This not only appealed to Andrew's kindly instincts, but also to his sense of fair play. It made Jesus seem more human for having made such extravagant claims – there is something of a megalomaniac in us all – and, because he was more human, more likeable, and certainly not to be blamed for what had been done in his name. If Christ was not God, then he had never had the power either to deceive or enlighten generations of gullible believers.

He had passed into the Jewish quarter of the Old City and came to the top of the steps which led to the Western Wall. Here he stopped and looked down on what remained of Herod's Temple. The view always astonished him for, even though – as Jesus had predicted – not one stone of the Temple itself remained standing, the massive blocks of the retaining walls were still in place; and now, as always, a row of pious Jews stood nodding and chanting as they prayed at this relic of their Holy of Holies.

The sight of these Hasidim with their frock coats, beards and ringlets, had always seemed bizarre to Andrew – sometimes even repulsive. Now, however, he felt a certain kinship with them. Why, after all, should it seem strange to him that they wore the costume of the Polish gentry in the eighteenth century when he was dressed in the habit of a medieval monk? Both bore witness, in their eccentric attire, to their faith in the same God. The Muslims, too, who had occupied the Temple Mount since Saladin had taken Jerusalem, believed like the Jews and Christians in the existence of a single God. Perhaps that was all that mattered – to believe and to acknowledge that belief, whether by chanting at the Western Wall, prostrating oneself in the direction of Mecca or singing vespers in a church. Was there not a residue of righteousness in all religions? Did it matter if one believed or disbelieved that God had given Moses the tablets of the Law, or that Jesus had risen from the dead, or that the Prophet Mohammed had ascended into heaven on the back of his horse, el-Buraq, from the rock beneath the golden dome which Andrew could see from where he stood? Did it not accord not just with charity, but also with common sense, to recognize that all religions, in their different ways, reflected elements of the same truth, just as water, glass, chrome or silver reflect the light of the same sun?

It was setting, that sun, sinking behind him, its last rays giving a pink hue to the honey-coloured ashlars of the Western Wall and reminding Andrew that he must return to sing vespers in the church of St Simon Doria. Whatever random thoughts had been passing through his mind, he retained a reflex obedience to the rules of his order.

The nine Simonite monks in residence in Jerusalem were a company mixed in age, nationality and occupation, united only in their common calling and faith. Dressed in their grey habits, and with their faces half hidden by their cowls, it was hard to tell who was a German, who an Italian, who an Irishman, who an Arab. The reading during supper in the refectory was in Latin – still the *lingua franca* of the Catholic Church – and since the monk at the lectern was the same young Italian who had shown Andrew to his room, he read with a certain fluency from Eusebius' *History of the Church*.

It was just as the Prior, Father Manfred, was about to give thanks to God for what they had eaten that the sounds of commotion came from the hall. Father Manfred hurried through grace and rapidly left the refectory. Andrew and the other monks followed and saw, as they filed out, the tall figure of their General, Cardinal Memel.

He was dressed in a black soutane with scarlet edging and a scarlet cummerbund as marks of his rank. There was a golden crucifix hanging from a golden chain around his neck, as befitted a man who was the titular Bishop of Ebolium. He was, when Andrew caught sight of him, laying a friendly hand on the shoulders of Father Manfred as he knelt to kiss the episcopal ring. Then he stooped to help the German Simonite to his feet, and turned to present the young priest who had accompanied him from Rome.

The monks coming out of the refectory hesitated for a moment, uncertain as to whether they should greet their General or humbly make themselves scarce. Since few of them, however, had ever seen Cardinal Memel at such close quarters before, and since he was a gaunt, handsome, genial man who looked more like a film star than a cleric, they could not bring themselves to disperse but stood in a cluster around him; and Cardinal Memel, alert despite his journey, and sensitive to the flurry of excitement, turned to welcome his fellow Simonites with the informality and friendliness of a modern Prince of the Church.

Father Manfred, a shy and pious scholar, introduced those monks whose names he knew, but since several, like Andrew, had only recently arrived, he became confused because he could not remember what they were called. They therefore introduced themselves – Father Xavier from La Plata, Brother Laurence from Cork, Father Ignatius from Cracow – filing past in a line like guests at a reception. Indeed, Father Manfred, taking the Cardinal's geniality rather more seriously than perhaps the Cardinal had intended, herded his flock into the monastery parlour and asked the Irish brother to open some bottles of Lebanese wine.

As they were walking from the hallway into the parlour, Andrew introduced himself to the Cardinal. At first, Cardinal Memel did not seem to distinguish him from the other monks, but the young priest who accompanied him moved forward and whispered in his ear. The Cardinal's expression became more serious, and he turned back to Andrew saying: 'Ah, yes. The young Englishman. Good. I'm glad you're here.' Then his expression changed back to that of the fêted film star, and he swam into the group of chattering scholars who, with the innocence of the pious, had grown tipsy with the excitement of the occasion even before tasting a drop of the order's Château Musar.

Later that evening, after Andrew had returned to his cell, he was summoned to the office of the Prior. It was a large room on the ground floor with, on one side, small barred windows giving onto the street and, on the other, larger ones which looked out over the cloister. These were shut, and, although a large fan turned slowly in the ceiling, the room was unpleasantly hot. As Andrew entered, he saw, in the dim light, the Cardinal seated on a sofa and the Prior, looking tired and miserable, on a wicker chair beside him. The young priest who had come with the Cardinal from Rome was standing behind them, his body propped against the Prior's desk.

Cardinal Memel stood up as Andrew came in. 'I'm sorry it's so stuffy,' he said, as if reading Andrew's thoughts, 'but we can't risk opening the windows. We mustn't be overheard.'

'Of course,' said Andrew.

The Cardinal extended his hand but, before Andrew could stoop to kiss the ring, he felt his own hand grasped and then shaken, and the Cardinal's other arm came around to take him by the shoulder and guide him towards a chair.

'You don't know my secretary, Father Pierre,' he said, nodding towards the pale young Frenchman by the desk.

'But you know Father Manfred, of course.' He turned briefly to the Prior. *'Sie kennen diesen Jungen schon?'*

'Natürlich, Eminenz.'

Cardinal Memel pointed to a chair next to the sofa and they all sat down in a circle, except for the secretary who remained leaning against the desk.

'Father Manfred knows why I am here,' the Cardinal began in his deep, drawling voice, 'and Father Pierre is also in our confidence, but it is of the utmost importance that no one else should know. The Holy Father does not want the news of the find to leak out before we are ready to react. He has authorized me to make a preliminary assessment of the claims made by your friend Professor . . .'

'Dagan,' said Father Pierre.

'Dagan. That's right.'

'Now, as far as I know, the Church has never pronounced upon the validity of the Slavonic additions to Josephus' *Jewish War*, let alone the Codex that turned up in Vilnius. However, the tendency among our scholars has been to accept their authenticity, and what reactions there have been to the Vilnius Codex have been affirmative. This does not mean, of course, that we can discount the possibility of a fraud or even a coincidence of some kind. Quite the contrary, we must bear that very much in mind. But we must not *close* our minds to the possibility that Almighty God now considers us ready for a new revelation that may alter our understanding of the Faith.'

Andrew nodded. The other priests were silent.

'Too often,' the Cardinal went on, 'the Church has been caught on the hop – by Galileo, by Copernicus, by Darwin. Too often, she has reacted to uncomfortable facts by burning those who brought them to her attention, or simply by anathematizing any awkward developments, as did Pius IX with his Syllabus of Errors.'

'Na, ja . . .' murmured Prior Manfred, nodding his head in agreement.

'Therefore, we must approach this discovery of Professor Dagan's with an open mind – not so open, of course, that it should endanger our fundamental faith and let in despair, but open with a total trust in Almighty God who, in his own good way and his own good time, reveals to his children the truths of his creation.'

He stopped, rather as if he had reached the end of a sermon, and stood up – not to go to an altar to say the Creed, but to suggest that they all should get a good night's sleep because they would need their wits about them the next day. Then he left the room, accompanied by the Prior, and Andrew prepared to follow them, but the secretary, Father Pierre, held him back.

Unlike the German Prior, who had appeared devastated by what he had been told, the alert young Frenchman remained quite calm. He asked Andrew, almost as a courtesy, whether he spoke French; but when it became apparent that, however adequate, Andrew's French did not compare with Father Pierre's exquisite English, they reverted to that language to go over the arrangements for the following day.

'It is unfortunate,' said Father Pierre, 'that the Cardinal is never willing to travel incognito. It means that there are many who will learn that he is in Jerusalem, and will wonder why. The Patriarch, for example, has not been informed, but he will certainly know by tomorrow morning. So will the Greeks and the Armenians, the Jesuits and the Dominicans. We have therefore prepared a story that the Cardinal is here for an informal conference of biblical scholars at the Ecumenical Institute at Tartur. Of course, there is no such conference, and his Eminence rarely has time to meet his fellow exegetes these days, but it was the best pretext we could come up with at such short notice.'

Andrew, who had not considered complications of this kind, merely nodded to signify his acquiescence to anything Father Pierre might propose.

'We have therefore arranged to travel tomorrow morning to the Institute, dressed in our clerical habits, and there to change into something less formal before returning to West Jerusalem, where Professor Dagan is to meet us. He has been entirely cooperative in making these arrangements. He is aware, I think, of the sensitivity of the Cardinal's visit.'

'Of course.'

'As the Cardinal told us just now, the Holy Father is particularly anxious that before the find is validated, the Church should not be seen to be taking it seriously.'

'But how . . .' Andrew began.

'Of course,' the young Frenchman interrupted, as if confident that he could express better than Andrew what Andrew intended to say. 'How can the Church validate or invalidate the find without investigating it, and how can it investigate it without appearing to take it seriously?'

'Yes.'

'That, my dear brother, is the kind of conundrum which is not uncommon in the Vatican.'

'Does the Cardinal himself intend to make the initial assessment?'

'Yes.'

'But . . .'

'But how can a biblical scholar decide upon an archaeological question?'

'Yes.'

Father Pierre gave a Gallic shrug. 'How indeed? He is not even much of a biblical scholar, and his theology is deplorable.'

'Then why was he sent?'

'He sent himself, *mon cher*. He was, most unfortunately, the first to know, and he told the Holy Father only yesterday when all his arrangements had been made.'

'But surely the Holy Father could have stopped him?'

'That might have been even more dangerous. At least, if his Eminence feels himself to be responsible to the Holy Father, he may think twice before he opens his mouth to the press.'

'Is he likely to do that?'

Father Pierre shrugged again. 'He is an American. He feels that the people have a right to know. And there is nothing he likes better than a Press Conference.'

'So what should we do?'

'Restrain him. Don't let him get carried away.'

'But is he likely . . . to get carried away?'

The Frenchman closed the folder that had lain open on the

124

desk, picked it up and started towards the door. 'The Cardinal has many virtues,' he said in a lowered voice, 'but humility is not preeminent among them. He is quite convinced that the Holy Spirit has already chosen him as the next Pope, and he seems to think that the best way to ensure this destiny is to run for the post as one would for the Presidency of the United States.' He hesitated at the door. 'Did you notice how he spoke German to Father Manfred?'

'Yes.'

'He can hardly speak German at all, but he likes to practise for his blessings *Urbi et Orbi*.' He mimicked a Pope giving his blessing from the balcony of St Peter's. 'And he chose me as his secretary to teach him French.' He opened the door and ushered Andrew out of the room. 'To be a candidate for the throne of St Peter's these days, you must be a graduate not just of a seminary but also of Berlitz.'

Thirteen

At seven the next morning a black Mercedes, having squeezed through the narrow streets of the Old City, drew up outside the Simonite monastery. Cardinal Memel, wearing his scarlet skull-cap and black, red-trimmed cassock, got into the back seat with Father Pierre beside him. Andrew, also wearing his Simonite habit, but clutching a hold-all containing jeans and a tee-shirt, sat beside the driver. Under the curious eyes of the passing Arabs, the car edged away, drove down past the Casa Nova hospice and left the Old City through the Jaffa Gate. It then crossed the valley of Hinnom and went out on the road to Bethlehem.

At the Ecumenical Institute everything was prepared. The Cardinal was led off in one direction by an older man whom Andrew took to be the director, while a younger man in an open-necked shirt showed Andrew and Father Pierre to two bedrooms where they changed from their habits into their more casual clothes. The French priest, whom Andrew met again in the corridor, looked much younger and more vulnerable without his habit – the *éminence grise* suddenly reduced to a precocious *normalien*. They followed the young man across the Institute garden to a second, smaller car – a white Peugeot – and waited beside it in silence until the Cardinal appeared, dressed in white cotton trousers and a white short-sleeved shirt as if ready for a game of tennis. They all climbed into the car, and the young man who had accompanied Andrew and Father Pierre drove them back into Jerusalem to the Staedtler Institute of Archaeology.

There Jake, who must have been waiting, stepped forward to greet them. Andrew presented him to Cardinal Memel, who shook his hand vigorously and put his arm around his shoulder as if Jake were yet another young Simonite monk. Andrew saw Jake wince at this avuncular gesture, which he was obliged to endure until they reached the entrance to the Institute. He then moved ahead to open the door, ushered them into the lobby, and led them up the stairs to Professor Dagan's office on the first floor.

The Professor and Anna awaited them. Andrew stepped forward to introduce the Cardinal and Father Pierre, winking at Anna, who responded with a smile. Professor Dagan offered them coffee, but the Cardinal said that he would prefer to move straight on. They therefore returned to the cars – the Cardinal and Father Pierre going with the Professor in the white Peugeot, while Andrew and Anna went with Jake in his little Subaru.

'Is that guy really a Cardinal?' Anna asked as they drove towards the Old City.

'He's the head of our order,' said Andrew.

'His predecessors,' said Jake drily, 'used to preside over the burning of Jews.'

'You're thinking of the Dominicans,' said Andrew.

'In 1486 the Simonites in Salamanca had a dispute with Rabbi Tagus to persuade him of the error of his ways. When he would not recant, they denounced him to the Inquisition and he was burned.'

'I didn't know,' said Andrew.

126

'You can never catch Jake out on a point of fact,' said Anna.

Following the Peugeot, Jake drove around the south of the Old City, skirting Mount Zion, and in through the Dung Gate. Here they were stopped by the police who, upon recognizing Professor Dagan, let them pass into the plaza where they parked their cars. The two groups got out, and followed the Professor across the plaza to the building adjacent to the Western Wall. Cardinal Memel, who had put on sunglasses, looked like a visiting American academic, and Father Pierre like a graduate student. At the entrance to the excavations, Jake and Professor Dagan took yarmulkas from their pockets and put them on their heads. Jake then took three paper skull-caps from a box by the door and handed them to the Gentiles.

'We are entering sacred ground,' said Professor Dagan. 'We must cover our heads.'

'I should have brought my own,' said Cardinal Memel, as he placed the little cap on his head.

They entered the excavations and made their way along a narrow passage towards the Western Wall. 'These foundations are from many different periods,' said Professor Dagan. 'Some Hasmonean, some Herodian, much of it used by the Umayyads as foundations for the structures overlooking the Temple Mount.'

They came out of the passage into a large, cavernous chamber formed by the span of an enormous arch, one end of which was embedded in the Western Wall. Dagan stopped. 'That's Wilson's Arch,' he said, 'named after your fellow countryman' – he inclined his head towards Andrew – 'who discovered it in 1868. The pillar is Herodian, but the arch itself was almost certainly demolished during the siege of Jerusalem by Titus, and rebuilt by the Umayyads in the seventh or eighth century. Now, if you will follow me . . .'

He led them down a flight of steps towards the Western Wall where half-a-dozen Hasidim were praying, and a group of Israeli schoolchildren were being lectured by their teacher. 'This is Warren's Shaft,' he said, 'dug by another Englishman, Captain Warren, which established that we are now standing at least four metres above the level of the Herodian pavement . . .'

Andrew had seen this before – so, too, had Cardinal Memel – and he could not tell whether Dagan did not realize this, or whether he was merely playing at taking an American colleague on a guided tour. Dutifully, Andrew peered down the shaft, and then followed the group towards the iron gate at the entrance to the tunnel.

Here Dagan stopped while Jake unlocked it. 'As you can imagine,' he said, 'the whole question of excavating around the Temple Mount is very delicate because we now pass under the Muslim quarter of the city. For that reason, this tunnel was not dug by the Department of Antiquities, but by the Department of Religious Affairs. Nevertheless, what has been uncovered is interesting, as you will see if you follow me.'

Jake had unlocked the gate and pulled a number of switches which lit a series of lights along the tunnel. He then stood back to let his father pass through, followed by Cardinal Memel, Father Pierre, Anna, and Andrew, before closing the gate and following at the rear.

The tunnel was long. The left side was made of concrete, so Andrew was unable to tell what soil or structures it had cut through; but the right side, being the Western Wall of the Temple Mount, showed all the exquisite craftsmanship of Herod's stonemasons. Every now and then, Dagan would stop to demonstrate, for example, how the unmortared joins between the blocks were so tight that it was impossible to insert a ten-agorot piece; or to point out the largest block in the whole edifice which, he estimated, would weigh four hundred tons.

As they proceeded, Andrew began to feel dizzy. He had visited excavations of this kind before – he had been deep into the pyramids in Egypt and the royal tombs in Mesopotamia – but, as they continued walking through the musty air, he became oppressed by the fear that there might be a fall of rock which would bury them alive. Of course, the thought was absurd because the tunnel had been in use for some time, but reason cannot always master the kind of irrational panic brought on by claustrophobia. Although they had been underground now for only a quarter of an hour, Andrew became convinced that this subterranean journey had lasted much longer, and to doubt that he would ever see daylight again.

He felt faint. He wanted to cry out, but dared not for fear that Jake and Anna would think him a fool. He kept his eyes fixed on the blue denim of Anna's jeans until Professor Dagan stopped once again.

'We have reached the point,' he said, turning to face the Cardinal, 'where Herod's retaining wall leaves the side of the Tyropean Valley and cuts into the bedrock beneath the Antonia fortress. To your right, you will see how the rock face is dressed to look like the wall. Further along, we come to the point where the wall cuts through the cistern, and where the Hasmonean channel bringing water down from the north of the city had to be dammed.'

Andrew peered over the shoulder of Cardinal Memel, and glanced cursorily at the narrow defile, but his eyes, like the Cardinal's, were drawn to the black hole in the Western Wall where one of the massive stones had been removed.

Dagan, too, seemed to appreciate that he must abandon his act and get to the point. He turned towards the wall and showed them the points where the solid rock ceased and the man-made wall resumed. Then came a pillar of bedrock, which must have stood in the centre of the cistern, with steps cut in the side to give access to the water. 'What we suspected,' said Dagan, 'but wanted to verify, was that this cistern was connected to a series of others, built beneath the Temple, to meet the considerable demands for water made by ritual purification. It therefore seemed plausible to go through the wall into the other half of the cistern, and from there to explore areas which have remained unknown, certainly since the destruction of Herod's Temple.'

'What about the Muslims?' asked Cardinal Memel.

'We felt it could be done without disturbing them,' said Dagan. 'It was a matter of cutting around a single block, and removing it from the wall.'

They turned to the wall and looked at the rectangular hole.

As they did so, Jake pulled a switch behind them and a yellowish light became visible from the other side.

'We can go in,' said Dagan. 'You will find a shelf of rock, when you go through, which is four or five metres above the bottom of the cistern. There is a ladder from there down to the floor. Please be careful where you walk. We have left everything exactly as it was found.'

He went to the wall, stooped, and went head-first through the hole. The others waited to follow him in the same order as before. Anna, standing in front of Andrew, glanced up at him uncertainly.

'Are you OK?' she asked.

He smiled to reassure her. 'A little dizzy, but I'll be fine.'

Anna went through the wall. Andrew followed and found himself standing on a narrow shelf of rock, looking down into the other half of the cistern.

Like others he had seen before, it had probably been a cave which had been extended and rounded off by masons. The lights which had been set up by the Israeli archaeologists were more than enough to illuminate the walls. Two of them were pointing down at what looked like a pile of rubble, laid out on a plastic sheet on the floor of the cistern.

Since Jake was now coming through the hole in the wall behind him, Andrew climbed down the ladder, but, as he reached the bottom and walked towards the plastic sheet, he stopped and started swaying from side to side. His dizziness had become acute, and he saw Anna, as she turned towards him, in a blur. He felt himself fall, then caught, held, and led back towards the wall.

'It's so stuffy,' he mumbled.

'Sure,' said Anna, who was holding on to one of his arms. 'You'd better sit down.'

With Anna on one side and Jake on the other, he leaned back against the rock.

'I'm sorry,' he said.

'Don't be silly,' said Anna. 'There's no air in here. And it's creepy. I'm not sure I want to see a skeleton, whether it's Jesus Christ or John Brown.'

Her words reminded Andrew why he was there – to use

130

his professional skill and judgement to form an opinion about something of overwhelming importance. The challenge restored him. He stepped forward.

'Rest a moment,' said Jake, holding on to his shoulder.

'No. You see, I'm the archaeologist. The others cannot judge.'

'There's plenty of time.'

'I'm fine, really I am.' Andrew stepped forward – the faintness was gone – and walked unaided towards Professor Dagan, Cardinal Memel and Father Pierre.

They stood looking down at a human skeleton which lay cradled in one half of an enormous earthenware jar. Andrew could see at once that the bones were exceptionally well preserved. He could tell, for example, that, although the body had lain in a foetal position at the bottom of the jar, it was that of a man around five and half feet tall, with short legs and a powerful torso. Some of the ribs on the left side had caved in but those on the right remained in place. The jaw-bone had become detached from the skull, but the skull itself was in good condition. The teeth, in particular, were as sound as those of many a living man, and suggested death at a relatively early age. Most startling of all, however, were not the bones or the teeth but the huge rusty nail which still ran through both ankles.

'Is this how you found it?' asked Cardinal Memel.

'More or less,' said Dagan. 'The storage jar lay on its side, and it was cracked. We did not expect to find anything of particular interest inside, and meant to remove it to the Institute to study its contents. We then realized that it would be impossible to carry it up the ladder and through the hole in the wall without disturbing the contents, so we laid it on this plastic sheet and opened it just as you see it now.'

'Nothing has been changed since then?'

'Nothing at all.'

'That is most interesting,' said Cardinal Memel, pointing to the nail which transfixed the ankles.

'It seems that the legs were twisted before being nailed to the cross,' said Dagan.

131

'There are other instances of crucifixions of this kind,' said Jake.

'And did you realize at once that it might be Jesus?' asked Cardinal Memel.

'It is not for me to say whose skeleton it might be.'

'No, of course not. But it was inevitable, finding a body in a cistern . . .'

'It was not so unusual to find a body,' said Dagan, 'because there are tombs cut into the rock all over and around Jerusalem, many of them close to cisterns. What was unusual was to find the body in a jar, not in an ossuary.'

'Of course.'

'If the family or the friends of a dead man had taken the trouble to bury him deep beneath the Temple, you would assume they would have placed the body in a decorated ossuary, or even a sarcophagus. It also seemed curious that so much trouble had been taken to bury the body of a criminal in this way.'

'So you thought that it might be Jesus?'

'I had to be careful. I did not wish to look foolish, like Sukenik.'

'Who was Sukenik?' asked Cardinal Memel.

'The father of Yadin. After the war, in a tomb in Talpirth, he found an ossuary with a graffito which seemed to suggest that it contained the bones of Jesus.'

'And it didn't?'

'No. His inferences were successfully refuted by your compatriot, Kane.'

'But it must have occurred to you . . .'

'Certainly, when I examined the skeleton, and found marks consistent with what was said to have been done to Christ . . .'

'The nail through the ankles?'

'Yes. And look at the skull.'

Cardinal Memel took a pen-torch from one of his pockets and a magnifying glass from another, crouched and peered through the glass at the skull. 'Yes. That's extraordinary.' He looked up and turned to Andrew. 'Here, Brother,' he said in an excited tone of voice. 'Come and look at this. You can actually see traces of the crown of thorns.'

Andrew knelt down and, sure enough, on the surface of the skull, he could see a faint tracery of scratches.

'Because the cistern was airtight,' said Professor Dagan, 'the skeleton is better preserved than many others we have found. We have sent samples away for analysis and carbon-dating of both the bones and what remains of the skin. Preliminary reports suggest that there are chemical compounds within these fragments consistent with the theory that the lacerations could have been made by the curved spikes of plaited *Sisyphus spina Christi*, which was indigenous to Palestine at the time.'

'And the marks on the bones?' asked the Cardinal, turning his attention to the rib-cage of the skeleton.

'The measurements taken between the two incisions match the known width of the blade of a Roman spear.'

'But all this could be a coincidence,' said Father Pierre sceptically. 'There were many thousands of Jews crucified during this period. Many might have been given a *coup de grâce* with a spear.'

'And crowned with thorns?' asked the Cardinal.

The Frenchman shrugged. 'Perhaps it was customary to torment prisoners in this way.'

'Of course,' said Professor Dagan.

The Cardinal turned to Andrew. 'You're the archaeologist, Brother. What do you say?'

'We are trained never to jump to conclusions,' said Andrew.

'Of course,' said Michal Dagan. 'And these are not conclusions. These are only preliminary findings, but we thought it proper to involve others at once.'

'And the Church appreciates your so doing,' said Cardinal Memel.

'I was thinking less of institutions,' said Dagan drily, 'than of my fellow archaeologists, particularly Father Lambert.'

'Of course, of course,' said the Cardinal, glancing at his secretary. 'And he, quite clearly, was convinced.'

133

'When did it occur to you,' asked Father Pierre, 'that it might be the body of Christ?'

'As a speculation? Almost at once.'

'You remembered the Vilnius Codex?'

'Yes.'

'And put two and two together?'

'Not at once. But when we found the marks on the bones . . .'

'You realized that it might be Christ?'

'I realized that I should call Father Lambert.'

Cardinal Memel looked back at the skeleton. 'Just think, gentlemen. If Father Lambert was right, then we are looking at the earthly remains of our Lord and Saviour, Jesus Christ.'

'"I have gazed upon the face of Agamemnon,"' said Father Pierre scornfully.

'What's that?' asked the Cardinal.

Father Pierre turned to Andrew. 'Wasn't that what Schliemann said when he discovered the gold mask of a king at Mycenae?'

'Yes.'

'And was it Agamemnon?'

'It is now thought it was not.'

'Father, Brother,' said the Cardinal reprovingly. 'This is not the moment for *bavardage*. I should like to suggest, if our Israeli hosts do not mind, that we stand and say a prayer together.'

He grunted, slightly, as he got to his feet. Father Pierre gave Andrew a covert look as if to say: 'What a clown.' But in obedience to their superior both he and Andrew stood beside the Cardinal with bowed heads and clasped hands while Professor Dagan and his two children withdrew discreetly to the ledge of rock.

'Almighty God and Father,' prayed Cardinal Memel in his deep bass voice, 'you have in your mercy drawn back the veils of mystery over the meaning of our existence and your creation, enabling us to rise out of our condition of sinful ignorance into a life of grace and truth. Help us now, we beg you, to understand the true meaning of what we see before our eyes, so that we may go forth from this cavern beneath

134

the foundations of your holy Temple, and carry its message to the waiting world.'

Walking back down the long tunnel to the plaza in front of the Western Wall, Andrew's thoughts and feelings about what he had just seen were constrained by the role he had adopted in the cistern, of an archaeologist whose judgement could affect the future history of the world. He even wore a thoughtful and slightly self-important expression, as if pondering a question of science, not reconsidering a matter of faith.

When, at last, he took off his paper cap and stepped out into the hot, bright sunshine, he did not drop this role for that of an anguished believer who had just had the rug pulled out from under his feet. Instead, he felt a sudden, irrepressible burst of high spirits which made him want to run across the plaza and jump for joy.

He told himself that it was only relief at escaping from the confines of the tunnel which had changed his mood in this way; and he was restrained from obeying the impulse to run, skip or even smile by the presence of the Cardinal and Professor Dagan. He confined himself to catching Anna's eye, and giving the kind of complicit wink that one mischievous child directs at another, which elicited from her one of her wry smiles. It was only when he reached the car that he understood that the relief he felt was not just at escaping from the tunnel, but also at returning unaffected by what he had seen.

He knew, of course, that it would be irresponsible and unprofessional to reach any fixed conclusion without further painstaking research. Even then, it was unlikely that anyone would ever be certain one way or the other. Father Lambert had apparently accepted that the balance of probability came down in favour of the hypothesis that this was the skeleton of Jesus Christ: what made Andrew so happy was that, unlike Father Lambert, he had discovered the truth before it was too late.

He knew that this was an entirely egotistical reaction, and for a moment felt the usual twinge of bad conscience; but then that twinge was overridden by the liberating realization that if Christ did not rise from the dead, then all the struggle to be unselfish was futile. What was the point, now, of continuously chastising himself for being what he was – someone young, healthy, intelligent and, at that particular moment, in enormously high spirits?

They drove back to the Staedtler Institute in the same cars as before. Andrew sat in the back of the Subaru, Anna next to Jake in the front. She turned towards Andrew. 'What did you think?'

'It could be Jesus,' he said.

'Do you really think so?'

'In itself the discovery of a skeleton with those marks, and hidden like that, would lead one to wonder. But add to that the quite separate discovery of the fragment of Josephus. Clearly, Father Lambert thought that proved it was genuine.'

'Doesn't that upset you?'

He looked perplexed. 'It should, shouldn't it? But somehow it doesn't.'

'The French priest seemed sceptical,' said Jake.

'I think he was just playing the Devil's advocate,' said Andrew. 'Or perhaps one should say, the advocate of the Risen Christ.'

Jake did not laugh. 'Will he influence the Cardinal?'

'I doubt it. He was only chosen as his secretary to teach him French.'

They reached the Staedtler Institute, where the Cardinal was already taking leave of Professor Dagan with one of his vigorous handshakes. 'This has been a most memorable occasion, Professor,' he said. 'One way or the other, it has been a most memorable occasion.'

'For me, too,' said Dagan.

'Now I know you won't expect me to pronounce on your find before I have had time to think about what I have seen, and discuss it with some of my colleagues. I would be grateful if you would continue to regard our visit as confidential until we are ready to make the Church's position clear.'

'Of course,' said Michal Dagan. 'As I have told you, the government, and I myself, are all too aware of the implications of this find, and are most anxious to cooperate with the Christian Churches.'

136

With a few more courtesies of this kind, the clerics took leave of the Israelis. Andrew, suddenly realizing that he was to part from Anna, drew her aside and said: 'Can we meet later on? Where will you be?'

'Call me at home. I'll be there this afternoon.'

She smiled, then followed Jake and her father towards the entrance to the Institute. When she reached it she turned and waved to Andrew as he was driven off in the white Peugeot with Cardinal Memel and Father Pierre.

Fourteen

The three Simonites could say little in the car because of the driver but, upon reaching the Ecumenical Institute at Tartur, Cardinal Memel instructed them to change back into their clerical clothes and then meet him in the garden. When they reassembled, the Cardinal was accompanied by Prior Manfred, and by the thin, grey-haired man wearing a beige jacket and open-necked shirt who, when they had arrived that morning, Andrew had taken to be the director of the Institute. However, the Cardinal now introduced him as 'Father van der Velde, whom we have taken into our confidence in this matter', and Andrew realized at once that this was the distinguished Dutch Dominican from the Ecole Biblique.

This priest now led the four Simonites to a seminar room where they sat down around a polished table. Father van der Velde brought in a jug of fruit juice and five glasses on a tray. He filled the first for Cardinal Memel, who now that he was wearing his red-trimmed cassock and scarlet cummerbund took on some of the dignity of a Prince of the Church, then the other glasses for the other monks, before sitting down with them to listen to the Cardinal.

'I have told Prior Manfred and Father van der Velde what we have seen this morning,' said Cardinal Memel to the two younger men, 'but I think that, having heard from me, they

137

should also hear from you – particularly from you, Brother Andrew, because of your archaeological expertise.'

Andrew blushed, a little awed by this formal confrontation with such eminent priests. Father van der Velde, who seemed so modest in pouring out the fruit juice, was well known as one of the most eminent and influential theologians in the Roman Catholic Church – a Dominican who had served as a *peritus* during the Second Vatican Council, and who had gone on to work so hard for the reunification of the different Christian Churches that he had become known as 'the apostle of ecumenicism'. He had occasionally been rebuked by theologians like Cardinal Ratzinger, and whenever his name had come up in conversation with Father Lambert, Andrew had noticed that tight look which came onto his face when he had difficulty in suppressing uncharitable thoughts.

Now, under the scrutiny of this penetrating theologian, as well as that of the General of his order, Andrew became confused. He dared not give free expression to the wild and heterodox thoughts which were running through his mind, yet he knew that as the pupil of Father Lambert he was expected to have something to say. 'You will appreciate,' he began, 'that it is difficult to form any judgement of my own on the archaeological data because I have not had the opportunity . . .'

'No, sure,' the Cardinal interrupted. 'But what were your impressions?'

'My impressions? Well, clearly this was the skeleton of a crucified man with marks on the bones consistent with the descriptions in the Gospels of what Our Lord suffered. It is in a cistern which matches the location of the cistern in which Pilate, according to the Vilnius Codex of Josephus' *Jewish War*, buried the body of Jesus of Nazareth. Therefore, at first sight, it seems, or rather it seemed to Father Lambert who was a far greater archaeologist than I am – it seemed that this was indeed the mortal remains of Our Lord.'

Father Pierre opened his mouth to protest, but Cardinal Memel held up his hand to silence him. 'How can you be so sure,' he asked Andrew, 'that the whole thing is not a hoax?'

138

Andrew, who had hardly considered the possibility, felt like a student who had forgotten an essential point in an essay. 'I cannot be sure. I cannot even speculate one way or the other until I have made a more detailed study of the find, but I know Professor Dagan – I have known him for some years, because he was not just a colleague but also a close friend of Father Lambert's – and it is inconceivable to me that he would have anything to do with a hoax.'

'And clearly Father Lambert thought the same.'

'Yes. And then there is the Vilnius Codex. That too would have to be a fraud.'

'But why?' asked Father Pierre.

'Just a moment,' said Cardinal Memel, holding up a hand to restrain his secretary. 'Before we move on to you, Father, I should like to be sure that Brother Andrew has had his say.'

'There is nothing I can think of at this moment to add to what I have said,' said Andrew, as he might have done at the end of his Confession.

'Very well. Father Pierre. *On vous écoute.*'

'I think it would be absurd,' said the young Frenchman, arching his eyebrows with Gallic contempt for the illogical, 'to accept one hypothesis or the other at this stage.'

The Cardinal frowned at the word 'absurd'. 'No one suggests,' he said, 'that we either accept or reject any hypothesis. However, we do have to decide whether or not Professor Dagan's discovery merits an investigation by the Catholic Church. If we decide that it does, then we are, to some extent, acknowledging the possibility that he may have discovered the mortal remains of Our Lord Jesus Christ. If we do not, however, we are open to the charge – which has been made over and over again in the Church's history – that we are afraid to submit the tenets of our faith to any kind of scientific scrutiny.'

'A comparable case was the Turin Shroud,' said Father van der Velde in a quiet, high-pitched voice.

'Exactly,' said Cardinal Memel. 'And there the Holy Father himself authorized the carbon-dating of the fragment of cloth.'

'Certainly,' said Father Pierre, 'if *prima facie* evidence emerges that this skeleton is that of a crucified man from the period of Pontius Pilate, then there will be speculation that it is the body of Christ.'

'And the Church will be asked to comment.'

'Yes. But as well as investigating the archaeological data, if that must be done, we should also investigate the possibility of a fraud.'

'Undoubtedly that will be done,' said Cardinal Memel. 'But do you feel *now* sufficiently confident that it is a fraud to advise that we should denounce it as such?'

Father Pierre hesitated. 'I mistrust the Jews,' he said.

'What motive would they have for a hoax of this kind?'

He gave another shrug. 'They have always been the enemies of Christianity.'

'I think that is untrue,' said Father van der Velde.

'Yes. I too,' said Prior Manfred.

'Certainly,' the Dutchman went on, 'there have been attacks on Christian churches here by some fanatics, but the Israeli government has always shown great sensitivity about our feelings for the Holy Places.'

'Of course,' said Father Pierre. 'Pilgrimages are a source of foreign currency. But even here they try to denigrate our faith by turning the Holy Land into a Disneyland.'

'How do you mean?' asked Cardinal Memel.

'They take pilgrims to an old Turkish caravanserai and call it the Inn of the Good Samaritan. Think how many thousands more would come to see the Body of Christ.'

'I cannot believe,' said Andrew, 'that Professor Dagan would be party to a hoax for the promotion of tourism.'

'Nor does your hypothesis deal with the necessary link between the discovery of the cistern and the Codex in Soviet Lithuania,' said Cardinal Memel, 'unless, of course, you are suggesting some collusion between the Israelis and the Russians.'

'It seems very unlikely,' said Father van der Velde. 'What interest would the Russians have in a fraud of that kind?'

'The discrediting of Christianity,' said Father Pierre.

'But as I understand it,' said Father van der Velde, 'the

Soviets under Gorbachev are seeking to rehabilitate Christianity, not discredit it.'

'That is also my understanding of the international situation,' said Cardinal Memel.

'But surely,' said Prior Manfred, who until this point had remained largely silent, 'surely we are approaching this question from the wrong direction.'

'How do you mean?' asked Cardinal Memel.

The face of the pious German was creased and twisted with the evidence of much anguish. 'What we are asking, are we not, is whether this is a fact or is not a fact – whether these bones are the bones of Jesus of Nazareth. But surely we should be listening in our hearts for the voice of God to tell us.'

'Certainly,' said Cardinal Memel.

'I feel sure,' Prior Manfred went on, 'that this discovery is sent to test us – but in what way, *das weiss ich nicht*.'

'Blessed are those who *have* seen and yet still believe, perhaps?' asked Father Pierre.

'There is a certain levity in your attitude, Father,' said Cardinal Memel to his secretary, 'which seems to me, in the circumstances, inappropriate.'

'Yet,' Prior Manfred went on, his agitation forcing the words out like puffs of vapour from a steam engine, 'yet he is right to refer to doubting Thomas because perhaps, if these are the bones of Christ, then they are uncovered to test us further, to see if our faith in Christ can survive despite the evidence that there was no bodily resurrection.'

'Are you suggesting,' asked Cardinal Memel, 'that it does not really matter whether these are the bones of Our Lord or not?'

'*Ja . . . nein . . . das ist . . .* that is to say, when it is established, if it could be, that they are, then does that mean that all our faith is vain?'

'Those are the words of St Paul,' said Andrew.

'Yes, but St Paul is not Jesus,' said Prior Manfred. 'There are many things he said which the Church now rejects – about the position of women, for example. And there are many theologians and exegetes who have for some time harboured doubts about the bodily resurrection of Christ.'

'Certainly,' said Cardinal Memel.

'And these doubts have not destroyed their faith,' said the German Simonite, 'so why should it destroy ours?'

There was an almost crazed look in his eyes as he spoke. It was quite evident to Andrew that, for all the reassurance that his arguments conveyed, he was closer to a crisis than any of the others. It was apparently evident to the Cardinal, too, because he turned from Prior Manfred to Father van der Velde. 'You, Father,' he said, 'are more up to date than any of us, I think, on the latest developments in biblical exegesis.'

The Dutch Dominican sat back in his chair and reached into the pocket of his jacket. 'I am very much of the opinion of Father Manfred,' he said, taking out a packet of Gauloises and looking down at it as if wondering whether to smoke a cigarette. 'We may look at the question of whether Jesus rose from the dead or not in a literal sense – and whether, in consequence, the skeleton discovered by Professor Dagan could be his – without doubting any article of the Nicaean Creed.'

'Go on,' said Cardinal Memel.

'For some time, as most of you know, many theologians and exegetes, such as Father Schillebeeckx in Holland or Father John Coffey in Sydney, have had grave reservations about accepting that the Christ of the Resurrection was the physically reanimated corpse which was placed in the tomb. The belief arose for several reasons. It is much easier to grasp the concept of resurrection from the dead when it is presented as physical reanimation, particularly in the context of the Pharisaical tradition among the Jews which, unlike the Greek philosophical tradition, made no distinction between body and soul. However, the evidence of the Gospels themselves hardly sustains such a hypothesis, for though it is clearly stated that the body was gone – and we need not doubt that – it is also quite apparent that those who saw the risen Lord did not at first recognize him as Jesus.'

'Mary Magdalene,' said Cardinal Memel, 'thought he was a gardener.'

'And the two disciples, on the road to Emmaus, walked with him and talked with him without realizing who he was.'

'Exactly,' said Father van der Velde, in the tone of an approving tutor. 'And if you read the Gospels simply as narratives, they all founder when it comes to the risen Lord. Until the crucifixion they read as clear, straightforward statements of fact, yet after the Resurrection they are meandering and confused. The fact of the Resurrection itself is dramatic, but the events leading up to the Ascension, and the Ascension itself, come as an anticlimax, almost as if the Evangelists as authors did not know what to do with Jesus after he had risen from the dead. Is he a man or is he a spirit? On the one hand, they are eager to show that he is flesh and blood, eating with the apostles on the shores of Lake Galilee. On other occasions, however – in the upper chamber in Jerusalem, for example – he appears to them out of thin air.'

'Yet,' said Prior Manfred, 'it was there that Christ showed Thomas his wounds and told him to touch his wounds, and it was there too that he blessed those who believe without seeing.'

'Yes. But believe what? That he rose from the dead, certainly, but must it be in a literal sense? Were those wounds bleeding? Were they dressed? And where did Christ go when he disappeared once again into the ether? And was it the same Christ who appeared to St Paul on the road to Damascus *after* the Ascension?'

'St Paul certainly thought so,' said Cardinal Memel.

'*Ja, vielleicht* . . .' muttered the old German, shaking his head.

'The Evangelists,' Father van der Velde went on, 'do not tell us very much about what Christ did after his Resurrection. The detailed account of his life before the crucifixion is in marked contrast to the vagueness of their account of the hundred days or so after the Resurrection, and the Ascension itself would seem to have been omitted from early versions of St John's Gospel and is certainly less vivid than, for example, the descriptions of the Transfiguration.'

143

'Are you suggesting, then,' asked Cardinal Memel, 'that Our Lord did not rise from the dead?'

'The question we must consider, your Eminence, is not "Did Christ rise from the dead?", because it is an article of our faith that he did, but "What do we mean when we say that Christ rose from the dead?", or "In what way did Christ rise from the dead?" Is it possible, we must ask ourselves, that Christ rose from the dead in a way that left his body itself on earth?'

'For God, anything is possible,' said Cardinal Memel.

'So the answer must be yes, because the Jesus of before the crucifixion did not disappear into thin air, whereas the risen Jesus did, and so, we must suppose, was physically real only in a spiritual sense and not in an actual, scientific sense that would exclude the existence of his mortal remains.' He paused and looked down at his packet of Gauloises, as if considering, again, whether it would be appropriate to smoke.

'I follow your theology and your exegesis,' said Cardinal Memel, 'but how does this hypothesis explain the empty tomb? Was that a hoax by the apostles to help us believe in the Lord's spiritual resurrection?'

'That is most unlikely,' said Father Pierre, 'because the Pharisees believed that those saved would rise again with a new body.'

'That's quite true,' said Father van der Velde. 'The disciples could plausibly have claimed a resurrection even if the tomb had not been empty. Moreover, the passages in the Gospels which describe the finding of the empty tomb, though they contradict one another in places, are nevertheless as vivid and convincing as the descriptions of Christ's crucifixion. Yet, if one accepts that Peter, John and Mary Magdalene did find the tomb empty, but that Christ did not rise from the dead in a literal sense, then who removed the body and how was it done?'

'It must have been the disciples,' said Andrew, remembering what Father Godfrey had done with the corpse of Father Lambert. 'They were the only ones with anything to gain.'

144

'But the chief priests were aware of that,' said Father van der Velde. 'They knew that Christ had in some sense predicted his own resurrection, and that his disciples might therefore steal the body and claim that he had risen from the dead. That was why they asked Pilate to place a guard over the tomb – which, according to both the Evangelists and Josephus, he did.'

'Josephus states, I seem to remember,' said Cardinal Memel, 'that the Jews also put a guard of their own at the tomb.'

'I know. But that is unlikely. Remember, it was the Sabbath, and no Jew could bear arms on the Sabbath.'

'So they had to get Roman soldiers to guard the tomb.'

'Precisely. Now, even before the discovery of the Vilnius Codex, which suggests that it was Pilate who ordered the removal of the body from the tomb, it had become clear to many exegetes that it was quite probably removed upon his orders. We discovered this by approaching the question from another direction – looking back, as it were, upon the Gospels with the benefit of our knowledge of the Acts of the Apostles, which come after them in the canon but were almost certainly written before. To begin at the end, we have St Paul sent to Rome for trial on charges brought against him by the chief priests. Why to Rome? Because Paul was a Roman citizen, certainly, but what is interesting if you read between the lines of Luke's narrative is the almost amicable relationship between Paul and the Roman authorities. When Paul is threatened with assassination by the Jewish leaders, the Roman tribune in Jerusalem provides a cohort of Roman soldiers to escort him to the safety of Caesarea; and once he is there, Pilate's successor, Festus, invites him to preach before King Agrippa and his sister, Princess Bernice.'

'Wasn't that because Paul was a Roman citizen?' asked Cardinal Memel.

'Or was it Roman policy to protect the fledgeling Christian Church?'

'And what about Nero?' asked Father Pierre.

'But that's just the point. We are so used to thinking of our martyrs in the Roman arenas, and the persecution of

Christians under Nero and the later Roman emperors, that it seems inconceivable that, in those early years in Palestine, it was Roman policy to *encourage* the spread of Christian teaching. Yet there is further evidence to suggest that this was in fact the case. Remember that power was to some extent shared at that time between the Roman procurators and the leaders of the Jews. But one power which was reserved to the Roman procurator was the power of sentencing a man to death. This was why the Jews were obliged to ask Pilate to authorize the crucifixion of Jesus.'

'Why did he agree?' asked Father Pierre.

'Because he was afraid of a riot if he refused,' said Cardinal Memel.

'That is what the Evangelists imply,' said Father van der Velde, 'but is it consistent with the fact that Festus would not hand over the lesser figure of Paul? Or was it, as Josephus states, because Pilate was bribed by the Sadducees?'

'That is more likely,' said Prior Manfred, 'from what we know about the behaviour of Roman procurators at the time.'

'Then why,' asked Father van der Velde, 'did the Evangelists not say so? Why, indeed, did they make Pilate out to be a reasonably decent man? Was it not because they themselves were being protected by the Romans and did not want to offend them?

'Look at the martyrdom of James, the brother of the Lord,' Father van der Velde went on, 'which is described by Hegesippus and also by Josephus in his *Antiquities*. He was the leader, you will remember, of the Christian Church in Jerusalem, and was widely respected by both Christians and Jews. Ananus, the chief priest, wanted to get rid of him but he dared not while there was a Roman procurator in Palestine. It was not until the interregnum between Festus and Albinus that he took advantage of the absence of a Roman procurator to condemn James, a misuse of his power for which he lost his position as chief priest. Look, too, at Peter who, soon after Pentecost, was arrested and imprisoned by the chief priests, and was then miraculously released by an

146

angel. Now an angel, as we all know, was the conventional device used by the Evangelists to describe divine intervention in the affairs of men, but is it not possible that it was the Roman authorities who secured his release? Is it not even possible that the sudden change which came over the apostles at Pentecost, when they no longer cowered afraid in an upper room, but came to speak openly of Christ in the market place, came about not just because of the descent of the Holy Spirit but because of assurances by the Roman authorities that Christian preachers would be protected? Is it not even conceivable that the hearing of the apostles by many men of different nationalities – each in his own tongue – came not as a result of a miracle, but because the Romans themselves provided interpreters to spread the message of Our Lord Jesus Christ?'

'But why?' asked Cardinal Memel. 'What interest could the Romans have had in promoting the Christian Church?'

Father van der Velde leaned forward with an animated expression on his learned face. 'Here, too,' he said, 'the riddle seems insoluble. There are no records of the government of Judaea at that time. But, again, as with our biblical exegesis, we are looking too closely for details and not enough at the whole. It is only when we stand back, mentally, from our detailed and specialized studies, and consider the Roman predicament in its widest sense, that it suddenly becomes clear why Pilate should have wished to promote the Christian religion.

'Consider the task assigned to him, and then the problems he faced. Palestine was essential to the Roman empire because it controlled the eastern seaboard of the Mediterranean – "our sea", as they called it. Should the ports of Sidon, Tyre, Caesarea and Jaffa fall into the hands of the Parthians, the Romans' unconquered enemies in Mesopotamia, then the Parthians could threaten the sea routes from Egypt to Italy along which were carried the cargoes of grain upon which Rome itself depended.'

'But what had this to do with a new religion?' asked the Cardinal impatiently.

'It had everything to do with a new religion,' said the

147

Dutch Dominican, 'because the stability of Palestine had so much to do with the old one. The Jews considered themselves the chosen people. It irked them to submit to the Romans, to pay taxes to Caesar, to be ruled, in effect, by men they despised because they were pagans. They were by nature a volatile, almost ungovernable people. The Romans, when they could, preferred to delegate their authority to Jewish kings like Herod, or his sons Antipas and Philip; but when those kings proved ineffective, like Archelaus in Judaea, then they had no alternative but to impose direct rule from Rome.

'Yet, however firm that rule, they lived in constant fear of a rising in Israel which would give an opening to the Parthians. And the Jews themselves, at the time of Our Lord, were in a state of incipient revolt, not just as a reaction to the Roman occupation, but in anticipation of the advent of their Messiah – the all-conquering king promised by the prophets, who would lead them, God's chosen people, to power and glory. All evidence we have – and there is much of it – suggests that the Jews at the time of Pilate were in a fever of Messianic anticipation, and that almost no one thought of this Messiah in terms other than those of military conquest and political power.'

'Of course,' said Cardinal Memel. 'So along comes a leader who says that his kingdom is not of this world.'

'Precisely. Jesus of Nazareth, with his meekness, his humility, his injunction to love one's enemy, to return evil with good, to turn the other cheek, and, above all, to render unto Caesar the things that are Caesar's – here was the ideal man, from the Romans' point of view, to divert all this Jewish rebelliousness into a harmless religion. If the Jews could be persuaded that their Messiah was leading them to paradise in another world, and that it really did not matter who ruled them in this one, then Pilate's task would be made much easier. Moreover, since Jesus had made cryptic references to rising again from the dead, and would do nothing to save himself from crucifixion, Pilate must have felt that he could kill several birds with one stone. He appeased the Sadducee establishment, as represented by the chief priests, by taking their bribe and crucifying their troublemaker. Then he spirits away the body, under cover of the Sabbath, and protects Christ's disciples when they step out into the street proclaiming that Jesus has risen from the dead.'

He stopped – his eyes bright with enthusiasm, his Gauloises forgotten.

'But did this theory of yours,' asked Cardinal Memel, 'predate or postdate the discovery of the Vilnius Codex?'

'Please,' said Father van der Velde, 'this is not *my* theory, but the conclusion reached by several theologians and exegetes, and it was evolved some time before the discovery of the Vilnius Codex. A certain caution had to be maintained, as I am sure you will understand, in expressing the theory in public. Many of us held posts in Catholic universities and would have undoubtedly lost our jobs if we had promulgated theories of this kind.'

'I cannot imagine them going down well with Cardinal Ratzinger,' said Cardinal Memel with a laugh.

'Particularly as they are not susceptible to any kind of proof. Even with the discovery of the Vilnius Codex, which seemed to confirm much of our theory, we could not prove that the theory was correct. Even now, with Professor Dagan's find beneath the Temple, nothing can be proved, but evidence is accumulating which suggests that Christ did not rise from the dead in the literal sense that has hitherto been supposed.'

The Cardinal sat back in the practised manner of a chairman who wishes to conclude a meeting. 'Father van der Velde, fellow monks of St Simon Doria, I want to thank you for what you have done today. We should each now go and ponder on these things in our hearts, but maintain the strictest secrecy as before. I myself shall make my report to the Holy Father, and it will be for him to decide how to handle Professor Dagan's find. I can tell you now, however, that my advice to him will be that it must be taken seriously, and that far from representing a threat to our faith, it may be a vitally important sign of the times – the culmination of the new spirit in the Church which came with Vatican II, and

149

the portent of a new maturity in our relationship with our Creator. Remember the Apostle Paul. "When I was a child, I spake as a child, I understood as a child, I thought as a child: but when I became a man I put away childish things." It may be that now the Deity who is the source of all life and all good and all understanding considers us ready to discard the props of the miraculous which have hitherto sustained our faith, and to walk freely towards a full and rational understanding of the bond between God and man.'

Fifteen

After the departure of the three Simonites from the Staedtler Institute, Anna followed her father and brother up into her father's office, but sensed at once that they wished her to leave. Indeed, Professor Dagan said to her: 'I think it would make your mother happy if you went home for lunch.'

She left them and caught a bus to Rehavya. Her mood, for all the comforting smiles that she had directed towards Andrew, was as black as it had ever been. Her father's find, which should have excited her – not just as his daughter, but as an archaeologist in her own right – had done nothing to relegate the private preoccupations which tormented her whenever she returned to the bosom of her family in Israel. She had come, certainly, to witness her father's triumph; but, as she had looked down at the skeleton marked by a spear and a crown of thorns, she had been overwhelmed not by excitement or exaltation but by acute irritation with her brother Jake.

There was something about his manner as he escorted them underground which exasperated her – an aloofness, a reticence, a conceit, and that same sneer which he had so often directed towards her when, as a child, he had been told secrets which had been kept from her. To be sent home to have lunch with her mother inevitably exacerbated her irritation, and Anna became exasperated with herself for being caught up in this way by the emotional reflexes of her childish self. She had told herself in the aeroplane, the day before, that she was now an adult with adult feelings, yet no sooner did she set foot in Israel than she was drawn back into the passions provoked by her immediate family.

The contrived way in which her father had embraced her at the airport, and a similar reserve in her mother's kiss when she had arrived at the flat in Rehavya, had made Anna feel angry; and the polite questions over supper about her life in London had only reminded Anna of how little either of her parents seemed to care about what she was doing. That night – the night of her arrival – she had cried under her sheets, muffling her sobs in the pillow. She could have coped with the coldness of her parents if she had had Henry waiting for her in London. She could have managed her jilting by Henry if she had found affection at home; but this double rejection – one explicit, one implicit – was more than she could bear.

She had been distracted from her misery the next morning by the visit to the excavations beneath the Temple Mount; but now that she had returned home, she felt once again all the wretchedness and resentment of the night before and prepared to face her mother in an angry frame of mind.

Rachel Dagan seemed surprised to see Anna. She was watering the plants on the balcony, and looked down at the watering-can as if wondering whether she could go on with what she was doing or should abandon it to talk to her daughter.

'Can I get a drink?' asked Anna.

'Help yourself,' her mother replied. 'There's lemonade in the icebox.'

Anna went to the kitchen and poured herself a glass of homemade lemonade. She took it onto the balcony, which was just wide enough for two battered canvas chairs and an old *chaise-longue*. Anna sat down on the *chaise-longue* and pulled back the hem of her divided skirt to let the sun shine onto her knees and shins. She sipped her lemonade and watched her mother.

Rachel Dagan was small, like her daughter, but while

151

Anna had her father's sharp but delicate features, Rachel's were more rounded and bland. Her spirit was also quite different from Anna's, so that while Anna's face was lean from the many changes of expression which reflected her changing moods, Rachel's was plump and smooth, not just because she had grown heavier over the years but because her character was consistently placid, her mood always calm.

As if to match this psychological trait, her voice was soft and her movements gentle. Anna had never known her to be angry; at worst, if crossed or frustrated, her grey-green eyes would widen and her reticence give way to silence. In general, however, she remained patient and even-tempered – the calming, soothing influence in a highly strung, idiosyncratic family.

It was because Anna was temperamentally so different that she had found it impossible when growing up to model herself upon her mother. The primary influence had always been her father who, though shy and introspective to the outside world, played the part of a pasha in his own home, sometimes sulking, sometimes raging, if his wishes were thwarted.

Anna had often discussed her parents with her Aunt Miriam in London, and it was partly because she sensed that Miriam had feelings for her brother Michal similar to those felt by Anna for Jake, that the niece got on so well with her aunt. 'You must always remember,' Miriam had said, 'that your father had no parents after the age of fourteen. He was always looking for a mother, and he found her in Rachel.'

'So she was too busy mothering him to mother us?' Anna had asked.

'Perhaps. Who knows? It sometimes happens that way.'

Now, on the balcony of the flat in Rehavya, as Anna watched her mother, she felt aggrieved towards the woman whose gentleness and calm seemed like a varnish to protect her from any involvement in the lives of her own children. The silence, clearly, was to save her from comment; the patience was to save her from action. Her obligations – or so it seemed to Anna – only extended to the delicate handling of her husband's fragile ego.

152

Rachel Dagan, as if sensing some of these angry thoughts in her daughter on the *chaise-longue*, prolonged the watering of her plants for as long as she could, but when it was clear that the cactuses and geraniums were already sodden, and that any more water would merely spill from the pots onto the tiled floor, she put down her watering-can, looked at her watch and said to her daughter: 'Are you hungry yet? Would you like some lunch?'

'Why don't you sit down? We could talk.'

'Yes. If you like.' She sat down, upright on one of the canvas chairs. 'What would you like to talk about?'

'Don't you want to know about the visit to the dig?'

Rachel Dagan looked away. 'I think three archaeologists are enough for one family.'

'But you must feel *something* about Dad's find.'

'Of course I do.'

'Pleased?'

'For him, yes, but I also feel . . . afraid.'

'Why?'

'Because it will make people angry.'

'Revolutionary discoveries always do.'

'I know. And your father, of course, was prepared for anger and controversy, but not for the death of Father Lambert. That upset him. He wanted to bury the skeleton and pretend that it had never been found.'

'So why didn't he?'

'Jake would not allow it.'

'What the hell had it got to do with Jake?'

'He was working with him. He persuaded him to go into the cistern.'

'I don't understand why he left the IDF,' said Anna.

'He is still in the IDF,' said Rachel. 'They gave him leave to help your father.'

'If Dad had needed help, he could have called on me.'

'You would have had to serve in the army.'

'He could have fixed that.'

'He thought you were better off in London.'

'Out of the way.'

Rachel looked at her daughter with a nervous expression in her eyes. 'We only want what is best for you,' she said.

'You know,' said Anna, sitting up on the *chaise-longue* and shaking her hair over her eyes to hide the tears, 'you always say that, but now, aged twenty-two, looking back over my life, I feel that you've always wanted to get rid of me.'

Her mother did not immediately deny it. 'It was very difficult,' she said, 'because you were in school when we were in America, and when we came back, we thought it best to leave you there.'

'But not Jake?'

'Jake was always an Israeli.'

'Like Dad and you?'

'Yes.'

'But not me?'

'You never learned Hebrew.'

'It seems to me now,' said Anna, her voice wobbling with a mixture of misery and anger, 'that you never really wanted me to become an Israeli.'

'That isn't true.'

'Or that you didn't care whether I did or didn't, whereas Jake . . .'

'Your father always wanted a son.'

'And you?'

'I wanted to make your father happy.'

'But not a daughter.'

'God gave you to us . . .'

'I was an *accident*?'

'Nothing from God can be called an accident.'

'But I was unexpected?'

'I was already forty . . .'

'Then why the fuck didn't you abort me?'

'Anna, dear,' her mother said gently.

'Can't you understand what it was like for me, growing up with this sense that I was less loved and less wanted than he was?'

'We did want you, Anna. We did love you. But you must realize that we were . . . inhibited.'

'What?'

154

'By our own inheritance. Our own childhood.'

'Why should that mean that you loved me less than Jake?'

Rachel sighed – a horrible sigh for Anna, because it signified that her mother could not deny that they had indeed loved Jake more than they had loved her. 'You must try and understand,' she said in her calm, almost monotonous voice, 'what your father suffered as a child.'

'I know,' said Anna impatiently. 'I know all that. I've heard it a thousand times.'

'It was not just that he and Miriam lost their parents in the camps. That was bad, but it happened to others. Worse, however, were the years before. You see, his father was a rich and successful man, one of the best lawyers in Hamburg. Nor did he think of himself as a Jew, but simply as a cultivated, urbane, liberal-minded member of the German middle class. They did not go to the synagogue. Your father and your aunt did not even to go a Jewish school.

'Then came Hitler and the first Nuremberg laws, which said that Aryans could not be employed by Jews. First, the servants had to go from their house – even the old cook who had worked for them for twenty years. Then the secretary from his practice, and then one by one his German clients left him, so that his practice contracted. He could only act for Jews. They had to sell their large house outside the city and move into a flat in the centre of town. Then the insults started. Once, he was taking your father for a walk in the park when a group of stormtroopers stopped him, spat at him, shouted "*Juden 'raus*", and kicked him out of the park – kicked him, literally, the father in front of his son.'

'Why didn't he leave?'

'To go where?'

'The States.'

'To do what? He was now old. He was becoming deaf. He only spoke German and only knew German law. And it wasn't easy to find a sponsor.'

'What about Eleazar?'

'He offered to take the children, but he wouldn't sponsor your grandparents because he might have had to pay for them for the rest of their lives. Also your grandfather was an optimist. Even when he had to sew a star of David on his suit he thought that the bad times would pass, that Hitler would mellow, that all would be well.'

'But they sent Dad and Miriam to America . . .'

'Yes. Because they saw the war coming and sent them to Chicago.'

'To their Uncle Eleazar?'

'Yes. He wasn't their uncle, only a cousin, a vulgar man who lived in a nasty apartment with his Irish housekeeper. The two children thought that they had come on holiday, but they never went back. For a time there were letters, then postcards, then news from friends and the Red Cross. Then nothing.'

'They were taken off?'

'Yes. The first time, when they came for your grandfather, a doctor friend gave him an injection which made it look as if he had had a heart attack. But they came again and took your grandfather and grandmother, your great-uncle and your aunts, they took them all to Riga and they were never heard of again.'

'I know, Ma,' said Anna – her voice softer and less aggressive than it had been before, 'and it's all terrible, but we can't go on agonizing about it for ever.'

'I don't want you to agonize,' said Rachel Dagan. 'I only ask you to try and understand the effect of it all on a boy who first sees his parents humiliated and then learns that they have been gassed and burnt.'

'It must have been bad.'

'It was. He has never got over it. Always, within him, is his anger – his desire to do something to save them, or to take revenge on those who treated them in this way.'

'But how could he?'

'How, indeed? He fought in the war, in the last war, but against the Japanese, not the Germans. Then, after the war, we all hoped that justice would be done, but soon we were told to forget about the Nazis because the Communists were the enemy now. But your father could not forget, so he came to Israel – not just because there were great opportunities here for an archaeologist, but because he felt that here he could be proud to be a Jew.'

'I don't know why he can't just forget about being a Jew.'

'As your grandfather forgot?'

'That can't happen again.'

'Don't be so sure.'

'It's more dangerous for Jews in Israel than it is in Europe or the States. You don't dare go to the Old City, or even take a walk in the park.'

'That's only because of the *intifada*.'

'Which has made Jews into torturers and killers.'

'That may be true of some,' said Rachel Dagan, 'but here at least we are masters of our own fate. And that is what your father wanted – not just to be in control of his individual destiny, but to have a son who would be untainted by the shame he felt at his father's humiliation. It is not true that Michal loves Jake more than he loves you, but Jake is everything that he wanted and needed in a son. He is clever. He is brave. He is proud. Even his worst qualities – his contempt for the Arabs and the Bedou – delight your father, for he sees in him a phoenix which has risen out of the ashes of Auschwitz.'

Anna sat back, the tears gone from her eyes but not the look of resentment. 'But do *you* go for all that crap?' she eventually asked her mother.

'What . . . crap?'

'The phoenix rising from the ashes?'

Rachel turned away as if to hide her reaction to Anna's question. 'You should understand,' she said to Anna, 'that men are different to women . . .'

'Humph.'

'And while women are often content with a home, men . . . their pride – their self-respect even – depends on the fortunes of their tribe, their nation.'

'You mean that Dad felt like a wimp because his father was kicked around by the Nazis, but Jake feels like a man because the boot is now on his foot and he can kick around the Arabs?'

'It isn't as simple as that. Jake, and your father through

157

Jake, can respect themselves now as part of an ancient nation. They are no longer the *schnorrern* in Poland or the dentists in New Jersey. They are the masters in the land given them by God.'

'But that's fantasy, Ma, and you know it. I very much doubt that either Dad or Jake really believe in God except as an excuse for screwing the Arabs. Even if they do, it's plain as hell to me that if God ever did give Israel to the Jews, then he changed his mind and took it away from them a couple of thousand years ago. I mean, Dad can dig up the whole fucking country, and all he's ever going to uncover that's authentically and undeniably Jewish are a few piles of stones from the time of Solomon. The Hasmonean remains are really Greek, the Herodian remains are really Roman, and everything else is either Christian or Muslim.'

'That is not true, Anna.'

'Look around you, Ma. What do you see when you look at Jerusalem? Turkish walls, Christian churches and on top of it all the golden dome of a mosque which has been sitting on the site of the Temple for at least thirteen hundred years.'

'But there are Jewish monuments . . .'

'Sure. The Hilton, the Sheraton and the Laromme.'

'You are too harsh, Anna.'

'Well, if I am, it's because I feel cheated.'

'No. You have not been cheated.'

Tears returned to Anna's eyes. 'I have, Ma, because you let me out of this crazy country to see it all from the outside, and then you didn't really want me back because I couldn't and wouldn't swallow the mad myth which makes Dad and Jake feel like real men.'

'We need a myth,' her mother said gently.

'Perhaps we do,' said Anna, tears now dribbling down her cheeks, 'but you never thought about a myth for me. You left me to salute the Stars and Stripes, then sent me to sing God Save the Queen, so I'm left without a myth or a country or a family . . .'

'We didn't mean it that way,' said Rachel Dagan.

'You may not have meant it,' said Anna, 'but it happened,

and you let it happen because you cared more about them than you did about me.'

'Not them, Anna,' her mother said in a voice so low that it was almost a whisper, 'but him perhaps . . .'

'Then him, yes. You were such a perfect fucking mother to Dad that you had nothing left for me.'

'He was the first, Anna.'

'Then why did you have me?'

'You came . . .'

'Well, I wish to God that you'd aborted me and fed me to the dogs . . .' And with that she got up and shut herself in her room to sob once again into the pillow.

She slept and did not wake until around five, when she heard her mother tapping on the door. 'Anna. The telephone. It is Andrew.'

Anna got off her bed and went out into the living-room. Her mother was not there. The telephone lay on its side next to the receiver.

'Hi,' she said, trying not to sound sleepy.

'Anna?' He seemed agitated.

'Yes.'

'Are you busy?'

'No.'

'Could we meet?'

'Sure.'

'Can you get to the Jaffa Gate?'

'Yes.'

'I'll wait for you there.'

Anna was glad to escape from her parents' flat. If she could have done, she would have left Israel that evening and returned to London. However, going to meet Andrew amounted to much the same thing: he now seemed her only friend.

He was sitting on the steps beneath the citadel, wearing the same jeans and shirt he had had on that morning. Since Anna had expected him to be back in a Simonite habit, or at least the kind of dark, quasi-clerical costume that he wore when he was in London, this struck her as odd but agreeable:

159

he was decidedly better-looking when not dressed as a priest.

When she came closer, and he stood to greet her, she sensed at once that he was in an unusual mood. His manner was almost frenetic, like someone who has missed a night's sleep but has kept awake by drinking frequent cups of strong coffee. He said at once: 'I am glad you could come,' as if she was doing him a great favour in meeting him in this way. 'Where shall we go? Would you like a drink? Or shall we go for a walk? Where can we go? There's a nasty little café over there. The rest seem to be shut because of the strike.'

'They'll be open in the Jewish quarter.'

'That's true. Let's go there.' They started walking towards the Armenian Patriarchate. 'And if nothing's open, we can take a cab to my hotel.'

'Your hotel?'

'Yes. I've taken a room at the American Colony. Just for a night. I could probably stay longer but I don't know what it costs.'

'I thought you were staying at the monastery?'

'I was, but suddenly . . . Well, that's what I wanted to tell you. I've decided to leave, for the time being . . . probably for ever. The order, that is . . . and, having made up my mind to do that, it suddenly seemed quite wrong to go on living as a Simonite, even for a day or an hour or even a minute longer. So I rushed out into the street with my bag, but then I thought it was discourteous just to leave like that, so I went back and told the Prior – he's a nice old German – and he was very sympathetic. I think he was upset about what we all saw this morning – and he rang the American Colony.'

'But why? Is it because of Dad's find?'

'Yes, well, not just the find as such but more what we made of it afterwards – especially Father van der Velde and Cardinal Memel.'

'Do they know you've left the order?'

'No. They went straight from Tartur to the airport.'

'What did they think of the find?'

'Different things. Father Pierre – that's the Cardinal's

secretary – thinks that the whole thing is a fraud, but the other two seemed to accept that even if this particular skeleton was not that of Christ, it is almost certainly somewhere else, because he almost certainly did not rise from the dead in the literal sense that we had always supposed.'

'And is that what you believe?'

'Yes, I think I do, not just because Cardinal Memel and Father van der Velde believe it, or even because Father Lambert seems to have come away convinced that it was the body of Christ, but really because it suddenly seems to me wrong to insist upon something so inherently improbable when doing so separates us from others who believe in God.'

'But surely the whole point of Christianity is that Christ was the Son of God?'

'Yes. And the whole point of the Muslim religion is that Mohammed was God's prophet, and for the Jews it was Moses, and for centuries now we have been slaughtering one another – and people are being killed now here in Israel because the Muslims insist that Mohammed rose up to Heaven from the rock under the Dome, and we insist that Jesus rose from the dead from under that kiosk in the Church of the Holy Sepulchre, and you insist that God gave you Palestine.'

'I don't insist on anything.'

'No, of course, not you, but your father and Jake.'

'Sure.'

'What struck me yesterday, even before I saw the skeleton, was that if there *is* a God, and that God wants us to love one another, then we should build on what we have in common, and not insist on the things which divide us.'

'And what do we have in common?'

'Our faith in God, whether we call him God, Yahweh or Allah.'

'And if you don't have that faith?'

'Then build on our common humanity.'

They had reached the Jewish quarter and came to a café, where they sat down and asked for two glasses of Coke. As Andrew sat opposite her at the small table, Anna watched him uneasily – wondering, paradoxically, whether his speaking such sense was a sign that he had gone out of his mind.

'All this . . .' she began cautiously.

'All what?' he asked.

'All this belief in the same God and a common humanity – isn't it a kind of change-around from what you believed before?'

He gave a self-deprecating smile. 'Like St Paul? A vision on the road to Damascus? Yes, I suppose it is. But it makes me feel . . . I don't know . . . so excited and happy and free – like getting out of prison or leaving school.'

'I can imagine.'

'My only sorrow is the thought that Father Lambert must have come to just the same conclusion, but, because he was so much older, felt that he had wasted his life.'

'I know.'

'He must have realized, as I do, that once you accept Jesus as just one among many good men – one of the best, certainly, but not the unique source of truth – then you can take from his teaching whatever leads to the common good, and discount some of the harsher ideas which really, when one thinks about it, serve no purpose at all.'

'Such as what?'

Andrew blushed. 'Well, celibacy, for example. It only entered anyone's head because Jesus blessed those "who made themselves eunuchs for the sake of the Kingdom of God", and St Paul built on that, teaching that it was good to be married but better to be celibate. And then along came St Augustine who, to judge from his *Confessions*, was obsessed with sex, and couldn't distinguish love from lust.'

'And you?' she asked, looking at him with a trace of her old mockery. 'Can you distinguish love from lust?'

He blushed again. 'I think so, yes. And anyway, perhaps lust isn't as bad as it's been made out to be.'

'So it's off to the flesh-pots of Egypt?'

He laughed and said, with a rather hollow bravado: 'No, I'm not suddenly desperate to lose my virginity.'

'Father Lambert was.'

'Because he was in love.'

162

'So if you were in love . . .'

He looked away, as if to avoid her eye. 'When you are committed to celibacy, you have to discipline yourself to prevent your thoughts from wandering in certain directions, and you have to cultivate a certain mistrust of your body, not because your body is bad in itself, but because its appetites and passions can lead one astray.'

'But now you think they're a good thing?'

'Yes, now I do.' He looked up at her earnestly, his glass empty on the table. 'It must be difficult for you to understand, but my concept of celibacy was tied up with my belief in the Resurrection. It was as if the sexual act somehow initiated the decay of the flesh, as a fig must split open to release its seed. The Resurrection of Jesus, like the Assumption of Mary, was linked in my mind to their virginity. Then, suddenly, this afternoon, when I realized that Jesus, and Mary too, had a body like yours or mine, which flourished when they were living but eventually putrefied like the corpse in the cistern, then virginity seemed absurd – in fact not just absurd, but wrong, sterile, a denial of life. And that's what suddenly made the monastery seem intolerable – the thought that behind those doors were fifteen or twenty wretched men struggling to suppress their God-given desires.'

'And Father Lambert reached the same conclusion?'

'I felt all the time as if his spirit were hovering over me, guiding my thoughts in that direction.'

'But he had Mrs Dunn. He knew the difference between love and lust.'

'So do I.'

'I'm not sure I do.'

'Perhaps you've never been in love.'

She thought of Henry and frowned. 'It's all more complicated than you imagine.'

'I dare say.' He smiled.

'You can love someone who doesn't love you.'

'I'm sure.'

'Or fancy someone you don't love.'

'Or love someone without realizing it.'

'Sure. Or not know what the hell you feel.'

'Of course.' He hesitated – his voice now calmer than it had been before, as if he had reined in his bolting thoughts and had brought them under control. 'But you see, I have an advantage over you.'

'What's that?'

'Well, you went onto the pitch before you knew how to play the game, but I have had a long time to learn the rules, watching from the sidelines.'

'A substitute?' She looked up at him with one of her little sneers but met only an expression of tenderness.

'A substitute? Yes,' he said. 'I could hardly expect to be anything more.'

Anna opened her mouth to make some ironic rejoinder but was suddenly struck by the thought that, if Andrew was so sure he could distinguish between lust and love, it was because he felt he loved someone already; and if he loved someone already, it had to be her because she was the only girl he knew. And this realization filled her with panic, not just because it is always awkward to be faced, suddenly, with love or desire from an unexpected source, but also because, a week before, she had slept with his brother and Andrew did not know.

Yet – again to her own confusion – the idea that Andrew might love her, and unwittingly follow on where his brother had left off, did not appal her as she might have expected. Indeed, it had no sooner entered her head than the kind of vague admiration she had felt when she had seen him waiting at the Jaffa Gate returned as a brief spasm of sexual desire. She shifted in her seat, as if someone might notice, and said, because she had to say something: 'Do you think I could have some more Coke?'

'Of course.' He smiled and turned to call the man who had served them.

Anna noticed, when he faced her again, that he had the kind of sardonic smile on his face which was more usually found on hers – as if he was more in control of what was going on between them than she was, and was amused to see her floundering in her confused and contradictory

164

emotions. Was he so assured because he had declared himself? *Had* he declared himself? And did he also understand that, after a couple of years of comradely friendship, she too now considered him in a different way?

Yet, she told herself in the cynical tone she always adopted in her inner monologues, if he did think he loved her, it must simply be because she was the only girl he knew. It was inevitable, once he had abandoned his commitment to celibacy, that he would think of her in such terms; and, all at once, with an anguish which belied the cynical tone of her thoughts, she became afraid that the friendship he had felt for her had only ever been the sublimated love of a celibate monk. Now it had surfaced as sexual desire, it would wane with its satisfaction, as sexual desire, in her experience, always did. She would have gained one more lover, but lost her only friend.

The Coke came. They sipped it but did not speak, and the very fact that their earlier chatter had stopped so abruptly told Anna that Andrew, though he had said nothing to state it, and had heard nothing from her, was quite aware that they had established a bond of a quite different kind. Yet if, as she now knew, they were destined to become lovers, it was in a way that she had never known before, not ever imagined. He had said nothing; he had done nothing; no pass had been made, no innuendo slipped into a casual conversation; only that humble acknowledgement that he could but serve as a substitute for someone better.

He was silent now, as if also aware that anything either might say would be beside the point. He seemed shy, certainly, but not awkward or uneasy. His manner was that of a bridegroom who, after a long engagement, had finally reached the day of his wedding. She, too, looked back on their friendship as upon the courtship of an arranged marriage, with Providence the matchmaker and love an unexpected surprise.

When they had finished their drinks, they went out into the warm streets again and walked towards the Temple Mount to watch its honey-coloured ramparts turn pink from the light of the setting sun. There they held hands, as did a number of other courting couples. Then, as the sun set, both declared that they were hungry. They went back into the Jewish quarter to eat pancakes and drink beer at a table in the open air. Again they hardly talked because there was nothing now to say. Only when they had eaten did Andrew ask: 'Will your parents wonder where you are?'

'I guess they will if I don't go home.'

'And will you go home?'

'Do you want me to?'

'No.' He shook his head almost sadly.

'Is there room at the inn?'

He smiled. 'I think so.'

'Good. Then I'll call them from there.'

Sixteen

On the day that Andrew and Anna left for Israel, Henry awoke as usual at seven o'clock in the morning and went barefoot to his bathroom. There, as he rinsed his face after shaving, he saw a scarlet stain in the soapy water.

He was at once seized by panic. He spat into the basin: there was blood, too, in his saliva. He went pale, imagining that these were signs of internal bleeding; that his lungs or his liver or his kidneys had ruptured, and that in half an hour he would be dead.

A few moments later, after further spitting into the basin, he saw that the leak came from his nose, and could be stanched with a paper handkerchief. Still with the ambiguous taste of blood in his mouth, he shuffled through to the kitchen to make some coffee, feeling relieved to be still living and foolish that he had thought himself so close to death.

This was not the first such scare. Three months before, he had panicked because his weight had begun to go down. He had imagined some malignant growth devouring all the nourishment that would normally have gone to his body. He then remembered that he had given up alcohol for a spell, and that, since he was used to drinking several glasses of whisky every evening, he had reduced his consumption of calories by around a thousand each day.

Now, as he sat down to his breakfast of freshly squeezed orange juice, freshly ground coffee, wholemeal toast and thick-cut marmalade, with a copy of the *Financial Times* on the table in front of him, Henry tried to return to the solitary contentment he usually felt at this moment of the day. However, the fear he had felt, while it did not persist, left a residue of anxiety of an imprecise kind. It was not that he feared death, which he supposed was simply oblivion; he was, rather, annoyed in advance by the business of dying, just as he was exasperated when any of his machines broke down. He expected his body and his brain to function as efficiently as the engine of his BMW. He was tormented by petty malfunctions, like nosebleeds or toothache, far beyond the parameters of the pain itself.

He was equally fastidious about his clothes. When he had finished his breakfast he went to his dressing-room, where nine suits awaited him on heavy mahogany hangers. Before deciding which to wear, he thought of the day's appointments. Having chosen an appropriate suit, with shirt and tie to match, he dressed in front of a full-length mirror, inspecting each garment as he put it on for signs of wear, ready to throw it aside for the husband of his Spanish cleaner.

Once, he had been as demanding about the furnishings of his flat. A mark left by a glass on the leather top of his club fender, or by a greasy hand on the arm of his sofa, would have led him to call in the cleaners and, if the stain could not be removed, have the upholstery renewed. If, now, he tolerated the odd sign of grime or wear, it was not because it did not pain him, or would cost too much to make good, but because he could not be bothered to telephone the shops which had provided the furniture, or the girl who had decorated his flat.

As a result, although he seemed to others to be a man in control of his own fate, Henry felt the victim of a creeping decrepitude brought about by the weakening of his will. Far from the heroic destiny he had once envisaged, he now foresaw nothing but a grumbling war of attrition against dirt, dilapidation and disease, ending in a final defeat by cancer, a heart attack, emphysema or a stroke.

Only the demands made upon him by his work distracted him from this pessimism. That morning, having dressed, he drove from Belgravia to Soho, left his car in a garage, and walked from the garage to his office. It occupied one floor of an old brick building, with an architectural practice above and a cutting-room below. At ten, he held a meeting of his editors and researchers to discuss a newsletter on barter in international trade.

This, Henry believed, would increase over the next decade. Many countries in Africa and Eastern Europe were virtually bankrupt, their currencies worthless, their credit exhausted. Even the Russians needed most of the hard currency earned from the export of oil to import food for their hungry population. Those Western businesses who wished to trade with the Soviets in the future might have to return to the kind of barter which had existed at the time of Ivan the Terrible, when English merchants had exchanged pitch and iron for Russian furs and timber.

With this newsletter on barter in mind, Henry had arranged to have lunch with Edward Meredith, a friend from his days on the *Economist* and now the Moscow correspondent for a London daily. They usually met when Meredith was in London, and on this occasion – eager to pick his brains – Henry had asked him to lunch in a restaurant in Charlotte Street.

On his way to meet him, Henry was crossing the east side of Soho Square when a woman came out of St Patrick's Church whom he recognized but could not place. It was too late to avoid her, so he smiled and prepared to walk past, but she stopped and greeted him.

'I thought you might not remember who I was,' she said with a coy smile.

'Of course I do,' he said.

'I was reminded of you because I met your brother the other day.'

'Andrew?'

'Yes. I had heard about him from the Simonites, but I never realized he was your brother.'

Henry now remembered that this was Veronica Dunn, the woman seduced by Father Lambert. 'We're very different,' he said.

'I rang him this morning but they said he was away.'

'He went to Israel.'

She nodded – a grave expression on her face. 'Did he go because of . . . Father Lambert?'

'Yes.'

'To find out what might have happened to him there?'

'He knew already.'

'He didn't tell me.'

'He was very agitated.'

'Why? What was it?'

'It appears that Professor Dagan has discovered the skeleton of Christ.'

'Ah.' She made a sound – half an exclamation, half a cry – and a look passed over her face of mixed pain and relief, as if Henry had just removed the point of an arrow from her flesh. She listened gravely as he explained to her about the Vilnius Codex and the discovery of the jar in the cistern.

'And Father Lambert believed it was Jesus?'

'So it would seem.'

'The poor man.'

'It seems to explain why he killed himself.'

'Yes.' She nodded with the same grave look on her face, then frowned as some anxiety came into her mind. 'And your brother?' she asked. 'How did he take it?'

'He was shocked, I think, but also glad to know the truth.'

'What truth?'

'That Christ did not rise from the dead.'

'Is that established?'

'Why yes, surely, if Father Lambert accepted it.'

'Can we be sure that he did?'

Henry frowned. 'I should have thought so, from the very fact that he took his own life.'

She closed her eyes for a moment and Henry, afraid that

169

she might be about to faint, led her across the street to a bench in the garden of Soho Square.

'There might have been other reasons why he took his own life,' she said as they sat down.

While sympathetic to her physical frailty, Henry was irritated by this refusal to face the facts. 'You can't deny, surely,' he said, 'that his suicide now seems certain to have been an act of despair?'

'Of course,' she said. 'I am sure . . . I have reasons of my own for believing that that afternoon he was in a state of great confusion . . . perhaps despair. He doubted, yes, he doubted, but . . . you are not a Catholic, are you?'

'No.'

'I thought not.'

'Why?'

'Because you cannot understand doubt unless you have known faith.'

'They are both attitudes of mind.'

'No.'

'What are they, then?'

'Faith, is to find God. Doubt is to lose him, or rather, to lose sight of him.'

'And hadn't Father Lambert lost sight of God, or at least God as he had previously conceived of him?'

'We all lose sight of God from time to time. He withdraws.'

'Why?'

'Perhaps to teach us that he is a person, not an attitude of mind.'

Henry frowned, annoyed that this woman was trying to evade the ramifications of her lover's suicide. 'I dare say,' he said, 'that Father Lambert had had doubts before . . .'

'Grave doubts.'

'Any sane man would.'

'Any man at all.'

'All the same, the doubt he entertained that afternoon – knowing, as he did, that Dagan had found the body of Christ . . .'

'He cannot have known it.'

'Why not?'

170

'Because he had not had time to study the findings.'

'That's true, but *prima facie* . . .'

'*Prima facie*, it was enough to make him vulnerable to doubt, but that is precisely how we can know that he was not convinced, because he behaved irrationally, chaotically, absurdly . . .'

'In killing himself?'

'And in other ways.'

'What other ways?'

'I think you know.'

'Andrew did mention that . . .'

'I don't blame him. He's young.'

'But that – what he did to you – was not the act of a man who still believed in the Resurrection.'

'It was the act of a man wrestling with Satan.'

'Satan?' He gave a sniff of involuntary derision.

'If you don't believe in God, then I dare say you don't believe in Satan.'

'I didn't know that anyone did these days.'

'That only goes to show his cunning.'

'Why?'

'Because, *prima facie* . . .' – she repeated Henry's Latin tag with an ironic smile on her lips – 'there is so much evil and suffering in the world that it should be easier to conceive of an evil creator than of a good one.'

'Does one need to conceive of a creator at all after Darwin?'

'He explains how one thing turned into something else, but he doesn't explain how the first thing came out of nothing.'

'And a God, I realize, provides an easy answer,' said Henry scathingly, 'particularly if he is all-powerful and totally mysterious.'

'But he is not totally mysterious. He makes himself known.'

'To whom?'

'To anyone who prays and listens.'

Henry scowled. He disliked her archness and her complacency. 'How lucky you are to have all the answers,' he said.

'But I don't,' she said.

'Well, you seem better equipped than Father Lambert was to cope with the news of Dagan's find.'

She looked suddenly perplexed. 'He went through periods of great depression.'

'About his vocation?'

'No, no. He never doubted that.'

'About what, then?'

'About the state of the Church.'

'It's surely in better shape now than it has ever been.'

'In most ways, yes. But even when the Popes were utterly corrupt, they maintained the claims of the Catholic Church to be the only institution founded by God.'

'And don't they now?'

'A year or two ago – you may remember it – our present Pope held a meeting in Assisi of the heads of several different religions – not just bishops from other Christian denominations, but a Muslim, a Hindu, a Shintoist, even a Red Indian chief or medicine man.'

'I remember. They were photographed together.'

'Exactly. And that photograph seemed to proclaim that the Pope now accepted that the Catholic faith was just one among others. He may not have intended to say that, but that was its effect, and to Father Lambert this was very disheartening.'

'It seems to me to be stating the obvious.'

'Of course. But what is obvious to those who doubt is not obvious to those who believe.'

'So faith can not only move mountains, it can see through them too.'

'It is quite as valid a way of knowing what is true as deductions based upon archaeological data.'

'So it can rise above awkward facts like a skeleton found just where Josephus said it was buried, with marks consistent with what the Evangelists say was done to Christ?'

She smiled. 'I really think that it is faith of a different kind which makes you so sure that those bones are the bones of Jesus.'

'Why?'

'Because, after so many years, it is quite impossible to know something like that.'

'They found the body of Tutankhamun after many more years than that.'

'Certainly, but in that case there were inscriptions . . .'

'And here there is the description of Josephus.'

'Discovered when?'

'A couple of years ago.'

'Isn't that in itself an unlikely coincidence – two finds which fit so neatly together, within such a short space of time?'

'Are you suggesting that the find is a hoax?'

'Yes.'

'Will you bet on it?'

'If you like.'

'Whose judgement will you accept? An archaeologist's? Or must it be the Pope's?'

'I'll accept yours.'

'My judgement?'

'Yes. If you look into it.'

'But I'm not an archaeologist.'

'If it is a fraud, then it isn't really an archaeological question.'

'No. It would be personal, or political.'

'There may be some link, if *my* hypothesis is true, between Vilnius and Jerusalem.'

'Possibly.'

'Some complicity between two people.'

'Yes.'

She stood up. 'I must go.'

'And what is the wager?' asked Henry, glancing at his watch, then also getting to his feet. 'Ten pounds? A hundred pounds?'

'It is worth more than that, surely.'

'A thousand?'

'I think bets of this kind are usually in a different currency.'

He was puzzled. 'Dollars?'

'Souls.'

'Ah. You mean I'm playing for my soul?'

'And I for mine.'

'Very well.'

'Ring me when you know.' She held out her hand and he shook it – whether to say goodbye or seal their wager he did not know – before walking towards Oxford Street.

Henry was now late for lunch and found Edward Meredith waiting at his table. After his encounter with Veronica Dunn, he was particularly pleased to join his sceptical friend. He had changed a little since he had last seen him – his hairline an inch or so further back on the brow; his eyes a little more bloodshot and bleary; his face heavier around the jowls; but his personality was the same, and they at once reestablished the familiar manner of their early days in journalism. After conventional enquiries about the well-being of his wife and children, Henry plunged straight into the question of the Soviet economy.

'It's a fascinating time to be there,' said Meredith, 'because the country is doubly bankrupt – economically bankrupt and ideologically bankrupt. You are right about barter – they're reduced to that, not just in their trade with hard-currency nations, but also with other socialist countries which don't want their worthless roubles. Even in trade between the Soviet republics themselves, they may be reduced to barter. I wrote a piece about a paper-mill in Lithuania which suddenly stopped receiving pulp from Siberia. The director telephoned the saw-mill and was told that they would only continue to provide the pulp in exchange for sausage, cabbage, beer, potatoes and beans. It's a most extraordinary situation. Anything could happen . . .'

They ordered their lunch – not sausage, cabbage, beer, potatoes and beans but *feuilleté d'escargots*, rack of lamb, *fraises des bois*, a half bottle of Chablis and a full bottle of Clos de la Roche.

'I gather, from what you write in your paper,' said Henry, 'that the Lithuanians are determined to secede.'

'So are the other two Baltic republics, and possibly Armenia and Azerbaijan as well.'

'Will Gorbachev let them?'

174

'It's difficult to see how he can stop them, except by using brute force, which would lose him the support of the West.'

'Are they viable, these republics, as independent nations?'

Meredith shrugged. 'With a little help from their friends. Particularly Lithuania.'

'Why?'

'Because its industries are advanced by Soviet standards, and its agriculture retains some of its efficiency from the time when the land was privately owned. But, above all, because of the Catholicism of the Lithuanians, which has kept them socially and culturally distinct.'

'Is the Church still that strong?'

'As in Poland, it is the principal ideological opposition, and until recently was ruthlessly persecuted.'

'And now?'

'Now there's a thaw. The Archbishop has been released from house arrest and given back his Cathedral.'

'A change of heart?'

He looked doubtful. 'More a change of tactics.'

'Could the Communists still see it as in their interest to discredit the Catholic Church?'

'Yes, I should have thought so. Why do you ask?'

Henry hesitated, then said: 'My brother . . .'

'The monk?'

'Yes. He's stumbled on a story which might interest you.'

'About Lithuania?'

'Indirectly. But if I tell you, it would have to be off the record.'

'Very well.'

Henry leaned forward, and in a quiet voice told Meredith the story of Dagan's find.

'And you really think that it could be the skeleton of Christ?' Meredith asked him when he had finished.

Henry shrugged. 'I don't know. If he didn't rise from the dead, he has to be buried somewhere.'

'Of course. But this body would never have been identified if it was not for the Vilnius Codex.'

'So, if the Codex is a fake, then the find must be a hoax.'

'Even if the Codex is genuine,' said Meredith, 'the find

could be a hoax because this man Dagan might have put a skeleton into the jar and the jar into the cistern.'

'It would be difficult, wouldn't it, to make it convincing?'

'Not really. It certainly wouldn't be difficult to find the skeleton of a crucified man, since thousands were executed at that time in that way, and then to add the marks of the thorns and spear. Nor would it be hard to fake the Codex . . . if, that is, the forgers had access to the laboratories of the KGB.'

'Would it be possible for a private individual to fake the Codex?'

'In Russia? Unlikely.'

'Could the Israelis have smuggled it into the country?'

Meredith hesitated. He was said to have links with the intelligence services and now, certainly, seemed to be considering not just what he knew but how much he could say. 'They might have smuggled it in,' he said, 'but there would have to be half-a-dozen people to connive at a fraud of that kind – people placed, moreover, in the right positions: the monks in the monastery, the officials in the library and, of course, the young woman who discovered it.'

'Miss Vesoulis.'

'Yes. She would have to be part of the conspiracy, and I should have thought it would be beyond the capacity of Mossad to position people in that way. In Israel, certainly. In the West, probably. But in the Soviet Union, no.'

'But would it be possible for the KGB?'

'Of course. You see, what Mossad and the KGB have in common is that they enrol almost every citizen as a potential auxiliary, so you can never say precisely that anyone either is or is not an agent. Through zeal in Israel, and through fear or opportunism in Russia, anyone can be a kind of stringer – asked to report on a colleague or perform a small part in a much larger intrigue.'

'So it is not impossible that the Codex is forged?'

'Not impossible, no.'

'Improbable?'

Again Meredith hesitated. 'One would have to come up

176

with a motive, not just for forging the Codex but also for collaborating with the Israelis.'

'Who are surely the Soviets' enemies rather than their friends?'

'In theory, certainly.'

'What would be the motive?' asked Henry.

'Well, if one discounts the theory that it is an elaborate and expensive practical joke, then one must assume an intention to discredit the Christian religion.'

'Yes,' Henry agreed, 'and one can concede that both the Soviets and the Israelis are to some extent antagonistic towards Christianity.'

'They have that in common.'

'But it would surely be inconsistent for Gorbachev on the one hand to stop persecuting the Christian churches, and to try to enlist their support for his policy of *perestroika*, and on the other to play a dirty trick of this kind to discredit them.'

'I don't think that necessarily follows. Gorbachev may well feel that while it is a mistake to make unnecessary enemies anong believers, Christian beliefs are nonetheless absurd and reactionary superstitions.'

'So he could be behind a fraud of this kind?'

'I doubt that he would be behind it, but he might have allowed it to placate those opposed to his policy of religious toleration.'

'Could it have been done without him knowing about it?'

'Certainly, and here the fact that the Codex was discovered in Lithuania may be relevant.'

'Why?'

'Because Lithuania is the only one of the Soviet republics with a Catholic population. And there, as in Poland, the Church is the only institution which can effectively oppose the regime.'

'But all that is in the past, surely? The persecution has stopped.'

'Only direct persecution. Atheism is still the ideology of the state. Gorbachev, for quite practical reasons, may want to enlist the support of the Christian churches for his particular faction in the Party, but he must still counter a Church which implicitly denies his right to rule.'

'I don't follow,' said Henry.

'It is misleading,' said Meredith, 'to see the Communist Party simply as a political party. In the eyes of its members it is more than that – it is, in fact, more like a Church.'

'In what way?'

'In the West the legitimacy of a government depends upon democratic choice. In Russia it comes from its historical mission to lead mankind towards the socialist millennium.'

'But they surely don't believe that today?'

'You would be astonished how many still do – not least because it justifies their right to rule.'

'So your hypothesis would be that some Old Believer in the Lithuanian KGB dreamed up a scheme to discredit the Christian religion?'

'Yes. Or, if not discredit it, remove its otherworldly expectations, so that Christians, like Communists, can set their sights on a paradise here and now.'

'But how could they think that a hoax of such a kind could work?'

'Why shouldn't it work?'

'Because in the end they would be shown up.'

'Perhaps. Perhaps not. But by then the damage would be done. Remember the Zinoviev Letter, or the Protocols of the Elders of Zion.'

'But doesn't your hypothesis presuppose collusion with the Israelis?'

'Yes.'

'So some link would have to be established between the Soviets and Professor Dagan.'

'Yes. And that, of course, makes it less plausible if, as you say, Dagan is a man unlikely to commit fraud.'

'I don't know him myself, but my brother is sure he would be incapable of it.'

'And do you trust your brother's judgement?'

Henry frowned, then said: 'Not really, no.'

'The way to proceed,' said Meredith, taking an address book from his pocket, 'if you really want to get to the bottom of this, is to find out what you can about the people who were involved in the discovery of the Codex. Ask the Lithuanians here in London about this Miss Vesoulis. Ring this man.' He wrote a name and a number on a piece of paper. 'He may know of her. Or he can find out. Lithuania is a small country. Almost everyone knows everyone else.'

Seventeen

When Henry got back to his office, he returned to work on the question of barter but found that his mind was unable to concentrate on the papers spread out on his desk. Normally, he could interest himself in matters which others found intrinsically dull; now, some irritating inner voice kept whispering that matters like the convertibility of the rouble were trivial compared to the authenticity of Dagan's find.

At four he gave up and sent for one of his researchers, a girl called Sandy Wells, who though plain and unimaginative, could speak German and Russian and unearth information in a short space of time. He told her to give up her enquiries into contracts within Comecon and go instead to the British Museum to find out what she could about the Vilnius Codex and the Slavonic additions to Josephus' *Jewish War*.

She looked surprised but, since Henry paid her salary, she did what she was told. Henry then rang the number that Meredith had given him and asked to speak to Algirdas Sostakas. The voice which responded sounded cautious until Henry mentioned Meredith's name.

They agreed to meet at six at a pub in Notting Hill. The bar, when Henry got there, was not crowded, and he recognized Sostakas because of his blonde moustache and Baltic physiognomy. He was forty to forty-five years old, perhaps the child of a refugee from the Second World War, but he nevertheless spoke English with the accent of someone who knew it only as a second language.

179

He ordered beer, Henry whisky, and once they had glasses in their hands they left the bar and went to sit at a small table.

'It's very good of you to see me,' Henry began.

'Mr Meredith tells me that you are a very old friend.'

'You spoke to him?'

He shrugged his shoulders as if to say: 'What did you expect? I had to make sure.'

'Did he tell you what I wanted to know?'

'He said you would explain.'

'It concerns a Codex – a fragment of an ancient manuscript – in the State Library in Vilnius. It disappeared during the First World War, but was discovered four or five years ago in an Orthodox monastery.'

'You want to know if it is a fake?'

'Yes.'

'You are buying it?'

'No. But its authenticity has certain political implications.'

'There are many fake icons, fake manuscripts, fake relics. They earn currency that way. Dollars. Deutschmarks.'

'I realize that. But this Codex would have to be faked for a specific political purpose.'

'By Chekists?'

'Yes. If by that you mean the KGB.'

'We know, more or less, who are Chekists.'

'Here the conspiracy, if there is one, would implicate Orthodox monks as well.'

'Many of them are Chekists, especially in Lithuania.'

'And officials at the State Library, in particular a Miss Vesoulis.'

Sostakas took out a grubby scrap of paper and scribbled down the name with a ball-point pen.

'We are also curious to know,' said Henry, 'if any of the people involved in the rediscovery of the Codex have any links with Israel.'

He nodded. 'Many Chekists are Jews in Lithuania.'

'Why?'

'You know our history?'

'Not well.'

'In Lithuania there were always many Jews. In the cities, especially – in Vilnius and Kaunus. They were always on the side of the Russians. They didn't want an independent Lithuania. For this reason, and because they were in the cities, many of the Bolsheviks were Jews. They helped the Soviets when they invaded our country, with arrests, deportations, torturing and liquidations. In some areas, most of the militia were Jews. They closed our churches and imprisoned our priests.'

'And later,' said Henry tartly, 'they paid the price.'

'Of course,' said Sostakas. 'When the Germans came, we killed them.'

'All of them?'

'Most of them.' He did not seem displeased. 'Some escaped to Russia and came back at the end of the war.'

'As KGB?'

'Of course.'

'And today?'

'Also today.'

'Is it possible that any of these would have links with Israel?'

He frowned. 'I don't know, but I can enquire.'

'How long will it take?'

'A telephone call.'

'Is that safe?'

'We have ways of putting things. "How is my cousin Vesoulis? Is she still working at the State Library? We should like so much to know what she is up to these days." If it sounds innocent, it does not trigger the tape-recorders of the Chekists.'

'You must let me know if you incur any expenses.'

'Please.' He held up his hand as if Henry was pressing a banknote into his hand. 'It is a pleasure to do a favour for a friend of my friend Meredith.'

From Notting Hill, Henry drove back to his flat in Eaton Square. There he played back the messages on his answering machine, poured himself a drink and lay back on the sofa.

He was expected to dinner by some friends, but he knew

181

he could not face it and waited for the strength to telephone to say that he was ill. He told himself he was tired, and certainly his limbs felt weary; but the reason he balked at the thought of a social occasion was his consuming curiosity about Dagan's find.

When Anna had first told him that her father had discovered the skeleton of Christ, he had been neither particularly surprised nor particularly interested. Now, he realized, the truth or falsity of her claim could not only affect the psychological state of those who had faith, like Andrew or Veronica Dunn; it could also have considerable political ramifications all over the world – in Eastern Europe, in Africa, in Latin America.

Isolated for so long among like-minded agnostics, whose values were all of a secular kind, it came as a shock to Henry to realize quite how many people throughout the world still believed in the Resurrection of Christ. Seldom since adolescence had he himself stopped to consider questions of this kind. There had been moments, mostly on holiday, when, staring at the stars, he had been awed by the mystery of infinity, and had wondered about the origin of the universe; but, almost at once, when he had returned to London, he had been distracted once again by the practical concerns of his daily life.

Now, however, he had the uneasy feeling that there might, after all, be more to life than he had supposed; that perhaps the imperatives of instinct did not lead to fulfilment; and that perhaps the faculty of reason, unique though it was to the human species, was insufficient to explain the mystery which lay in the kernel of the human condition.

He sat up, put down his glass, and made the telephone call to the friends who were expecting him to dinner. The wife answered. He lied about a sudden sickness. She spoke the appropriate words of sympathy, but he could tell that she did not believe him.

He went out onto the small balcony at the back of his flat – a space between the sloping roof and the parapet. He watered the plants he kept there – a camellia, some herbs, and a bay tree – and breathed in the scented air of the

London summer. This taste of nature did nothing to calm his mind; and while he picked the chives and parsley for an omelette for supper, he continued to think about the skeleton, and grew increasingly agitated by the thought that, if reason could not explain the human condition, it was unreasonable to be sure that there was no God. Nor could it be impossible, if there was a God, that he should have been born a Jew, have died on a cross, and, after dying, have risen from the dead.

If such a story was not certainly false, then it must be possibly true. Thus, incontrovertible evidence – even evidence which pushed the balance of probability one way or the other – would be of critical importance, not merely to those political developments in different parts of the world which were influenced by people's religious convictions, but also to the individual speculations of a man such as Henry about the value of his actions or the meaning of his life.

He cooked his omelette and ate it in the kitchen, his mood swinging between excitement and gloom. He still felt a repugnance for religion, and thought it absurd to suggest that a God powerful enough to bring the whole universe into existence should choose to become a sweating, defecating, human being. Yet he had to acknowledge that, if there was a God, then what appeared absurd to us might seem sensible to him. He would be privy to knowledge beyond the range of human understanding which made it necessary for God to become man to enable man to become a god.

Yet if he, Henry, were potentially a god – a creature whose existence would continue beyond death, but one whose condition in that dimension would be determined by his attitude to the crucified Jew, then, clearly, his life up to that point would have earned him not bliss but torment. So too would the lives of almost everyone he knew. It followed, if there was a God with power over the destiny of human beings, that the first prayer to be addressed to him should be a plea to be spared this awesome choice: to be reassured that Professor Dagan was right, that the skeleton was that of Jesus of Nazareth.

As if in answer to that prayer, the telephone rang and

Henry heard, on the other end of the line, the flat, matter-of-fact voice of his researcher, Sandy Wells.

'I thought you'd like to know what I've uncovered so far,' she said.

'You shouldn't be working so late.'

'It's OK. In fact, it's all quite interesting. You see, there's really quite a lot of controversy about the Vilnius Codex and the additions found in the Slavonic version of Josephus. There are those English scholars who accept them, like Thackeray and Williamson; then there are those like Shurer, who think they are medieval forgeries; and then there's this third guy, Eisler, who thinks that they're basically genuine but have Christian interpolations.'

'What do you think?'

'Well, I think one's got to accept that the Slavonic version is derived from an early edition of Josephus written in Aramaic for the Jews in Babylon. There are passages which don't exist in the Greek version but which are unmistakably by Josephus. It's also clear how such an Aramaic edition should end up in Vilnius. I don't know whether you want to go into details . . .'

'Yes.'

'Well, really, it boils down to the links between Babylon and the Byzantine Empire, and the Byzantine Empire and Russia. It's more than likely that if such an edition of Josephus did exist, then it would have ended up in Constantinople and been known there to scholars of the Orthodox Church. The most plausible theory is that it was translated into Old Russian in the fifteenth century by members of a Judaizing sect of the Russian Orthodox Church which, when finally suppressed by the Tsar, took refuge in Catholic Lithuania.'

'Might they have inserted the references to Jesus and John the Baptist?'

'It's conceivable, certainly. But it's hard to think of a motive.'

'To prove that they existed?'

'Of course. That's the obvious motive. But before the late

eighteenth century no one doubted that they existed, so why should some medieval forger go to all that trouble?'

'So you think that the additions were definitely written by Josephus?'

'Yes.'

'What about the Vilnius Codex?'

'That's more complicated. It existed up to the First World War, but it was one among dozens of manuscripts scattered around in different places. They certainly knew that there was a Slavonic version as far back as 1893, but this guy Alexander Berendts who was piecing it together died in 1912. Then came the war. The Germans invaded Lithuania; the Russians retreated, taking the Vilnius Codex with them. It was thought to have been given to the State Archives in St Petersburg and destroyed in the fire there in 1917. That's why the publication of Berendts' work by Konrad Glass in 1920 did not include it. But given the chaos existing in Russia in 1917 it is quite plausible to suggest that the Codex was left in the monastery for safe-keeping.'

'So you think it's genuine, too?'

'It's impossible to be certain, but, if it stands up to carbon-dating, then I'd say that, on balance, yes, it's the real thing.'

He rang off, elated by a most extraordinary sense of relief. Only a forged Codex could justify doubting the integrity of Dagan. If the Codex was genuine, then the find was genuine, and Jesus of Nazareth had not risen from the dead. He was not, then, a superhuman being embodying the way, the truth or the light but a Middle Eastern sage with a number of interesting ideas which had been and always would be interpreted in a number of different ways.

Or rejected altogether . . . As Henry stepped back from the abyss of Christian belief he felt a sudden surge of physical well-being, like a man who wakes up to find himself cured of a debilitating disease. Life – life on the earth and in the air – appeared once again as something of extraordinary beauty. Why had he faltered? Was there not art to entertain him, women to love him, men to esteem him and continents to be explored? What dreadful doubt had tempted him to accept the morbid philosophy of the crucified Jew? He was not a god but a man – a beast at the pinnacle of evolution – and he would live his life to the full until he returned like Jesus of Nazareth to the dust from which he came.

The telephone rang again. It was the Lithuanian, Sostakas. 'Mr Nash?'

'Yes.'

'Are you alone?'

'Yes.'

'Good. I have been talking to my friends in Vilnius. They have news of your friend, Miss Vesoulis.'

'Yes.'

'She is, almost certainly, what we suspect. She was given the job at the State Library without proper qualifications.'

'Is it known why?'

'She had powerful friends.'

'In the Party?'

'Even more powerful.'

'In the KGB?'

'That's what they think.'

'And she was the one who discovered the Codex?'

'One month or so after she was appointed, the monks handed over their archives. There were many documents, and Miss Vesoulis was given the job of sorting them out. Very soon, she found the Codex, translated it, and published her findings.'

'It sounds as if she knew it was there.'

'Not only that. My friends tell me that it was most unusual for someone so young to have a paper published in the *Soviet Archaeological Review*; and even more unusual for a paper to be published so soon after being submitted.'

'So there are signs of a helping hand.'

'Yes.'

'Do they know whose?'

'It is suspected. A man named Gedda. A Jew.'

'Ah.'

'He is her lover.'

'And what else besides?'

'He is a Soviet expert on Middle Eastern Affairs.'

'An academic?'

186

'At one time. But now a diplomat of some kind. You should ask our friend Meredith. He knows, I am sure, about Gedda.'

Henry telephoned Meredith. 'I've been talking to your Lithuanian friend,' he said.

'Did he help?'

'He's found a link between Miss Vesoulis and a man called Gedda.'

'Gedda. Yes. I should have thought of him.'

'Who is he?'

'A diplomat, so called. He was here in the embassy back in the Seventies. We threw him out.'

'For spying?'

'Yes.'

'And now?'

'At one point he was in Damascus as part of the Military Mission.'

'Would he have had contacts with the Israelis?'

'Not in Damascus. There aren't any. But he would have had links with Syrian Intelligence, and access to their agents in Israel.'

'So he could have had the Codex forged?'

'Certainly.'

'And planted the skeleton in the cistern?'

'Not without help from the Israelis.'

'Dagan?'

'Yes. Unless Dagan himself has been duped.'

'So we need to find a link between Gedda and either Dagan or some other Israeli.'

'Yes. And since Gedda himself won't have gone to Israel, it's a matter of finding an Israeli who was in Moscow some months before the Codex was found. Or, if not Moscow, Damascus.'

'You said there were no Israelis in Damascus.'

'None by choice. But the Syrians took prisoners during the war in Lebanon. Get one of your researchers to go back over copies of the Israeli papers, or just the *Jerusalem Post*, to see if someone, say a student of Dagan's, was taken prisoner in the Lebanon and later exchanged.'

Henry sighed. 'It all seems far-fetched.'

'More far-fetched than finding the body of Christ?'

'Perhaps not, except . . . it must be somewhere.'

'What?'

'The skeleton of Jesus.'

'Why?'

'Because he can't have risen from the dead.'

'Nothing is impossible for God.'

'Do you believe that?'

'If there is a God, it's only common sense.'

'And is there a God?'

'That's a very deep question, Henry. We must talk about it some other time.'

Eighteen

Anna was awoken at dawn by the cry of a mullah from a nearby mosque calling the faithful to prayer. She moved in the bed and sensed that she was naked. All at once she remembered everything that had happened the day before. She remembered it vividly, yet she knew that dreams can leave a strong residue of feeling and was therefore afraid to open her eyes for fear of finding herself in her parents' flat in Rehavya. But there were no mosques in Rehavya, and she could still hear the mullah. She could also sense the even breathing of a body beside her, and slowly moved a leg across the mattress until it came up against Andrew's side.

She barely touched it: she did not want to wake him until she had put her thoughts and feelings in some order. It was not easy. Usually, when she first awoke, she went through a self-analysis which could be reduced to one question: am I happy or sad? Sometimes the answer was happy; more often it was sad; but today there were so many different factors to consider – so many undigested experiences – that she could not at first decide. She thought of Henry in London, then of her mother and her tacit admission that Anna had indeed been less loved than Jake; and finally, of course, there was Andrew – his unspoken declaration and then the sudden metamorphosis from friend to lover.

The speed with which it had happened had confused her then, and it continued to confuse her now. She could not decide, in thinking about the night before, quite who had seduced whom. Certainly, it could hardly be said that she had had designs on him, since she had never thought of him as anything more than a friend; yet, when it had become clear that he loved and wanted her, her body had reacted even before her mind. Was this what was meant by falling in love?

If so, it was not at all how she had imagined it. She had always envisaged an older man – suave and masterful – who would bear down on her with glowing eyes and bend her to his will. Andrew, however, had made no demands; he had simply proceeded as if their making love was the natural and obvious thing to do. Clearly, he had never done it before, but he was neither awkward nor inept, hesitant nor apologetic. Nor did he act the part of the virile lover, as so many previous boyfriends had done, by tearing off her clothes and throwing themselves at her body. Instead, he had been gentle, thoughtful and above all astonished, as if the sight and feel of her body was yet more beautiful than he had imagined.

Her first thought, when it was done, was how unlike his brother Andrew was. The memory of Henry, however, had at once provoked both anxiety and shame as if, retroactively, she had been unfaithful to Andrew. She was afraid of what he would think if he ever found out that Henry had been her lover, or quite how recently she had been in his brother's bed.

The same thoughts came back to torment her now. If she did not tell him, would he not find out from Henry? If she did tell him, would he not be disgusted that she had transferred herself so easily from one brother to the other? Would he not, in any case, come to despise her for the speed with which she had let herself be seduced? Yet she had not been seduced. They had known each other too long; they

189

were too good friends; it had been as if the house were already built, and all that remained was to go through the door. But would he think of it in the same way?

She waited for him to wake, listening to his quiet breathing. The sun shone in through the curtains. She could not see a clock, but guessed that it must be already eight or nine in the morning. Her thoughts returned again to her father, her mother and Jake, but now they seemed like beings in a different world. How could she have cared whether or not they loved her as a child, when her childhood was over and a new life with a new love had begun? How could she have ever thought that she had loved Henry, with his cold manipulation of both her body and her soul? And the beefy boys – the soldiers and the students? How could she ever have allowed them to defile what had been made so precious by Andrew's caresses?

He stirred, turned, awoke. He sat up abruptly, looked at the window, rubbed his face, then turned to look at her and smiled. '*Benedicamus Domino*,' he said.

'I beg your pardon?'

'It's what they say in the monastery to wake you up in the morning.'

'*Benedicamus Domino*?'

'*Deo Gratias*. That's what you answer.' He kissed her, then took hold of the sheet beneath her chin and gently pulled it down to her stomach. 'You know,' he said quietly, 'when at times as a monk I did let my thoughts stray a little down forbidden paths, they never went further than imagining how wonderful it would be to lay one's head on a girl's bosom.'

She looked down over her chin. 'I'm afraid they don't make much of a cushion.'

'They're fine,' he said, smiling, resting his head gently between her small breasts. 'Do you think,' he asked, 'that we could get breakfast brought up to the room?'

'Sure.'

'I also used to dream of that – breakfast in bed on the first morning of one's honeymoon.'

'Is this our honeymoon?'

190

'Isn't it?' He sat up and looked into her eyes. 'Aren't we married, really, after last night?'

'If you say so.'

'I do.'

'And want to be.'

'I do.'

'So do I, I guess.'

He leaned forward and kissed her. 'Then I pronounce us man and wife.'

They both wanted to leave Jerusalem and go back to London but their tickets could not be changed without paying a great deal more money. They moved to a cheaper hotel in West Jerusalem. Andrew insisted that Anna tell her parents where she had gone, but he did not himself tell Prior Manfred. 'There's nothing much I can do until I get back to England,' he told her. 'Then I'll go and see Father Godfrey and formally resign from the order.'

The hotel was small and smelly, and their room intolerably stuffy, but the joy they both felt in one another's company made them oblivious to any discomfort. Privacy was all that they required. Already familiar as friends, their chief pre-occupation was with the pleasure they could exchange with their bodies. They lived off felafels, coffee and Coca-Cola and often ate and drank in bed.

On the Sunday they took a bus to Jericho. Because of the *intifada*, there were fewer tourists than usual and Andrew became afraid that perhaps Anna was in some danger; but since he himself was so patently European, and Anna leaned on his arm, the Arabs they met were friendly – the shop-keepers too friendly, badgering them to buy their postcards, carpets and Bedouin bracelets before the strike closed their shops at midday.

Before the Arab restaurants closed, they ate at a table shaded by a vine. In the great heat of the afternoon, they went to visit the ruins of the neolithic city uncovered by Kathleen Kenyon in the 1950s. There, for a moment, their conversation became that of two archaeologists, but as they walked back into the centre of Jericho to take the bus back into Jerusalem, they returned to the inanities of lovers.

Anna was sick in the night. Andrew, sympathetic to her suffering, rose early to bring her mineral water and a glass of sweet tea.

'I already feel much better,' said Anna, sitting up in bed and propping her slight body against the wall.

'Good.'

'It must have been the salad at Jericho.'

'Of course.'

'Or a bug.'

'Yes.'

'Do you feel OK?'

'Me? Yes. Fine.'

She frowned. 'You look kind of funny.'

'How?'

'Well, the expression on your face.'

He gave up trying to hide his smile. 'I'm sorry,' he said, sitting down on the bed and taking hold of her hand. 'It's just that I know that sickness in the morning sometimes means that a woman is pregnant.'

'Not in my case.'

He blushed. 'It's quite likely, isn't it, after what we've done?'

'Not unless . . .' She stopped and looked away.

'What?'

She turned to him again. 'It isn't very likely.'

He stood and walked towards the window. 'It would be wonderful, wouldn't it, if our first child was conceived here in Jerusalem?'

'I guess it would.'

'God knows where we will live. Perhaps Henry will lend me some money for a deposit on a flat, and then I can get a mortgage on my salary from Huntingdon.'

She looked at him from under her brow. 'You were serious, weren't you, about getting married?'

He turned to her, beaming. 'We can't get married. We *are* married.'

She looked away, avoiding his eyes.

192

He smiled, mistaking the reason for her confusion. 'I promise you, that's theologically sound. The church only blesses a marriage. The state only registers it. A marriage itself is made between two people who commit themselves to one another for ever.'

'And you really feel committed to me for ever?'

'For more than for ever – for eternity.' He came back to the bed. 'I always thought it was a little unromantic of Our Lord to say that there was no marrying in Heaven and now, well, now I feel I am entitled to believe that there is.'

'But what happens if I don't make it to Heaven?'

'Oh, you will. St Paul said that Christian wives could save their pagan husbands, so it must work the other way around.'

She looked down at the bedclothes. 'Listen . . .' she began.

'To what?'

'To me.'

He looked into her eyes with a mock-serious expression. 'I am listening.'

'We've known each other for a long time.'

'Yes.'

'And in some ways we know each other very well.'

'Yes.'

'But there are things about me that you don't know.'

'I'll have time enough to find out.'

'But when you find out, you may not like it.'

He smiled. 'I can't imagine disliking anything about you.'

'But you know, for example, that I've had other boyfriends.'

He blushed. 'Yes. In the past. Of course.'

'In the recent past . . .'

'I don't really need to know.'

'Are you *sure*?'

'Why do you ask?'

'Because I love you now,' she said, 'and I want to love you always, and I think I can and I will love you always, but I'm afraid that in a month or a year you might find out something about me that will give you a reason to leave me.'

'I'll never leave you,' he said.

Tears had come into her eyes. 'I've always been left before.'

'I wouldn't leave you, ever, and I couldn't, now that there's a baby.'

'There isn't a baby.'

'You can't be sure.'

'Of course I can be sure. I'm on the pill.'

'Oh.' It was as if she had hit him.

'And that isn't all. I had a boyfriend in London.'

'I didn't know.'

'He didn't want you to know.'

'Why not?'

'Because it was Henry.'

He said nothing but avoided her eyes.

She cried quietly. 'I'm sorry, I'm really sorry. I wish to God I'd knever known him or any of those other morons . . .'

He looked at her and took her hand. 'It isn't your fault,' he said.

'If I'd known, I'd have waited.'

'For what?'

'For you.'

'But you couldn't have known.'

'I did dream of you,' she said. 'Not of you, Andrew, but of someone who would love me immediately and for ever.'

'And I *will* love you for ever,' he said. 'All this, really, it can't make a difference if you're sure.'

'What?'

'Well, that you love me and not him.'

'I *am* sure . . .'

'But a week ago . . .' He said this as if for the record – not as an accusation.

'Yes.' She nodded. 'A week ago I was with Henry. I didn't love him but I didn't leave him. And he chucked me after three months to the day. And I won't pretend that there weren't times when I was happy with him up to a point; because I never knew if the kind of love I imagined actually existed. Now I know it does and, well, just like you said, I feel that we're married, and I never felt that before.'

He smiled. '"If ever any beauty I did see, which I desired, and got, 'twas but a dream of thee."'

She looked at him suspiciously. 'Who said that?'

'John Donne.'

'I guess that's about it.'

He kissed her lightly on the lips. 'We both have a past, haven't we? A week ago I loved that bizarre idea of God as a celibate, crucified Jew. And I didn't leave him, he chucked me by showing up in that cistern. So let's forget our pasts and think of now and the future.'

'Sure.' She smiled through her tears, leaned forward and hugged him. Then, because she wanted to sleep, she sent him to visit the Rockefeller Museum.

Nineteen

He could have taken a bus or a taxi, but he chose to walk, weaving his way between the other pedestrians on the crowded pavement of the Jaffa Road, or stepping onto the street and dodging the taxis and buses as he walked towards the Old City.

He was in no hurry; he was only going to the museum to kill time while Anna rested. Yet he took long strides, and had an anxious look on his face, as if he were late for some appointment or impatient to get to work.

Since it was a weekday morning, this businesslike manner blended with the bustle of those around him. His thoughts, however, were anything but businesslike. They were in complete confusion; for, while he was not the first young romantic to discover that love sometimes follows an uneven course, there were ways in which his case was an exception – even unique.

He had had no experience whatsoever of emotional exchanges with women. Even before he had decided to

195

become a Catholic or a Simonite monk, he had been sufficiently shy, romantic and frightened of girls to have got no
further than a quick kiss at the end of a teenage party.
Whereas most of his contemporaries had, by the time they
reached the age of twenty-eight, been through one or two
affairs from which they had learned something about love,
Andrew had been through none. His only knowledge came
on the one hand vicariously from his brother's cynical
adventures, and on the other from the blend of romanticism
and sentimentality which so often affects the attitude of the
clergy towards the love they have sacrificed to pursue their
vocation.

It was this innocence which had led Andrew to take Anna
back to his room at the American Colony Hotel. There had
seemed to him at the time an inexorable logic which made it
right and proper that he should. He had not considered that
he had fallen in love with Anna since coming to Jerusalem,
but that he had suddenly understood the true nature of the
affection he had felt for her now for almost two years. His
commitment to celibacy was, as he had explained to Anna,
bound up with his belief in the divinity of Jesus. Purity –
even virginity – was necessary for the sanctification of the
body which, like Christ's, would rise from the dead.

Even while he believed this, he had been aware of the
argument against it which Henry, and also Anna, had tacitly
presented – that celibacy was unnatural and, therefore, by
definition, the symptom of a neurosis. So, when he had seen
the skeleton of a crucified man buried beneath the Temple
Mount, and had believed that it was that of Jesus of Nazareth, he had found himself without the foundation upon
which his commitment to celibacy was based. The first
hypothesis being no longer tenable, the second took its
place; and, all at once, he felt cured of that neurosis which
had seen sexual longing as a serious sin.

The departure of the ascetic, however, did not mean the
arrival of a cynic like his brother. There remained the
idealism about love embalmed from his adolescence. He had
therefore made for the only girl with whom he could plausibly consider himself to have been in love. Moreover, because

he had not felt that he was falling in love, but merely recognizing something for what it was, it never occurred to him that Anna would not recognize it too. He knew, of course, that she had had boyfriends in the past; but she herself had told him how transitory and unsatisfactory these liaisons had been. He also knew – or so he had thought – that she had no boyfriend in London, because she would certainly have told him if she had. He therefore assumed, because he had been not just her closest but almost her only male friend in London, that she too must have been deceived about the true nature of the bond between them; or, quite possibly, not deceived at all, but heroically reticent about the real nature of her feelings in deference to the vows he had taken to lead a celibate life.

Thus, with the sublime egoism of the young man in love, he had taken it for granted that his love for Anna would be not just requited, but consummated there and then. A blend of fashionable theology and heady romanticism had convinced him that, after two years of sublimated courtship, it would be wrong to wait a moment longer. As he had explained to Anna, a wedding only blessed a bond which was formed by a couple's commitment; and she had seemed to accept in its entirety his understanding of the way things were. If she had said very little that first evening, as they had walked through the streets of the Old City, he had assumed it was because everything was clearly stated by the touch of their hands and the look in their eyes.

And the certainty that she too had recognized that she had loved him when they had only professed to be friends had given him great confidence as a lover. He knew that, if he bungled things in bed, it would make no difference to such a deeply rooted affection. As a result, his body had not let him down, but had enhanced and strengthened the new-found emotions in ways he had not imagined. He had anticipated the delight of his own senses, but not the joy it would give him to bring about such ecstasy in another; nor the beauty he would find, even after the demands of his instincts had been met, in the shape and texture of Anna's body. To be able to run his hand over her undulating skin,

197

or gently to implant kisses wherever he chose, made him happy in a way he had not envisaged and could not explain.

As they made love again and again, he became almost afraid of the power he possessed to transform Anna from an alert, intelligent, sarcastic girl into a whispering, clinging creature craving his attentions. Even as he was taken up by his own rapture, he was astonished – almost envious – of her complete oblivion as, with her mouth half-open and her eyes half-closed, she murmured like a mystic in an ecstatic trance. No wonder, he thought, that sex so obsesses the human race. Why should anyone ever want to do anything else?

In those first days with Anna, they had indeed done little else – eating and sleeping only to recover their strength to make love again and again. However, from the beginning, thoughts had come unbidden into his mind which suggested that all was not as straightforward as it seemed. He had found, for example, when he and Anna were discussing Father Lambert's seduction of Veronica Dunn, and he told her how Father Lambert had apologized not for what he had done but for what he had done badly, that a cruel grin crossed his face, and a callous laugh accompanied his conjecture as to whether Father Lambert had been unable to finish what he had started, or whether it was all over before it had properly begun.

It was only the next morning, in that limbo between sleeping and waking, that he had inwardly flinched as he recalled this ridicule of the man he had loved so much. Without mentioning it to Anna, he quickly repented of his cruel thoughts, even disowning the arrogant young male who had had them. Then, out in the street, he had been ambushed by another, contradictory and shameful sequence of thoughts and emotions when he had seen, walking towards him, wearing shorts and tight tee-shirts, two tall European girls – Dutch or German. One of them was not only pretty, but gave Andrew a fleeting glance of interest, which, involuntarily, he returned, wondering, before he was aware of what he was doing, what it would be like to sleep with her – wondering, and then wanting to try her for size, to give her the benefit of that skill and vigour which had left Anna with such a fresh complexion and happy smile.

Again, he had soon repented of these wayward thoughts, and even considered going to the nearest Catholic church to say a decade of the rosary before the Blessed Sacrament – the kind of penance he would have imposed upon himself in his days as a Simonite monk. Now, however, such a practice seemed slightly absurd. Moreover, since he was constantly in Anna's company, he could hardly go into a church and fall to his knees without her knowing what he was doing; and, for a reason he could not fathom, he felt inhibited – even ashamed – about being seen by her at prayer.

Clearly, on that first night in the American Colony Hotel, it would have been inappropriate to kneel at his bed as he usually did to say his night prayers: and the next morning, too, since they had breakfast in bed and did not get up until lunchtime, he missed the moment to say his morning prayers. Nor, at midday, when he heard the Angelus ringing from one of the churches in the Christian quarter, did he stop to say that ancient prayer as he did in the Simonite monastery. This omission came not from a deliberate decision to stop addressing the God in whom he still believed; rather, it seemed tactless to make these outward displays of an inward disposition in front of someone who did not share it.

The first excuse he made to himself was that these practices were part of the discipline of a Simonite monk; and that, since he had abandoned his vocation, he could abandon them as well. However, he knew that prayer was not simply for priests, and was obliged to admit that, since recognizing his love for Anna, he had hardly thought of God at all. Clearly, he still believed in him. Why else should he suffer from those stabs of remorse after scoffing at Father Lambert, or lusting after the girl with the flirtatious eye and long brown legs?

One afternoon, on the pretext of going for a copy of the *Jersualem Post*, he had gone into a church and said a quick prayer of repentance. He had felt absurd as he did so, since

199

it was Anna, not God, who had been cheated by his lecherous thoughts; and he was perplexed to discover, in recalling this sin, that he did not feel quite as ashamed of it as he should. It was as if the change he had made in leaving the Simonite order, and living with Anna, had not resulted in a straightforward metamorphosis from celibate monk to devoted lover, but had rather fragmented his personality so that two or even three different characters now lived within the same mind – the kind and humble Christian; the loyal and devoted husband of Anna; and this new, strutting embodiment of brute nature that gloried in what was healthy, strong and triumphant and despised what was feeble, needy and poor.

The confusion was made worse by the impossibility of discussing it with Anna. When he returned to the hotel after praying in the church, she had asked him why he had been so long, and he had lied incompetently about the difficulty of finding a newspaper. She had looked at him with an amused smile, as if realizing that he was up to something, while knowing that it could not be anything particularly bad. He had longed to throw himself at her feet and confess his worthlessness, but could not bring himself to disillusion her by revealing that, only days after declaring his lifelong love, he had fancied a girl he had passed in the street.

Equally, it had seemed impossible to tell her about his remorse over scoffing at Father Lambert for, if to confess the first would make him seem lecherous and faithless, to admit the second would make him seem humourless and prim. He had therefore kept silent about both matters, playing the role of a cheerful, debonair lover, sinking yet more deeply into a bog of deception.

Then came their trip to Jericho, Anna's sickness and the question of a child. If Andrew had decided, upon leaving the Simonite monastery, that everything Christ had taught was bunk, then it would have been easy to disown his Catholic conscience; but because he still thought of himself as a Christian, he still reacted involuntarily in a Christian way. Imbued with the Catholic teaching that sex was meant

200

by God for procreation, he had justified the pleasure he took in it by the fact that it would end in the conception of a child.

Anna's blunt statement that she could not be pregnant because she was taking the pill had first shocked him for its reflection on the morality of what *he* had done; it was only later that he came to see what it implied about Anna. Not knowing that women sometimes take the pill simply to regulate their menstrual cycles – and Anna being too proud to pretend that this was the case – he assumed that she had been taking it because she had been sleeping with some other man. He had not asked her who it was. He had turned the other cheek. And he had been struck a second, harder, blow when she had told him that the other man was Henry.

This had shocked him on so many different levels, and in so many different ways, that he had been quite unable to consider how he should react or what he should say. Anger, jealousy, embarrassment, disgust, disillusion, all swirled around in his mind to the extent that he might have said or done anything – strangled her, left her, kissed her – had not the lingering monk, whom he had tried so hard to shake off during the days which had gone before, stepped forward with the reflex gentleness and humility which came from the years of religious life.

This gentleness, however, was most tenuous: the violent emotions were not dissipated, they were merely concealed. Certainly, in telling Anna it did not matter that she had been to bed with his brother – that the past was past – he had wanted it to be true. However, as he walked towards the Rockefeller Museum, he remained confused and tormented, both by the knowledge that Henry and Anna had been lovers, and by the exposure of his own credulity. He was embarrassed to recall his conceited assumption that she had been in love with him for the past year. Why had he not wondered about the men she might have loved before? He had known that she had boyfriends; he should have known that she would have gone to bed with them. The answer was, that he had not stopped to think about possible boy-friends, and what they might have meant to her, because he had not really thought about her at all; and, when he had agreed, with such modesty, that he could only claim to be a substitute, he had not meant a substitute for some other lover who had let her down, but for some more eligible candidate with better prospects who would present himself in the future.

That she had had lovers before, he now acknowledged, should have come as no surprise; that she had had one so recently might be disagreeable, but, if it was over, it was something that might be quickly forgotten. That it was Henry was almost more than he could bear, because he had always somehow blamed his brother's behaviour on the depravity of his women. To make love out of wedlock was one thing; to make love out of love was quite another and, since Henry so clearly did not love his girlfriends, Andrew had always taken it for granted that they did not love him and slept with him simply to gratify their vanity or their lust.

It therefore seemed that he had to look upon Anna as a girl of this kind, or as an exception; but this alternative seemed almost worse, because it implied that she had loved Henry as sincerely as she now purported to love him – willing, perhaps, to marry him and bear his children. That Anna, at one point, might have been prepared to do that was even more painful to consider than that she was simply depraved. It was better not to think about it at all but distract himself, for the time being, by concentrating on the exhibits in the Rockefeller Museum.

He had been there a number of times before, often with Father Lambert, and perhaps because of this Andrew now found that the exhibits depressed him. He remembered how excited the Professor had been when showing Andrew the bowls, glasses, ossuaries and sarcophagi from the time of Christ; and he imagined the despair that must have entered his heart upon realizing that the skeleton in the cistern might one day have pride of place between the prehistoric Galilee skull and the remains of the Bronze Age man from Mount Carmel.

In the Northern Room he paused in front of two Romanesque friezes from the façade of the Church of the Holy

Sepulchre. One of them depicted the life of Jesus; the other had figures of animals, plants and naked human beings. The dragons, he remembered from Father Lambert's explanations, represented heresy, the Antichrist and the Devil. The sirens were temptation and female lust, while male lust as well as pride and arrogance were represented by the centaur. The birds symbolized parsimony while lechery was embodied in a naked man.

Andrew stood for some time staring at this marble frieze. Pride, heresy, lust – how simple things had been for these crusading craftsmen and how simple they had been for him. How clear had been the distinction between truth and falsehood, good and evil, love and lust. Lust – there she was, the siren on the frieze. Was Anna such a siren? Had she not herself confessed that she could never distinguish love from lust? Had she gone to bed with him so easily just to satisfy a sudden urge of the flesh? And was he, too, no more than that figure of lechery, deceiving himself that he loved her because, like Father Lambert with Mrs Dunn, he was determined to indulge an instinct he had repressed for so long?

And was it simply his pride which was affronted by the knowledge that she had slept with Henry? He looked again at the centaur. Pride, arrogance and male lust. Was that all that upset him – that another man had made love to her? That she had responded to Henry and perhaps half-a-dozen others in the same way as she had responded to him? Yet how could he be jealous retrospectively unless conjugal love, like divine love, was outside the strictures of time? Was he so entrapped by Christian concepts that he must always think in terms of an eternity that was as much the past as the future?

He went through into the next room and looked at the stucco figures from the Hisham Palace near Jericho – snarling lions and big-breasted girls whose jovial smiles seemed to ridicule the torments depicted in the frieze next door. Could he escape, he wondered, from the tentacles of a Christian conscience? Could he ever bring himself to enjoy pleasure for its own sake without seeking to give it some justification?

Was love itself, perhaps, just an unreal idealization of a crude, atavistic instinct?

She had said that, even when sleeping with Henry, she had known that she did not love him, and had dreamed of a love that was eternal – a love she now felt for him. It was only her body which had sought its own satisfaction, and the body, he knew, was something distinct from the spirit. But was it? Why had she hidden her affair with Henry, and why had Henry too insisted that Andrew should not know? Had each felt embarrassed or ashamed? Had she sensed, as he had supposed, that already in her friendship with Andrew there were the seeds of the love which they now recognized and enjoyed? If so, then their friendship had already been corrupt, because she had deceived him daily about Henry, just as Henry had deceived him about her. The complete candour and trust which was both a sign of love and one of its principal delights was in reality only a sham. Always in the mind of the other there was some calculation, some pretence. Had he not hidden from her his lecherous feelings for the long-legged girl? Had he not lied about going to pray in the church? Did lovers often lie, he wondered? Were there wives, perhaps, who faked ecstasy with their husbands or husbands who, to allay their suspicions, made love to their unloved wives?

He looked at his watch. It was twelve. Never before had he felt quite so oppressed by the complexity of human relations; and while he did not doubt for a moment that he loved Anna, he left the museum and made his way back to the hotel with a certain trepidation.

Twenty

While Andrew was at the museum, Anna slept – tired after both a broken night and their anguished conversation. Soon after eleven, she was awoken by the ringing of the antique telephone which stood on the table next to the bed.

It took her a moment to realize where the sound came from, and when she saw that it was the telephone she hesitated to pick it up, knowing that only her parents knew where she was. However, it continued to ring, and to silence it she picked it up.

'Anna?'

'Yes.'

'This is Henry.'

'Where are you?' His voice was so clear it seemed as if he might be in the next room.

'In London.'

'How did you know I was here?'

'Your mother gave me the number. Is it a hotel?'

'Yes.'

'Why aren't you staying at home?'

'There wasn't room.'

'Have you seen Andrew?'

'Yes.'

'Is he all right?'

'Yes.'

'It seems he's left the Simonite monastery and they don't know where he's gone.'

'He's OK.'

'Tell him to ring me.'

'Sure.'

'Now listen. There have been some developments here in London.'

'To do with what?'

'The Vilnius Codex. I can't tell you much over the telephone, but if you can I'd like you to make a few enquiries at your end while you're there.'

'What kind of enquiries?'

'Have you heard of a man called Yehuda Louvish?'

'No.'

'He was an officer in the army during the war in Lebanon who was captured by the Syrians and later released. Find out, if you can, what he is doing now.'

'I'll do what I can.'

'Be discreet.'

'OK.'

He paused on the other end of the line, then asked: 'Are you all right?'

'Why shouldn't I be?'

'You sound funny.'

'I've been sick but I'm fine now.'

'When are you coming back to London?'

'Next Friday.'

'And Andrew?'

'Him too.'

'There's a lot I'd like to ask you, but it can wait.'

'I'll get him to call you.'

'Good. As soon as he can.'

She put down the telephone in a rage, yet she was not sure quite why she was angry. At first, she thought she resented the nonchalant way in which the lover who had dumped her was so quick to make use of her in one of his investigations. Then she ascribed it to the retrospective remorse she felt when reminded of his existence and their former liaison. Finally, after brooding about it, she realized she was angry with Henry because his call had implicitly suggested that the Vilnius Codex might be a fake.

He had not said as much, but what else could he have meant by 'developments' which led to an officer in Israel? If the Codex was a fake, then the find might be a fraud, and if the find was a fraud, then the reason for which Andrew had abandoned his vocation would be invalid. It was this thought which filled her with dread, and the dread which inspired the anger against Henry as the bringer of bad news. What, to him, was no more than a puzzle – an amusing distraction from industrial law and trade regulations – was to Anna a matter of life and death.

It was not a question of whether Jesus of Nazareth had risen from the dead, but whether Andrew believed it or not. Certainly, he had said that he would never leave her, and he had undoubtedly meant what he said. Certainly, too, despite all her disappointments in the past, she felt she could trust him never to leave her for another woman; but that first wife, the Catholic Church, whom he had loved so well for so long – that was another matter. He had left her because he felt she had cheated him. What if he were now to discover that in fact she had been true? That it was not Jesus who had deceived him by pretending to rise from the dead, but Anna's father and other unknown Jews?

As she considered the matter, the suggestion that her father might be party to a hoax seemed absurd. She knew that his devotion to archaeology was more important to him than almost anything else – more important, certainly, than his feelings for his family. Then she remembered the conversation with her mother about her father's commitment to Israel. Was it possible that, for the sake of Israel, he might take part in a deception – or, at any rate, turn a blind eye?

The idea redoubled her dread, not because it would put her father's livelihood and reputation in jeopardy, but because it threatened her bond with Andrew. To have found a love which she had barely dared to imagine – a love that was fresh, equal and eternal – only to see it threatened almost at once, was more than she could stand. Weakened by her sickness and a sleepless night, she wept for a while, her face once again squashed down into the pillow.

Even as she gave way to despair, however, certain practical considerations crept into her mind. At any moment, Andrew might return. He would ask her why she was crying. She would have to tell him of Henry's call. He might then ring Henry and learn what she had learned – that there was something fishy about the Vilnius Codex. She sat up, suddenly convinced that if somehow she could give Henry the information he wanted, then perhaps Andrew need never know. She got out of bed, her nausea gone, and splashed her face with the tepid water which trickled out of the tap of the basin in their room.

As she dressed, she wondered how she could find out about this Yehuda Louvish. She could ask Jake, of course, but, if there was a conspiracy of some kind, Jake was certainly in it. Then she remembered Joel Abramovicz, a young journalist she knew on the *Jerusalem Post* who was a specialist on defence. She picked up the telephone, got through to Abramovicz and arranged to meet him for lunch.

She left a note at the hotel for Andrew, saying that she had gone to see her father. It was the first lie she had told him since he had become her lover, and it pained her to deceive him, but she had no doubt that his happiness was irretrievably linked to hers, and no scruple should be allowed to inhibit her from doing what she could to protect it.

Joel Abramovicz was a *sabra* Israeli, but like Anna he had been to college in the United States and spoke fluent English with an American twang. He too was small, with curly black hair, thick-lensed spectacles and an eager, earnest face. He was waiting for Anna at the bottom of Ben Yehuda Street. They went for lunch to a restaurant nearby.

'What are you doing in Jerusalem?' he asked her. 'I thought you were studying in London.'

'I am,' said Anna. 'I'm just here on a visit.'

'To see the folks?'

'To see the folks.'

'How are they? I haven't seen them in some time.'

'They're fine.'

Joel sat at one of the small tables with a pitta bread filled with salad and felafel. Anna sipped a glass of orange juice.

'So how can I help you?' Joel asked.

'Do you know anything about an officer called Yehuda Louvish?'

'You're asking if *I* know anything about Louvish?'

'Yes.'

'Yes. I know a little. But Jake's the one you should ask. He works for Louvish.'

'Ah.' His answer was like the stab of a knife in her stomach.

'At least he used to. Last thing I heard was that Jake had left the army to help your father.'

'For various reasons,' said Anna slowly, 'I don't really want to ask Jake about Louvish.'

'He probably wouldn't tell you anyway. It's all top-secret stuff.'

'Mossad?'

Joel shrugged. 'Or Shin Bet. I don't know. It's often

difficult to know who answers to whom. During the war in Lebanon Louvish ran an outfit which answered directly to Sharon. He was one of his bright young men.'

'And now?'

'I don't know. There are rumours that he runs some kind of dirty tricks department.'

'Against the PLO?'

'Sure. But not just against the PLO. His speciality is covert propaganda.'

'Give me an example.'

Joel leaned forward and lowered his voice. 'The planting of *agents provocateurs* in terrorist organizations. That kind of thing.'

'What else?'

'War criminals. They know where they are and expose them as and when they're needed.'

'Needed?'

'To remind the world what happened, and why we're here.'

'And Jake works for him?'

'He certainly did.'

Anna looked down at her empty glass.

'Do you want some coffee?' Joel asked.

She shook her head and watched Joel as he turned to call the waitress and order some for himself. There was something very lovable about him. He embodied everything that she liked about Israel; he was alert, cultured and humane. Suddenly, she wanted Andrew to meet him, but the thought of Andrew reminded her of the Codex. She leaned forward and asked Joel: 'Is there any conceivable way in which Louvish could be linked to the Russians?'

He glanced at her with his eyebrows raised in surprise. 'You seem to know everything about him already.'

She felt the knife twist in her stomach. 'You mean there is a link?'

'His parents came from Russia just before the war in Europe. Louvish speaks Russian as well as Hebrew, English and Arabic. He's a very clever guy.'

'Is that the only link – that his parents came from Russia?'

'There's something else which has always seemed strange. In '82, when Louvish was in Lebanon, he was captured behind the lines.'

'By the PLO?'

'No. By Amal, the Shi'ite militia. They held him for a while, then he was handed over to the Syrians and taken to Damascus.'

'How did he get back?'

'That's the mystery. Suddenly, four or five months later, he reappeared in Israel.'

'Was there an exchange of prisoners?'

'That's what made it odd. Normally an officer of Louvish's rank would only be exchanged for several hundred Arabs. In his case, there were none.'

'You mean they just *gave* him back?'

'So it seemed.'

'Why?'

'No one knows. But the chances are that he did some kind of deal with either the Syrians or even the Russians, who would probably have interrogated him in Damascus.'

'But how could anyone trust him after that?' asked Anna.

Joel shrugged. 'Again, a mystery. You would think he would have been put on ice so far as counter-intelligence was concerned. In fact, it was soon after he came back that he was given his own department.'

Anna shook her head, as if in disbelief. In reality, she was beginning to see things all too clearly.

'He also has some strange political affiliations.' Joel went on.

'With the Likud?'

'Of course. And with the religious parties. But also with groups like the Temple Faithful.'

'Who are they?'

'A bunch of zealots, mostly Americans, who want to rebuild the Temple.'

'What about the mosques?'

'They'd be demolished.'

'But that's crazy.'

Joel shrugged. 'In Israel there's a thin line between what's

210

crazy and what's patriotic.' He finished his coffee. 'May I ask why you're suddenly so interested in Louvish?'

'When I can, I'll tell you, I promise.'

'Is there a story in it?'

She frowned. 'There could be. But I don't think it's one that can ever be told.'

They parted outside the sandwich bar – Joel to go back to the offices of the *Jerusalem Post*, Anna to walk to a bus stop, where she stood wondering what to do next.

Her most urgent emotion was to hope against hope that what seemed possible would not turn out to be true. She knew Andrew better than he knew himself, and recognized that a resurrected Jesus was her most dangerous rival. Her first impulse was to telephone Henry and tell him that there was nothing to link Louvish to either the skeleton or the Codex. Her second was to question her father. However strong the grudge she still felt against Michal Dagan for his shortcomings as a parent, she still retained such faith in his integrity as an archaeologist that it seemed impossible that he would have perpetrated a gigantic fraud.

She walked the short distance to the Staedtler Institute and turned up at his office unannounced. There, her father's secretary ushered her in as if she was expected; and Dagan greeted her as if he knew that sooner or later she would come to see him. He looked perplexed – even guilty – and Anna realized that he must have been told about the bitter conversation with her mother. He came forward to kiss her, but then hesitated, as if afraid of a rebuff, and, to cover his confusion, he showed her to an armchair as if she was a student or a junior lecturer.

'I was worried about you,' he said.

'I've been OK,' she said. 'I've been with Andrew.'

'Yes. I was told. He is a good friend to you, that young man.'

'Yes. A very good friend.'

There was an awkward pause, then Dagan said: 'Your mother told me about how you felt and . . . I am sorry.'

Anna was suddenly afraid that she would burst into tears,

so she said, somewhat sharply: 'I didn't come here to talk about that.'

'Very well,' he said sadly.

'I'd like to talk about it some time,' she said in a slightly kinder tone, 'but something more urgent has come up.'

'What is that?'

'The find . . . the skeleton.'

He frowned. 'What about it?'

'Dad, I need to know . . . I really need to know whether you found it by accident or not.'

His frown deepened. 'It was not by accident that we went through the wall.'

'But you had no idea there was a jar in the cistern or a skeleton in the jar?'

He avoided her eyes. 'I had no idea there was a jar or a skeleton, no.'

'Will you swear to that, Dad? To me – just to me – in the secrecy of this room?'

'Why? I don't understand. Why to you?'

'I can't explain just now, only it's very, very important.'

He hesitated and looked away from her. 'I can swear, of course, that I knew nothing of the jar or the skeleton.'

'And so when you knocked through that wall, it came as a complete surprise?'

'A complete surprise. We had not expected to find anything in the cistern.'

She paused. She knew that her father was not lying, but sensed that he was holding something back.

'Were you the first to go through the opening?'

'Yes. First me, I think, then Ya'acov.'

'Were you there when they removed the block?'

'Yes.'

'Did you see them remove it?'

'Yes. It took some hours.'

'Is it possible . . .' She hesitated, and frowned, trying to work out what might have happened. 'Is it possible that someone removed the block the day before, took in the jar, and then put it back again?'

'No.'

212

'Were you there the day before?'

'No.'

'So you can't be sure.'

'Ya'acov would have known. Ya'acov was there.'

She paused, then asked: 'When you found the skeleton in the jar, was it you who remembered the Codex from Josephus?'

'Yes.'

'*You* remembered it?'

He looked confused. 'Yes, it was me, or Ya'acov. I can't remember.'

'Jake?'

'Or me. Or Mordecai.'

She leaned forward and looked straight into her father's eyes. 'Dad, why did Jake get leave from the IDF?'

'It wasn't so much that he was given leave from the IDF, as that the IDF, for reasons of security, wished to go beneath the Temple Mount, and, quite rightly, Ya'acov persuaded his superiors that it should not be done without an archaeologist in charge.'

'Do you know why they wanted to dig beneath the Temple Mount?'

'Yes. It was to lay listening devices to eavesdrop on the organizers of the *intifada*.'

'Did Jake ever tell you who ordered the project?'

'He never told me precisely . . .'

'Was it Yehuda Louvish?'

'Louvish, certainly, is the officer in command of the department.'

'Do you know Louvish?'

'I have met him. He lives in Rehavya.'

'Did it occur to you, Dad, that Jake and Louvish might have faked your find?'

Never before had Anna seen her father look both so frightened and so ashamed. 'You must understand, Anna,' he said in a voice little louder than a whisper, 'that there are sometimes lines of thought which we cannot follow.'

'Because of where they might lead?'

'Yes. Because they might lead where you cannot go.'

213

'So it *did* occur to you.'

'Listen, Anna. You do not understand – you have never understood – what Israel means to me. It is everything, my dear, everything – not just a nation like any other nation, but the land of God's consecrated people. We have suffered for so long – for so very long – despised, humiliated, exterminated like vermin – until now, in this generation, we have won back what God gave us so long ago.'

'Dad, that's . . .'

'Let me finish. Anna, I know that you cannot see this, and for that I blame myself; and I am not asking you to see it now, but only to understand how *I* feel when, for the sake of Israel, I am asked simply to suspend for a moment my disbelief, to restrain certain thoughts, to let certain suspicions escape without pursuing them, to leave a few questions unanswered.'

'To perpetrate a fraud.'

His eyes widened with anger. 'A fraud? Is it a fraud? Or is the Christian religion a fraud? We know that the body of Jesus of Nazareth must have been buried somewhere, and I have found what I have found. It may or may not be the body of the Nazarene. That is not for me to say, and I have never said anything, one way or the other. I present my evidence to the Christians. It is for them to decide.'

'Christians like Father Lambert?'

He lowered his eyes. 'Yes. Like Father Lambert.'

'But you will be exposed, Dad, and ridiculed. We already know about Louvish . . .'

'Who knows about Louvish?' asked a voice behind her.

She turned and saw Jake standing by the open door.

'I do.'

He closed the door and came into the room. 'What do you know?'

'Enough.'

Jake smiled. 'Would you like to meet him?'

'Ya'acov . . .' Michal Dagan began.

He ignored his father but said to Anna: 'I am sure he would be happy to answer your questions.'

'I know enough,' said Anna.

214

'He could tell you more.'

She hesitated, curiosity struggling with her mistrust of her brother. 'When could I meet him?'

'Right now.'

She looked uncertainly towards her father, but his eyes, still afraid, were on his son. 'Ya'acov . . .' he began again.

'We'll see you later, Dad,' said Jake and, with an ironic bow towards his sister, he escorted her out of the room.

He drove her in his Subaru from the Staedtler Institute up through Me'a She'arim, across the old Green Line, and out of Jerusalem on the Ramallah Road. For a while neither of them spoke. Then Jake said, in just the same sneering tone with which he had put down his sister as a child: 'You should have kept out of all this, you know. You're way out of your depth.'

'You got me involved.'

'How?'

'In London. You asked me to ask Andrew to lay on a Catholic archaeologist to authenticate the find.'

'That didn't mean you had to fuck him.'

She turned to him, her face flushed with anger. 'Do you have bugs in every bedroom in Israel?'

'Knowledge is power.'

'Jesus Christ, Jake, what's happened to you? You were never nice, but now you're despicable.'

'Look who's talking.'

'I happen to love Andrew,' she said with as much dignity as she could muster.

'Last week you loved his brother.'

'Things sometimes happen that way.'

'What's so special about Catholics? Do they fuck better than Jews?'

'Henry isn't a Catholic. He's an atheist.'

'But Andrew's not just a Catholic, he's a Catholic priest.'

She blushed. 'He's not a priest. He's a monk. And he hasn't taken his final vows, and he still thinks Dad's dug up Jesus.'

'You haven't told him about Louvish?'

'No.'

'Lucky for him.'

'Why?'

'Because there are things it's better not to know.'

He slowed down as the road ran parallel to the wire fence of a military compound, the top festooned with coils of barbed wire.

'Do you really think you can get away with this thing?' asked Anna.

'Why not?'

'Because it's crazy.'

He stopped the car at the steel gates to the compound. 'You don't live here,' he said, showing his ID to a guard with a machine-gun. 'You don't know what we're up against.'

'Nothing's worth destroying Dad's reputation.'

'It won't destroy his reputation, it'll make it.'

The gates were opened. 'Not when the world knows it's a fraud.'

'The world won't know.'

'It will if I tell it.'

'And how will you tell the world?' he asked.

'I'll tell a journalist, I guess.'

The gates closed behind them. Jake smiled.

Twenty-one

The building they entered, though superficially like a court-house or a school, had the narrow windows of a fortress and the thick steel doors of a prison. They went up one flight of stairs, along a corridor, and came to a door which Jake opened with the familiarity of someone who knew his way around. They entered a small ante-room where a girl in uniform sat typing at a desk.

'Is the Colonel busy?' Jake asked her in Hebrew.

She shook her head. 'No. Go in.'

216

They went through into a much larger room, with a table and some chairs at one end and a large desk at the other. Blinds covered the windows, dissipating the light from the sun. There was no air-conditioning. One of the blinds flapped in front of an open window. On the desk there was a fan, and behind it, on the wall, a large map of Greater Israel.

As they came in, a man in uniform rose from his seat at the desk. He was aged around fifty, but looked vigorous and fit. His greying hair was shaved close at the back of his neck. His face and his hands were brown but, at the open neck of his khaki shirt, there were the blurred margins of a whiter skin.

As he crossed the room to meet them, he looked at Jake with a mildly puzzled expression.

'Colonel,' said Jake. 'This is my sister Anna.'

Louvish smiled and greeted her in Hebrew.

'My Hebrew isn't too good,' said Anna.

He nodded and pointed towards the sofa and chairs. 'Then let us speak English.' Jake and Anna sat down while Louvish looked into the ante-room and asked his secretary to bring some coffee. Then he too sat down, and leaned forward, his elbows resting on his knees, ready to hear what they had come to say.

'I brought her to meet you,' said Jake slowly, 'because she had lunch with Abramovicz, that journalist on the *Post*, and then went to my father to ask about you.'

He nodded, his expression unchanged. 'What did Ambramovicz tell you?' he asked Anna.

'Nothing,' said Anna. 'It wasn't him who gave me your name.'

'She had a call from London this morning,' said Jake, 'from the brother of the monk. He has been making enquiries about the Vilnius Codex.'

Louvish nodded. 'Has he made the connection?'

'Not yet, but he suspects it.'

'Has he spoken to the monk?'

'No.'

'So he is still convinced?'

Jake looked at his sister. 'I think so, yes.'

'And the Cardinal?'

'Yes.'

'So the leak is not yet large – simply the brother, Abramovicz and this young lady.' He turned to Anna with cold eyes but a benevolent smile.

'Joel knows nothing,' said Anna, 'and Henry – well, I don't know what he knows or how he knows it, but if the cat's out of the bag in London, you can't put it back in here in Jerusalem.'

Louvish seemed to ponder this for a moment. He then turned to Jake. 'Have you any idea how the brother in London came up with my name?'

'He has a friend with contacts through the British Secret Service with Lithuanian émigrés in London.'

'Will he have told them what he is after?'

'I doubt it.'

'So we have only to deal with him, with Abramovicz and with you' – he turned to Anna – 'to have a good chance of putting the cat back in the bag.'

'Yes,' said Jake, 'but we must think of my father.'

'Of course.' He continued to look at Anna like a headmaster pondering the problem of a troublesome child.

'The best solution,' said Jake, 'would be for Anna to persuade the monk's brother that you don't exist, or at any rate have nothing to do with the find.'

'Why should I?' asked Anna.

'To save your ass,' said Jake.

'To save Israel,' said Louvish.

'How does it save Israel to involve my father in some half-baked hoax which sooner or later is bound to be exposed?'

Louvish frowned, but his tone remained calm. 'I think you are wrong to say it would be exposed, because people believe what they want to believe and at this moment there are very many people who would like someone to dig up the body of Christ – and these people are not atheists or Muslims or Jews, who know quite well that he did not rise from the dead, but liberal Christian theologians who want to adapt their faith to the modern world.'

'So you're in the business of helping out Christian theologians?'

Louvish did not smile. 'No, I am in the business of helping my people, the Jews.'

'How does it help the Jews to dig up the body of Jesus?'

'I will tell you because I believe that, when you understand what we are trying to achieve, you will help us to achieve it.'

'Don't count on it.'

'No, I won't count on it. But I would ask you for a moment to be patient and listen. You see, I know, from what Jake has told me, that you have never felt you belonged here, but you have the intelligence to understand that there are others, like your father, your mother and your brother, who love Israel and would willingly die to protect her.'

'Sure.'

'The problem is that dying is often not enough. If there is a lesson to be learned from our revolt against the Romans and the consequent obliteration of the ancient state of Israel – ending, as you know, when Masada was taken – if there is a lesson to be learned from all they suffered, it is that courage and determination are *not* enough. There are times when brute force wins.

'Now, however you may feel about Zionism, we do have a state of Israel which has survived for forty years – and survived despite the enmity of all the countries which surround us. We have fought three wars against them, and we were obliged to act in Lebanon, where – you may or may not know – I was captured and taken to Damascus. For some months, I was held in solitary confinement. I had time to think – to consider the position of Israel, and compare the dangers which face us now with the dangers which faced us in ancient times. In both periods, we have shown courage and determination in pursuing our independence, but none of the countries now wishing to destroy Israel has anything like the power of Rome. The only nation in the modern era which can be compared to Rome is the United States, the champion, not the enemy, of Israel. If we have survived, it is because might as much as right has been on our side.'

'I don't suppose even Arafat would disagree with that,' said Anna.

'Of course,' said Louvish. 'All this may seem fairly obvious, but, when you are in solitary confinement, some of your thoughts are inevitably obvious. However, they proceeded to less obvious territory – namely the future. When I looked into the future, I became afraid. The support of this great power, on the other side of the world, for a small band of Jews clinging to the edge of Asia, arose from a set of quite fortuitous circumstances. The pogroms in Russia at the end of the nineteenth century drove hundreds of thousands of our people to emigrate to America. The descendants of these refugees, in the most populous states of the Union, ensure political support for Israel.

'What alarmed me, as I sat in my cell, was the realization that these fortuitous circumstances would change. There were, in the United States, only six million Jews. They could not hold the balance of power indefinitely, in California or New York. The growth of other states in America – Texas, for example, or Florida, with their large populations of Catholic Hispanics, or the Southern states, with their Baptists – could alter the balance of power. Even if it did not, the chances of the United States continuing to dominate the world as it has done since the end of the Second World War, seem small. Already, the economies of the East are growing more vigorously than the economies of the West. With economic strength comes political power. And why should the Koreans or the Japanese care about the fate of the Jews? Why should they jeopardize supplies of oil from the Arab countries to satisfy the aspirations of a small sect in the West?

'Of course, if things in Palestine were to stabilize, if our Muslim neighbours were to accept the state of Israel, the danger would recede with the passage of time. But, as I looked into the future, alone in my cell, I could only see further struggle and further bloodshed. Sooner or later, I knew, there would be an *intifada* of the kind we see today, particularly if we were to exercise our rights over the land we had reclaimed.

'Israel, after all, was only half-completed. Sure, we had won back the territory we believed was ours, but were we masters in our own land? We had Jerusalem, and we had surrounded the city with Jewish settlements. In the city itself, however, there remain the towers and domes and minarets of other religions; and, most blasphemous of all, there, where our Temple should be, on the site of the Holy of Holies, is the golden dome of a mosque. Clearly, Israel can never be Israel – can never believe in her inalienable right to return – until we remove the mosque and rebuild our Temple on its rightful site on the Temple Mount.'

'But that . . .' Anna began.

'Of course,' Louvish interrupted. 'It will double the number of our enemies. It will enrage the world. Yet how can we ever say that we have really returned – how can we prove that we have a God-given right to this land – if we dare not demolish a mosque and rebuild the very symbol of God's Covenant with our people?'

Anna glanced sideways at Jake, to see if he too realized that this man was mad; but the eyes of her brother were fixed on the lips of his superior officer with an expression of exhilaration and awe. She turned back to Louvish. 'Are you really serious?' she asked. 'You really want to pull down the Dome of the Rock and rebuild the Temple?'

'Don't you see,' said Louvish, 'that it has to be done – not as an exercise in archaeological reconstruction but as the tangible proof that our nation is reborn?'

'But that's crazy,' said Anna. 'You can't just pretend that nineteen hundred years haven't happened.'

'But you can,' said Louvish. 'Look at our language. Who spoke Hebrew a hundred years ago? A few old rabbis – and, even for them, it was not their mother tongue. Now we all speak it.'

'I know . . .'

'It was the vision of a few men that achieved it, and it is their work that is only half-completed. Israel still has some way to go before she is truly in possession of the promised land, and, as we proceed, we are certain to make still more enemies. That is why it is so important to consider how to make useful friends – or, at least, to keep the friends we have, particularly the United States, in a period when the influence of the Jews in America is likely to diminish.'

'And is digging up Jesus going to make you friends?' asked Anna.

'Yes.' He hissed out the word. 'Because, in America, besides the six million Jews, there are two hundred million Christians, and in South America there are millions more. In India, the Philippines, South Korea, China and Japan, the Christians are an influential minority. The whole of Western Europe is Christian, and so, beneath the surface, are the countries of Eastern Europe – even the Soviet Union itself. The one thing they all have in common is their belief that Jesus of Nazareth rose from the dead – a belief which is incompatible with any fundamental sympathy with Israel, because, at the root of Christian teaching, is the certainty that God's Covenant with us, his chosen people, ended with the death of Christ. He was the son of God. He abrogated the old Covenant and brought in a new one, replacing us Jews as his chosen people with all those who accepted that he was the promised Messiah.

'What struck me in Damascus, as I sat in my cell, was that, if these hundreds of millions of Christians could somehow be convinced that Jesus of Nazareth was *not* the son of God, but just one among other Jewish prophets, like his cousin John the Baptist, then they would have to accept that he was in no position either to make a new Covenant or to abrogate the old one. I understood, too, that the one article of Christian belief which confirms him as a superhuman being is his resurrection from the dead. If it could be shown that he had not risen, then it would have to be accepted that the old Covenant still stands.'

'You mean,' said Anna, 'that a billion Christians are suddenly going to become Jews just because you dig up the body of Jesus?'

Louvish laughed. 'I hardly think so, no. They would still be Christians, but the follower not of God but of an unusual man. They would no longer have grounds for that supposition which lies behind all Christian thinking – that, somehow, the obliteration of Israel by the Romans, culminating in the destruction of Jerusalem and the demolition of the Temple by the soldiers of Titus, was not only no more than what the Jews deserved for killing the son of God, but was also predicted by Christ as the necessary demonstration that the old Covenant was at an end.'

Anna again looked at Jake, and, although her instinct told her that it might be wise to appear convinced by what Louvish was saying, her irritation at the smug look on her brother's face got the better of her. 'If you'll excuse me saying so, Colonel,' she said scornfully, 'I think solitary confinement sent you slightly crazy. I know some Christians, and most of them don't think like that at all.'

Louvish did not seem discouraged by her reaction. 'Consciously they may not, but unconsciously they do. And for us time is running out. The sympathy we can still count on for what we suffered under Hitler will not outlive those who remember the last war. Certainly we can remind the young of what happened with trials of war criminals like Demjanjuk, but soon there will be no war criminals to uncover, and the images of suffering Jews will be replaced in the newspapers and television screens by images of suffering Palestinians as we put down their *intifada*. All the world will care about is the danger of war and the threat to their supplies of oil, and then the age-old hatred of the Jews by the Christians will rise to the surface once more, and it will be "'*raus mit den Juden*" all over again – '*raus* not from the ghettos of the European cities but from this ghetto here, between the River Jordan and the Mediterranean Sea.'

Anna scrutinized Louvish with a puzzled look on her face. She still thought that he must be mad, but he did not look mad, and she had to acknowledge that everything he said had a kind of inner coherence. It was not that she felt persuaded to approve of the hoax – she did not feel sufficiently involved with the plight of her people for that; but she could appreciate the logic of what Louvish was saying – that people's attitudes and convictions are malleable – and could accept, if marshalling support for Israel was his job in

223

counter-intelligence, that the plan to find the skeleton of
Jesus became a plausible project for covert propaganda.

Her attention turned to the mechanics of the thing. 'OK,'
she said to Louvish. 'I see now why you did it. But how was
it done? How did you come up with the Vilnius Codex?'

'Here,' said Louvish, 'providence came to my assistance.
As you know, I was originally captured by the Shi'ites in
Lebanon. After a certain amount of rough treatment by
them, I was handed over to the Syrians, who sent me to
Damascus for interrogation. They were rather more sophis-
ticated – certainly less violent – and seemed to accept quite
quickly the limits I placed upon what I would tell them.
They were principally interested in what they could extract
in exchange for me – in terms of prisoners we had taken and
hard currency.

'Our people, I like to think, wanted me back but the
demands at first were so exorbitant that they had to pretend
for a time that I was not of much value. That is why I was
kept waiting in Damascus. After a while, however, the
Soviets in Damascus came to hear of my capture and
expressed an interest in what I might know. One of their
men used to visit me almost every day – an urbane and
intelligent man called Gedda – Leon Gedda – who spoke
excellent Hebrew as well as Arabic, English, Russian, Polish,
even Lithuanian because he had lived in Lithuania as a child.

'His method of interrogating was far subtler than the
Syrians'. Where they had put quite straightforward questions which told me immediately what they wanted to know,
Gedda never put any questions at all. He always referred to
my interrogation as a chat, and arranged for it to take place
in a relatively pleasant room, with comfortable chairs and
decent coffee; and he left an open pack of cigarettes on the
table from which we each helped ourselves as we wanted.

'He also gave the impression of being genuinely more
interested in me than in what I had been doing behind the
lines in the Bekaa Valley. To get me to talk about myself, he
told me about his own life, and it turned out that, in our
pasts, there were several points in common. Not only were
we both Jews, but his grandparents, like mine, came from

Brest, but while mine had gone to Israel as Zionists, his had joined the Bolsheviks. His father, having fought against the Whites, had joined the Cheka, ending up in Vilnius as the coordinator of the Soviet campaign against the partisans.

'In 1949, his father had been taken prisoner in an ambush. Five days later his mutilated body was dumped in the main square of Kaunus. Gedda was then ten years old. From that date he vowed that he would follow in his father's footsteps and one day take his revenge.

'I cannot pretend,' Louvish said to Anna, 'that, after two months of solitary confinement, I was not vulnerable to Gedda's technique. He not only had great charm, but he also had a most infectious nonchalance, which seemed to suggest that he did not care what he said, so why, I thought, should I? I realized, of course, that this put me off my guard, and that I might easily forget what was secret and let slip some piece of classified information. Therefore, to protect myself, I decided to talk to him about what I had been considering alone in my cell – my plan to undermine the central tenet of the Christian religion by digging up the body of Christ.

'The idea seemed to interest him at once. At first I thought it was only from historical or political curiosity. We went back over the precedents for this kind of thing – the Protocols of the Elders of Zion, for example, or the Piltdown Skull. Then we moved on to the technology, and for a while I thought he was trying to find out what techniques we had evolved for forging documents or frustrating the effects of carbon-dating. He boasted of Soviet skills in this field. Indeed, even as we talked, he seemed to adopt my project as his own – returning to it day after day, often with answers to the questions of the day before.

'The problems, we soon decided, were not technical, because it would not be hard to find in Israel the skeleton of a man crucified in the first century of the modern era. The difficulty would be to identify it as the body of Jesus of Nazareth. Our first idea was to fake the pieces of wood or papyrus which Pilate had nailed to the cross, saying that this was Jesus of Nazareth, the king of the Jews. The objections to that were not technical, but were the same as any that could be made in respect of corroborative evidence found at the actual site – the whole thing could be a hoax.

'We arrived at two necessary conditions for the scheme to have a chance of success. The first was that the discovery should be made by an archaeologist with an international reputation whose integrity was beyond reproach. The second was that the critical corroborating evidence should be quite independent of the find.

'As to the archaeologist, well, there were several, but my mind settled upon your father first because of his reputation and second because I knew that I could call upon Ya'acov to help me. More intractable was the question of corroboration. We thought about it for days on end and came up with various ideas, all more or less improbable. Then Gedda remembered Josephus and the Slavonic additions to his *Jewish War*. What poetic justice if the man who so shamelessly betrayed his people in the first century could be used to help them in the twentieth. If I could think of a place where the body could be discovered which had some unique features not hitherto made public, then he would arrange for the discovery to be made in Russia of a hitherto unknown Codex which referred to the burial of the Nazarene in the same place.

'For days I racked my brains to consider where the body might have been hidden. Our hypothesis was the same as that of the chief priests at the time – that Christ's own disciples had stolen the body and smuggled it out of the city. I thought of sites in Galilee or Samaria where the skeleton might be found, but, not being an archaeologist, I was not familiar enough with any of them to know which of them would serve our purpose. The choice of a site to place a skeleton would have to await my return to Israel.

'By this time, it had become clear that Gedda would arrange my release. Quite what he told the Syrians or his superiors in Moscow, I do not know. He had no assurances from me that I would go through with the plan, but he was so eager to see it put into effect that he seemed prepared to take the risk that I might let him down. Only right at the end did I ask him why he or his government were willing to embark on a venture of this kind. He then explained to me quite candidly the difficulties being faced by the Soviet Union – how the economy was inefficient; how its failure to produce not just consumer goods but the minimal requirements of its people had led to widespread disillusion with the theories of Marx and Lenin upon which the whole legitimacy of the Communist state depended.

'There was a grave danger that the Soviet Union would disintegrate – each republic falling back upon the racial, national or religious ideologies of its bourgeois past to justify seceding from a now unwanted union. Russia itself might survive the demise of Marxist thought – and even Byelo-russia and the Ukraine, because they shared the same heritage of Orthodox Christianity. But the Muslim republics like Azerbaijan; or those whose populations were Lutheran like Latvia, and above all Lithuania, with its links with the Roman Catholic Church, would be overwhelmed by a popu-lar desire to secede.

'Of course, behind all this reasoning, there were Gedda's personal reasons for wanting to frustrate the rebirth of a nationalist, Catholic Lithuania. He was quite candid in his determination to prevent the ideological heirs of those who had murdered his father from taking power once again in Vilnius. There were others, he said, who thought like him, but how far my scheme had the backing of the Kremlin, I was never able to tell.

'He accompanied me as far as the border with Jordan. There we parted with a handshake – two Jews whom ideology had taken in quite different directions but who remained brothers all the same. Back in Jerusalem, I worked out with Ya'acov just where the skeleton should be found. Three months later, in Geneva, I handed Gedda the text of the new Slavonic addition. Five months after that came the news that a lost Codex of the Slavonic version of Josephus' *Jewish War* had been discovered in Lithuania.'

Louvish sat back in his chair, his explanation over. There was not, on his face, any expression of conceit, but simply the sombre look of an officer who had described the background to a necessary mission.

His eyes, however, remained fixed on Anna, studying her reaction. If she had been alone with him, he might have seen in her expression a certain admiration for the audacity of his scheme. She had no interest, after all, in sustaining the dogmas of the Christian religion; indeed, it was essential to her happiness that Andrew, at least, should continue to believe that there had been no Resurrection. However, Jake sat next to Anna, and the feelings of rivalry he provoked in her proved stronger than her caution. She turned away from Louvish and, with a look of sneering disdain, said to her brother: 'I suppose you provided the skeleton?'

'It wasn't hard to find.'

'And hoodwinked Dad?'

Jake shrugged. 'Sure.'

'Did he never suspect what was going on?'

Jake shook his head. 'People don't ask questions when they might get answers they don't want to hear.'

'And you thought that, if you could fool him, you could fool the world?'

'We don't need to fool the world,' said Louvish. 'Just some of the people some of the time will do.'

'Like Father Lambert?'

'Of course. If he had announced the find, it would have been front-page news; and any doubts expressed later would take up only a couple of inches on the inside page.'

'And now you expect Cardinal Memel to announce it instead of Father Lambert?'

'Yes,' said Jake. 'He was completely taken in.'

'And it didn't bother you to use him in that way?'

'No.'

'Or that it drove Father Lambert to suicide?'

'There are always unforeseen eventualities,' said Louvish.

'Like me.'

'Like you.'

'Well, I won't kill myself, I can promise you that.'

Louvish smiled. 'Not, certainly, while you're under my protection.'

'Thanks,' said Anna, 'but I can look after myself.'

'I'm afraid, given what you now know, that won't be possible.'

She looked from Louvish to Jake. Jake looked away. 'You mean I'm a *prisoner*?' she asked.

'You avoided the draft,' said Louvish. 'You are liable to three years in prison for that alone.'

'I was deferred . . .'

'Your deferment has just expired.'

'But you can't keep me quiet for ever,' said Anna. 'And then there's Henry. What are you going to do about him?'

Neither Louvish nor Jake replied.

Twenty-two

Michal Dagan returned home late that night in a state of some agitation. Rachel, his wife, seemed to realize this and served his supper in silence. Only when they were both sitting at table did she say that Andrew had telephoned an hour earlier, asking after Anna.

'What did you tell him?'

'That I didn't know where she was.'

She said this in a tone which suggested that her husband did know, but Michal Dagan said nothing.

'He thought that she might have had lunch with you,' Rachel said.

'She came *after* lunch,' said Dagan, as if the exact moment mattered, 'and then she went off with Ya'acov.'

Again Rachel waited for him to say more; but when he did not she swallowed the morsel of fish that was in her mouth, laid her fork aside and said: 'Did she come to talk?'

'Yes.'

'About you and her?'

'No.'

'About what, then?'

'The dig.'

'She wanted to talk *archaeology*?'

'Yes . . . Except it was more than archaeology.'

Rachel picked up her fork and put a piece of boiled potato into her mouth. She ate it methodically as she always did, waiting for her husband to go on.

'She asked me about Louvish,' said Michal.

For a moment, Rachel's jaws stopped moving. Then she swallowed what was in her mouth, and once again laid aside her fork. 'Why should she ask you about Louvish?'

'Because she suspects what we suspect . . .'

'Suspect?'

He flinched. 'Very well. What we know.'

Rachel shook her head. 'You must get out of this, Michal, before it gets worse.'

'Get out? How? I have found what I have found.'

'You have found nothing,' she said with unusual vehemence.

'How can you know that?' asked Dagan miserably.

'Because I know my son, and I know the influence that Louvish has over him.'

'Of course, of course, but if it is for Israel . . .'

'Israel can survive without lies.'

'You don't understand . . .' He got up from the table and crossed the room, as if unwilling to hear any rejoinder, but Rachel said nothing. She remained at table, finishing her food.

Michal sat down on the sofa and opened the evening newspaper, but his eyes would not focus on the words. It was as if, quite independent of the mind which directed them, they were terrified of reading the story of his extra-ordinary find.

For some time the old couple sat like this – the husband pretending to read the newspaper on the sofa, the wife methodically eating the supper she had prepared. The silence was like low cloud hiding peaks of antagonism and troughs of recrimination. It was finally broken by the sound of a key moving in the lock of the front door. Both looked towards the hallway to see Jake come in.

230

'Ah, Ya'acov, good,' said Michal, his expression changing to one of mute admiration for his heroic son.

Jake greeted his parents, then went into the kitchen to pour himself a drink.

'What happened to Anna?' shouted Michal after him in an almost jovial tone of voice.

'She's OK,' said Jake. He came back from the kitchen holding a glass filled with milk and sat down at the table next to his mother.

'Where is she?' asked Rachel.

'With Louvish.'

'Still?' asked Michal.

'She's been detained.'

Dagan went pale. 'Louvish detained her?'

'Yes.'

'Why?'

Jake shrugged. 'Because she asked too many questions.'

Dagan put down the unread newspaper. 'That is going too far.'

'She should have minded her own business.'

'It was her business. We made it her business.'

'Just as we made it the business of Father Lambert and drove him to suicide,' said Rachel, handing Jake a plate with fish and boiled potatoes, but looking, as she did so, at her husband on the sofa.

Dagan, with his elbows resting on his knees, hid his face in his hands.

'He didn't kill himself,' said Jake with an anxious glance towards his father.

'He's found hanging out of the window of his cell,' said Rachel, 'and he didn't kill himself?'

Dagan looked up at his son.

'We now know he was murdered,' said Jake.

'How can you know that?' asked Dagan.

'Louvish told me. We have his notebook.'

'But how? Where did he find it?'

'They killed him to shut him up.'

'Who?'

Jake shrugged. 'Some Catholic fanatic. A Jugoslav. They

231

caught him at Heathrow checking in for a flight to Zagreb. One of our people was working on security and found the notebook in his suitcase.'

'He knew what it was?'

'He had been briefed.'

'So what did he do?'

'He switched the notebook for a gun and then called the British police.'

'But who was this man?'

'A Croatian – a defrocked Franciscan from Mostar.'

'How did he know about the find?'

Jake shrugged. 'The Franciscans here run the Holy Places, don't they? Someone must have got wind of it – perhaps from Father Lambert.'

'But then why . . .'

'Whoever knew about it here must have alerted the order.'

'And they *killed* him?'

'Those Croatian Franciscans worked with the Ustasi during the war. If they could massacre hundreds of thousands of Serbs and Jews, why should they hesitate over a crazy priest?'

Dagan looked at his wife to see if she believed their son's story; but, at that moment, she rose to take some used plates into the kitchen. He stood, meaning to follow her, but instead paced up and down the room. 'Of course it makes much more sense if he was murdered, because I knew when he rang me that afternoon – I knew from his tone of voice – that he could not then, straight afterwards, have thrown himself out of the window. He was very polite, of course – he was unwilling to disappoint me – but he made it quite clear that, after thinking it over, he felt sure it could not be the body of Christ. So why, after that, should he kill himself?'

'It had to be murder,' said Jake.

'Yes. Of course. But if only the Croatian had known.'

'What?'

'That Father Lambert no longer believed in the find.'

Jake nodded. 'Then there would have been no need to kill him.'

232

Dagan returned to the sofa and sat down. Once again, he covered his face with his hands. Then he asked: 'But what made Louvish suspect that he had been murdered?'

'He knew about Father Lambert's call to you.'

'How?'

'He knew.'

'He tapped his telephone?'

'Perhaps.'

'Or mine?'

Jake did not answer.

'Of course,' said Dagan. 'It would have to be mine.'

'He has to know what's going on.'

Dagan did not dissent. Once again, he covered his face, as if blocking out the light would help him think. 'So, Louvish thought Father Lambert had been murdered,' he said to Jake, 'but how did he know that the notebook had been stolen?'

'If someone had taken the trouble to kill him, they would hardly have left the notebook with evidence that he believed in the find.'

Michal nodded. 'No, that's true.'

Rachel came back from the kitchen with a pot of coffee and a jar of Coffeemate. 'It seems to me,' she said quietly, 'that Louvish had a better reason to kill Father Lambert than any Croatian.'

Jake frowned. 'Why?'

'Because Father Lambert must have realized that the find was a fraud.'

'He never said that,' said Michal Dagan.

'But he said he was sure, didn't he, that it could not be the body of Christ?'

'Yes, certainly, but as a matter of faith, not of fact.'

'How much better for Louvish, then, to have people think that Father Lambert killed himself in despair, or that his fellow Catholics killed him to keep him quiet,' said Rachel.

'Then why wasn't the notebook left there,' asked Jake, 'for the monks to find with the body?'

'Because he had written nothing . . .'

'Then why take it?'

'To add something later or . . .' She hesitated.

'Or what?' asked Dagan.

She turned to her husband. 'To persuade you that Father Lambert was murdered by someone else.'

Dagan looked at his son.

'You make things too complicated,' said Jake.

'Perhaps Louvish,' said Dagan, 'is a too complicated man.'

'He is a simple man,' said Jake, 'who would die for Israel.'

'And kill for Israel,' said Rachel.

'Of course,' said Jake, looking defiantly at his mother.

'And expect others to do the same.'

'Of course,' said Jake again.

She looked into the eyes of her son. 'You were in London, Ya'acov . . .'

'Rachel, please,' said Dagan. 'How can you suggest such a thing?'

'And Anna?' she asked, without taking her eyes off her son. 'Is the same thing going to happen to her?'

Jake looked away. 'He won't harm her,' he said with an exaggerated bluster.

'Then what will he do with her?'

'Keep her out of the way until the story has broken.'

'And afterwards? Can he ever let her go – someone who knows so well just what has happened?'

Jake scowled. 'If he thinks she'll be sensible, he'll let her go.'

'When has Anna ever been sensible?'

Jake said nothing. His father got up from the sofa. 'You must speak to Louvish, Ya'acov. Tell him that things have gone far enough.'

'I can't,' said Jake. 'I'm going back to London.'

'To London? Why?'

'To fetch the notebook.'

'When?'

'Tomorrow. At six in the morning. On the British Airways flight.'

'Then I shall speak to Louvish.'

Jake shrugged his shoulders. 'Please yourself.'

*

The building where Louvish lived was not far from the Dagans' apartment, and, being one which housed several vulnerable officials, was guarded by a man wearing jeans and trainers with a machine-gun slung over his shoulder.

He recognized Professor Dagan and let him pass. Dagan climbed the stairs, the cool air, scented by pine and eucalyptus trees, coming in from the open windows at each landing. He rested for a moment on the first floor, and again on the second, but on the third walked straight to the door of the flat which belonged to Louvish. He knocked and waited, his face squarely in front of the peephole in the door.

Louvish himself opened the door. He was still wearing his uniform, but had changed his boots for sandals. He stood aside and asked Dagan in, as if he had half-expected such a visit so late at night, then led the way towards the living-room. Before either had sat down, Dagan said: 'Where is my daughter?'

Louvish raised his hand and made a soothing gesture to calm him down. 'She's perfectly comfortable and perfectly safe.'

'If she has been arrested,' said Dagan, 'I should like to know on what charge.'

'There is no need of a charge,' said Louvish, sitting down on a chair. 'There are the emergency regulations.'

'To deal with Arab agitators,' said Dagan, 'not patriotic Jews.'

Dagan was thinking more of himself than of Anna when he said this, because he felt that her detention was an affront to him, but it enabled Louvish to recover from the defensive posture he had held since the Professor had appeared at his door.

'But is she a patriotic Jew?' he asked. 'If I could be sure of that, I would let her go.'

Dagan was confused. 'She may not see things as you or I do,' he said lamely, 'but that is no reason to detain her.'

Louvish sighed and gestured to Dagan to sit down on a chair. 'You know quite well, Professor, that what you have discovered in that cistern is of considerable political significance. Already, one man has died as a result of it – your friend, Father Lambert, murdered, we now know, to prevent him authenticating the find. If news gets out in the wrong way, it could lead to riots and bloodshed, and destroy much of the good will which is felt towards Israel in other parts of the world.'

'There is no need to pretend any more,' said Dagan, his voice rising with his growing agitation.

'Pretend what?' asked Louvish coldly.

'That the whole thing is not a preposterous deception.'

Louvish neither frowned nor smiled. 'You only say that,' he said, 'because your daughter put the idea into your head. That is why she must be detained. We cannot have her influencing others in the same way.'

'It won't work,' said Dagan. 'No one will be taken in.'

'No one?' Now Louvish smiled. 'Didn't *you* believe in what you found? Didn't Father Lambert? Father van der Velde? And Cardinal Memel?'

'Yes. But they didn't know about the Vilnius Codex.'

'But you are a scientist, Professor, and I am a soldier. We deal in facts, not silly, unsubstantiated rumours. There is the Codex – it will undoubtedly be subjected to rigorous tests. There is the cistern. There is the jar. They too will be open to examination. And there is the skeleton which, as you know, is certainly that of a man crucified in the first century of the modern era. What else is asked of you but that you should attest to these facts as facts, and leave rumours and conjectures out of the equation?'

'I was confused, deceived . . .'

'Deceived? By whom?'

'By myself. By my own wish to discover something that would help establish our right to *eretz Israel*.'

'And your wish has come true,' said Louvish. 'If the find is announced by the right people in the right place, by Cardinal Memel or by the Pope in Rome, then it will establish beyond doubt in the Christian mind that God's Covenant with Israel still stands.'

'It still stands,' muttered Michal Dagan. 'Of course it still stands, and we know that Jesus of Nazareth did not rise from the dead – that, somewhere, there are the bones, or the dust from the bones that were his. And I wanted the bones in the cistern to be his. I was so determined that his was the body I had uncovered, that I ignored all my instincts as an archaeologist, instincts which told me that the whole thing was too improbable, too coincidental, too good, indeed, to be true.'

Louvish shook his head sadly. 'Those were the right feelings, Professor – not the selfish ambitions you now suppose them to be, but the culmination of all those aspirations which you have had for our people since you were a child. We have suffered, Professor – your parents and my grandparents, herded into gas chambers, then shovelled into ovens. They had no nation to protect them – nowhere to go – because for nineteen hundred years it had been accepted that God's gift of a nation to the Jews had been withdrawn; that the promised land was no longer Palestine but some mirage of paradise in another world.

'Yet you know – you *know* – that this *is* our land, and that the rock where our father Abraham was ready to sacrifice Isaac for the sake of the God of our people, and where Solomon built his Temple to house the Holy of Holies, you know, as I do, that this rock is the heart of *eretz Israel* and the foundation for a new Temple, which must be built and shall be built before our people can feel that they are truly home.'

Dagan shook his head. 'I don't know, I don't know,' he moaned.

'We both know,' Louvish went on, 'that, somewhere, there must lie the bones of Jesus of Nazareth. You know, too, that the longer those bones remain undiscovered, the longer a billion Christians are encouraged to believe that he was the son of God whom *we* killed by crucifixion, thereby bringing upon ourselves the well deserved punishment of expulsion from our homeland. You know, too, that only when those bones are found again can it be demonstrated that he was not superhuman, but a minor political agitator and would-be prophet. The bones have to be found; and people have to believe that they are the bones; and whether the bones you found in the cistern are the actual bones or not does not matter. What matters is that they *could* be the bones, because the bones do exist, and that, because of the Vilnius Codex, many will believe that they *are* the bones. Only then, after nineteen hundred years, will the vile blood-libel that we Jews killed the son of God be once and for all disproved, and will all the wretched humiliation and per-secutions which followed from that libel – right up to the gas chambers and ovens in which your parents died – be brought to an end as Israel is reestablished as the land promised by God to his chosen people.'

Dagan sat in silence, his head bowed, as if crushed by the weight of Louvish's argument. There seemed nothing he could dispute. What was asked of him but that he should connive at a lie? What sacrifice was that if it saved his people? Then he remembered his reason for coming to see Louvish that evening – the detention of Anna – and won-dered if he might not be expected to sacrifice something more.

'Ya'acov told me,' he said, 'that Lambert was murdered after all.'

'Yes,' said Louvish. 'By a Croatian.'

'My wife does not believe you.'

'We have the notebook to prove it.'

'She thinks that Ya'acov killed him.'

Louvish was silent for a moment. Then he asked: 'And what difference would it make if he did?'

'It would make a difference to me.'

'Struggle demands sacrifice, Professor. You sent your son to fight in Lebanon. You knew he would kill there.'

'I know.'

'And you were prepared to see him die.'

'Of course.'

'Did you love him less than you loved Father Lambert?'

'No.'

'Then why complain if it was his life and not Ya'acov's that was lost to further our cause?'

'Did he have to die?'

'He was the foremost Catholic archaeologist – and the first to see your find. His judgement was critical. If he had

238

believed the skeleton was that of Jesus, then his Church would have found it hard to deny it; and at first, as you know, it seemed he did. But then he called you from London and said he had changed his mind – and we had to resort to our second option and make it seem that he had committed suicide.'

'Why did you take the notebook?'

'Since he had written nothing in it about the find, no purpose would be served in leaving it there. Later, it could emerge that he had left the notebook here in Jerusalem, with a final entry giving the reason for his despair.'

'And this story about the Croatian?'

Louvish smiled. 'That was Ya'acov's idea, to spare your feelings.'

'To spare my feelings?' asked Dagan sceptically.

'And to allay your suspicions. He knew you would wonder why Father Lambert had killed himself so soon after calling you to say that he no longer believed in the find.'

'How considerate of my son.'

'He is a fine young man – not just brave, but also clever.'

'And Anna?'

'The same qualities but slightly distorted. Foolhardy, and too clever by half.'

'For which she must die like my friend?'

'Die? No, I hope it won't come to that,' said Louvish. 'But she must serve her sentence for avoiding the draft, and then . . . we shall see.'

'And what am I to do?' asked Dagan. 'What am I to tell her mother?'

'Tell her that no war is won by those who let pity rule their hearts. Tell her that she must be prepared to sacrifice her daughter just as you, like Abraham, are prepared to sacrifice your son.'

'I don't think she could bear it,' said Dagan.

'Then let us hope that Yahweh provides a ram caught in a thicket,' said Louvish, 'so that you can sacrifice that instead.'

Twenty-three

Michal Dagan left Louvish at around two in the morning and started to walk back towards his own home. When he had gone less than a third of the way, however, he was stopped by the thought that Rachel would be waiting for news of Anna. Knowing that she would see through any pretence or procrastination, he felt unable to face her.

He turned – not back towards Louvish's flat but in the general direction of the Staedtler Institute of Archaeology. He was tired – very tired – but so painful and confused were the thoughts tormenting him that, even if he had lain down on a bed, he would not have been able to sleep. He walked in the cool, quiet streets, hoping that a steady stride would bring order and calm.

If only, he thought, he could be governed either by emotion like Rachel or by reason like Louvish, and yet what contradictions there were in both the reasoning and the feeling. He had been prepared to sacrifice Ya'acov for Israel, so why not Anna? Was it because he loved her less that he felt so loath to lose her? Or was it because he was afraid of Rachel's reproach? She felt, he knew, that he loved his daughter less than his son and would never believe, if Anna now disappeared, that he had done what he could to save her.

What had Abraham told Sarah, he wondered, as he had set out with Isaac, their only son, with the fire and the knife in his hands? Had he told her what Yahweh had commanded him to do? Had she seen anything odd in the look in his eye? And if, like Isaac himself, she had known nothing of what he intended, what would Abraham have said when he returned?

Dagan shivered – not because of the cool night air, but with the dread with which he anticipated Rachel's reproach. She would know that he had connived at whatever Louvish had done; and she would think that he had abandoned Anna not from an excessive zeal for Israel, but from the lukewarm affection she inspired in him. And, of course, there would be truth in her suspicions. Dagan had to acknowledge that, while he had always been ready to sacrifice Ya'acov in the Lebanon, he could never, like Abraham, have raised his own hand to cut his throat.

Was he less reluctant to sacrifice Anna? As Rachel had told Anna, Dagan had never felt as fond of his daughter as he had of his son. Sometimes, to defend himself for this lack of affection, he blamed Anna for growing into someone so unlike what he thought a daughter should be. In a more honest frame of mind, he would recognize that the reasons he had put forward for leaving her to be educated in the United States had really been pretexts for banishing this cuckoo from the nest.

What would Abraham have done, he wondered, if he had had ambivalent feelings for Isaac? Would he have felt, as Dagan now felt, the sour bile of bad conscience as he prepared to sacrifice what was in fact no sacrifice at all? No. It was inconceivable, because Yahweh spoke so clearly to Abraham, and Abraham to Yahweh. Would that Yahweh would make himself so clear to Michal Dagan.

Yet Yahweh, to Dagan, was not someone who spoke in the ear or even the mind of a man. To him God's intentions were made manifest in the history of his chosen people. It was by studying the past that one could discern his will for the future; and, since the greatest evil of the age was undoubtedly Hitler's attempt to exterminate the Jews, so the greatest good must be the antithesis of that – the reestablishment of a Jewish nation. It was inconceivable that Yahweh could want anything different.

Why, then, did he feel so unhappy when he thought, not just about the fate awaiting Anna, but about the murder of Father Lambert? Why had Louvish admitted that Ya'acov had killed him? Was it to test the inexorable logic of his reasoning? Did he boast of his ruthlessness to prove his patriotism? Or to draw others into complicity with what he had done?

Again, as with Anna, Father Lambert had aroused ambivalent feelings in Michal Dagan. Certainly, he had been his friend, but also his rival. Was it not true that Dagan had asked him to come to Israel to authenticate his find, not just because he was the one archaeologist who could persuade the Christian Churches that the skeleton was that of Jesus Christ, but because Dagan had exulted in showing the Catholic monk that his beliefs about Christ's Resurrection were now proved to be absurd?

Had Dagan had no doubts about his own hypothesis? He could not now remember. If there had been any scepticism at the back of his mind, it had been quickly silenced by his Zionist zeal and professional ambition. What were Yadin's discoveries at Masada or Kenyon's at Jericho compared with Dagan's uncovering of the body of Christ? And what were the accomplishments of those Christian archaeologists like Father de Vaux, Father Vincent and Father Lambert compared with those of the Israeli, Michal Dagan?

Of course, when he had seen the effect of the find on Father Lambert, Dagan realized that any professional rivalry he might have felt was insignificant beside the theological significance of what had apparently been uncovered. He had noticed, too, that, despite the destructive effect of the discovery upon his own beliefs, Father Lambert had been sincerely pleased that such a triumph should crown his friend's career. Indeed, it was perhaps this humility – this fear that his own professional pride might impede his acceptance of what Dagan had found – which had prompted Father Lambert to authenticate the find so promptly and return to London in despair.

That would explain why, only a day later, he had telephoned Dagan to say, not just that he had changed his mind, but that he now felt that the skeleton could not be that of Jesus of Nazareth. The call, made only an hour before Father Lambert died, had been relayed by Dagan to Ya'acov in London, and then, presumably, by Ya'acov to Louvish in Israel – or, more likely, had been recorded through a tap placed on his own telephone at the Staedtler Institute, and replayed at once to Louvish. It would then have been a simple matter for Louvish to call Ya'acov in London and order the priest's execution.

Dagan, who until that moment only knew that he was walking away from Louvish and away from home, suddenly came in sight of the floodlit walls of the Old City. He was on Mishkenot Sha'anannim, near to the Montefiore Windmill. He sat down on a low stone wall facing the city, and forgot for a moment that he was cold, forgot, even, that he was tormented by so many contradictory emotions, and simply looked with rapture at his beloved Jerusalem. How could anyone who was not Jewish understand what the city meant to him? It was not merely the site of his people's historical glory, nor the tangible proof, after two millennia, that they had regained what was rightfully theirs. It was rather, like the empty tomb of Christian myth, the proof that, after their crucifixion – the holocaust – the Jews had risen from the dead.

He thought now, as he always did when he looked at the Old City, of his mother and father, and he prayed that somehow from the mysterious depths of She'ol they might see through his eyes that their suffering had not been for nothing. This time, however, the conjuring up of the image of his dead parents did not bring comfort and reassurance, but rather induced a spasm of that bad conscience which had disturbed him since parting from Louvish. However hard he might try to invest them with his own aspirations and ideas, he could not so mould his memories that the honest and amiable lawyer from Hamburg would condone what he had done. And his memory of his mother merged with the image of Rachel, and both women rebuked him with the same silent look of reproach.

'But I do it for you,' he said aloud, as if his father were standing there, confused and perplexed. 'Do what?' the old lawyer seemed to reply. 'Lie? Deceive? Murder? Your friend? Your daughter? For stones and rocks and sand? No, not for me, for that is what was done to *us* from generation to generation – by Titus and Torquemada, by Ignatiev and Hitler. And however many of us died, they never triumphed. *We* triumphed because we did not put our trust in stones and rocks and sand – in castles or palaces, synagogues or even a Temple – but because we put our trust in faith and rectitude, in patience, in humility and resignation to the will of Yahweh. Remember, Michal, the man I was as you sat on my knee and I puffed at my pipe – a victim, certainly, already a victim who was to be kicked out of the park by the Brownshirts; but warm, humorous, affectionate, kind, just, decent and honest. Those qualities are better monuments than all the stones and rocks and sand you will ever cheat and kill to conquer. And what are you, Michal, my son, but cold, loveless and afraid? And what is Ya'acov, raised in your image and likeness, but ruthless, fanatical and cruel? What monument are you to my suffering, whether or not you hold Jerusalem or live in Israel; whether or not you demolish the Dome of the Rock to build a new air-conditioned Temple of marble-faced pre-stressed concrete? No, Michal, my son, I suffered and your mother suffered, and that suffering brought us close to Yahweh. If you must build a monument, build one to us in yourself so that when we meet in She'ol we may know you and love you as our son.'

With no onlookers to inhibit him, Michal Dagan wept – sobbing not just at the rebuke implicit in the memory of his dead parents, but also and more normally because he was tired, distraught and confused. Until that day, he had been propelled through life by the clear and urgent mission to exact revenge and retribution for everything that his parents had suffered as Jews. Now, in one day, he had been forced to count the cost. In doing so, he had come to wonder not just whether the game was worth the candle, but whether it was worth playing at all.

In seeking to punish the elusive malefactor who had persecuted his people throughout history, Dagan now recognized that he had become malign himself – conniving through the most devious logic at the sacrifice of his daughter and the murder of his friend. The shock of understanding that, unwittingly, he had become party to something so patently wrong returned strength to his conscience, which, like Samson in the court of the Philistines, pulled away the two pillars upon which the edifice of his convictions had rested.

The tears which now trickled down his wrinkled, weather-beaten cheeks came not just from fatigue and remorse, but also, to his own astonishment, from an extraordinary sense of relief and joy, as if a spring which had been blocked for many years had suddenly been opened. What he saw for the first time was that the finest accomplishments of men and women lay not in nations and empires, wealth and culture, in palaces, temples, churches or mosques, but in those invisible and intangible thoughts and emotions which are imbued with gentleness, unselfishness and love.

He now understood that, for fifty years, he had suffered from a misconception. His father was not a Joshua who had failed but a Job who had succeeded – a man who was defeated and humiliated in the terms of this world, but heroic and victorious by the values of the next. Though persecuted by vile men, he had not been infected by their hatred. The pity he had felt was also for them. For that reason, even in Auschwitz, he had triumphed.

Very slowly it began to grow light. The street lamps lost their pointed brilliance and became superfluous. The moon-light evaporated, like a morning mist, as the first rays of the sun rose from behind the sparse hills of the Judaean desert.

Michal Dagan got to his feet. There were still traces of tears on his haggard face but the tears themselves had stopped. He shuffled out of the park and away from Mish-kenot Sha'anannim – not in the direction of his home in Rehavya, but down past the almshouses into the valley of Hinnom. Already one or two cars and buses were passing as he stumbled across the road which encircled the Old City, and climbed up the path towards the Zion Gate. He reached it just as the sun had risen, and shone obliquely onto the city wall. He stood there for a moment to recover his breath. A policeman looked askance at the old, unshaven man, coming so early to the Old City, but he made no attempt to stop Dagan as he walked through the gate.

Bent with exhaustion, he walked towards the Temple Mount. There, in a cool pool of shadow, two or three Jews were already praying at the Western Wall. He too went to the wall, putting on his yarmulka as he entered the enclosure. He did not stop to pray but passed straight through to the cavernous space below Wilson's Arch.

At the gate to the passage there was a sleepy guard, one of Louvish's men, who looked surprised to see the Professor. 'None of your people is here,' he said to Dagan.

'It doesn't matter,' said Dagan. 'I can manage on my own.'

The man looked perplexed but unlocked the gate and switched on the lights.

The air, which usually felt cool compared to the heat outside, now seemed hot and stuffy. Dagan, already exhausted, set off down the long tunnel. 'Vanity of vanities, all is vanity,' he muttered as he stumbled along beside the massive blocks of Herod's Western Wall. 'What profit has a man of all his labour which he takes under the sun? One generation passes away and another generation comes but the earth abides for ever . . . All things are wearisome . . . what was will be again, what has been done will be done again; there is nothing new under the sun.'

He reached the entrance to the cistern. Here, there was a switch for the lights inside and, since they had always been turned on for him by one of his assistants, it took Dagan some time to find it. When he did, he heard, through the rectangular hole in the wall, an echoing pop as the bulbs were lit. He crouched, climbed through, and then paused for a moment, standing upright on the ledge of rock, remembering the emotions which had overwhelmed him when he had stood there with Jake on the first occasion – the feelings of excitement, exaltation and triumph.

Now, it was as if that had happened not a month before but in some other life. As he climbed down the ladder onto the shale floor, he felt an excitement, a triumph and an exaltation of quite a different kind – and a sense of vindication, too, which went far beyond his own memories and experiences or the memories and experiences of his family or his race – reaching down into the innermost kernel of his being and out to the extremities of space and time.

Yet, while this emotion was overwhelming, it was hardly

coherent, and the thoughts which went with it were jumbled. It was here, just above him, under the Dome of the Rock, that Abraham had been prepared to sacrifice Isaac, and had found, instead, a ram caught in a thicket. To Dagan it seemed as if the ram had fallen into the cistern and was darting in and out of the shadows made by the lamps. At the same time, the spade he found at the foot of the ladder leading down from the ledge became the knife held in Abraham's hand as he raised it to sacrifice, not his son but the ram. But it was also a spade, a spade with which to dig a grave for his parents, and bury with them the rage and anguish which had possessed Michal since, as a child, he had seen his father humiliated in the park. And the skeleton he now saw, as he approached the contents of the broken jar laid out on the plastic sheet, became in his mind's eye the relics of those millions who had died – relics so terrible until that moment that he had never recognized them as an enduring and indestructible monument to his parents' quality of soul. With a great groan of final anguish, he raised the spade and brought it down, time and time again, to slaughter the sacrificial ram, to exorcize the black spirit of vengeance – and, finally, to reduce the skeleton of a crucified man to a thousand fragments of dust and bone.

PART THREE

Twenty-four

It was already midday in Israel, but ten o'clock in Britain, when Jake arrived in London on the British Airways flight. He was not armed but had in his hand-baggage all the equipment that is carried by a diabetic. There was a packet of disposable syringes, indistinguishable from the kind seen in a doctor's surgery, which would be used for the daily dose of insulin; and another, smaller, portable syringe looking something like a fountain-pen with which a diabetic could top up his dose of insulin while sitting at a table in a restaurant.

There were four small bottles with the syringes, each labelled insulin, and all but one containing insulin – the odd one being filled instead with a poison which stopped the heart. It was easily administered, left no trace in the blood, and had been used successfully to dispose of terrorists and their mentors in different countries of the world.

Jake passed through customs and immigration control without difficulty. The stamps on his passport showed that he had been in and out of Britain many times before. Since his only luggage was the bag he had had with him on the plane, he went straight from Terminal One to catch the Underground into central London.

If he had been in a hurry, he would have taken a taxi, but Louvish always scrutinized his expenses on missions of this kind, and reacted to any unnecessary extravagance as if it were a blow aimed deliberately at the faltering economy of Israel. Since Jake knew that his target, Henry Nash, would already have gone from his flat to his office, and that he would have no opportunity to deal with him until he went out for lunch, he had no reason to hurry into the city. He sat reading *Newsweek* as the train made its way through the suburbs of Hounslow and Hammersmith. At South Kensington, he changed to the Circle Line, catching a train to Victoria. There, he went to the public lavatory, shut himself into a cubicle, took the portable syringe out of his bag and filled it with a dose of the poison. He screwed on the cap and clipped the syringe to the inside pocket of his polyester blouson. He closed the bag, used the lavatory, then left to deposit his bag in a storage locker.

He was booked on the El Al charter flight which flew from Gatwick to Tel Aviv that evening. He studied the railway timetable to check the times of the express to the airport; then he went back to the Underground and caught a train to Piccadilly Circus. From there he walked to the Swiss Centre in Leicester Square, went into the café and sat down.

It was here that Aron – the operative who had helped him with Father Lambert – was to bring a photograph of the target. Jake already knew a certain amount about Henry Nash, and had formed a picture of him in his mind; but that was not enough to make a positive identification, and Louvish would be angry if he killed the wrong man.

If there was one emotion which dominated the many thoughts and feelings flitting through Jake's restless mind, it was the desire to earn Louvish's approval. His regard for his father amounted to nothing beside his admiration for his commander. Certainly, the Professor was a zealous Zionist who had raised his son to be brave and heroic, but the very longing had exposed him to Jake as a man who himself was neither.

Louvish, on the other hand, was as decisive in action as he was in analysis: the logic of the thought led inexorably to the enactment of the deed. No misgivings were allowed to impede the attainment of an objective: pity, said Louvish, was merely cowardice in a pleasing disguise.

Jake did not like to kill. The first time was supposed to be the most difficult, but in his case it had been the easiest, in the heat of battle in the Lebanon where his victim, given the chance, would have happily killed him. Later, in cold blood, on missions in Athens and Geneva, it had become harder; but even there the targets had been strangers in a crowd.

The worst had been the last, Father Lambert, because he had been kind to Jake since he was a child, and because he had looked at Jake and at Aron as they had dragged him to the window, not with hate or even fear but with a pity that did not seem at all like cowardice in a pleasing disguise.

Jake had understood quite clearly why Father Lambert had to die. There was never a flaw in the logic used by Louvish. He could see, too, why it was necessary to kill Henry Nash, and he told himself over and over again that he should no more flinch from sticking a needle into the arm of this Englishman than Judith had hesitated to hack off the head of Holofernes. Time might separate the one deed from the other, but the cause remained the same.

Only one thought worried him – that Louvish might judge it necessary to eliminate Anna too. It was unlikely that, if he did, he would involve Jake in her execution, but that did not resolve his anxiety. However much his sister had exasperated him over the years, she remained a member of his family, his people, his nation. Was not Anna one of those they were fighting to defend? Could it really be right to kill her? Or was it possible that, after all, Louvish's logic was somehow flawed?

He looked at his watch. It was a quarter to twelve. Aron should have arrived by now. What if he did not turn up? Jake could find the office, but how would he identify the man? He looked for a public telephone. There was none in sight. If he left the café, Aron might arrive and miss him. In any case, he knew the habits of a man like Henry Nash: he would not leave for lunch before half-past twelve. He could afford to wait. He could even wait until the evening – these things were better done in the rush-hour – and take a later plane, but he wanted to get back as soon as possible: he was afraid about what his father might do in his agitated state of mind.

That was why he must get back, yet Aron still had not come. It was now five to twelve. He stood up, left money for his coffee on the table, and went to look for a telephone. There was one outside in Leicester Square, but it was being used by a swarthy Lebanese. Jake could tell this from the man's accent as he chatted in Arabic, apparently to a girl, trickling a loathsome flow of pornographic innuendo down the line, unaware that anyone around him could understand what he said.

Jake turned away. He hated London. He longed to be out of these gutters, filled with human rubbish, and back in Israel, in the desert, with his comrades in arms. How pitiable were those who had never known what it was to fight in the heat, side by side with your friends, for a cause that had been ordained by Yahweh himself. How majestic it was, when they camped under the stars, to know that their lives were not to be lived out as ants in the antheap of a city like London, but as the heroes of Providence, reconquering and rebuilding the land of God's chosen people.

He found a telephone and dialled Aron's number. The girl answered. Aron had left over an hour before. There had been a call from Tel Aviv. That had held him up. And the traffic. Or the Tube. She did not know how he had travelled. Jake told her to tell Aron, if he rang in, to meet him outside the offices of the *Soho Newsletter*.

It was now a quarter past twelve. He had to start his surveillance soon, or risk losing the chance of finishing the job in the lunch hour. He walked up Dean Street, past a nightclub advertising non-stop striptease by big-busted girls. He shuddered. How vile, this wantonness of the Philistines. Never, never, would Jerusalem become like London. Never would a new Isaiah be able to say: 'What a harlot she has become, the faithful city . . .'

He came to the building which housed the office of the *Soho Newsletter* and walked straight past to the corner. He crossed the street and walked back down the other side. There was a small sandwich-bar, with three or four stools up against the counter. He could sit there and watch, but how would he know who to watch for? He would have to go to the office and try to find out. He crossed the street again and went straight into the old brick building, then up the stairway, with its bright green plastic banisters, to the first floor.

He did this with all the confidence of someone who

254

worked there. Only at the door to the office of the *Soho Newsletter* did he hesitate for a moment, not because he was afraid, but because he had entered on the spur of the moment and had made no plan of what to do. He knew that Henry was the managing director, and that he was Andrew's brother; he also knew that he was unlike Andrew in almost every way – an atheist, not a Catholic; a roué, not a prig.

He pushed open the door and found himself in a small foyer. He looked around at the wall. Perhaps there would be a photograph of the board of directors. There was none. There were framed prints; modern, tubular chairs; a table, with magazines on it; and a desk behind which a sharp-nosed girl sat answering the telephone and putting through calls.

She looked up as if to ask what Jake wanted, but as she did so the telephone burbled. She picked it up – her eyebrows still arched in the interrogatory look she had directed at Jake.

'*Soho Newsletter*,' she said in the sing-song voice of the trained receptionist. 'Mr Nash? One moment, please.' She pushed a button on the board in front of her, and turned back to Jake. 'I'm sorry . . .'

'I was wondering . . .' Jake began.

She was not listening. The light was still flashing on her console. She smiled up at Jake. 'I won't be a minute.' She picked up the telephone again. 'Sandy? Is Mr Nash in his office? Oh, I see. He can take it here, then. It's that young chap – Alistair something or other. Will you take it? Good.'

She pushed another button; another light flashed for a moment, then stopped.

She turned back to Jake.

'I was wondering . . .' he began again.

Again she was distracted. Two men, both in suits, one blue, the other grey, came out into the foyer from the passage behind the desk. 'There was a call for you,' the girl said. 'I put it through to Sandy.'

'Was it Alistair?' asked the man in the grey suit.

'I think so, yes.'

'About time,' said the man in the blue suit.

'Sandy can deal with him,' said the man in the grey suit.
They went out.

'I *am* sorry,' said the girl to Jake.

'I wanted to see Henry Nash,' he said.

'Oh, that was him who just went out of the door.'

'Which one?'

'The tall one.'

'I'll run and catch him.'

Out in the street, the two men were sauntering away from the office. Jake walked behind them, cursing the girl, because neither seemed taller than the other. They were both about the same age and, above all, they were the same type. The grey suit was better cut. The blue suit seemed crumpled. As he grew closer, he noticed that the man in the grey suit was an inch or two taller.

They came to the corner, stopped for a moment, finishing what they had to say, then parted – the man in the blue suit turning to the west, the man in the grey suit to the east. Jake went to the east, a short way behind, convinced that the man in the grey suit was his target. He felt for the syringe in his inside pocket, found it, but left it there. The street was neither empty enough nor crowded enough for him to prick him without running the risk of being seen. In a moment he would turn into Frith Street, or, even better, into Oxford Street, and there, quite safely, it could be done.

He removed his gaze from the back of the man's head, knowing that people could sense when they were being followed. When the man hesitated before crossing a street, he too stopped. Then, when the man crossed the street, he followed and found that they had come into Soho Square.

The man walked through the garden in the centre, where small bunches of office workers sat eating sandwiches and drinking juice out of cartons and cans. This would do. If he sat down on a bench, Jake would sit next to him. But it seemed unlikely, from what he knew of Henry, that he would take sandwiches from the pocket of his well-cut suit.

He did not stop and sit down, but walked straight through the gardens and crossed the street on the other side of the

256

square. There he hesitated, looked at his watch, then slipped furtively through the door of a red-brick church.

Jake frowned, wondering why an atheist should go into a church. He had looked at his watch. Perhaps he had an assignation. Churches, after all, were always used as a meeting place for lovers or spies. The newsletters involved covert connections. He must be using the church to meet a cautious informant.

Jake crossed the street and followed Henry into the church. He had been in churches before and always had loathed them. However beautiful the building, or rich the decoration, they were the temples of the enemy – stew-pots of that malign ideology which had persecuted the Jews since the death of Christ.

This one was ugly, and smelt of incense and candlewax. There was a lobby – empty but for a large marble bowl of holy water, and stands selling tracts of Catholic propaganda. Beyond, through double doors of glass, was the church itself – painted stucco, aping the baroque, with portraits above the altars of the Holy Family looking Irish or Italian – anything but Jewish.

At first the church seemed empty, but then he saw, kneeling before the statue of a woman, perhaps St Bernadette or the Virgin Mary, two Filippino women, and, right at the front, at the foot of the altar, the man in the grey suit, staring up at the figure of Christ on the cross.

Jake felt once again for the syringe in his inside pocket. This seemed as good a place as any for the job to be done. He took out the syringe, unscrewed the top, and, holding it behind his back with two fingers and the thumb of his right hand, he walked quietly down the left-hand side of the church.

When he was within fifteen feet of his target, he stopped and looked around. The church was still empty but for the Filippino women, and their eyes were fixed on the statue behind the bank of flickering candles. He looked back at the man, brought the syringe out from behind his back and stepped forward. At that moment, the figure in the grey suit

257

went down on his knees before the cross, lowered his head, and clasped his hands together in prayer.

Jake cursed inaudibly, turned, and went back down the aisle. Henry Nash was an atheist. He would not pray. He had followed the wrong man. In the foyer, he put the top back onto the syringe and the syringe back into his pocket. He went out into the sunlight of Soho Square. As he did so, he caught sight of Aron, looking for him among the people sitting on the benches. He crossed the street, went up behind him, and tapped him on the shoulder. Aron turned. He looked afraid.

'I was held up,' he said. 'There was a power cut on the Bakerloo Line.'

'Never mind,' said Jake. 'Did you bring the photograph?'

'Yes.' He reached into his pocket. 'But Louvish called. The mission is off.'

Jake took the photograph. 'Why?'

'I don't know. There are developments in Jerusalem. The whole thing is definitely off.'

He looked at the photograph. He had followed the right man.

'I'm not too late, am I?' asked Aron. 'You haven't done it?'

'No,' said Jake. 'I haven't done it.' He gave the photograph back to Aron. 'Did Louvish say what I was to do?'

'Go back as planned.'

Twenty-five

Three weeks later, Henry met Anna when she returned to London. She arrived on the same flight from Tel Aviv that Andrew had taken two weeks before. Henry greeted her as he might have greeted a sister, had he had one, or a very old friend. Neither said much as they walked to the car park, and even as they drove through the tunnel beneath the runway, they were silent – Henry apparently concentrating on keeping his silver-grey BMW in the flow of other cars leaving the airport, Anna staring ahead with a wistful look in her eyes.

It was only when they were on the motorway that Henry asked: 'Are you all right?'

'Sure,' she said shortly, but with a shrug, as if to add: 'As well as can be expected.' She turned towards him, and for a moment the wistful look left her eyes to make way for an expression of pained apprehension. 'But what about him?' she asked. 'Is *he* all right?'

Henry could not return her glance – he was driving in dense, fast-moving traffic. He simply nodded and said: 'Yes, I think so. For the time being.'

They drove on for some time in silence. Then, again with some reluctance, Anna said: 'Did he tell you?'

'What?'

'About him and me?'

'Yes.'

She paused, then said: 'I guess you think I behaved badly.'

'No, I don't.'

'I really loved him.'

'I know.'

'But once he knew about the hoax . . .'

'Why did you tell him?'

She gave a sad smile. 'At first, I didn't. When Louvish let me go, he was waiting at the hotel, and he was so happy to see me and I was so happy to see him that I just couldn't bring myself to tell him that everything Dad had found was phoney. I told him that Dad had had a brainstorm, and had destroyed the skeleton because Father Lambert's suicide had made him think that the find would lead to more suicides, riots and civil wars.'

'Did he accept that?'

'Sure, but then he would have accepted almost anything.'

'Why?'

'Because he needed to believe that Jesus definitely had not risen from the dead. It was all a package – the priesthood, celibacy and the Resurrection on the one hand; sex, me and the skeleton of Jesus on the other.'

'You realized that?'

'Yes.'

'Yet you told him?'

She sighed. 'It's hard to lie to someone you love, especially someone like Andrew. And then the whole thing got out of hand. Andrew felt he had to tell the Simonites what had happened. He went to see the Prior and then telephoned the Cardinal, who gave a press conference in Rome . . .'

'I read about it.'

'And when he was rebuked by the Pope the next day, Andrew felt that it was all his fault.'

'But Cardinal Memel said nothing about the find.'

'I know. It was all kind of theological. But Andrew felt sure that he would never have said what he did about the Resurrection if he hadn't seen the skeleton in the cistern. So he was all set to go to Rome and tell the Pope the whole story, and I could see him getting deeper and deeper into a lie, so I told him.'

'You knew the risk?'

'I guess I did, but I thought . . .' She sniffed. 'You see, one of his favourite sayings of St Paul was that the truth sets us free.'

'He still loves you,' said Henry.

'Sure. Like a sister.'

The cars in front of them slowed down as the motorway narrowed from three lanes to two, and then was carried on concrete stilts over Chiswick.

'So what happened after you told him?'

'It was terrible. Much worse than I had imagined.'

'How?'

'He withdrew into himself, but at the same time pretended that nothing had changed. But I knew that, well, he was suffering – that he was even forcing himself to make love to me when he didn't really want to.'

'He felt guilty?'

'Guilty. Ashamed. Disgusted. He came to see me as Eve who had inveigled him into eating the forbidden fruit, and as a result he would never make it back into the Garden of Eden.'

'The idea of Hell was always very real to him,' said Henry.

260

'You can say that again. But, you see, he'd promised never to leave me. He'd said we were married in the eyes of God, so he was completely caught.'

'Poor Andrew.'

'Sure, poor Andrew, going to bed each night as if he was getting into his coffin, making love to me with a look of doom on his face, and afterwards – Jesus – it wasn't a matter of post-coital sadness, it was post-coital despair.'

The trace of a smile came onto Henry's lips. 'Poor Anna,' he said.

'In the end I couldn't bear it. I told him to go.'

'And he agreed?'

'He didn't want to go. He didn't want to stay. But he felt he had to go to Rome anyway, to tell Cardinal Memel that the whole thing had been a fraud. So I suggested that he go back from there to the monastery in London – for a while, at any rate, to think things over.'

'And he agreed?'

'He didn't want to leave me, but I persuaded him that Dad was still in a bad way, and that I needed to be alone with him for a while.'

'Which was perhaps partly true?'

She shrugged. 'Sure. Dad did have a kind of breakdown. I think he still can't forgive himself for Father Lambert's suicide. I'm sure that's why he smashed the skeleton, though Ma says he did it to save me from Louvish. He's certainly fed up with Jake for landing him in the whole shemozzle, and only wanted me and Ma with him. So we went off to Galilee, and Andrew came back here – miserable but relieved.'

'Yes,' said Henry. 'That's how I found him. Miserable but relieved.'

They had reached Kensington. 'Are you staying with your aunt?' Henry asked as he waited at a red light.

'Yes, but you don't have to take me all the way there.'

'Of course I will, but perhaps you'd like some supper first.'

'I'm not hungry, but I'd like to talk.'

The car moved forward again.

'What I really hate about the Christian religion,' said Anna, 'is that it talks about loving one's neighbour, but when it comes down to the business of Heaven and Hell, it's every man for himself.'

Again a slight smile came onto Henry's lips. '*Sauve qui peut*,' he said.

'Precisely.'

'I think, to give him his due,' said Henry, 'that Andrew's dilemma was a little more complicated than a straight choice between being saved as a priest and being damned as a lover.'

'Did you talk to him about it?'

'Yes.'

'What did he say?'

'His thoughts were very confused,' said Henry. 'I was worried that he was heading for a breakdown.'

'So was I. That's why I thought he should go home.'

'I'm sure it was the right thing for him to do at that time.'

'And have you seen him since?'

'Yes. He's much calmer.'

She scowled. 'I bet the monks are glad to get him back.'

'I'm not sure they know how nearly they lost him.'

'His confessor must know.'

'Of course.'

They turned into Eaton Square and stopped outside Henry's flat.

'I feel as if I've been away for years,' said Anna.

'A lot has happened in a short space of time,' said Henry.

He brought her suitcase up to his flat, because she said she wanted to take a shower. It was a sign of how much had changed that neither seemed embarrassed by the intimacy of the position in which they were placed. The condition of Henry's flat suggested that he too had altered in some way which was not at once apparent in his manner. Where, before, the living-room had been kept scrupulously tidy, with every rug and cushion in place, there was now a certain chaos in the room, with odd books in haphazard piles and letters left unopened on the table.

So preoccupied was Anna with her own state of mind that she did not notice the untidiness of his flat, nor that his manner had subtly altered from the sardonic charm which had once so enraptured her to a kindlier, more tentative approach. When she returned from taking her shower, wearing fresh clothes, he handed her a glass of wine with a look of great solicitude, as if he cared for her now far more than he had ever done before.

'You said you thought,' she said as she took it, 'that things were more complicated with Andrew than they seemed.'

He sat down opposite her, but, rather than sink back into the cushions of his plush sofa, he perched on the edge, holding his drink between his knees.

'Do you find Andrew naïve?' he asked.

She seemed hurt. 'No. I don't think he's naïve.'

'Perhaps that's the wrong word,' said Henry.

'He's kind of unspoilt and uncompromising . . .'

'Yes. Uncompromising and unspoilt. That's what I mean. He has never had to live his life at odds with his ideas. He has never had to settle for anything other than a clear conscience.'

'Yes.'

'Whereas others – most of us, I would say – muddle along, if only because we are not quite clear what our conscience is telling us to do.'

'Yes.'

'Some of us, even, are not even sure that there *is* a right path or a wrong path . . .'

'Yes.'

'Most trust to a kind of gravity which will pull us, like a meandering river, down towards the sea.'

'I guess that applies to you and me . . .'

'But not Andrew. Ever since he was a child he was determined to be on the right side of the law, and he was always very anxious that there should be a law to give an inflexible structure to his life.'

'Why?'

'I don't know for sure. I'm not a psychoanalyst. But I think an analyst would say that it was partly because our mother was such a bully, and yet so erratic, that we never knew where we stood with her, what would make her pleased with us, or what would put her in a rage.'

'He told me . . .'

'While our father, who might have provided some consistency in our lives, was a weak man who could not stand up to her and, eventually, as you know, ran off with his secretary leaving us at the mercy of our mother until, in Andrew's case, he came upon Father Lambert.'

She drank from her glass and nodded to Henry to go on.

'Now Father Lambert not only exemplified all those qualities which had been so poorly represented in our father; he was also the priest of a religion which offered a definite and detailed code. It inevitably appealed to someone like Andrew, who had always wanted to know whether he was doing right or doing wrong.'

'Sure.'

'So he found, both in the man and in the religion, a clear answer to what the Freudians might call the yearning of his super-ego, and a way to cope with the frightening urges of his libido. The libido, however, can never be successfully repressed or denied. If it cannot flow on the surface, then it runs underground and in his case, I suspect, expressed itself in his affection for you . . .'

She nodded.

'And only surfaced again as undisguised sexual desire when, for a moment, your father's claim for his discovery enabled Andrew to throw off the inhibitions implicit in his commitment to a priestly vocation . . .'

'Go on.'

'At first he thought he was in paradise, but quickly discovered that life outside a monastery is neither as innocent nor as simple as it seems.'

She blushed. 'Because I told him about you?'

He looked at her but did not blush. 'Yes. He said nothing at all to suggest that he blamed either of us for what had happened, but clearly he had had as idealistic a conception of sexual love as he had of everything else, and to discover so soon that we make mistakes or, rather, that we settle for

264

the relative while awaiting the absolute, threw him into confusion.'

'For me he was the absolute,' said Anna.

'I know. And I am sure that in time he would have realized that. But before he could recover from that first confusion, he suffered the second setback, the discovering that the find was a hoax, and he felt impelled to return to the structure which had served him so well before, but within which he had committed himself to the celibate life of a monk.'

Anna stood up. 'Shall we go eat?' she said abruptly, to hide from Henry her burgeoning tears.

'Yes.' He finished his drink and together they went down into the warm streets and walked to a restaurant in Chelsea. There, after they had ordered, Anna described in greater detail what she had learned from Louvish.

'Will the story get into the press?' Henry asked her.

'I don't think so. Cardinal Memel didn't mention it. Louvish certainly won't leak it. Nor will Dad.'

'And you?'

She shook her head. 'No. It would ruin Dad.'

'What will he do now?'

'Ma wanted him to go back to the States, but he won't hear of it. He says he now loves Israel more than he did before.'

'But not in the same way?'

'Not at all in the same way.'

'And Jake?'

'He's gone to Gaza.'

'And you?'

She looked sad. 'After the Congress of Biblical Archaeologists at Oxford, I guess I'll go back to the States.'

'You're giving up on Britain?'

'I think Britain gave up on me.'

'I'm sorry.'

'It's funny,' she said. 'I've been dropped before, and I've felt bad about it at the time, but I've never before felt that it needn't have turned out like this, and I've never hated a rival like I hate the Catholic Church.'

265

Henry looked perplexed. 'Can you blame the Catholic Church for our emasculating mother?'

'No. But, as you always said, the Simonites are short of vocations, so don't tell me that, now they've got him back in their clutches, they aren't painting me as a Jezebel who will lure him out and lead him to damnation.'

'And will you?'

'What?'

'Try and lure him out?'

'I don't even know if he'll see me.'

'I'm going to visit him tomorrow. I'll find out.'

Twenty-six

At ten the next morning Henry went to the Simonite monastery, where Gerry, the porter, called Andrew down from his cell. He was wearing the grey habit of the order, with a rope tied around his waist. Though calm, he seemed thin, and had a tired look on his face, as if he had been fasting or keeping an all-night vigil.

He greeted Henry with a kind of measured friendliness and led him back to his cell. Henry, who loathed all institutions, but felt particularly repelled by the mixed smell of floor polish, incense and the monks' breakfast which always permeated the air, followed him obediently up the stairs.

'They moved me to another cell while I was away,' said Andrew, as they walked along the corridor on the second floor.

'Promotion?'

'In a way.'

They reached the cell, and Andrew opened the door before standing back to let his brother go in before him.

Henry looked around at the book-lined walls. 'Who was here before?'

'Father Lambert.' He closed the door. 'It was much simpler to move me up here than to move all his books and papers down to my old cell.'

266

'But doesn't it give you the creeps?'

Andrew frowned. 'It reminds me, naturally . . . but that's as it should be.' He directed Henry towards the wooden armchair and himself sat down at the desk.

'You seem to be busy,' said Henry, glancing at the pile of papers.

'I've not only been asked to clear up his papers, but also to take over some of the things he was to do for the Congress of Biblical Archaeologists.'

'They must be relieved that you came back.'

Andrew blushed. 'I'm also relieved to have something to do.'

'Of course. And I won't waste your time. I just wanted to see that you were all right, and to tell you that Anna came back last night.'

'Ah, good. I must ring her,' he said in a tone of contrived detachment.

'She'll be at the Congress. Her father's coming too. But then she means to go back to America.'

He frowned. 'Won't she finish at Huntingdon?'

'I don't think so.'

'No, well, I can see why she might not want to. She only came, after all, to study under Father Lambert. Without him, it's only to be expected that she might go elsewhere.'

'I don't think that it's because of that that she's leaving,' said Henry.

Andrew looked out of the window. 'No. There must be other reasons. I realize that.'

'Do you realize that she still loves you?' asked Henry.

Andrew's expression did not change. He still looked out of the window at nothing in particular. 'And I still love her,' he said in a flat tone of voice. 'There was never any question of an absence of love.'

'I know, but . . .'

'It was only a matter of what kind of love it should be.'

'Are you sure . . . are you absolutely sure that you know what kind of love it should be?'

He sighed and looked back into the room. 'She agreed,' he said in an irritated, almost exasperated tone of voice, 'we both agreed, that we weren't meant by God to be man and wife.'

'How can you be so certain?'

'I can be certain because, well, because at the root of what took place between us was the lie – the biggest lie of the Prince of Lies – that Jesus did not rise from the dead. And I believed that lie because I wanted to, just like Father Lambert, and like him I ignored all the usual procedures, and spurned all reasonable doubt, and I seduced Anna just as Father Lambert seduced Mrs Dunn. But, while he died in despair, and in mortal sin, God in his mercy has given me the chance to redeem myself and repent.'

'I can see that,' said Henry gently, 'or, rather, I see quite clearly how it can seem like that to you. But I wonder if God would want you to save your soul at her expense.'

'But don't you see,' said Andrew urgently, 'it isn't just a question of *my* soul? If it was just that, it would be easy.'

'You mean that hers is at risk?'

'Not hers. *His.*' He looked back towards the window.

'Father Lambert's?'

He nodded.

'You feel that by becoming a Simonite monk, you can save his soul as well as your own?'

'Yes. By seeing it through, right to the end, my life for his life – a return, no more, for what he did for me.'

'But that's . . .' He was about to say 'mad', but stopped himself for fear of tipping his brother over the edge. Instead he said: 'It makes God seem vengeful – to try and placate him in that way.'

'It's not to placate God, it's to cheat the Devil.'

'You mean the Devil can claim the soul of Father Lambert . . .'

'Unless I offer up my life to expiate his sin, just as Jesus did for the sin of Adam.'

'So it is not to save *your* soul that you have returned?'

'No. His.'

'And if you were to discover, somehow, that he had died in a state of Grace?'

'Then, of course, there would be no debt to pay. But I

268

found him there, hanging, and I heard from her lips of his sin with a woman, and I saw the skeleton, and, like him, I doubted, and I denied Christ's divinity – so easily, so quickly, so shamelessly . . .' He shuddered.

Henry shifted in his chair. 'You may like to know,' he said, 'that I went to see Veronica Dunn.'

Andrew looked up suspiciously. 'When?'

'Yesterday. Before I fetched Anna from the airport.'

'Did she ask to see you?'

'No. I had promised to tell her how things turned out . . .'

'Of course. She must have been relieved to know it was a hoax.'

'She knew that already.'

'How?'

'From faith. She said she always knew. In fact, I'd made a bet with her about it and went to tell her that she'd won.'

'And was she all right?' asked Andrew.

'Yes. She seemed fine.'

'I'm glad.'

'She was worried about you.'

He frowned. 'She shouldn't be.'

'We agreed . . .'

'What?' asked Andrew, almost irritably.

'It's awkward for me to say this,' said Henry in a quiet but deliberate voice, 'given what passed between Anna and me, and what passed between her and Father Lambert, but we both agreed – we both felt quite certain – that you are not meant to be a priest or a Simonite monk but Anna's husband and the father of her children.'

'Meant by whom?'

'By . . . God.'

'But you don't believe in him.'

'I'm no longer so sure . . .'

'Take care,' said Andrew gravely. 'Don't believe unless you must. Faith is a terrible burden.'

'Didn't Christ say that his yoke was easy and his burden light?' asked Henry.

'Yes,' said Andrew sadly, 'and at times it is. But at other

269

times God withdraws and the Devil renews his temptations – to give up, to abandon one's vows and solemn resolutions.'

Henry smiled. 'Am I an agent of the Devil?'

Andrew did not smile. 'Are you? I don't know. Not knowingly, certainly, but perhaps . . . you mean well, I know, but love is so complicated – so selfish, sometimes, and at other times so pure.'

'Has it occurred to you,' asked Henry, 'that perhaps, before making any final decision, you should seek advice of some kind?'

'I have my confessor.'

'A Simonite?'

'Yes.'

'You should consult a priest, perhaps, who is not a Simonite, or a lay counsellor of some kind.'

'Do you mean a psychiatrist?'

'I suppose I do.'

He laughed. 'I'm not mad,' he said, 'or only in so far as anyone who aspires to be holy will always seem mad.'

'I didn't mean to suggest that you were mad,' said Henry, 'but only, perhaps, that you were unhappy.'

'Of course I suffer,' said Andrew. 'If I didn't suffer, then what would I have to offer to save his soul?'

'And *her* suffering?' asked Henry. 'What should she do with that?'

'Endure until it passes,' said Andrew, 'and then find a better man than me.'

Sensing that the conversation had become too painful for his brother, Henry talked a little longer about other things and then told Andrew that he must leave. He insisted that he could see himself out and left his brother at the door of Father Lambert's cell. Impatient to escape the claustrophobia which always came over him in an institution of this kind, he made his way back along the polished corridor and down the heavy wooden stairs.

At the entrance, however, he was waylaid by the porter, who asked if he could spare a moment to speak with the Prior. He was led back along the corridor on the ground floor and shown into Father Godfrey's study, with its comfortable armchairs and the portrait of St Simon Doria on the wall.

Father Godfrey rose from his desk as Henry entered and, with a friendly gesture, guided him towards one of the chairs. 'I'm so glad you could look in,' he said. 'I knew you must be worried about Andrew . . . so were we, so were we . . . and I wondered how you found him? Whether, indeed, you are reassured?'

Not knowing what the Prior knew – or whether he was Andrew's confessor – Henry looked at him uncertainly. Father Godfrey, as if realizing that Henry might feel constrained, lowered his voice and added: 'He has told me everything, I think, of what happened in Jerusalem – certainly about the skeleton, the deception and Miss Dagan.'

'It seems clear to me,' said Henry, 'that the two are very much in love and should get married.'

Father Godfrey frowned, as if pained that anyone should speak so bluntly. 'You may be right, you may be right,' he muttered, 'but it seems to us that that was the aberration . . .'

'What?'

'The love affair. A result of the shock, surely, at seeing what appeared to be the skeleton of Our Lord.'

'A shock which some might say brought him to his senses.'

Again the Prior frowned. 'I know, of course, that you are not sympathetic to the idea of the religious life, but I would have hoped, for your brother's sake, that you would try and judge his case with some objectivity.'

'I am no longer so opposed to the religious life as you assume.'

'You can see its value?'

'Clearly, if one accepts that Jesus was God, then one might feel that he wished you to devote your life to him in an uncompromising way.'

The Prior looked relieved. 'Then you accept that his vocation might be genuine?'

'It could be, but I am convinced that it isn't.'

'Even though he has felt it, now – apart from this short aberration – for over six years?'

'Yes.'

'What makes you so sure?'

'I know him very well. He is very open, affectionate and kind.'

'Of course. But these are qualities which may suit a priest as well as a married man.'

'I know. And if I felt that God *did* want him as a priest, I would do nothing to dissuade him. But I can see so clearly the psychological forces which have driven him to it – above all, his obsession with Father Lambert . . .'

'I know, I know. He was always very influenced by Father Lambert, and naturally feels an obligation towards him.'

'And is that a proper basis for a religious life?'

'Not in itself, no, but as a manifestation of love . . .'

'To give up his life for the sake of another?'

'"Greater love hath no man . . ."'

'But does God bargain in that way?'

'He does, yes, or so it would seem from Scripture. Look at Lot, who haggled to save Sodom, or even the barter implicit in the new Covenant – our salvation in return for the sacrifice of Christ.'

'And you are happy to have Andrew back on that basis?'

The Prior avoided his eyes but said: 'It is not for me to turn away someone whom God has called to join our order.'

For a moment, Henry felt impelled to argue further, but he knew that it would be futile – not just because Father Godfrey seemed so determined to hold on to Andrew, but because Henry himself no longer felt certain that what the Prior said was untrue.

He left, and escaped from the gloomy monastery into the street. He walked towards his car, which he had parked at a meter. When he reached it, he stopped, turned, and looked back – not at the grim monastery in which Andrew was imprisoned, but at the shabby church which stood next to it, with grass growing in its gutters and weeds from the crevices between the wide, worn steps: and, just as three weeks before he had felt curious enough to enter St Patrick's in

Soho, so now he turned and went back into the church of St Simon.

It was cool and musty, with the sombre green light of dawn. There was a particular smell – a mixture of condensation on the tiles of the floor, and smoke from the guttering candles in front of the statue of the Virgin and St Anne. He walked down the right aisle, looking up at the stained-glass windows representing the Father, Son and Holy Spirit; then at the painted bas-reliefs at each station of the cross, depicting the suffering of Jesus in Jerusalem. What trouble and expense had gone into the decoration of this church with works of art which were now ignored. How incongruous that, in an age when man finally seemed to have mastered the world with steam, gunpowder and reason, these painters and sculptors of the Victorian age should have returned in their imaginations to the Middle Ages.

Yet, even as he thought this, Henry found himself kneeling at the foot of the altar, just as he had done at St Patrick's in Soho. Then, he had not prayed; he had merely been curious to see how it felt to adopt such a posture before an invisible deity who might or might not exist. Even now, he did not pray, but looked at the stone table at the top of the flight of steps. Behind it was the tabernacle – a little cupboard covered with embroidered cloth; and beside it, on a bracket set into the wall, was a brass lamp in which burned a candle in a red glass bowl – the sign, Henry knew, that there was consecrated bread in the tabernacle.

So this, he thought, is the Holy of Holies of the new Covenant, just as the innermost courtyard of the Temple in Jerusalem was the Holy of Holies of the old one. That had been at the heart of one of the greatest monuments of the ancient world; this was at the centre of a decrepit old church in Paddington. Yet the first, for all its magnificence, could hardly be compared with the second if it did indeed house the living God.

He looked above the tabernacle to the figure of Christ on the cross. He imagined Andrew kneeling before this same cross, begging to be forgiven for the sin of loving Anna. As he imagined this, and thought with despair of his own inability to help her, or to save his brother, he found himself speaking, not to the figure on the cross nor to the man it depicted, but to the presence hidden in the tabernacle. 'Let him go,' he said in the silence of his mind. 'Let him go, and I will believe in you, in what you taught, yes, even in your Resurrection. Let her be happy with Andrew, and let Andrew be happy with her, and, if you need a life to atone for the wretched Father Lambert, then take mine. Show him the way out, as you show me the way in. Cut through his guilt and neurosis as you cut through my egoism and doubt. Is it much to ask? Didn't you walk on the water? Didn't you feed five thousand on a few loaves and fishes? Didn't you bring Lazarus back to life? Didn't you raise yourself from the dead? Then please perform a small miracle – raise Andrew from this gloomy mausoleum and let me give my life in his stead.'

Twenty-seven

Among the delegates to the Congress of Biblical Archaeologists at Oxford there was a Jesuit from a Canadian university, whom even Father Lambert in his most charitable frame of mind had found difficult to endure – not because he was malicious or cantankerous, but because he was a tenacious and indefatigable bore.

He had once been told that he looked like Teilhard de Chardin, and the comparison had gone to his head. He walked with a furrowed brow, as if he were considering the deepest mysteries of our existence, and he spoke with the slowness and the solemnity of a sage. During the first days of the Congress, Andrew had always to have his wits about him to avoid being cornered by this Father Stephen Driffield in one of the halls or quadrangles for one of his 'little chats'. Luckily, having taken on Father Lambert's duties as one of the coordinators of the Congress, he had an excellent excuse to move away whenever the old priest approached him.

His duties also distracted him from the more painful presence of Anna, who was there with her father as a member of the Israeli delegation. He did what he could to avoid her, since every glimpse provoked anguish of a most confused kind. He could see that she too did what she could to shun him. This compounded his remorse – it seemed to prove that he still caused her to suffer. There were moments when he thought they should meet on their own, but became afraid that if they did all his pious resolutions would crumble – that he would feel powerless not to embrace her and kiss her and drag her to his room in the college where he was lodging.

Every night during the Congress, he lay awake on the narrow bed which belonged to a student during the term, tormented no longer by gentle fantasies of laying his head upon her bosom, but by savage, unsubtle sexual desire. Even when he was able to banish these coarse fantasies from his imagination, he could not rid himself of the memories of her perfect face and sour smile.

He knew, of course, that they were sent by the Devil to tempt him. So, too, the longing he felt to care for her, to protect her, and to make her laugh, which came over him when he caught sight of her across a quadrangle or at one of the lectures, was merely a subtler wile of the same Satan who, with Father Lambert within his grasp, was determined not to be cheated.

His resolution to save the soul of his patron and mentor was bolstered by his role as his understudy at the Congress. The delegates had been told that Father Lambert had died of a stroke the month before. Many of them had known and admired him, and came to Andrew to express their sorrow – among them, the dreary Father Driffield. Luckily, there were so many others around that Andrew could escape from him without seeming impolite. He avoided him again when the old Jesuit tried to collar him after Andrew had delivered the paper that Father Lambert was to have given. On this occasion, too, there were many others who crowded around him to discuss the paper or to talk of Father Lambert – among them, Michal Dagan, who clasped Andrew's hand

275

and held it, saying in a low, hoarse whisper: 'What I would give to have had him read that paper.'

Andrew nodded. 'I know.'

'But at least there is no Cardinal Memel.'

'No.' He glanced at Anna, but she had moved behind her father so that her face was hidden.

Dagan turned to his daughter. 'Have you arranged to see Andrew while we are here?' he asked.

'He's very busy,' said Anna drily.

'But not *so* busy, are you,' asked Dagan, turning back to Andrew, 'that you can't have supper with old friends?'

'No, of course not,' said Andrew.

'This evening, come this evening, and we will have supper.'

'That would be kind but . . .'

'No buts. Come to my room in Balliol at seven. We will drink a glass of sherry – isn't that the thing? – and then go out to a restaurant.'

Andrew looked again towards Anna. She remained hidden behind her father. 'Thank you, yes,' he said lamely. 'At seven. I'll be there.'

They moved away. Andrew turned to the other delegates, and then went to the organizer's office to deal with a furious quarrel which had broken out between a Frenchman and an Iraqi as to which of them had first uncovered the entrance to a Hasmonean tomb. He had intended to listen to a paper by an American archaeologist – an old friend of Father Lambert's – on cuneiform tablets from Carchemish, but, realizing that he had already missed the first half-hour, decided to go back to his room.

As he passed through the gate, he saw the figure of Father Driffield walking slowly along the other side of the quadrangle, holding his conference papers in one hand, and his empty pipe in the other.

Since the route to Andrew's room led through the passage between the two quadrangles, he stopped and stepped back into the shadows of the porter's lodge for fear that the Canadian Jesuit would see him. When he saw him disappear beneath the arch, he cautiously continued.

The senior common room of the college, in which the delegates to the conference could, if they wished, take tea, gave on to the passage between the two quadrangles. As he passed it, Andrew saw through the door the solitary figure of Father Driffield sitting alone at a table. The sight of the garrulous old Jesuit – whom the other delegates undoubtedly found as boring as he did, and so went to the same pains to avoid – gave Andrew a pang of bad conscience. So, although neither hungry nor thirsty, and with a number of other things he wanted to do, he went into the common room himself, filled a cup with tea from the urn on the trolley, and sat down on a chair next to the priest.

'Ah,' said Father Driffield, his face lighting up as he saw Andrew. 'Playing truant too, eh? Couldn't face old Dormer riding his hobby-horse about the Hittites.'

'No.'

'Well, I've always thought he made much too much of that find of his which was, what, fifteen years ago? And he's been giving the same paper ever since.'

'Yes.'

Father Driffield glanced from his half-drunk tea to his empty pipe – the prop he used to string out his endless stories, sucking it, lighting it, puffing at it in the middle of a sentence to prevent anyone else breaking in. Now, however, because he was in the common room, he hesitated to light it, but instead took up his cup of tea. 'You know, Lambert didn't think much of him – Dormer, that is. He never said as much, in so many words – he was too charitable a man to do so – but I could tell, I could tell . . . No, he didn't think much of Dormer.'

'He had to be invited.'

'Of course, of course. You couldn't avoid it but' – he sipped his tea – 'there are a great many men in our field who hold chairs at important universities, but who, when you come down to it, have accomplished very little, while others, like Lambert – well, of course, Huntingdon is important, very important, but he should have been here at Oxford – Regius Professor, if there is one.'

'Yes,' said Andrew, scorching his tongue in his impatience to finish his tea.

'Do you know,' said Father Driffield, 'that I must have been one of the last people to have seen poor Father Lambert alive?'

Andrew put down his cup. 'When was that?'

'I've been in Rome, at the Institute, but I stopped off here on my way from Montreal – when was it? About a month ago – to see a colleague at Farm Street, and as I was leaving I ran into Father Lambert. He was leaving, too, so we walked up into Grosvenor Square and sat on a bench and had a chat.'

'But when was that?' asked Andrew again.

'I can't remember the date exactly, but he'd just got back from Israel, and someone told me he died later that very day. If he did, he certainly went straight to Heaven, because he'd just received the sacrament of Reconciliation from that old priest of ours – I forget his name, a severe old man. Father Lambert said he always went to him, because he was one of the few who didn't make your excuses for you.'

'But what time of day was it?' asked Andrew. 'Can you remember that?'

Father Driffield picked up his cup and slowly sipped his tea – delighted to have aroused Andrew's interest and determined to spin out the story. 'It must have been, well, around four or five in the afternoon, and overcast, a little cool for that time of year, so after we parted, I went for some tea at the Connaught. You know, it's part of my English heritage as a Canadian that I always like a cup of tea around four or five in the afternoon . . .'

'And you say he'd been to Confession?'

'Yes, although we call it Reconciliation now . . .'

'Are you sure?'

'Well, of course I'm sure, because he told me about that old priest – I wish I could remember his name – and then went on for some time about the sacrament – how important it was, and how neglected these days. He said hardly anyone goes – they're happy to settle things in their own conscience. Yet it's one of the promises which Our good Lord made to his disciples – 'those whose sins you forgive, they are forgiven' – which proves to us that he really was the Son of God.'

'Did Father Lambert say that?'

'Sure he did. He was in a funny mood. As you probably remember, he wasn't usually very talkative, but that afternoon I could hardly get a word in edgeways. He went on about faith and doubt and Almighty God retiring, momentarily, from our lives to teach us that we are lost without him. Then he returns, and you feel the warmth of Grace all over again, and all doubt and confusion vanish in the light of Grace, and you see all over again how extraordinary and wonderful it is that there is a God who loves each of us enough to bring us into existence, not just as an animal or an insect or a plant but as an eternal being who can choose to love him or reject him, but who, even if he does reject him by sin, just as St Peter did, and St Paul and St Augustine – in fact, almost every saint has sinned in his time – how, even then, one can repent and know with absolute certainty, after the words of absolution, that every sin is forgiven.'

Andrew was silent, his head bowed. Father Driffield glanced at him, as if expecting an interruption, but, seeing there was none, he drank from his cup and continued: 'He was also very interesting about Grierson's discoveries in Ugarit. I'd wanted to tackle him on that for a long time, and as soon as he'd said his piece about Reconciliation, which was, I have to admit, a little pre-Conciliar for my taste, I managed to get him onto the question of Grierson's method, which I criticized in a paper you may have seen in the *Saskatchewan Archaeological Review . . .'*

Andrew left him talking and staggered back to his own room, his mind grappling with all that he had just been told. How could he make sense of what had happened? Father Lambert had returned from Israel convinced that Christ had not risen from the dead. In his despair, he had turned to Mrs Dunn. Had he then repented? Had he then believed? If he had believed, repented and then confessed his sins, how could he, in the space of an hour, have fallen back into a state of such despair as to buy a clothes-line and hang himself from his window?

But if he had not hanged himself, then someone must have killed him – and all that hope returned which Andrew had felt at the beginning. If Father Lambert had been murdered, it must have been to prevent him from denouncing the find. It followed that he must have died for his Christian witness, and his soul, far from being ensnared by the Devil, was already in Heaven wearing a martyr's crown.

Andrew knelt and prayed as he had never prayed before – a mixture of thanks and pleading for what he now suspected to be true. For, if it were true, he was released, and he could run to Anna as he had so longed to do, and beg her to have him after all. How could he find out? How could he know for certain? Who could have killed him and why? The thoughts and prayers ran round and round in his head until he realized, suddenly, that it was seven o'clock when he was expected by the Dagans at Balliol College.

He washed, changed his shirt and combed his hair, and walked from his college to Balliol, his mind still filled with confusing thoughts. Some of the delegates returning from Dormer's lecture greeted him as he passed but Andrew did not see them. Indeed, so pressing was the riddle which obsessed him that, no sooner had Michal Dagan admitted him to the large panelled room which he had been assigned for the Congress, and poured him a glass of sherry, than Andrew blurted out what he had heard from Father Driffield.

Michal Dagan was alone – Anna was expected – and he listened to what Andrew said with a bowed head.

'Of course, it must all seem nonsense to you,' said Andrew, 'but to me, it is completely confusing because, if Father Lambert had really repented and confessed his sins and believed them forgiven, then why on earth should he hang himself from the window of his cell?'

For a while Michal Dagan sat in silence, his head still bowed, his face hidden. Andrew, who had, until then, been so preoccupied with his own agitation that he had not noticed the old man's reaction, realized that his words had

had a considerable effect. He waited in silence for Dagan to reply.

Eventually, Dagan looked up. There were tears on his cheeks. 'I shall tell you,' he said slowly, 'no matter what happens as a result. Lambert – your Father Lambert – did not hang himself. We killed him – not me, but Ya'acov on the orders of Louvish – because Lambert telephoned me in Jerusalem that afternoon to say that he now believed that the skeleton I had found could not be that of Jesus of Nazareth. But my telephone was tapped. Louvish heard this and he thought that his purpose would be served just as well if he made it seem that Father Lambert had taken his own life in despair. There was his notebook, you see – he thought he would have written in it that he accepted the find – but Ya'acov found that he had written nothing in it, so he took it away to forge some entries and plant it, if they needed to, on someone they could make responsible for his murder.'

Andrew was weeping.

'Poor Father Lambert,' said Dagan.

'No, no,' said Andrew. 'You cannot imagine how happy he must be.'

'Happy?'

'Yes, now, in Heaven.'

The old man shrugged. 'In Heaven, yes, perhaps, who knows?'

Half an hour later, Anna came to her father's rooms to find Andrew and the Professor laughing together, having drunk two-thirds of the bottle of sherry.

'You know, I think it is because he is drunk,' Michal Dagan said to his daughter, 'but this crazy young man says that he is no longer going to be a monk and wants instead to marry you. I warned him that life would be more peaceful as a priest, and that you aren't at all an easy person to live with, but he says he knows you very well, and he thinks you will get along, and he asks me if I will let you get married.'

'I asked him, I mean,' said Andrew, 'if he minded if I were to ask you.'

'Of course, of course,' said Michal Dagan. 'But what notice

281

would she take of my opinion now, when she has never paid any attention before?'

'I'm sorry,' said Andrew, blushing, and hardly daring to look at Anna, 'but might you – I mean, after everything – might you consider, well, marrying me after all?'

This time she did not hide behind her father, but with a shrug and one of her sour smiles said, 'Sure.'